"You are a woman of great courage to face those cutthroats."

His fingers closed around hers as if she were a lifeline. Her late husband's hands had always been smooth and soft, the hands of a gentleman, so unlike this man's calluses which bespoke hard work. She marveled at their size and at the tingles that traveled up her arm.

A flush crept over her face as she realized the direction of her thoughts. "I saw a cruel act and felt compelled to intervene. I could do nothing less."

His eyes darted over her face and he said in a stronger voice, "They might have turned on you."

"I'm an excellent shot."

"And did you not consider that you may have been in danger from me as well?"

She suspected many women found him a very great danger, but not for the reason he spoke.

Swallowing against a dry mouth, she lifted her chin. "You hardly looked dangerous at the time. And I daresay you lack the strength to offer any threat now."

The barest hint of a smile twitched his lips.

D1482353

Praise for *THE GUISE OF A GENTLEMAN*

"Combining Jane Austen with swashbuckling adventure, *THE GUISE OF A GENTLEMAN* is a fine specimen of pirate romance!"
~*USA Today* bestselling author Jennifer Ashley

The Guise
of a
Gentleman

by

Donna Hatch

The Guise of a Gentleman

Cover Art by *Rae Monet*

The Wild Rose Press
PO Box 708
Adams Basin, NY 14410-0706
Visit us at www.thewildrosepress.com

Publishing History
First English Tea Rose Edition, 2010
Print ISBN 1-60154-701-3

Published in the United States of America

Dedication

To Vicki, Frances, Jennifer,
and to all my sister writers at ANWA,
Desert Rose RWA and Beau Monde RWA.
I couldn't have done it without you!
Also, to my parents for always believing in me.
And most of all to my husband,
who'd look great in an eye patch!

CHAPTER 1

England, 1819

Lily Standwich was a traitor. Elise choked on her tea, hoping she'd simply heard wrong. But no, Lily had indeed betrayed their pact.

Seated in her front parlor, Elise set down her teacup with a bit more force than she ought to have on the Chippendale table. "Married? Lily! What are you thinking?"

"Oh, good heavens, I'm only forty-two, not a hundred. Why, my hair isn't even gray yet." Lily smoothed her dark hair and nibbled her biscuit as if she hadn't just delivered such shocking news.

Sinking back against the parlor settee, Elise could only stare. She and Lily had shared so many confidences and reassured each other about the freedoms and pleasures only a financially stable widow could enjoy. Now, they would lose that common bond. Elise would grow old, alone, while all her friends moved into a world dominated by husbands; world of which she was not a part. Not that Elise wanted a husband ever again.

Until a moment ago, she'd believed Lily felt the same way. When did Lily change her mind?

Elise sputtered. "Yes, but...but why?"

Lily gave her a look one normally reserved for a slow-witted child. "I love him. And I want to spend every moment with him, day and night."

Dismay weighted Elise's heart. She knew her friend had been spending time with the widowed Mr. Harrison, possibly even indulging in clandestine meetings with him, but taking a lover hardly equated marriage. Elise would never take a lover, and she'd vowed long ago she would never remarry, a vow Lily had also made. And broken.

Elise shook her head in disbelief. "Are you sure that's what you want?"

Using her fingers, Lily ticked off a list of Mr. Harrison's attributes. "He has money of his own, comes from a good family, already has two sons, so there's no need of an heir." She moistened her lips, her expression turning earnest. "But it's more than that. We truly enjoy one another's company. He treats me like a queen. For the first time in years, I am truly happy." Lily delivered her last sentence with such dreaminess, Elise half-expected her friend to be jesting. She wasn't.

Elise felt as if the world were tilting slightly to one side. A knot formed in her stomach. She stared absently at the blue and lilac patterns on the carpet and tried to sort her tangled thoughts. "But you had no intention of remarrying."

Lily heaved a sigh. "I know I'd often said that. But it was just noise to try to make us both feel better about our widowed state. What else should I have done? Confess I was dying of loneliness?" She touched Elise's arm, her voice hushing. "I have a chance to be happy again. Can't you be pleased for me?"

Her face warming with shame at her own selfishness, Elise managed a wan smile. "Of course. I apologize. I'm just surprised."

"I understand, my dear." Lily eyed her with apprehension. "We're having a *soirée* in two weeks' time to celebrate. Will you come?"

Elise retrieved her tea cup and sipped to give herself time to form an answer. The familiar emptiness in her heart returned. "You know I dislike large gatherings."

"It wouldn't hurt you to make a few social appearances now and again."

Sighing, Elise nodded in resignation. "I suppose you're right. Charlotte Greymore has been telling me the same thing. Just yesterday, in fact. Yet, it doesn't seem right going to events without Mr. Berkley at my side."

Lily patted her arm. "He was a good man, and you made a lovely couple, but he would not wish you to mourn all your life, any more than John would have wished it for me."

Elise looked down at her clenched hands. "Perhaps not."

"There are any number of eligible gentlemen in the area. It's possible someday you, too, will remarry and find happiness again."

"You know I plan to remain a widow."

"Nonsense. You are, what—? Eight and twenty? Hardly in your dotage. A lady as young and lovely as you should not remain at home alone."

The usual discomfort arrived that always came on the heels of a compliment. Her late husband had often told her she was comely, but he had seen her through the eyes of love. She knew she had little to tempt a man.

It didn't matter. She would never remarry.

Elise shook her head sadly. "I'm happy for you, Lily, but please do not expect me to follow in your footsteps."

"Think of your son. A boy needs a father's guidance."

She knew Lily did not mean to sound callous, but although Edward had been gone for five years, Elise still missed him. No man would ever take his place. And she had no desire to announce to the world that she had ceased mourning him, lest a gentleman entertain the idea she might engage in a liaison. Not that she'd have suitors stumbling all over themselves in the attempt.

She folded her arms. "I'm not willing to consider remarrying. I'm surprised after all our discussions on the subject over the years you would think I'd so easily change my mind just because you did."

"You're right. I'm sorry. I know this must seem very sudden to you, given all our talks. I'm happy. And I want you to be happy, too." Lily paused. "Do come to my party. This will just be a few friends, not a big, elaborate *fête*."

Spurred by a sense of duty to her friend, Elise nodded. "Very well, I will attend and toast to your happiness."

Lily smiled. "Excellent. Most of the guests will be old friends. There will be only one new face."

"New face?" Suspicion curled in her stomach.

"Jared Amesbury has returned to England and has let Richfield Manor for the summer."

Elise raised her brows. "Richfield Manor has not been occupied for as long as I can remember."

"I suppose Mr. Amesbury wished to rusticate after such a long time overseas. I knew his mother, the countess. Lovely lady. She passed on two years ago. His father, the Fifth Earl of Tarrington, is well-respected, and his children make him proud."

The names meant nothing to Elise. She had lived in this summer home in the country just outside Brenniswick since her marriage to Edward nearly ten years ago. Before that, she lived a quiet life a few miles to the north and had traveled very little either before or after her marriage, though she'd spent much of her youth poring over travel books and dreaming of far-away lands awash with adventure. She and her father had often spoken of trips they planned to take. Those plans ceased upon his untimely death. Many dreams died with him. The rest of her dreams died with Edward.

Lily leaned forward, her brown eyes twinkling.

"I visited Mr. Amesbury upon his arrival. He has grown into a most handsome man. Educated at Cambridge. I believe he served in the Royal Navy during the war. Or was he a privateer? I forget. No matter. He would be a most welcome addition to Brenniswick, don't you think?"

Elise folded her arms and said firmly, "I'm not interested in meeting eligible bachelors or widowers."

"Of course not, dear," Lily agreed too quickly.

Elise suspected agreeing to come to the *soirée* had been a mistake. Despite her promises to the contrary, matchmaking appeared to be high on Lily's menu. Elise had no desire to taste that dish.

"The *soirée* is two weeks from tomorrow."

Elise took her hand. "Lily, I wish you and Mr. Harrison all the happiness in the world. He's a fine man and is fortunate, indeed, to have you."

Lily smiled, looking relieved. "I can't tell you how much it means to hear you say that. I feared you'd be disappointed or feel abandoned."

How well Lily knew her. But no amount of enticement would have made Elise say anything to hurt her friend. Instead, she again squelched her own feelings and wished Lily happiness.

After Lily took her leave, Elise stood motionless in the foyer, her emotions spinning like dust motes in the sunlight which rained over her.

Her friends were moving on without her.

Charlotte Greymore had married two years ago to a fine man she'd loved for years. Now Lily would remarry. Elise would have to face widowhood without her two dearest friends. Oh, they'd see one another from time to time, but things would be different. She'd be alone.

Nonsense. She had her young son and a large estate to manage for his inheritance. What more did she need? Certainly not a man!

She took her foolish emotions in hand and wrestled them into submission.

In the nursery, she checked on her son who sat reading with his nurse, although Colin looked as though he'd rather be chasing frogs by the lake. Colin perked up at her arrival, but she laid a finger over her lips and gestured to his nurse. His shoulders slumping, he sat back on his haunches and propped his chin on his fist. Smiling, she retrieved her hat, gloves and riding crop. As was her custom, she also picked up her double-barreled rifle before heading for the stables.

Prince's welcoming whinny met her. At the door, she paused to breathe in the scent of hay and horses. Edward had detested the odors of the stables and always had the stable lads bring his horse to him, tacked up and ready to ride. In contrast, Elise liked the earthy stable smells. They resurrected fond memories of her dear father.

Matthews, the head groom, whistled as he attended his duties at the far end. Elise entered the darkened interior and moved to Prince's stall. Prince whinnied again.

"Hello, Prince." She set down her gun and ammunition and opened the gate. Upon entering his stall, she rubbed the horse's muzzle and ran her hands down his neck and back.

Prince put his head over her shoulder and, using the underside of his chin, he pulled her against his neck for a horse hug. She wrapped her arms around him, savoring his sweet, musty scent and his genuine affection. His lips nipped softly at her neck, and the hairs on his chin tickled.

He'd been a first-rate hunter in his prime, much like the horse she'd ridden at her father's side in local fox hunts in her youth, to her mother's disapproval. When she'd turned sixteen, her mother had announced that Elise needed to give up her wild ways and begin acting like a lady. Too grief-stricken over the recent loss of her father, Elise had bowed to her wishes. She never participated in another fox hunt and married the perfect gentleman.

"Mornin', Mrs. Berkley," Matthews called.

"Good morning," she called over her shoulder.

Matthews threw the tack over the gate where she could easily access it and left her alone with her horse. After tying up Prince so he wouldn't move about, she brushed him, rubbing her hands along his rich, chestnut coat. Grooming her horse always calmed her when she was troubled, and Lily Standwich's announcement had left her decidedly troubled.

She and Lily had turned to one another in their mutual grief when they'd been widowed, and that common link sealed their friendship. Now Lily would remarry.

"I don't understand Lily," she muttered to Prince. His ears swiveled back to hear her as she brushed his coat to a shine. "You won't catch me falling for a man or walking meekly into a second marriage."

On cue, Prince whinnied and shook his head.

She laughed softly. "You and Colin are the only ones I could ever love now that Edward, God rest his soul, is gone."

Elise had loved Edward, of that there was no question. She'd earnestly strived to be the perfect wife and to conduct herself in all ways to make him proud. Allowing another man into her life would be a betrayal of Edward's memory. Besides, liked being own mistress. Was the love of a man truly worth giving up one's widowhood liberty?

Elise set aside the brush and tacked up Prince. After stopping for her gun, she led him outside.

"Nice day for a ride," Matthews said. He spotted her rifle and made a grunt of satisfaction.

He gave her a leg up and stepped back. He'd finally stopped asking to accompany her. It simply wasn't done for a lady to ride alone, but now that Edward was gone, Elise often did things that simply weren't done. Besides, they were in Brenniswick, hours from the nearest city. Nothing dangerous ever happened in Brenniswick.

Prince danced against the reins, and she let him have his head. They galloped, leaping over stone fences and hedgerows, avoiding her tenants' homes and crops. Nearing the north edge of her land, she slowed to wend her way through a grove of birch. Sunlight slanted through the leaves, illuminating patches of soft earth which muted the sound of Prince's hoof beats.

A disembodied male voice shattered the peace in the woods. "I don't care what you do to the boy. He means nothing to me."

Startled, Elise reined. Prince let his breath out in a whoosh and then quieted as Elise stroked his neck. Not even birdsong broke the afternoon's silence. A prickle ran down the back of her neck.

A sharp, mirthless laugh erupted from the trees. "You care, or you wouldn't have come for him. Talk, or the boy dies." The second man's voice raised chill bumps on her arms.

A child cried out in distress and broke off.

Elise's imagination painted frightening reasons why a child might be silenced so abruptly. With quickened heartbeat, she urged Prince toward the direction of the voices.

The first voice floated through the misty air. "Kill the whelp; I don't care. It won't change my answer." The voice ended with a strangled grunt.

With her pulse hammering in her throat, Elise eased her loaded rifle out of its resting spot by her knees.

Following the voices, she walked Prince forward,

his footsteps muffled in the damp loam. At the edge of a clearing within a hollow, she pulled him to a stop. The scene that met her exceeded her fears. Her heart nearly leaped from her chest.

Like entertainers in a play, three men and a small boy performed a deadly act. A man with a large, plumed hat slowly pulled a rope stretched over the limb of a nearby tree. The rope encircled the neck of a second man who stood on his toes in a desperate attempt to keep the noose from cutting off his breath.

Shock rippled through her, robbing her breath. He was being hanged.

Only a few paces away, a third man with long, black braids straddled the boy lying on his stomach on the dirt. The ruffian fisted one hand in the boy's hair, pulling the head back. The other hand held a knife against the young victim's exposed throat.

The man holding the rope spoke in a faintly Spanish accent. "Then Santos will carve him up. Slowly. Since you don't care."

The child appeared to be eight or nine, not much older than Elise's son. He squeezed his eyes closed, and the pain and terror in his expression twisted her heart.

"Stop!" the man in the noose gasped. "Let the boy go."

The captors exchanged knowing glances. "I knew you were bluffing," sneered the man with the rope. "First you watch Santos kill the pup, then your turn," the hangman said. "Unless you talk."

The man being hanged twisted against his bonds. "I told you, Leandro, someone else took it. I don't have it and I don't know where it is."

"Then you are of no use to me alive. I still owe you for killing Macy. I will enjoy watching you die a slow death. But first, the boy. Santos, slit his throat. Slowly."

Horror froze a knot in Elise's stomach.

A curved sword hung from Leandro's belt, but Elise saw no sign of a gun. The boy emitted a cry of pain and fear. Her heart lurched, demanding action. Anger surged, followed by determination. She raised her rifle to her shoulder and sighted down the left barrel at Santos who threatened the boy.

"I'll tell you," the man in the noose man gasped. "Let him go and I'll tell you."

"Gentlemen!" Elise's voice rang out with more confidence than she felt. "Remove your hands from the boy. Release the man. Get off my land."

Every eye turned to her, and mouths dropped open. Whether their surprise stemmed from her sudden appearance or her boldness in addressing them, she did not know.

The ruffians made no move. Perhaps they needed more encouragement. She braced herself against the rifle's kick and squeezed the front trigger. The ground erupted in a tiny explosion where the ball impacted inches away from Leandro's feet. Yelping in surprise, the Spaniard released his hold. The hanging man fell to his knees and collapsed face-down.

Prince, the hunter that he'd been for years, remained calm.

Leandro kicked the motionless man on the ground. Elise's stomach tightened at the brutality. She squeezed the second trigger which fired a ball through the other barrel. The ball hit the ground at the horses' hooves in the clearing.

With remarkably calm fingers, she began the reloading process, but before she could fire another shot, the scoundrels scrambled to their horses. Leandro glowered down at his former victims, his face twisted in rage. Even at this distance, Elise felt his malignant hatred. He galloped away with Santos following him until the trees swallowed them.

Still lying on his stomach, the boy dropped his head into his arms, his shoulders shaking silently. Elise spurred Prince to the hollow. Before Prince fully stopped, she slid out of her saddle and rushed to the lad. Terrified, he shrank from her.

She halted and laid the rifle at her feet. With her hands held out, she spoke in soothing tones. "It's all right. They're gone. I'm a friend. I'm here to help."

He lifted his head and stared at her with large, dark eyes.

She tried to smile reassuringly. "Don't worry, I won't bite. Those blackguards nearly got the better of you, didn't they?"

With his frightened eyes still upon her, he pushed himself to a seated position and hugged his knees. Except for a shallow cut on his neck, he appeared unharmed.

Choking noises from the fallen man snatched her attention. How could she have forgotten him? Alarmed, Elise dashed to his side and fell to her knees. His face and neck were mottled and purple. With trembling fingers, she ripped off her riding gloves and pulled at the tight knots.

Elise continued to work at the noose, breaking her nails as she tore desperately at the ropes. The instant the rope around his neck had loosened, the stranger gasped and coughed. When she enlarged the loop enough, she slid it over his head and cast it aside. The rope had bitten into his skin, and bruises surrounded a raw wound.

"Those scoundrels," she muttered, her heart squeezing in sympathy for the injured man.

The boy crawled closer, warily eyeing her. Tears and grime streaked his face. Blood dripped onto his shirt from his throat.

"It's all right now," she soothed the boy. "Did they hurt you elsewhere?"

The child blinked and wiped his nose on his sleeve. Without speaking, he shook his head. He wore the coarse clothes of a field worker, but they were in good repair. He looked anxiously at the gasping man lying face-down at her side.

She returned her gaze to the man. "Sir?"

With his face turned away, he continued to cough and wheeze.

"Sir? Can you hear me? Those men are gone. The boy is well. You're both safe. Sir?"

She shook him gently, unsure if he were even conscious. Or did coughing signify consciousness? She had no idea. Except for his attempts to breathe, he made no effort to move. His harsh breathing continued, but the coughing abated.

Hoping to rouse him, she ran her hand over his head as she would a distressed child. His sable brown hair curled slightly over her fingers as she stroked it. In a flight of fancy, she imagined the sun had also run its fingers through those thick waves, leaving lighter streaks behind. When her hand encountered a bump on the back of his head, he hissed in his breath and pulled against the binding which secured his wrists behind his back. Wishing she had a knife, Elise turned her attention to the cords. As she worked at the knots, the rough jute bit into her flesh, her bleeding fingers staining the rope.

The bound man wore no coat; only a dirtied linen shirt, breeches, and heavily creased, leather boots. No gentleman would go about so roughly clad. He must be a craftsman or tradesman, she mused. With his powerful, muscular body, she could easily imagine him as a blacksmith or a pugilist. He could be a sailor, but Port Johns lay a two-hour carriage ride away. Few sailors ventured this far inland, preferring to remain in the port town.

His identity mattered little. At the moment, her most pressing concern lay in seeing to his welfare.

At least he breathed more easily now. Once Elise loosened the knots around his wrists, the man wrenched his hands free and rolled over onto his back, chest heaving, eyes closed.

Elise caught her breath. A shiver raced through her nerves.

He was without a doubt the most handsome man she'd ever seen. He appeared perhaps thirty, with a deeply suntanned, clean-shaven face. Dark brows arched over his closed eyes. His long lashes no doubt drew envy from women, but nothing effeminate touched his rugged face. He had the kind of strong features, square jaw, and well-formed mouth that would have fascinated a sculptor. Unlike most men in her social circle, his features possessed a certain hardness which hinted at a life of struggle. Typically, that edge only appeared on the visages of the impoverished or those who had returned from the horrors of the Peninsular War.

A horse nickered. Fearing the ruffians had returned, she reached for her rifle and came to her feet, but only saw a blue roan thoroughbred standing in the shade, its reins dragging on the ground. She listened. Except the wind in the trees, she heard no other sound. No one else appeared to be nearby.

She looked back at the roan, the horse of a wealthy man. Had this man stolen it? Had she unwittingly aided a horse thief? That might explain the hanging, however illegal. But no, the Spaniard, Leandro, had been demanding information.

The boy remained curled up, watching her with enormous eyes. He pointedly glanced at her gun and inched further away.

"You've nothing to fear from me, lad. I'd never shoot a little boy." She poured a teasing tone into her voice. "Unless, of course, you don't eat your vegetables."

He studied her warily and heaved a shuddering

breath. A glimmer of a smile touched one side of his mouth.

She returned her gaze to the stranger and sank back down beside him. One eye had swollen and discolored, and he bled from a cut at the corner of his lip.

Resting her hand on his chest, she leaned over him. "Sir, can you hear me?"

He opened his eyes. Vibrant blue-green, they possessed a penetrating quality that left her feeling strangely revealed. Astonished at the quickening of her pulse under his focused stare, she swallowed.

"My lady," he said hoarsely. In direct opposition to his attire, his accent bespoke good breeding.

Despite his rough clothing, an air about him mocked the idea that he could be some kind of servant. Moreover, his features looked decidedly patrician. The by-blow of a nobleman, perhaps?

He gazed at her with unnerving intensity. "Are you the angel who rescued me?" He lapsed into coughing again.

With effort, she found her voice. "I'm no angle, sir. However, you're fortunate I happened along. You'd surely be conversing with St. Peter if those ruffians had their way."

"I doubt I'd be allowed anywhere near the pearly gates." He touched her face as if to assure himself she truly existed. The intimate contact startled her. The gentleness of his caress surprised her more.

She never expected a soft touch from such a large and heavily-calloused hand. Nor did she foresee the delicious warmth that traveled through her body in response. Shocked more at her own reaction than his bold behavior, she moved out of reach. To her dismay, a small place in her heart cried out for more.

He lowered his hand and glanced up. "José, lad, are you all right?"

"Aye, sir, well 'nough," the boy replied in an accent Elise could not place.

Relief touched the man's face. Then he refocused those aquamarine eyes upon Elise. "I'm in your debt, my lady."

"Think nothing of it, sir."

"You are a woman of great courage to face those cutthroats."

He reached for her hand, and his fingers closed around hers as if she were a lifeline. Her late husband's hands had always been smooth and soft, the hands of a gentleman, so unlike this man's calluses which bespoke hard work. She marveled at their size and at the tingles that traveled up her arm.

A flush crept over her face as she realized the direction of her thoughts. "I saw a cruel act and felt compelled to intervene. I could do nothing less."

His eyes darted over her face, and he said in a stronger voice, "They might have turned on you."

"I'm an excellent shot."

"And did you not consider that you may have been in danger from me as well?"

She suspected many women found him a very great danger, but not for the reason he spoke.

Swallowing against a dry mouth, she lifted her chin. "You hardly looked dangerous at the time. And I daresay you lack the strength to offer any threat now."

The barest hint of a smile twitched his lips. He opened his mouth as though to say more but refrained. Instead, he said, "I'm grateful to you. Now we must leave or risk them returning."

Without letting go of her hand, he tried to rise. Instead, he sucked in his breath sharply, his features twisted in pain, and eased himself back down. Elise bit her lip in sympathy and almost wished she'd shot the villains instead of the ground.

After breathing against pain, he glanced at the boy. "José, lad, are you sure you're all right?"

"Aye, sir."

"Then shimmy up a tree and see if you can spot them."

José clamored up a nearby tree and peered out over the countryside. After a moment, he called down, "I see farms, sir, and open fields. No riders."

"Keep a sharp eye out, lad."

Elise turned her mind to the man's well-being. The bruising around his eye had darkened and it had swollen nearly shut. Looking for bloodstains, she made a visual perusal of his body. She found none but wondered what hidden injuries he'd suffered.

He closed his eyes, and his face relaxed. "Your hands are so soft," he whispered, his fingers tightening over hers. "My mother used to stroke my hair like you did a moment ago." He brought her hand to his face and pressed it against his cheek as if hungry for human touch.

Torn between wanting to comfort him and achingly aware of the impropriety of his conduct, she turned her hand over and rested it against his cheek. She couldn't remember when she'd touched a man in such an intimate manner. It felt right somehow.

And that terrified her.

She slowly removed her hand. "Are you well enough to be moved? Or should I send for a doctor?"

"Not necessary. I merely need to rest a moment." Again those vivid eyes fixed upon her. The corners of his mouth lifted. "Your timing could not have been better."

He slowly pushed himself up, breathing harshly against hidden pain, but then steadied himself. As he leaned forward and shifted his position, his unbuttoned shirt exposed a shocking amount of his chest. Muscular and broad, it provided a tempting sight. She'd never even seen Edward so scantily clad. Her late husband had been the perfect English gentleman, always immaculately dressed.

She flushed deeper when she realized she had failed to look away from the indecent sight of this stranger's *dishabille*. Guilt tugged at her heart for betraying Edward's memory by looking at another man so wantonly.

The stranger ran his tongue along his lip and she watched the motion as if hypnotized. He returned his attention to Elise. His eyes softened. "My beautiful angel." He cupped her cheek, leaned in, and kissed her softly.

Too startled to react, she froze.

His lips brushed against hers, light as a whisper and more provocative. His fingers slid to the back of her neck and held her firmly in place. His thumb stroked her cheek while his lips grew more insistent. The passion contained in such a gentle contact astonished her. For a blissful moment, she allowed her lips to melt into his, reveling in the long-absent touch of a man. An altogether unfamiliar longing began in the middle of her stomach and spread outward.

Edward had always been careful and controlled as if he feared he would sully her. This stranger, though gentle, kissed with passion, stirring a fire within she'd never known.

Remembering herself, she gasped and pushed against his chest. Even in his weakened state, he held her with surprising strength. When she pushed harder, he released her. Slowly. The desire lurking in those aqua depths excited and frightened her.

She held on to the fear. It was safer.

"Sir, you have taken unkind advantage of me," she accused, her breathing ragged. Her traitorous lips ached for another kiss. "I am not a common wench to be used at whim."

"No, there's nothing common about you," he murmured, his thumb caressing her cheek. Wickedness joined the desire so clear in his eyes.

Appalled at her lack of self-restraint, she reached for something stronger than fear to protect herself from him—from herself—and seized anger. She sat further back, beyond his reach. "You must be half-mad from your ordeal to be behaving in such an atrocious manner!"

His eyes glittered with a devilish light. "I'm a healthy man who knows a brave and beautiful woman when I see one. Clearly, I'm in my right mind." His recovering voice, rich and deep, rippled over her like a physical caress.

Infuriated that a stranger could have such power over her, she frowned. "You speak as a well-bred gentleman, but you certainly do not behave as one."

He flashed an unrepentant grin. "I've had years of practice rejecting my upbringing."

The unsettled feeling in her stomach annoyed her as much as his shocking actions. "Perhaps I should have saved only the boy and let your friends have you."

He lay back down, lacing his fingers behind his head, and laughed with abandon, the sort of truly mirthful laugh that invited one to join in.

She resisted. "Pray tell me; why you were being threatened by those men?"

Still amused, he tilted his head. "Are you always this direct?"

"Under unusual circumstances."

"Two men threatening to kill another man and a boy is not a circumstance you normally encounter?"

"Do not mock me, sir."

"But you make it such fun. Your cheeks grow pink when you are riled. Or flustered. You're really quite lovely."

Since getting a straight answer seemed unlikely, Elise thought it best to flee this dangerously handsome man and his irreverent allure. No man had ever tempted her like this. What was the matter with her?

She pulled on her gloves, gathered the skirts of her riding habit, and stood. "Since you appear to be sufficiently recovered, I shall leave you."

He grinned up at her. "Where have you been all this time, my angel?"

She picked up her gun and raised her chin. "Married to my husband," she replied primly. "Good day, sir."

"Wait," he called, undaunted. "What is your name?"

She stowed the gun on the saddle and turned back, holding Prince's reins. After dredging up every ounce of haughtiness she possessed, she looked down her nose at him and hoped he'd believe her façade. "As it is unlikely that you and I shall ever meet again, it hardly matters."

His compelling laugh rang out again. "Then I shall just have to call you Angel."

Far from being offended by her rebuff, he dared laugh at her. Twice! Annoyed more than she'd believed possible, she led her horse to a nearby boulder to use as a step. After mounting and settling herself upon the side-saddle, she looked back with a frown, partly to reassure herself that he suffered no dangerous injuries, partly to restate her disapproval of his conduct.

Most of all, to show him that she felt nothing whatsoever for him.

Or his scandalous kiss.

Still lying on his back, his eyes traveled lazily over her figure as if what he saw pleased him in an ungentlemanly way. "Farewell, my angel."

"Humph." She turned her horse to the narrow path.

His laughter chased her as she left the hollow.

She paused at the rise and looked out. The valley lay below her in every direction. No other riders appeared to be in the vicinity. It would be safe to leave the man and child here without fear of further encounters with ruffians.

She glanced back to see the boy helping the man to his feet, both speaking a language she could not identify. Spanish, perhaps? As she watched, they mounted the blue roan and rode off in the opposite direction. Despite his obvious pains, his laugh rang out over the valley again.

Fighting a smile of her own, she shook her head at the man's audacity and tried to banish the memory of his hands on her face and his lips on hers.

Most of all, she tried to banish the unwelcome awareness he'd stirred within her. The scoundrel! The next time she saw a man in danger, she'd keep her distance.

CHAPTER 2

In his bedroom in the manor house he'd let for the summer, Jared waved off his valet hovering anxiously nearby.

"No, Gibbs, no need to contact the constable. The villains are, no doubt, long gone by now."

Frowning, Jared examined the bloodied ring around his neck in the looking glass and suppressed a shiver at the memory of the noose. His lip and one eye were swollen and had already turned interesting shades of purple. Each time he drew a deep breath, searing pain flared in his ribs. The bump in the back of his head where he'd been struck throbbed in earnest.

Few could have managed to creep up and clout him on the head. Apparently, Leandro had been less drunk than usual, or Jared surely would have heard him coming.

"A doctor, then, sir?" the valet persisted.

"Not necessary. No serious harm done." Nothing a good bottle of rum wouldn't cure. Since English gentlemen normally avoided such crude liquor, he'd have to settle for brandy. Perhaps being landlocked would have a few advantages, after all.

He cursed his stupidity at letting down his guard. When José had gone missing, Jared's instincts had screamed of sinister forces at work. He'd shed his gentleman's clothing and gone out after the boy alone, unwilling to trust any of his new staff. None of them knew his secret life.

He should have used more caution. Though he had eliminated most of his enemies before he left the sea, his safety remained far from sure. His recklessness had placed José in mortal danger. Jared's hands clenched and a sick dread knotted his stomach. He harbored no doubts that Leandro and his toady, Santos, would have killed them both. Painfully. It would have been a pity, too, with all the work he had yet to do.

But no one, except the British Secret Service, was supposed to know he'd come to this quiet village. Especially not Leandro. His presence might ruin everything.

And he was so close to freedom.

"Then I shall prepare your bath, sir. Dinner will be served shortly." Gibbs's statement brought Jared back to the present.

"Very good, Gibbs."

"And sir, you have an appointment with your tailor tomorrow morning."

"Ah, yes, Lady Standwich's *soirée*. Don't I have anything formal enough for that?"

"Oh, no sir. You'll need a black superfine for a *soirée*."

Jared frowned as he considered enduring another session with the tailor. His favorite manner of passing the time did not involve standing in his skin while a man with pins in his mouth measured, tucked and poked. However, since his assignment depended upon fitting in with polite society, he would bear it without complaint.

"Very well. I'll go to Port Edmunds and submit myself to the tailor's torture." Besides, he needed to check on his ship.

Jared was almost certain Gibb's lip twitched into a smile just before he gathered up Jared's clothes and left. Jared sank into the slipper tub. The warm water soothed his soreness but not the pain in his ribs where Leandro administered his parting shot. The damage would be inconvenient but not crippling. He leaned back and drew a breath, his tension fading.

José was safe. Because of the courage of an angel, they'd survived the afternoon. At the moment, little else mattered.

Gibbs bustled in, added a log to the fire, and meekly offered a towel. A week ago Jared had forcibly taught his new valet that he was fully capable of drying himself. As he dried himself, he smiled at the memory of the valet quailing under his wrath.

Gritting his teeth, he remained still while the uncomfortable business of being dressed by another person commenced. With all the layers of clothing polite society demanded—shirt, collar, waistcoat, frockcoat, and especially the cursed cravat with its complicated knots—he had to admit he would never have managed without Gibbs's practiced hands.

One thing for pirates; they dressed more comfortably than the civilized gentleman. And when Jared had posed as the pirate Black Jack, his devil take-it attitude had won him the freedom to dress however he pleased rather than as some dandified weakling enslaved by fashion.

A footman came in as Gibbs finished tying the dratted neckwear. "Mr. Greymore is here, sir," he announced.

"Excellent. Ah, show him into, er…" He'd fallen dreadfully out of practice.

"The drawing room, sir?" the footman offered.

"Yes. The drawing room. Quite."

"Here, sir, for your face," Gibbs said.

Jared drew back as Gibbs came at him with a silver tin of—good grief! Was that powder? "Oh, no. No, no, no."

Patiently, Gibbs held it out so Jared could see that it lacked any terrifying properties. "Sir, your face will draw attention. This will just—"

23

"No. I am not putting on that stuff. Put it away before I get my sword."

With a frown of resigned disapproval, Gibbs stepped back. "As you wish, sir."

Jared knew he looked disreputable, like he'd gone five rounds with the champ in fisticuffs, but there was nothing—outside of wearing make up, for heaven's sake—that he could do about it. Besides, little shocked Greymore.

Unlike his normal lope, Jared descended the stairs with all the dignity of a duke. It made for a better image. It also hurt less. He refrained from tugging at the annoying cravat.

He hadn't been in the drawing room since his arrival the previous week. The draperies were thrown wide, and the afternoon sun shone onto the carpeted floors in distorted squares from the leaded glass. No fire burned in the fireplace, and the only sound in the room came from the ticking of a mantle clock. The servants had swept away the last vestiges of dust and neglect in the house. It didn't even smell closed-in anymore.

A dignified gentleman wearing an immaculate suit waited by the windows. About ten years Jared's senior, Greymore had recently developed a few grey hairs near the temple, giving him a refined, distinguished appearance. Though slightly shorter than Jared, and a tad portly, he possessed a commanding presence.

"Greymore," Jared greeted.

The man turned with a smile and clasped his hand. His bright, sharp eyes swept over Jared. When he caught sight of Jared's swollen and bruised face and what little of his neck the cravat did not cover, alarm replaced his smile.

"Good grief! What happened to you?"

"Merely a misunderstanding," Jared replied.

He might trust Greymore with his life, but he

trusted no one with all of his secrets. He went to a side table and poured port from a crystal decanter into two glasses.

"Is that a rope burn?" Greymore persisted.

"An enthusiastic wench, to be sure. Fortunately, this time she used only a rope and not a chain." He grinned and handed Greymore a port.

Greymore frowned, clearly not believing a word, and sipped the port. "You are the most closed-mouthed man I've ever met."

"I've developed a dreadful habit of preferring to live."

Heaven knew he'd made enough bargains with the devil to live another day. Today was the second time he'd faced the embrace of a noose.

It was, however, the first time he'd met an angel.

Greymore eyed him with speculation. "For the first few months on the Peninsula, I wasn't sure if I could trust you, not withstanding the Secret Service's assurances."

"I'm sure you weren't alone in that uncertainty."

"But Rebecca believed in you. And you saved my life. Twice."

Pain flared at the mention of Rebecca. Stifling it, Jared swirled the port and took a long drink. The liquid warmed him, numbing the ache in his ribs. And in his heart. He summoned a wry grin. "I have my moments. Few, but they do exist."

"I brought the information you requested." Greymore retrieved a letter from a hidden inner coat pocket and handed it to him. "These gentlemen in the county have a vested interest in shipping. Some are owners, others are merely investors. On the next page, you'll see the name of each ship in their fleet, and which ones have reported losses due to pirates. There's also a list of cargo stolen."

Jared scanned the names. Using the Black Jack

alias, he'd been the pirate to take some of them. The *Intrepid* had been the one with the newly married couple traveling on board. The husband had glared at Jared murderously, watching for any sign that his wife would be molested. The bride had eyed him with revulsion and terror.

Those were aspects of piracy Jared would not miss.

"How can I help you?" Greymore's voice brought him back.

Jared drew a breath. He needed to learn to trust sometime. He pulled at the cravat and decided which of his many secrets he'd need to reveal in order to complete his task.

"We have proof of a coalition of pirates. There have been a shocking number of hits on the most heavily-laden merchant ships over the last four years. Someone is passing information from the shipping business to a leader of the pirate ring. The leader goes by the name *O Ladrão*, but we don't know who he actually is."

"*O Ladrão*? What does that mean?"

Jared quirked a wry grin. "It means 'the thief' in Portuguese. *O Ladrão* then sells information to other pirates in his organization in return for a percentage of the plunder. There are at least three men between *O Ladrão* and the pirate captains. None of the informants know the identity of anyone in the ring except the one man directly below him to whom he passes on the information."

Again, he felt Greymore's eyes upon him. The unspoken question, 'were you one of those pirate captains,' hung in the air, but Jared volunteered nothing.

Greymore chewed on his lower lip. "We created those miscreants when we turned respectable merchants into privateers during the war."@

"After the war ended, privateers turned to

outright piracy instead of returning to honest work. And someone is organizing a number of them."

"A pirate coalition," Greymore said thoughtfully. "A chilling thought. What do you know?"

"I've followed the trail here to a member of the gentry or the aristocracy. Find him, we find *O Ladrão*."

Greymore frowned. "What do you propose? Search houses looking for incriminating evidence?"

Jared couldn't resist needling him a bit. "We could try to get hired on as someone's servant and eavesdrop, but that would take an awfully long time if we do it for every house here."

Greymore's frown deepened. "That, and I'm well known here. But you aren't the only one good with disguises."

Grinning, Jared waved him off. "I don't think we'll need to resort to that." He read through the list again. "Many of the members of the *ton* have shares in shipping. None of these names here have any obvious connections; all have suffered losses due to pirate attacks." He looked up from the paper and stared, unseeing, out the window. "I wonder if *O Ladrão* has allowed his own ships to be boarded to throw suspicion off himself. The goods might be sold at a smuggler's port and thus the losses could be recouped."

"Hasn't the navy shut down all the smuggling coves?"

"They've made a valiant attempt. But I know of three that remain undisturbed."

"What's your plan?"

"Garner invitations to social events so I can meet people here. Then keep my mouth shut and listen. Maybe I'll hear something interesting."

"Hmm. I read somewhere that an unwed gentleman who has money must invariably be looking for a wife. If word gets out that you're wealthy, and unmarried, all the mamas will throw parties for you."

Jared made a face and replied with great reluctance, "I suppose that's one option."

"We'll have to make up some wild story about how upright and virtuous you are, or everyone will see you for a rake and lock up their daughters. You'll receive few invitations."

"You've always been good at telling tales. Very well. Tell your friends I'm an upstanding gentleman seeking the peace afforded by the countryside."

Greymore wagged a finger at him. "See to it that you behave in a manner that would not contradict that story."

Jared held up his hands in surrender. "I will be the picture of propriety. Although it's gatherings which attract men folk that I want, not marriage marts filled with desperate and conniving mothers. I didn't come here to get leg-shackled."

"You'll meet the men because the ladies will have their husbands call upon you and invite you to hunt or have dinner and so forth in order to determine your suitability for their daughters. They'll fall all over themselves to meet you."

"I'm only a second son."

The older man waved that off. "You're the son of an earl, and you've amassed a fortune. Trust me, they'll consider you ideal. Besides, women with no taste find your looks tolerable."

"Your flattery makes me blush," Jared murmured with a wry grin that pulled at his sore lip.

A picture of shallow, grasping women flashed into his mind, like sharks in a feeding frenzy. More of the same. At least the women here wouldn't be afraid of him.

"It's my money women find attractive," Jared added.

"Right," Greymore said dryly. "And it's been how long since you've slept alone?"

"A gentleman wouldn't tell." Actually, Greymore would be disappointed to learn the truth. People often assumed by his playfulness and impulsive acts that he was a philanderer. He'd have to work on his demeanor and be the kind of man fathers would trust with both their daughters and their secrets. Especially their secrets.

Greymore snorted. "Just don't seduce any virgins."

"What do you take me for? I never seduce virgins."

Greymore pinned him with a searching stare. Jared resisted the urge to tug at his cravat. Cursed thing!

Greymore removed his accessing gaze and finished his drink. "Mr. Hogan is rather fond of faro, and we're having an evening of games at his house two days hence. Care to join us? It would be the perfect way to introduce you to the others in the area."

Jared groaned. "I haven't played faro in years. I suppose I should plan to lose heavily."

"They'll love you for it. Especially if you lose."

Jared made a sound that was partly a laugh, partly a snort. "No doubt."

"And I'm hosting a riding party in three weeks."

"Perfect. And Lady Standwich has invited me to her soirée in two weeks."

Greymore's eyebrows rose. "How'd you manage an invitation from Lady Standwich?"

"Connections, dear fellow," he replied, a bit smug.

At the thought of a social affair involving ladies, a sudden hope flared. The soirée might prove more useful than he originally thought. His angel's genteel demeanor, cultured accent, and the cloth of her expertly tailored riding habit firmly proclaimed her a noblewoman. She'd no doubt be a member of the same elite social circle in which Lady Standwich traveled.

And yet, the haughtiness he often encountered in peers and their kin remained absent in that lady. She'd attempted to emulate that attitude after he kissed her, but her anger and indignation only masked her true emotions.

Emotions which clearly surprised and frightened her.

"Say, Greymore, do you know a lady in this area with brown hair and grey eyes? She appeared perhaps five and twenty. She's pretty and very proper."

"That describes about half the women in the county," Greymore replied dryly.

"This one is special."

Greymore rolled his eyes. "You are here to fulfill an assignment, not bed every poor, hapless woman who has the misfortune of crossing your path."

"None of the women I bedded were hapless or misfortunate," Jared replied with a wounded tone. "And might I remind you most of them are the seducers? I had to be the gentleman and oblige their whim. Think of how rejected they would have felt had I refused."

Greymore made a scoffing noise. "I don't know if I should admire you or despise you."

Jared smirked. "It's a curse to be irresistible to women, but I do my best to survive."

"I'll be sure to keep any future daughters of mine under guard when you're in England," Greymore said.

"How is marital bliss?"

Greymore softened. "Unlike anything I imagined. She adds a dimension to my life that I find most gratifying."

"Not dreadful to be tied down?"

"Anchored, my man, not tied down. She gives me purpose and meaning."

"Careful, old friend, you are beginning to wax poetic."

"Perhaps, but I see things differently now. Having a wife and a child on the way makes me want to be a better man."

Jared shrank back with exaggerated fear. "I hope it isn't contagious."

Greymore clapped a hand on his shoulder. "One day the elusive Jared Amesbury will stumble into the lure of matrimony. I only hope I'm there to see it."

Jared shivered. "A cage is not for me."

Unbidden, an image of a lovely angel with soft hands and concerned eyes returned. She possessed a sweet, uncomplicated beauty that brought out a protective side he did not often indulge. Her gentle touch had soothed him. Between her tender hands and the compassion in her eyes, she reached a spot in his heart he had not known existed. She'd shown remarkable courage and a healthy wit.

The lady claimed to be married, and he sensed no duplicity in her, but the unpracticed, hesitant way she had kissed him revealed her inexperience.

Her husband, should he actually exist, was either a fool who neglected her or a prude who knew nothing about pleasuring a woman. Perhaps he was an impotent fossil.

Despite the brave lady's assurance, Jared knew their paths would cross again.

He hoped his next encounter with her would again be sans husband.

CHAPTER 3

Wearing her chemise, stays, and underskirts, Elise sat at her dressing table while her maid arranged her hair. After winding small strands into loops and pinning them into place, the maid curled the ends. Pink rosebuds peeped out from her brown curls, and slender tendrils curled around her neck. The rest of her hair showered down the back of her head in ringlets.

"I'm not taking my bows to the queen, Morrison."

The aged maid smiled. "It's your first real social gathering in years, ma'am. Might as well create a sensation."

"My presence alone will create a sensation," Elise said dryly. "The neighbors have labeled me a recluse."

"You never looked at your new gown when it arrived, ma'am. I would've liked to have seen it on you sooner, so I could make any necessary alterations. I can't believe you wouldn't go for more than one fitting."

Elise waved a hand. "My modiste has never sent an inferior gown yet, and my figure hasn't changed since my last order. Although she nearly suffered an apoplexy when I requested an evening gown in this color."

"It has been far too long." Morrison retrieved the new gown with a flourish and helped Elise into it. As she buttoned up the back, she gushed, "Lovely shade. So nice to see you in something other than your usual somber colors."

As she stood watching her reflection in the long mirror, Elise had to admit the dress was magnificent. Her customary drab colors always made her skin looked pallid. The deep rose, almost burgundy, with a paler pink sheer overskirt, gave her fair complexion a healthy glow. Tiny pink satin rosebuds lined the sweetheart neckline and trailed down the sides of the parted overskirt in front. Satin roses also touched each capped sleeve.

The lifting of her spirits at the flattering shade and style of her evening gown fell as she realized that by wearing such a creation, she'd officially come out of mourning. It seemed a betrayal to Edward.

Then another thought struck her. Would the gentlemen view it as an announcement? She hoped not. Not that they would be interested, anyway.

Morrison glanced inquiringly at her. "Are you unwell, ma'am? You've grown suddenly pale."

"No, Morrison. Unfortunately, my health is wonderful, and I feel compelled to attend the soirée as I'd promised."

Grinning, Morrison tied a cameo-adorned ribbon around Elise's throat. "Don't you fret, ma'am. Just a dinner party, like any other. Five years is a long time to mourn. It's good you're returning to society again, if you don't mind me saying so."

"I fear Lady Standwich's reasons for inviting me are not as benign as she claims."

"Oh?"

"She seems to feel it her duty to help secure a second husband for me, despite all of our previous conversations to the contrary."

"She did well when she introduced you to your dearly departed husband," Morrison pointed out.

"I've a son to raise and an estate to manage. I have neither time nor desire for courting nonsense. Or husbands."

"Mother, you're beautiful," seven-year-old Colin

declared.

Elise turned from her looking glass to smile at her son standing in her doorway. She crouched down and opened her arms in invitation. The child dropped a book with a thud and ran to fling his arms around her neck.

"My son, you are beautiful." She kissed his towhead and pushed his hair back away from his cherubic face. "Mother is going to Lady Standwich's dinner party, so you be good and remember to say your prayers."

"Yes, Mother. Do angels hear my prayers?"

"Yes, my love. God and His angels."

"And Father is an angel?"

"He is. And he's watching over you, so be good."

"Yes, Mother."

Colin, barely two years old when Edward died, didn't remember his father, but Elise tried to impress upon her son that he'd been an exemplary gentleman. She hoped Colin would emulate his father as he grew into adulthood.

"What are you reading, son?"

Colin retrieved the book lying on the floor where he'd dropped it, and held it out to her.

Elise sighed. "Another book about pirates?"

"Yes, Mama, but this one's a navy captain who hunts pirates," he said, part sheepish, part defensive.

She watched him dubiously. "Very well, if it doesn't glorify wicked men who harm others."

Colin peered at her from under his golden lashes. "But pirates aren't all bad, are they, Mother?"

"Pirates lie and steal and hurt innocent people, Colin. Don't you think that makes them bad?"

"Suppose they have no choice?"

"Men can always choose to behave with honor, Colin," she said sternly. "Never forget that."

He considered momentarily. "Father would never have been a pirate, would he?"

Elise almost laughed out loud at the ridiculous image of her immaculate Edward wearing an eye patch and brandishing a scimitar. "Absolutely not. He would never have thought of stealing or harming anyone."

Colin's shoulders slumped in defeat.

"Remember the word I use to describe him?"

He thought for a moment and grinned. "Inter-gritty!"

She smiled. "Integrity. It means he behaved as he ought, even when it wasn't convenient."

A footman approached. "The coach is ready, ma'am."

"Thank you, Albertson."

She kissed Colin again and gathered him close. "I will see you in the morning, my love."

He snuggled into her. She inhaled his clean child's scent and held onto him as long as he let her. After a moment, he wriggled away and trotted out.

Elise rose and donned her gloves and a wrap. Lady Standwich and her soirée awaited. Hopefully, the dear woman's apparent designs on finding a new husband for Elise could be thwarted without embarrassment to either of them. Or to the prospective suitor, whoever the unfortunate gentleman might be.

Inside the Standwich home, Elise waited in the reception line to greet the hostess, nodding politely to others in attendance, many of whom she had not seen since Edward's death. She smoothed the folds of her gown with trembling hands. Then she chastised herself for her anxiety. She knew these people. Some of them, such as Lily, she'd known since her childhood.

Inside the drawing room, murmuring voices and soft laughter rose above clinking glasses and footsteps. Bejeweled ladies in clouds of perfume glided by.

Lily held out both hands to her. "Elise! How delightful to see you, my dear. What a lovely gown."

Elise stared at Lily. She was positively radiant as she stood next to Mr. Harrison.

"How kind of you to say. And may I say you look lovely as well?"

Lily smiled graciously and turned to her affianced. "I believe you know Mr. Harrison."

"I do, indeed. Congratulations on your upcoming marriage, Mr. Harrison."

"I am undeserving of this lovely lady, but selfish enough to ask her to have me, regardless," Mr. Harrison replied.

Elise smiled politely while he and Lily exchanged loving glances.

"Thank you for coming," Lily added. "I cannot tell you how honored we both are that you've come."

"It's my pleasure."

Aware of the line of guests waiting to greet the hostess and the man at her side, she inclined her head and moved away. She declined a drink and moved to the open doors leading out to the gardens illuminated by colored paper lanterns. The breeze carrying the scent of jasmine and honeysuckle stirred her dress as she stepped into the meticulously tended garden.

She'd expected a terrible sense of betrayal for attending her first social event since Edward's death, but only felt vaguely out of practice. And guilty for not being more grieved.

A fountain splashed into a pond where candles floated like glowing lily pads. The tiny flames cast swirls of light on the dark, rippling water. She skirted the pond, watching the reflections.

"Mrs. Berkley?"

She turned to face a lean man a few years older

than herself. "Lord Druesdale."

"Wonderful to see you after such a long time. You look lovely as ever." He bent over her hand.

"How kind of you to say."

"Druesdale, on the prowl already?" came a deep voice.

She looked up into a pair of aqua eyes set in a handsome face. And caught her breath. Her heart stalled.

The man she'd rescued from hanging, and who'd kissed her, grinned down at her. Drawing a shaky breath, she stepped back.

His dark hair had been styled in the latest fashion; short at the sides and back, tousled and curly on top. She knew first-hand his waves were his own and not the result of a valet's hot-iron. Meticulously dressed in a suit of superior quality, so unlike his attire in the woods at the time of the near hanging, he watched her, completely poised. All signs of the man struggling to draw his breath had vanished. Even the bruises had faded. She wondered if the rope burns were still underneath his expertly tied and creased cravat.

For an instant, she almost preferred the opened shirt. Then she flushed at her own brazenness.

His eyes glinted as if her discomfort pleased him in an unwholesome way. She remembered the feel of his lips against hers. Her face flamed in embarrassment and in another, more secret, fear.

Lord Druesdale turned to the gentleman. "Whenever I have the attention of a beautiful lady, you always appear. I liked you better when you were abroad."

The newcomer chuckled without taking his eyes off Elise. She swallowed, reduced to a state of speechlessness under this handsome, virile man's stare.

Lord Druesdale cleared his throat. "Mrs.

Berkley, may I present the Honorable—" he coughed delicately, as if he found the term amusing "—Jared Amesbury."

Ah. So this was Jared Amesbury. Elise found it difficult to believe that the man she had saved from near death could be the same respectable gentleman of whom Lily Standwich had spoken so fondly. The knowledge left her with more questions than answers.

Mr. Amesbury's teeth flashed white in the dim light. "Mrs. Berkley."

"Mr. Amesbury."

Appallingly flustered, she almost refused his offered hand. He kissed the back of her hand, and when he straightened, his fingers remained closed over hers a second longer than they ought. She remembered his touch without the protection of her gloves, and the warmth that contact had invoked. She hoped the garden's darkness would shield her expression.

"Lord Druesdale, may I have a word?" someone outside her line of sight called.

The lord scowled at Mr. Amesbury as if he had designed this need for his absence, and bowed to Elise. "Forgive me, Mrs. Berkley, I appear to be wanted. I hope to see you again shortly." He shot Mr. Amesbury an indecipherable look, bowed to Elise, and moved away.

Mr. Amesbury moved closer to Elise. Her heart pounded as he neared. He looked smug as if he knew her thoughts.

"Despite your earlier refusal, I'm glad to finally learn your name. At least, part of it. What is your Christian name?"

"Missus," she said through clenched teeth, and turned to leave.

"Wait. Please don't go."

The desperation in his softly spoken words

arrested her movement. Slowly, she turned back to him. His disconcerting eyes traveled over her face with such intensity it seemed a physical touch. She wondered if he looked at every woman thusly and decided he probably did. The rake!

"I wanted to thank you again for your assistance in the woods." A seductive tone rumbled his voice.

"You're welcome," she snapped. Her own rudeness shocked her, but this womanizing cad deserved to be brought down a peg or two.

"And to apologize," he added, unperturbed. "I offended you the other day. I do not wish to destroy any chance I might have in the future to become better acquainted."

"I believe we are too well acquainted already."

"But I'm in your debt. Please allow me to thank you properly." His lazy smile and smoldering eyes made her wish she had worn a dress with a higher neckline.

She nervously touched the cameo on the ribbon at her throat. "It's not necessary to thank me. Besides, I doubt I can trust your definition of 'properly.' "

He laughed softly. "You're a wise woman, Mrs. Berkley. However, I have something less nefarious in mind." He executed a courtly bow. "I thank you, madam, from the bottom of my heart, for coming to my rescue."

From an inner coat pocket, he retrieved a velvet drawstring bag, opened it, and inverted it in his hand. A perfect, pink pearl lay in his palm.

He held it out to her. "There is an island where the natives harvest these from the ocean. The chief gave this to me to thank me for saving his son. I give this to you to thank you for saving the boy and me. I hope you will accept this token of my gratitude. And, I hope, as an apology."

She stilled at his unexpected words.

He added, "I offended you with my impulsive behavior, and I humbly beg your forgiveness." A smile lurked around the corner of his eyes despite the contrition in his tone.

Had a man ever left her so thoroughly confused? He was a muddle of a perfect gentleman and an incorrigible tease. Truly he was a cad. She'd just have to ignore those annoyingly elemental stirrings; they would be extremely inconvenient if she, as a mother and widow, followed them.

She indicated the pearl. "Truly, this is not necessary."

"Please take it." He grinned with roguish charm. "Otherwise, I'll be honor-bound to find some other way to thank you."

Something in his tone dispelled her guard. Laughing softly at his audacity, she picked up the pearl and admired it. "Very well, I accept, lest you become even more outrageous in your expression of gratitude."

A place in her heart was touched that he'd be so thoughtful as to have brought her a gift that possessed sentimental value, rather than merely one of monetary worth. Not that she should be accepting either one from a stranger, but somehow, she could not refuse.

Archly, she said, "And as you were clearly not in your right mind after such a terrible ordeal, I will forgive you for your misconduct." She wrapped the pearl in a lace handkerchief and put it in her reticule.

His smile appeared both wicked and relieved. "I cannot express how much that means to me. I have thought of you often since that day."

"You, sir, continually breach the boundaries of propriety," she managed, wishing she could slow down her traitorous heart and force it to accept her decision to dismiss him as beneath her notice. But she couldn't simply dismiss someone whose very presence filled the entire garden, and whose thoughtfulness touched her more than she cared to admit.

She almost uttered a sound of disgust. When had she become so easily ensnared by the charms of a libertine? She took another step backward and lost her balance. With a cry, she teetered at the edge of the pond.

His hand shot out to catch her by the arms. Laughter leaped into his eyes while he slowly pulled her in to his broad chest. He smelled clean and earthy and so very masculine. For one brief moment of insanity, she enjoyed his nearness, his arms around her making her feel safe, protected, desirable.

Where had she left her wits?

"Thank you," she whispered, dropping her eyes and shrugging off his hands.

His hands fell to his sides. "Do you really fear me so? Or is it that this isn't proper, either?"

"Of course this isn't proper. And I'm wise to mistrust a man whose conduct and intentions are questionable, at best. Unless I have my gun, of course."

His lazy laughter rang out, filling her with slow warmth.

She barely controlled the impulse to smile. Instead, she raised her chin while trying to look appropriately irritated. "You laugh at me, sir?"

"You are a sheer delight." He enclosed one of her hands between both of his. Though terribly, terribly improper, the possessiveness of his gesture felt oddly sweet. "Do you know that in many countries, once a person has saved the life of another, that person must remain with his savior until the debt is repaid? If we were to honor that, then I must be with you, watching over you, every minute of every day."

41

She considered remaining in this man's presence every moment of every day. Definitely not. Her sensibilities would never survive it.

She disentangled her hand and said primly, "Fortunately, we do not have such an inconvenient custom in England."

He chuckled. "I think you don't really mean that."

That sensual quality entered his voice, bringing to mind a stark remembrance of his kiss. She watched his gaze focus on her lips. She felt them part of their own volition as she remembered how soft and warm his lips were, the way she'd tingled at the touch. The way she tingled again now just remembering it.

For one brief, horrifying moment, she had the insane hope that he would kiss her again. Longer. Over and over...

She took herself in hand and drew a shaky breath. "Do you always accost women in this manner?"

"Only those who capture my interest. You see, I've never met an angel."

An angel? That was probably the loveliest thing any man had ever said to her. Too bad she harbored secret desires that contradicted such a compliment. Too bad it came from a scoundrel who probably used it with every woman he hoped to seduce.

"You, sir, are a dangerous flatterer."

He laughed with abandon. "You might as well tell me your name. I'll find out anyway."

She lifted her chin defiantly. "Very well, in exchange for a satisfactory explanation of your straits that day on my property, I will tell you my name. But you do not have permission to address me by it."

"I fear I may not be able to resist."

"Exercise a measure of control."

"Hmmm. Like the control I exercised when I kissed you?"

Her face flamed. "No!" she whispered tersely.

"I assure you, I was tempted to do far more than I did."

Arrogant wretch! "Then truly you are no gentleman."

"You're right. I only pretend to be. No doubt my mother would be horrified." A brief shadow touched his face. Sadness? Grief? Regret?

"My given name is Elise," she heard herself say.

"Elise," he repeated in a tone approaching reverence.

"But you do not have my permission to use it."

One corner of his mouth turned up, dispelling the earlier show of emotion. "Yes, ma'am."

A flare of light in the heavens caught her attention, and she watched a star streak across the darkened sky. "Look. A falling star."

"Make a wish," he suggested.

"I have no need of wishes. I have a home and a son and everything I need. I'll make one for you. What do you wish?"

"Freedom."

She blinked, taken aback by his unexpected answer. "Freedom from what?"

The light in his expressive eyes dimmed. "I can't tell you."

When he said nothing further, she ignored her upbringing and asked, "Why can't you tell me?"

A self-deprecating smile touched his mouth. "You already dislike me. If you really knew me, you'd be repulsed."

She touched his sleeve. "I never said I dislike you. Besides, we're virtually strangers; why should my opinion matter?"

Rigid with tension, he looked down at her hand resting upon his arm, his lashes concealing his eyes.

Very quietly, he replied, "It matters."

Stunned, she waited. Again, the guise of a playful rogue had fallen away and genuine loss shone through. His gaze locked with hers then, and he looked like a lost child. A deep and poignant sadness entered the aquamarine depths of his eyes, holding her in its grasp.

Seized with an overwhelming desire to discover the source of his haunting pain, coupled with the urge to offer comfort, she cast about for a method to cheer him.

She indicated the starry sky. "Then I'll make a wish. I wish for you to have all the desires of your heart."

He looked at her in wonder. Just when she'd begun to think she'd been wrong about him, the wickedness returned in the lopsided upturn of his mouth. "Even if my heart desires you?"

"I…" Her heart thumped and tightness coiled in her abdomen.

Suddenly terrified at the realization that, on at least one level, she did desire him, she fled to the safety of the brightly lit drawing room. Ordinarily she would shun bright lights that might reveal her discomfort, but she'd be safer inside away from him. From herself.

She halted. In exchange for her given name, she'd demanded an explanation regarding the noose and the men who'd been threatening him, yet he'd managed to distract her without answering her question. And she'd still given him her name. She clenched her teeth. Rogue!

Charlotte Greymore approached wearing a wide smile. "Elise, you look magnificent."

Elise touched her gown self-consciously. "How do you feel, Charlotte?"

"I am quite well, no need to worry. Are you all right?"

Elise laughed softly. "I'm not the one increasing, Charlotte."

Glowing with happiness, Charlotte placed a hand on her slightly rounded abdomen. "I'm over the sickness, and aside from some fatigue, I feel wonderful."

"I'm glad to hear it. And I'm glad you aren't going to be ill the entire nine months as was I."

Charlotte smiled and glanced over her shoulder at her husband. Mr. Greymore stood laughing in a circle of men.

"I'm in need of the ladies' retiring room." Charlotte blushed. "Excuse me."

Elise watched her pass her husband, touch his arm, and leave the room. Charlotte seemed happier than ever now that she'd wedded her childhood sweetheart. But then, Mr. Greymore was a remarkable man.

"Mrs. Berkley. How delightful to see you."

Elise turned to see her neighbor, Mr. Bradford. Edward and Mr. Bradford used to banter good-naturedly about the rightful ownership of the lake that spanned their adjoining land.

"How are you, Mr. Bradford?" she asked, swiftly regaining her comportment.

Slightly younger than she, Mr. Bradford had fine features and curling blond hair. She'd always thought him a pleasant man. After he'd buried his wife only months ago, the perpetual laughter had left his eyes.

He blinked and looked away. "I'm well, thank you. I miss Emma, of course, but we are getting along."

Elise felt a twinge of guilt. "I must apologize for having neglected you during this difficult time. I should have been there for you more."

His eyes widened in surprise. "You didn't neglect me. You've always been most kind. And my daughters adore your Colin."

Lily announced, "Ladies and gentlemen. Dinner is served."

Mr. Bradford bowed to Elise and moved to another lady he'd been assigned to escort into the dining room.

"It is my pleasure, Mrs. Berkley."

She looked up into Mr. Amesbury's eyes. He'd reconstructed his mask of careless charm, and his self-possession appeared firmly in place.

She shot a scathing glare at Lily for pairing her with Mr. Amesbury for dinner, but her friend only looked pleased. Resigned, Elise placed her hand on his offered arm. He was a large man, strong and muscular, and there was something world-weary about his face.

Those moments of vulnerability she'd seen in him moments ago in the garden touched her inner needs to soothe and comfort. She wanted to learn his secrets, heal his hurts.

But that would be unwise, considering she had no desire to risk placing herself under the thumb of a man.

"Are you trying to divine my thoughts?" he asked.

"I'm not sure I dare venture into such dangerous territory."

Softly chuckling, he led her to the dining room, following the other guests according to rank and precedence, and pulled out her chair for her before taking his place at her right. Lord Druesdale sat at her left. Directly across from her sat the young widower, Mr. Bradford. She felt like a fish in a glass bowl on display for a dozen hungry cats.

Mr. Amesbury settled next to her looking amused and satisfied. As servants brought each course, Elise concentrated on her food and tried to politely include both gentlemen next to her, so as not to show any favoritism. She did not wish to give any sign that might be misconstrued as preference.

A guest sitting further down the table caught her attention momentarily. Lord Von Barondy, a viscount, was a middle-aged man with thinning hair and sharp, darting eyes. He and his wife were respectable members of the community. Privately, Elise found them both terrible boors.

"Yes, I suppose I have had a run of good luck," the viscount said, his chest puffing out. "It's nothing terribly magical, really, just a series of good business investments. I fear I have a weakness for spoiling my lovely wife." He glanced at the lady beside him.

His wife, several years younger and wearing an enormous diamond and ruby necklace, smiled at him. He glanced fondly at her, and Elise felt a pang in her heart. Her own dear husband had looked at her that way in rare, tender moments.

Elise redirected her gaze to her plate and unclenched her hand.

"I wish I knew your secret," Mr. Bradford replied.

The viscount's wife fidgeted with her necklace with several bejeweled fingers as she ate, as if assuring herself all remained in place.

Von Barondy waved a hand magnanimously toward the other guests. "Let us not bore the ladies present with business. We're here to enjoy ourselves. Business can wait. Besides, you don't expect me to reveal all my methods for success, do you?"

Mr. Amesbury kept his focus upon his plate, giving no indication that he neither heard the exchange nor was even aware of the speakers. Yet, something about his stylishly bored manner gave her pause. It seemed too deliberate.

She frowned. Deliberate stylish boredom? She watched him with greater focus. He gripped his fork tight enough to whiten his fingertips. An alert stillness suggested he knew at that very moment the precise location of everyone in the room and the topics they discussed.

He glanced at her. His eyes widened briefly in surprise at her unabashed stare. A mischievous grin slid into place. Again, it appeared forced. Then his eyes took on a rakish glint.

"Having trouble keeping your eyes off me, eh, Mrs. Berkley?" he murmured in a voice only she would hear.

She glared.

One corner of his mouth lifted and then he turned to speak to Mrs. Carson sitting to his other side, his voice calm, his demeanor relaxed, and the illusion vanished.

Elise shrugged off the foolish notion. She must have imagined it. After all, she'd not kept the company of gentlemen in years, so what did she think she knew about them, or him in particular? Keenly aware of his presence, her eyes repeatedly moved to him, but she fought to direct them away. If only he weren't so uncommonly handsome!

He turned to her and leaned in close enough to send her heart flipping. The knots in her stomach made it difficult to eat. She glanced at him, wondering if he knew his effect upon her. Probably. The blackguard.

With perfect propriety, he murmured, "Are you enjoying your dinner, Mrs. Berkley?" His hand toyed with his glass, reminding her of his gentle touch despite his scars and calluses.

She swallowed. "Of course." She did not dare mention in front of other guests that he sat too close.

"Pray, tell me, Mrs. Berkley, have you any interest in Egyptian artifacts?" Lord Druesdale said.

Desperate to prove to Mr. Amesbury that he had no effect upon her, she gratefully turned from Mr. Amesbury to Lord Druesdale. "I, ah, no. That is, I have not become familiar with the subject. I read a great deal, but that is not a subject I have studied." She cringed, fully aware at how badly she was failing at her attempt to appear calm.

"Pity," replied Lord Druesdale. "It's fascinating. I was a member of Napoleon's excursions into Egypt and was present during some impressive and historic finds."

"Yes, I had heard," Mr. Amesbury rumbled. "While some of us were fighting a war, you were consorting with the enemy." There could be no mistaking his accusing tone.

Druesdale stiffened. "I was present as a scholar, not as a supporter."

The tension between the two men crackled. Elise felt as if she'd been caught in the crossfire of a duel.

"Your presence alone could be considered support," Mr. Amesbury shot back.

"I wouldn't expect you to understand."

They stared at each other hard until she feared they'd actually come to blows. Then Mr. Amesbury glanced at her. "Forgive us, Madam. You mentioned you enjoy reading. What do you like to read?"

"Oh, many things. I especially enjoy novels by Ann Radcliff and Sir Walter Scott. I recently read one called Frankenstein—"

"Novels? You surprise me," broke in Lord Druesdale. "I thought you the type who reads ladies' magazines, looking at the latest fashion plates and needlepoint patterns."

"I enjoy a wide variety of subjects."

"Poetry?" asked Mr. Amesbury.

"Not so much. I think Byron is one of the better poets, but he can be a bit dark for my taste."

"Ah, you prefer the romantics such as Wordsworth, Coleridge," said Druesdale.

Elise found her attention so neatly divided between the gentlemen on either side that she hardly knew where to look.

"If you must know, I read the newspaper more than anything else." She glanced at Druesdale, who looked faintly scandalized. Through the corner of her eye, she observed Mr. Amesbury. One side of his mouth twitched in amusement. In his eyes shone approval.

Elise blinked. Approval? Most men, Edward included, disapproved of ladies reading the newspapers, viewing them as too sordid for a lady's delicate nature.

Recklessly, she added, "In particular, I applaud the prison reforms and have made a number of contributions toward charities who seek change. I also support the idea of an educational system for the poor to give them the opportunity to improve themselves, although we may not see such a program during our lifetime."

She looked at them in turn with a challenging lift to her chin. Lord Druesdale stared with raised brows.

Mr. Amesbury grinned. "What an independent and forward thinker you are, Mrs. Berkley. You would like my sisters."

She searched for signs of mocking or condemnation, and found none. Astonishing.

After dessert had been served, the guests raised their glasses in toasts to the upcoming wedding between Lady Standwich and Mr. Harrison. Elise offered a toast she hoped sounded heartfelt and congratulatory. Lily positively glowed as she beamed at her intended, and Elise squelched her selfish disappointment at Lily's decision to remarry.

As dinner ended, the hostess stood and nodded to the men. "Gentlemen. You are most welcome to join us in the drawing room when you are so inclined." She gave an affectionate smile to Mr. Harrison, who visibly softened when their eyes met.

The ladies rose and followed her out, leaving the gentlemen to their own discussion. Grateful for the separation from the man whose very presence threatened her safe existence, Elise went with the ladies.

As conversation buzzed around her, her thoughts returned to Jared Amesbury. She puzzled over his moments of vulnerability in the garden, and over her desire to soothe him. And she recalled how much he'd needed her aid in the woods. How long since she'd had any desire to offer comfort to a man? How long since one had needed her?

She realized that she'd desperately missed being needed. Colin needed her, of course, and her servants and tenants depended upon her, but that was different. None of them needed her as a woman.

Then again, as much as she'd loved Edward and enjoyed their comfortable companionship, she wasn't entirely sure he'd ever actually needed her, either.

She sat stunned by the revelation of her own loneliness.

The shields, built up by years of fooling herself, fell away, revealing the chasm in her life. The chasm in her purpose. The chasm in her heart. Her hands shook, and she stared unseeing at the wall behind Lily's head. Then she gave herself a scolding for sinking into self pity and reminded herself that widowhood was wonderful.

At the moment, she had trouble listing reasons why.

The gentlemen joined them, and she sensed Mr. Amesbury the moment he entered the room. Like a great, hungry panther, he prowled closer. The image shattered when he halted, offered a slight bow, and politely indicated an empty place next to her on the settee.

"May I?"

She thought she heard a sound of annoyance

from Lord Druesdale who had reached her at almost the same instant, but forgot him the moment she looked up into Mr. Amesbury's face. The intensity in his eyes drove away her powers of speech. She swallowed against a suddenly dry mouth.

Though increasingly desperate to escape his unnerving presence and regain her self-control, Elise pulled her eyes away and nodded toward the empty seat. "Please."

The seat sank under his weight. She smelled his clean, masculine scent. Acutely aware of him, and disturbed by her reaction, she adjusted her skirts, flicked off an imaginary speck, and looked for something else to do to keep her eyes off him. Her earlier compassion for him vanished, leaving her only with the desire to escape his disturbing effect.

"Lady Standwich seems delighted at the prospect of her upcoming nuptials," Mr. Amesbury commented benignly.

"I can't imagine why," she said before she realized she'd spoken her thoughts out loud.

"You don't approve of her match with Mr. Harrison?"

Ashamed, she hastily added, "It isn't that. He's a fine man. It's only that I'm surprised she's decided to remarry."

"Are you? Why is that?"

She paused, unwilling to reveal too much. "We spent much time discussing how well we've adapted to widowhood and how we never planned to wed again and give up our independence. Her change of heart seemed sudden."

He shifted, bringing his leg near enough that she felt his warmth. A stirring began deep inside, so basic, so elemental in its origin that it seemed at once familiar and foreign. It frightened her. She inched away.

"Have I done something to offend you, Mrs.

Berkley?"

Keeping her eyes averted, she shook her head. "No, of course not."

"Why do you look distressed?" he persisted.

"You are far too attentive."

Grinning, he leaned close. "I don't think I've ever been accused of being too attentive before. I have, however, been accused of just the opposite on more than one occasion." His breath stirred the tendrils at her neck.

Her heart flittered and then pounded. She made the mistake of looking at him. The twinkle in his eye and irrepressible grin should have disarmed her. Instead, annoyance flared that he could so easily sweep away her sensible nature.

"You are bold, sir," she hissed through clenched teeth.

"I am," he agreed in a low voice. "So bold that I hope to hear you call me Jared some day."

She shivered at the indirect caress of his warm breath on her skin and kept her gaze downcast rather than meet that unnervingly direct stare. What had happened to her defenses? It was like trying to ward off a hurricane's blast with a mere parasol.

"Sir, that is hardly appropriate."

"Then I shall persist until it becomes appropriate."

Her gaze shot to his, her breath catching. If her heart beat unevenly before, it positively raced now with his mouth only inches away. A longing to move closer and feel the passion of his kiss surfaced once again. Horrified at her shameless desire, and the guilt that reared its accusing head, she looked away. She barely heard the other guests laugh and chatter.

His eyes glittered as he shifted closer.

"You're infuriating," she managed through clenched teeth as she tried to put on what others would see as a lighthearted smile so as not to betray anything was amiss.

He grinned wickedly. "Are you sure it's I who infuriates you? Or is it your unwilling attraction to me?"

Her smile tightened. "Arrogant, as well."

"I believe the word is 'perceptive.' Although, bold, infuriating and arrogant are all words that no doubt fit. Trust me; I've been called things much less flattering. You do owe me an apology, you know."

Taken aback, she stared. "Oh?"

"You led me to believe you are married, Mrs. Berkley."

"And so I was. For five wonderful years."

"I'm very glad to learn that I shall not have to duel your husband for you."

She swallowed her initial shock at his outrageous statement and lifted her chin. "Since you would surely have lost to my husband, it is fortunate for you no such thing will happen."

He grinned, handsome and dangerous. "I might surprise you."

She truly hoped he was joking. At the moment, she could not be certain of anything. Even herself. She bit her lip.

Lady Standwich stood and invited anyone interested to join a game of whist. She directed players to tables, making sure people were paired as she wished. She partnered Elise with Mr. Bradford, and as Elise took her place, she noticed both gentlemen at Elise's table were widowed. Determined to be polite, but wishing she could escape, Elise played the most miserable hands of whist ever. However, Mr. Bradford remained perfectly gracious about their losses.

Finally, Elise rose, bid them all good night, and signaled a footman to ready her carriage and bring her wrap.

"Lily, thank you for inviting me to your dinner party. I had a lovely time." She almost added 'despite your attempts to foist me off on the bachelors and widowers' but she held her tongue.

"Thank you for coming, Elise. It meant the world to me."

Elise turned to Mr. Harrison next to Lily. "Again, congratulations and I wish you both much happiness. Good evening."

They bid her good night and returned to their guests. As she waited near the door for her coach, she felt a presence.

"Mrs. Berkley, I'm sorry to see you leaving so soon."

Bracing herself, she turned to Mr. Amesbury.

"I had hoped you would partner me for the next game." The gentle seductiveness in his voice chased away any retort she might have made.

He raised her hand to his lips and actually kissed the back of her hand. She pulled her hand from his. Heaven help her if he ever kissed her hand without the protection of her gloves.

"Please don't do that," she pled weakly, too tired to spar with him.

He paused, the humor leaving his face, and he studied her carefully. "Why are you afraid?"

She looked away before she got so lost in those beautiful eyes that she forgot herself. "Anyone who calls herself a lady would be foolish not to fear you."

When he remained quiet so long, she dared to look up at him, expecting to see anger. Instead, his expressive mouth curved. In place of its usual sly wickedness, his smile was soft, regretful. "I would never hurt a lady."

She remembered his strangely powerful kiss and her foreign reaction to it. Their eyes locked, and she felt as though her soul were laid bare. All her loneliness, those long, sleepless nights, and her efforts to remain strong rose up to taunt her.

"Good night, Mr. Amesbury." She fled to the safety of her waiting carriage. A quick glance out of the window proved that he watched her.

Elise closed her eyes, refusing to look up at the sky and risk seeing another falling star lest she be tempted to make a wish. An involuntary smile stole over her face, and for just a blissful moment, she allowed herself to bask in the warmth of his attention. Something about his outrageous behavior appealed to the suppressed adventurer in her. She should have been appropriately horrified.

She promised herself the moment she arrived home she would repress it, never to indulge in it again.

How was it possible that a stranger stirred her womanly desires more powerfully than Edward had in five years of marriage? And what did that say about her loyalty to her beloved husband?

CHAPTER 4

Jared lounged in an armchair beside the fire in his bedchamber and picked up a book. "Thank you, Gibbs. That will be all." He opened the book and pretended to read.

"Very good, sir. Rest well."

Out of the corner of his eye, Jared saw the valet leave. Alone now, he took a candle to the dressing room and kneeled next to a sea chest beside the clothes press. After unlocking the chest, Jared retrieved a bag and pulled out its contents.

Grimly, he fingered the clothes he'd worn as a pirate. He could not explain why putting them on tonight seemed distasteful; they were comfortable and familiar, and for a change, clean. He should be grateful to have them. Best of all, the pirate's garb did not require the cursed cravat.

He swallowed his revulsion and dressed. After all, he couldn't very well meet with his former shipmates dressed as a gentleman; they'd have trouble recognizing him as it was.

After donning a cloak, he tucked his usual assortment of guns and knives about his person.

At the door he listened. No one stirred. He blew out the candles and stepped into the corridor, waiting until his eyes adjusted to the gloom before he crept forward.

Careful to keep his weight evenly distributed lest he cause the floor to squeak, Jared left the house and moved to the stables. He whistled.

An answering whistle came and a child's voice called out, "Cap'n?"

Jared let out his breath in frustration. "José, lad, you can't call me that here on land."

The boy stepped out of the shadowy interior of the stables leading Jared's blue roan. "Sorry, sir." He rubbed Aries's muzzle. "He don't scare me no more, sir."

For a lad who'd spent most of his short life on board a ship, he'd taken to the horses well. Jared hadn't dared leave the boy in the company of his crew in Port Johns; no telling what might happen to him or how many ways he'd be corrupted or harmed.

Of course, Jared hadn't managed to keep the boy safe on land, either. Leandro had seen his weakness for the lad and it nearly cost both José and Jared their lives.

What in the world had he been thinking when he so openly pursued Elise Berkley the other night? She was exactly what he did not need. He wouldn't make the mistake of forming any kind of attachments again. Worrying over José's safety was enough. He did not need another weak spot where his enemies could strike.

Jared took the reins and patted Aries. "Well done, José. Now go to bed. I'll untack and rub him down when I return."

José nodded and trotted off as Jared mounted and headed toward the nearest village. On the outskirts of Brenniswick, Jared slowed his mount as a shadow detached itself from an alley. After confirming the silent figure as his first mate, Jean-Claude Dubois, Jared continued to the tavern, confident the man would guard his back. Dubois followed at a discreet distance.

As he approached the tavern, Jared glanced about cautiously and paused to listen before he dismounted. Inside the tavern, he found a seat where he could keep an eye on the door and windows. One never knew when a quick escape would be necessary or when an ambush lay in wait.

Moments later, Dubois took up a defensive position in the opposite corner. The barkeep barely glanced at either of them as he brought drinks.

Jared took a long drink of cheap, watered-down ale and waited for his quartermaster. He didn't have to wait long. Another cloaked figure slipped in quietly. Jared noted with satisfaction that Dubois remained alert and had not missed the new arrival.

His quartermaster slid into a chair at Jared's table. "Jack. I hardly recognized you all cleaned up," he said with a lilting islander accent.

"Anakoni." Jared rubbed his smooth-shaven face where his beard had once been.

The Hawaiian fixed a searching stare upon Jared. "You wanted to see me?"

"Leandro paid me a visit." Jared omitted mention of Leandro putting a noose around his neck.

Anakoni started and then frowned. "He's here?"

Jared had made a career out of knowing when people were lying and when they were truthful. Anakoni clearly had no knowledge of Leandro's appearance. Which meant someone else had sold him out. And he had yet to discover how Leandro found Jared, or why he'd recognized Jared without his pirate's guise. As Jared sipped his ale, he speculated on possible traitors.

Anakoni digested the news momentarily and then pinned Jared with an accusing stare. "He's still after you for killing Macy?"

"It gets worse. He thinks I hid part of the booty somewhere. At least that's his excuse for leading his crew on a merry chase for me."

As Anakoni's eyes bored into his, Jared imagined the man reaching for his knife under the table. "Did you? Hide part of the booty?"

Jared suppressed a wry smile. Killing one's captain paled in comparison to the crime of stealing another's fair share of plunder.

"No. You were there. We went back for it, and it had been dug up. Someone double-crossed us."

"I'll see what I can find out," the islander said. "I don't suppose you'll tell me where you're staying?"

Jared looked at him askance. He'd only trusted Dubois and José with his whereabouts and his dual identity, although his story to them lacked a number of telling truths.

A brief smile twitched the other man's face. "Right. I'll send word through the normal channel if I need to contact you."

After Anakoni left, Jared made eye contact with Dubois. His first mate nodded once and slipped out of the room. Jared waited a moment and then slapped down his coin on the table. With his hands resting on his weapons, he stepped outside and paused to listen and scan the area, waiting for the prickly feeling at the back of his neck that warned him of danger. Nothing.

Jared retrieved his horse and rode to a darkened field with a clear view of the countryside for miles around. The small dark lump in the middle of the field might have been mistaken for a rock. At Jared's approach, the lump rose and sprouted legs.

"*Mon capitaine.*"

"Dubois. It wasn't Anakoni."

"*Non.* I didn't think it would be." His French accent lightly touched his words.

"To be honest, I didn't, either. Any other ideas?"

"It could be any member of the crew."

"None of them know I'm in Brenniswick. I suppose it's possible Leandro might have tailed us, but we were careful to avoid that."

The thought chilled him. He'd gone to the family estate to visit Cole and his new bride before coming here. If he'd been tailed, then he'd unwittingly led dangerous men literally to Cole's door.

No. He'd been very careful. More likely, someone had stumbled onto one of the crew in Port Johns. But how they'd gotten to José this far inland remained a mystery. Jared hated that kind of mystery.

"I'll find out who tipped him off and how much he knows." Dubois paused, eyeing Jared shrewdly. "Something you want to tell me, *Mon Capitaine*?"

Jared shook his head. This near the end, he could not afford the luxury of trust. He only hoped when this was all over, he could convince his crew to cooperate with the authorities and be spared the noose.

Soon, he would be free. But free to be whom?

He'd assumed so many roles over the years that he wondered if he knew who he really was. Or who he would become if he had no role to play.

Jared Amesbury, second son of the Earl of Tarrington, had been pretending to be others for so long, he wondered if that man existed.

Would he shed all his personas, only to discover no one there?

****

Days later, the sun shone on Jared as he sauntered along the main street of Brenniswick. As his thoughts tumbled, he strolled as if he were nothing more than a country gentleman out for a bit of fresh air. He nodded absently to people he passed and forced himself not to tug at his cravat.

He stepped into a cool shadow and looked up. He'd wandered near the steps of a church. He cringed. The last time he'd been in a church was in Havana where he'd impersonated a priest and helped rob the place. He thought plundering the church had been a bit extreme, however his men had certainly enjoyed themselves. Jared grinned at the fond memories.

He missed the sea. At first, the thought of being

landlocked had seemed horrible, and while it had not proven as bad as he had feared, he missed the freedom of commanding his own ship and having nothing barring his way.

Of course, he'd been playing a role then, as well. What surprised him was that he actually missed his mates. Though thieves and scoundrels, most of them were surprisingly decent men. All had secrets and pasts they never discussed, and Jared had found unexpected kinship in them. He had fit in with relative ease, once he got over his fear of waking up to find his throat slit.

Even his brother Cole had thrived in the freedom outside the strictures of the navy's discipline.

"Hold my hand and remain close, my love." A feminine voice brought up Jared's head.

A slender figure in an understated blue gown moved into Jared's line of sight. Elise Berkley's lovely face and pleasing form enraptured him. Her attention remained fixed upon a small boy whose hand she held, and she did not see him.

Drawn to her, Jared maneuvered himself into better position to watch.

The child looked up at his mother and nodded solemnly. Mrs. Berkley smoothed the boy's blond hair and touched his cheek in a gesture that took Jared's breath away.

Underneath a tasteful bonnet, her carefully braided hair had been wound into a large coil, hinting at its length and thickness. Jared pictured it loose, blowing in a sea wind, swirling around her back and waist. Her modest, subdued gown failed to hide her appealing, womanly curves. He wondered if he could encircle her waist with his hands. Then, as his eyes moved downward, following the curves of her body, he wondered a great deal that no gentleman ought to imagine about a respectable lady.

He let out a strangled breath. What made him think he could ever pass himself as a gentleman if, every time he saw this lady, all he wanted to do was throw her over his shoulder and carry her off?

Mrs. Berkley looked in his direction. Alarm replaced her soft expression. Women recoiling from him in fear had been the worst part of piracy. Jared's stomach twisted to see fear in Mrs. Berkley's face.

His heart chilled. He glanced down, half expecting to see himself clad in only a pair of breeches and boots with a cutlass in his hand. No, his suit looked perfect for the part of an earl's son; tasteful and expensive. Even the cursed cravat remained in place. He looked back up at Mrs. Berkley to see that her alarm had vanished, replaced by cool reserve.

He cursed himself. He should not have kissed her. And he had not improved matters by his forward behavior at Lady Standwich's soirée. He'd spent the better part of the last fifteen years in the company of villains and was out of practice for the more perilous kind of lifestyle to which he endeavored to return. He feared he'd never earn her trust. And why should he? He was a scoundrel. Only a foolish woman would ever feel safe in his presence.

He took command of his thoughts and swept off his hat. "Good day, Mrs. Berkley."

For an instant, he thought she would give him the cut direct, but her gentle nature, or perhaps impeccable manners, won.

"Good day, Mr. Amesbury." Her tone was painfully cool.

Jared inwardly winced. He diverted his attention to the boy holding her hand.

She stepped protectively closer to the child, as if she feared Jared would snatch him up and spirit him away. "My son, Colin. Colin, this is Mr. Amesbury."

The boy solemnly shook his hand, and Jared marveled at the child's soft, smooth hands, so unlike José's.

"I'm very pleased to make your acquaintance, young Master Berkley," Jared said. "How old are you?"

The flaxen-haired child puffed up his chest. "Just turned seven, sir."

"Ah. Growing well, I see."

A slow smile spread over the child's face. "Are you a pirate?"

Jared's heart stopped. What about him could have given that away?

A small laugh escaped Mrs. Berkley, and Jared could only gape at the lovely sound.

With a charming blush touching her cheeks, she hastened to explain, "He's been reading stories about pirates, and it's his dream to meet one. I thought he understood how vile they are, but he seems to have become somewhat confused by the lessons he's supposed to be learning. I apologize if his question offends you."

Finding his breath and coaxing his heart to restart, Jared held back a sigh of relief. He sat on his haunches in front of young Colin and lowered his voice to a conspiratorial whisper. "I used to be a pirate, you see, but I realized the error of my ways and have reformed." Admiration shone in the boy's face.

"You oughtn't encourage such a fantasy, Mr. Amesbury," she scolded gently.

"What makes you think I'm untruthful?" He grinned.

She glanced at him from under lowered lashes, no doubt remembering his attire the first time they met and assessing the possibility he might be telling the truth. "You being a pirate would explain your

The Guise of a Gentleman

rather extraordinary situation the first time we met."

Jared laughed uneasily and was suddenly glad for the cravat and all it symbolized. "That would be an explanation, but I assure you I am merely a gentleman with a far less nefarious past. However, any woman with a double-barreled rifle is clearly no one with whom a pirate would dream of tangling."

"You should be grateful I have such an unfashionable skill with firearms," she said a bit testily.

"Oh, indeed I am grateful." He grinned wickedly, secretly relieved he'd managed to change the topic. "If I have failed to express it to you, I am certain I can think up another way to show you."

With a blush, she took a step back. Then a gleam entered her eye. She glanced up at the church and said in a falsely sweet voice, "Then if you're so grateful, are you going to church?"

Jared froze. Go to church? Clearly, she was testing him. "Of course I'm going to church." He looked up at the imposing structure and wondered if lightning would strike before or after the walls came down. "I never miss a Sabbath." Unable to resist, he glanced at the boy. "All reformed pirates go to church."

With an uncertain smile, she led the way up the stairs toward the open doorway.

Colin turned around "So were you a pirate, or not?"

Jared winked and laid a finger over his lips with a meaningful glance at Mrs. Berkley.

Colin smiled broadly and fell back a step. "Were you the captain?" he whispered.

Jared nodded once.

Rapture overcame the child's face. Jared hoped such an innocent would never have an opportunity to learn the truth about real pirates who were nothing like the romantic heroes of the stories this boy no doubt heard.

"I'm learning to fence," Colin whispered. "I can fight with you if your ship gets boarded."

Jared nodded solemnly. "I can see you'd be a good man to have in a fight, but I told you I'm reformed."

Colin's enthusiasm fell. "Oh, right."

Jared paused inside the doorway to allow his eyes to adjust to the gloom. When they were in the midst of plundering a ship, he and his crew wore a patch over one eye so when they ventured into the darkened hold, they could switch the patch to the other eye and see with the eye that had already adjusted to darkness. It came in handy for dispatching foolish lurking heroes bent on protecting the ship's stores.

Without the eye patch to aid him, he waited and blinked while Mrs. Berkley settled her son in a pew. Half-amazed that the building still stood and hadn't been blackened by lightning, Jared hesitated in the aisle.

As a child, when he went to church with his family, they'd had their own family pew. What did newcomers do?

In an act of pity, Mrs. Berkley scooted over and patted the bench next to her.

Gratefully, he took a seat at her side, sitting close enough to feel the warmth of her body. Her subtle perfume wafted past him, and he inhaled deeply. "Thank you."

A faint smile tugged at her rose-petal lips, but she turned her head forward, leaving him to admire her profile instead.

She had a small, upturned nose reminiscent of a child's, but her lush, full lips reminded him of how soft and pliant they had grown with his mouth upon them. Her kiss had been hesitant, inexperienced, but full of yearning. He ached to possess them again and taste their promising sweetness. Had she truly been celibate during her widowhood? If so, she was either refreshingly pure or totally devoted to her late husband. Either way, his chances with her remained abysmal.

He refused to admit how much that bothered him.

Mrs. Berkley wore a guarded expression but little Colin peered at him, wide-eyed and curious.

Jared winked at the boy and smiled at the mother.

She pretended not to notice, but her lips twitched. Mesmerized by that full, almost pouting mouth that called to him like the lure of a siren, Jared swallowed and pretended to study the stained glass windows.

The next hour reminded Jared why he hadn't spent much time in church. As the vicar droned on, Jared alternated between wondering what kind of money any number of expensive items in the church would bring to his crew, and attempting to keep his thoughts pure about the enticing Mrs. Berkley. Surprised his evil thoughts failed to call down the wrath of heaven, he mused if he'd ever enter a church without fearing he'd rock the walls. He squirmed.

At the conclusion of the service, Jared offered Elise Berkley his arm. She hesitated, glanced at her son's beaming face, and relented. Jared's chest swelled as he escorted the lovely lady down the aisle and back outside. He paused to greet the vicar who heartily welcomed him, and moved into the sunshine.

Colin looked up at him. "Mr. Amesbury, do you like to fish?"

"I do, young Master Berkley. I spent much of my childhood dangling my legs in the pond catching fish."

"We have a lake. There's some really big fish there."

"Caught any?"

"The ones I catch are small. I always throw them back."

"I'll bet you catch the big ones someday."

"I wish you could fish with me. Mother does sometimes, but she doesn't like the worms."

Mrs. Berkley smiled sheepishly.

The boy went on. "Mrs. Robbins hates to go. Sometimes the gamekeeper takes me, or the cooper, but they haven't much time. Perhaps you could?"

Jared glanced at Mrs. Berkley, but she only appeared amused, not guarded. He looked down at the lad. "I'd love to fish with you. But you must ask your mother first before you extend any invitations, agreed?"

Mrs. Berkley glanced at him in surprise. Jared almost quipped that he might appear to have the manners of a savage, but he actually understood social customs and courtesy. Whether or not he chose to remember them was an entirely different matter. Then Mrs. Berkley looked Jared in the eye and smiled brilliantly.

Jared nearly fell to his knees.

He'd never seen anything so beautiful in all his life. The curve of her mouth and the tiny dimple that appeared mesmerized him. More astonishing was the pleasure in her expression. She seemed perfectly at ease, her smile genuine. That she would be looking at him and smiling seemed too good to be true.

As she turned her focus to Colin, tenderness and affection crept over her face. Deep inside his long-silenced heart, an awakening stirred.

"You have my permission if you'd like to invite Mr. Amesbury to fish with you, Colin," she said.

Amazed she appeared to have changed her opinion of him, at least to some degree, Jared managed a slight bow. "I'm honored you would trust your beloved child to my care. And I promise not to corrupt him with my former pirate ways." He knew she would believe him to be joking, only feeding the child's fantasies, but he enjoyed seeing the glimmer of doubt.

He nearly smacked his own forehead. What was he thinking? He must keep his aristocratic role in place if he hoped to succeed.

Jared straightened, adjusted his demeanor. "I look forward to it, young sir," he said with all the formality of a duke at court. He escorted the lady and her son to their waiting carriage. He handed them in then executed a proper bow. "Good day, Mrs. Berkley."

Her gaze lingered, probing, but Jared remained respectful and aloof, the perfect English gentleman. He smiled, careful to do so without any trace of impudence or rakishness, and then walked away. He felt Elise Berkley's gaze upon him, but he continued on to his own carriage.

José, taking to his new role as a tiger, greeted him with a wide grin as he leaped down from the carriage where he'd been holding the reins. "Purty lady, hey, Cap'n?" He sobered instantly and ducked his head. "Sir. Sorry, sir. Won't happen again, sir." The boy clamored back to his place behind the seat.

"I know it won't, José." Jared snapped the reins and guided his team out onto the street. He glanced back at the Berkley carriage as it drove off in the opposite direction.

Jared ground his teeth. Staying focused normally presented no challenge for him. Why did he find it difficult to do so in her presence? Most of the seductions in which he'd indulged had been either to further his disguise or to glean information. He seldom indulged in casual physical relationships; he couldn't afford to take the chance of inadvertently doing or saying something to reveal his true purpose.

Nor risk becoming emotionally attached.

His enemies would not hesitate to exploit any vulnerability he revealed. And the results would be deadly.

CHAPTER 5

In Lily Standwich's parlor, Elise sat surrounded by friends she'd known for years, her mind far away. While the ladies gossiped and enjoyed their tea, Elise remained silent.

Something about Jared Amesbury did not add up. One moment, he seemed a heartless philanderer. The next, a perfect gentleman. Then a playful rogue peeked through that poised demeanor.

That alone did not disturb her since many gentlemen often had sides to their personalities they did not reveal to society. But underneath Jared's practiced urbane boredom lurked wariness. Even when his stance appeared relaxed, he remained motionless, alert, watchful. He moved with silent, predatory grace, every motion of his body carefully calculated. He never made an unconscious move. Even his casual air seemed planned, as if he were a highly skilled actor playing some role.

However, these impressions—gained yesterday while at church, and once during the dinner party at Lady Standwich's home—were so fleeting that she could not be certain she hadn't simply imagined them.

And she still had failed to discover why she'd found him wearing the clothes of a common man, and even more peculiar, why he'd been in a noose. Despite her questions, she hadn't obtained a satisfactory answer.

But the intoxicating gratitude with which he had looked at her after she'd chased away his enemies, and the gentle, passionate kiss continued to invade her recollections with disturbing frequency. And his behavior since that day did nothing to lessen her response to him. If anything, it increased.

Lily's voice drew her in and Elise realized the ladies were discussing the very object of her thoughts.

"I understand Mr. Amesbury was in the war, but I forget if he served in the navy or aboard a privateer. He has traveled extensively since the war ended."

"My husband said he was unequaled in the hunting party last week," Mrs. Hogan said.

"He probably boxes as well. He's as large as a pugilist." Mrs. Carson giggled.

Lily took charge of the conversation again. "His elder brother has assumed the role as head of the family while their father convalesces by the seashore. The earl's health has declined since his beloved wife's death."

"My son went to Cambridge with a Christian Amesbury," Mrs. Hogan commented.

Mrs. Standwich nodded. "That would be the youngest brother. In my opinion, Christian is the best of the very fine lot. The pride and joy of his parents. Also a gifted artist, although they hope he becomes a man of the church."

"What more do you know of his family?" asked Mrs. Hogan.

Briefly, Elise wondered if Mrs. Hogan's question stemmed from her interest in him as a potential son-in-law. Had he given her any reason to think he might consider courting her daughter?

That Jared Amesbury might be turning one of those ready, lazy smiles upon Miss Hogan—or anyone else, for that matter—left her strangely unsettled.

"I hadn't seen Jared Amesbury since his

childhood, but I've endeavored to welcome him here for his mother's sake. Lady Tarrington was one of the dearest ladies I've ever known." Lily punctuated her statement with a firm nod.

Elise looked up. "Lady Tarrington. I believe I met her once." A vague memory arose of a kind lady with rich, dark hair.

"Of course. You would have undoubtedly met her when you were in London. Everyone adored Lady Tarrington. Hostesses considered their soirées and musicales successful if the Earl and Countess Tarrington attended."

"I wonder if Mr. Amesbury is a church-going man," mused Mrs. Hogan.

Elise smiled at the memory. "Apparently, he is. Colin and I met him on the steps. Colin reads stories about pirates. He's fascinated with them. He asked Mr. Amesbury if he were a pirate."

Gasps and laughter followed her statement.

"I was a bit embarrassed," Elise admitted.

"Was he insulted?" asked Mrs. Hogan.

Elise smiled. "No. He took it all in good humor. He even played along with him and said he was a pirate formerly, but had seen the error of his ways and reformed."

Mrs. Carson leaned in, her eyes sparkling. "He did? Hmm. He does have an unrestrained grin that makes one imagine all those years abroad have been spent in piracy."

Exclamations of mingled shock and delight followed.

"Oh, good heavens! You've been reading far too many novels, Frederica," scolded Lily.

Mrs. Carson only smiled smugly. "You did say he'd been at sea. Privateering and piracy are very close, you know."

Elise interjected hotly, "Except that one is honorable, in defense of one's country, and the other is disgraceful and vile."

Apparently pleased with her wildly overactive imagination, Mrs. Carson added, "I wonder how many women he's compromised. I might not resist if he tried to compromise me." She giggled again.

"Frederica, shame on you," Charlotte Greymore scolded.

But the young woman looked satisfied rather than contrite. Mrs. Carson's husband was at least forty years her senior; perhaps she had unfulfilled fantasies. But that did not excuse her wanton suggestion. Or the ridiculous idea of Mr. Amesbury as a pirate.

Elise's thoughts drifted back to the first time she'd met Jared Amesbury. Dressed as he had been that day, he'd certainly appeared the way she'd imagined a pirate would look. And the way he'd drawn her to him and took command of her mouth...

A delicious ripple shuddered her body. She chastised herself. There could be any number of explanations for his odd apparel. And for the rough men who'd captured him and threatened him and the boy. And the unusual nature of his dangerous predicament.

Her heart stalled. He had told Colin he was a reformed pirate.

Immediately, she dismissed the thought. Clearly, he said that to feed a little boy's interest and imagination out of a sense of playfulness in reply to Colin's question. She recalled his concern and affection for the child who'd been with him. Few men she knew showed such fondness toward children. He had certainly made a fast friend out of Colin. She'd never heard of a pirate possessing a shred of compassion or decency. Even the legendary Sir Francis Drake had been reported to be thoroughly ruthless.

And the tales of cruelty and torture committed

by the new scourge of the seas, Black Jack, made her shiver. He'd committed all manner of murder and mayhem over the last three or four years, at least. Mr. Amesbury couldn't be part of a group that vile.

"Mrs. Berkley? Elise?"

Elise blinked. Every eye on the room observed her in curious silence. She swallowed. "I beg your pardon?"

Mrs. Carson tittered. "Dreaming of pirates demanding your virtue?"

"Frederica, really!" Lily fixed a look of remonstration, but Mrs. Carson did not have the grace to look contrite.

Charlotte turned to Elise. "We're having a riding party on the morrow, if you care to join us."

Elise asked, "Should you ride in your present condition?"

"Oh, my time is months away. Still, I'll ride slowly, never above a walk," Charlotte said. "Will you come?"

"Certainly I will."

Lily looked smug. "Excellent. Then we'll have an even number."

Elise stiffened. "Are you inviting several men in need of wives, perhaps?"

"Oh, it will be a very mixed group, I assure you." Her twinkling eyes belied her benign tone and Elise inwardly groaned.

"If Mr. Amesbury has been a sailor, he might not be much of a rider," suggested Mrs. Hogan.

"If memory serves, he went to sea at the age of thirteen or fourteen," Lily said. "Adequate time to learn to ride well before he departed."

"I imagine he excels at everything," Mrs. Carson declared. "And I'm sure he was properly trained in horsemanship in his youth, even if he's been at sea all these years, plundering and compromising—"

Indignation welled up and Elise interrupted

sharply, "I think it's terrible that you would even suggest that a perfectly respectable man could be anything as horrifying as a pirate."

Again, silence descended as all the ladies watched her. A satisfied smile touched Lily's mouth. Charlotte looked amused.

Elise could almost hear their thoughts and hurried to explain herself. "It's wrong to spread rumors, especially ones based on imagination."

"Quite right," Lily agreed too quickly.

Charlotte's soothing voice broke in. "I'm sure Mr. Amesbury is a fine horseman. He wouldn't have done so well on the hunt, else." She smiled at Elise. "My Mr. Greymore thinks highly of him. They've known each other for years. I'm sure he'd know if his friend had ever been a pirate, so we can stop speculating now." She glanced at Mrs. Carson in remonstration.

Mrs. Carson folded her arms, with a calculating glint in her eye. Mrs. Hogan tapped her chin in thought.

Elise ground her teeth.

"There are so many injuries and even fatalities on those wretched fox hunts," Charlotte continued. "I fear for my husband every time he goes."

Her statement prompted a new discussion on the pleasures and evils of the hunt, and Elise gave Charlotte a smile of gratitude for so skillfully changing the subject.

As they prepared to leave, Charlotte said, "Shall you all come to Greymore Manor on the morrow?"

They agreed and bid each other farewell. As the others filed out of the room, Charlotte Greymore drew Elise aside.

Charlotte lowered her voice. "I met Mr. Amesbury when he arrived here this summer. He's certainly charming."

Elise looked away. "I can't imagine why you

think I care."

Charlotte kept her own counsel, wearing a mysterious smile, and merely bid her good day.

Clearly Elise needed to disabuse Lily of her misconception that she, in any way, thought to remarry. While the other ladies dispersed, Elise lingered until they were alone.

Lily turned back to Elise expectantly. "You might as well come back in and sit down, since you have something on your mind." Lily put her arm around Elise and led her back into the parlor. As they sat together, Elise twisted her fingers together.

"What is it, my dear?"

"I hold you in the highest regard." Elise paused, not wishing to offend her friend.

"Just come out and say whatever it is you wish to say."

Elise drew a breath. "I have no wish to remarry. Ever. Please stop arranging opportunities for me to meet gentlemen."

Lily laid her hand on Elise's arm and smiled indulgently. "My dear, I understand. Rest assured, I'm not trying to foist any gentleman upon you."

"Then the riding excursion?"

"Just a bit of a diversion. Perfectly harmless. Why, most of those in the party are already married."

"And you wanted an equal number merely to avoid awkwardness, not because you hoped some kind of romance would develop?"

Lily smiled. "My, how suspicious you are."

"Based on precedent."

"Since you broached the subject, is there anyone in particular you'd like to include? A pirate-turned gentleman, perhaps?"

"Oh! Please don't let that vicious rumor spread. How perfectly deplorable to even say such a thing!"

The gleam in Lily's eyes returned. "Since you've

chosen to champion him, perhaps I should—"

"Lily, please," Elise broke in. "I'm not his champion. I hardly know him. I simply don't subscribe to unwarranted gossip regarding anyone. You know that."

"True." The gleam deepened. "I promise to dispute the claim whenever I hear it and rise to the defense of the very handsome Mr. Amesbury as handily as you do."

Elise frowned. "Why does that not comfort me?"

****

On her way to the stables for her habitual ride, Elise walked through the gardens, stopping to speak with the head gardener and to ask after his family.

A childish laugh carried on the breeze. She raised her head to find two figures on the far side of the lake. Veering away from the stables, Elise strolled to them, smiling as she saw Colin and Mrs. Robbins sailing paper ships.

Colin tossed a pebble at one of the ships, causing it to wobble in the water.

"Huzzah! A direct hit, mateys. Load the guns again, ye swabs! Fire!" He tossed another pebble at the ship. It tipped over and begin filling with water. "Now, mateys, board the ship and take her plunder!" A moment later, the ship sunk. Colin cheered.

"Colin."

At her reproachful voice, he looked up. His grin faded and a decidedly guilty expression crossed his face. "Mother. We were just sailing ships."

"Pirate ships, perhaps?"

"Yes, Mother," he whispered.

She crouched down and held out her hand. He glanced at Mrs. Robbins, whose expression looked equally guilty, and trudged to Elise.

Putting her arm around him, she looked him in the eye. "Beloved. Pirates are not proper examples for a little boy who wants to grow up to be a gentleman like his father. Pirates are thieves and murderers, and have no hope of ever finding the happiness of home and family. They have no conscience and no peace. Would you want to always be looking over your shoulder, worried that the authorities would catch you, worried that your own shipmates would kill you and steal your treasure?"

He considered. "No."

"They are bad men, Colin, without loyalty or friend. And they do terrible things to their victims."

Colin remained silent for a moment. In a very small voice he said, "Some of them are good men. Mr. Amesbury is."

Elise looked out over the lake and chose her words carefully. "It's possible Mr. Amesbury actually served as a privateer during the war instead of being a real pirate. If so, then he served king and country. It's also possible he only played with you when he said that. If you remember, you asked him if he were a pirate. That was not information he volunteered."

"Maybe. But I'm sure he really was a captain of his own ship."

She smoothed a flaxen curl away from his forehead. "Why do you say that, my love?"

Colin cocked his head to the side "He walks like a captain and talks like he expects everyone to obey him."

Elise nodded. She'd ceased to be surprised by her young son's astute observations. For a child his age, he had a better grasp of the nature of people than many adults. She agreed with Colin; Jared Amesbury certainly possessed a commanding, authoritative air.

But then, he'd been born the son of an earl, so perhaps that demeanor came with his breeding. However, second sons often did not reflect the same self-assured stance as heirs, unless they held a position of leadership.

"I believe you're right. He probably was captain or at least a high ranking officer," she conceded. "However, he's a kind gentleman. I can't imagine him doing the deplorable acts pirates commit."

"No. He wouldn't hurt anyone. May I invite him to fish?"

Elise swallowed, uncertain why the thought of having the charismatic Jared Amesbury here filled her with mingled anticipation and dread. With the glaring exceptions of the stolen kiss, and parts of their conversation at Lily's dinner party, he'd behaved the perfect gentleman. Sunday past, he'd conducted himself with absolute propriety. And she held no reservations about allowing him to spend time with Colin. Instinctively, she knew he was honorable.

A tiny part of her missed the irrepressible rogue who made suggestive innuendos with merely a glance. With warmth flooding her cheeks, she quickly suppressed that indecent thought.

"Please, Mother? After church you said he might."

"You're right, son. A person must always keep one's word. Very well, ask Mrs. Robbins when your schedule will best allow for a fishing outing and you may write a letter inviting Mr. Amesbury. After your studies are completed and your tutor is satisfied, understand?"

He nodded vigorously.

She glanced at Mrs. Robbins over Colin's golden head and received a nod in acknowledgement. To Colin, Elise said, "He may be too busy, so we must respect his time."

"Yes, Mother!" He let out a whoop and ran back to the house.

Elise smiled as she watched him run and skip.

Colin turned and called, "Coming, Nurse?"

"Coming, young Master Berkley." Mrs. Robbins

grinned at Elise. "Do you wish me to arrange a time when you can join them?"

"No," Elise answered too quickly. She adjusted her tone to one of serenity. "No, don't concern yourself with my schedule. Just accommodate Mr. Amesbury's. I will join them if I am able."

Mrs. Robbins nodded, dropped a quick curtsey and went after an impatient Colin. Elise made a mental note to be far too busy to join a fishing party including Mr. Amesbury. She liked her safe, predictable world with no unexpected surprises.

A capricious, unpredictable man like Mr. Amesbury would only turn it upside down.

CHAPTER 6

Inside Greymore's study, Jared sipped a port. "The informant could be anyone who has access to the records. It could be even the lowliest clerk."

"And you're sure the leader, this *O Ladrão*, is a member of the nobility here in this area?" Greymore asked.

"Without a doubt. The trail led here."

Greymore stared out the window, swirling his drink. "How many other Secret Service Agents do you know?"

Surprised at the sudden change of topic, Jared swiftly considered his response. Seeing no harm in the truth he replied, "Three others besides you. Rebecca, for one."

Greymore nodded soberly. "I didn't know she was an agent until after she'd been executed."

Jared sat with forced casualness but his hand shook slightly. "I begged her to leave when she thought Boney had grown suspicious, but he always confided so much to her that she wanted to wait and see what other information she could coax out of him."

The information she'd seduced out of Napoleon had been instrumental in some of the battles won against his French troops. Some had speculated the Corsican Monster might have won the war if he'd been more cautious about what he told his various mistresses.

"Her efforts were not in vain." Greymore eyed him as if searching for signs of grief.

Jared met his gaze blandly, confident his

practiced mask of indifference remained in place even while thoughts of Rebecca overcame him. Her death had come as a crushing blow.

Jared tamped down the memories. "Why do you ask?"

Greymore shook his head, looking weary. "Just curious. I've known few. Most were killed during the war. Others, like me, have more or less retired. You're weary of it, too, aren't you?"

Jared uttered a short laugh. "I can't wait to finish this last assignment and walk away. Far away."

A footman entered. "Mrs. Greymore wishes me to inform you your guests await.

"Tell her I'll be right with her." Greymore turned to Jared with a wry smile. "Shall we join the others?"

Jared nodded. "This may be a good opportunity. One never knows when a careless word might slip, and a riding party may be a casual enough affair to loosen tongues. If Lady Fortune smiles upon me."

Greymore donned a frockcoat and hat. "Any suspicions?"

"At this point, no one is above suspicion. In particular, Lord Von Barondy. Something about that man seems off."

"Von Barondy. A viscount. Generally well-respected."

"A friend?"

"Acquaintance, merely. Not that I'd let it interfere with an investigation."

Jared nodded. Greymore would scrutinize a friend with the same professionalism as a stranger. "There was something evasive about him at Lady Standwich's dinner party."

"His wife is extravagant. Few men could afford to keep her. Could be a motive, I suppose, although most gentlemen just build up a mountain of debt and make token payments. He's in the riding party today." Greymore opened the door.

"Excellent."

Voices and laughter spilled from the front parlor. Following Greymore, Jared automatically scanned the faces of those in attendance, and out of habit, noted the location of every door and window. Someone stepped aside and Jared's gaze fell on Elise Berkley. Wearing a dark green riding habit, she sat on the far side of the room, talking with Greymore's wife. His heartbeat quickened, and he found himself standing in front of her.

He greeted the hostess first. "You're looking lovely as usual, Mrs. Greymore."

"How kind of you to say. And thank you for joining us today." Mrs. Greymore greeted him politely, but her eyes were only for her husband.

Greymore and his wife gazed at each other with such affection that an uncharacteristic sense of emptiness surfaced in Jared.

Greymore's young wife smiled graciously. "Mr. Amesbury, I believe you're acquainted with my friend, Mrs. Berkley?"

Elise Berkley regarded him with heightened curiosity and deep speculation, as if she'd recently learned something new about him and couldn't quite decide if it were true.

"I have had the distinct pleasure." Careful to keep his expression and tone benign, Jared inclined his head.

Mrs. Berkley maintained her assessing perusal. Jared raised a brow. Few English ladies would look so boldly upon a gentleman. As he returned the stare, he could not help but notice the creamy radiance of her skin, or the way her lips parted. Her tongue slid out to moisten her lips, but she seemed to realize her action would draw attention to her mouth, and pulled her tongue back inside. She lowered her eyes, not in a false attempt to appear demure, but out of discomfort, if her slow blush were any indication. Though her beauty rivaled that of any temptress, her sweetness dashed any hope of proving himself worthy of her attention.

No scoundrel such as he had a prayer of winning the favor of an angel.

He reminded himself that he had no intention of developing an attachment which risked distracting him from his assignment.

Or leaving him vulnerable to his enemies.

Mrs. Greymore turned to two other ladies seated nearby. "May I present Mrs. Hogan and her daughter Libby?"

Jared affected a slight bow to the lady and her very young daughter. "Delighted to meet you. It was a pleasure meeting your husband earlier."

Mrs. Hogan smiled. "He spoke well of you, Mr. Amesbury."

Recognizing the matchmaking glint in her eye and the way she purposefully glanced at her daughter, Jared bowed again, excused himself and made a strategic retreat, annoyed that it took him away from the lovely Mrs. Berkley.

As the party headed outside to their waiting horses, Jared watched Lord Druesdale work his way through the crowd to Mrs. Berkley's side.

"Mrs. Berkley, if I may have the honor?" Lord Druesdale offered his arm.

Mrs. Berkley took it without a second look at Jared and allowed him to help her mount her horse.

Jared gritted his teeth and squelched his sudden irritation. It mattered not whom Mrs. Berkley favored. And he would work better without pleasant distractions.

As Jared mounted Aries, he noted with satisfaction that Von Barondy had indeed joined the riding party. While the group headed out across the fields, Jared maneuvered Aries away from the Hogan family and edged near Von Barondy. He listened to idle conversation around him, paying special attention to anything involving the viscount.

Lord Druesdale's attention remained fixed upon Mrs. Berkley. She answered his questions graciously, and even posed a few thoughtful questions of her own. However, she showed him no special preference.

Why Jared noticed, he refused to examine too closely. He certainly didn't care. He had come here to fulfill an assignment. Then he'd try to start a new life without the Secret Service, pirates, or intrigue.

He idly scanned the terrain and vegetation, his ears trained on the conversation, but the discussions remained on politics and the races and other manly subjects. Nothing regarding shipping, nor pirates, nor business arose.

Then Greymore called to Lord Druesdale. After an apology to Mrs. Berkley, Druesdale eased his horse back to ride beside his host.

Mrs. Berkley looked out over the horizon, as if she longed to be in another place far, far away. Jared noticed Mr. Bradford, a widower he'd met days earlier, often watched her, his mouth working as if trying to muster the nerve to speak to the lady. Clearly both Bradford and Druesdale had good sense.

Against his better judgment, Jared maneuvered next to her. "Mrs. Berkley, I received an invitation from your son to join him fishing at my earliest convenience."

She glanced at him but quickly averted her eyes. "He'll understand if you are indisposed, Mr. Amesbury." She spoke politely, but without any true warmth.

He chose to ignore both her tone and his desire to discover the reason behind it. Instead he quirked an irreverent grin. "What? And lose my excuse to spend an afternoon in indolence?"

After another brief glance, she smiled faintly.

"Perhaps I merely flatter myself, but I believe Colin would be disappointed if I failed to fish with him."

"He would indeed." Again, she kept her gaze averted.

Curious as to why the lady who'd looked so boldly at him moments ago now refused to make eye contact, Jared looked down. His clothing all appeared proper; tasteful, fashionable yet understated. Even the cravat remained undisturbed. His boots shone from the attention Gibbs had shown them. He'd left his weapons at home. Most of them.

"Have I something stuck in my teeth?" He bared his teeth.

That won him a startled look of puzzlement. Her eyes focused on his mouth before darting away. "No."

He hesitated, dismayed how much her opinion mattered. In a hushed voice, he said, "Have I offended you in some way?"

"No." She continued to pointedly keep her eyes off him, but an expression akin to distress flickered over her features.

At a loss, Jared waited, but she made no further comment. Why this seemed so important to him, he could not begin to guess. "Would you tell me if I had?" he asked gently.

Her eyes shot to him again, but this time her gaze lingered as if she tried to divine his character, but feared to truly see it. "You're very candid."

"I am." He stared unseeing over the landscape. "I was as a child, too. My father despaired of my impetuous nature and my unfashionable habit of speaking my mind."

Strange that he'd find a career which required that he speak more lies than truth when his nature begged to be forthright. But his present career had not been entirely his choice. And he did take a certain delight in playing a role.

Jared glanced at Mrs. Berkley. Something about her awoke a long-denied desire to express his thoughts. A desire to confide. A desire he'd smothered for years in order to stay alive.

He added, "Perhaps you bring out the candid side of me. You were uncomfortably honest regarding your opinion of me the first time we met."

Her lips twitched in amusement. "Your actions demanded swift retribution."

"No doubt. But underneath that serene exterior is an articulate and intelligent woman who does not hesitate to express herself. I find that strangely refreshing."

"Most men find it strange and annoying."

He chuckled. "Men with small minds are threatened by intelligent women."

"And your mind is expansive?"

"I've discovered intelligence does not only smile on one gender. In fact, women seem to have a certain intuition that often eludes men."

Mrs. Berkley turned her head and looked him fully in the eye. Speechless, he beheld her radiant beauty. For a fleeting moment, a haunted look entered her eyes, as if something caged begged for freedom. It occurred to him that she was trapped alone in her world of etiquette. Then she shut it behind a carefully constructed mask of serenity.

"You have a most generous attitude, Mr. Amesbury."

He quirked a grin. "Does that mean you'll fish with us?"

She turned away, a smile touching her lips. "Perhaps."

"You aren't speaking freely anymore."

A tiny frown creased her brow and she held her

luscious lower lip between her teeth. Jared knew he was staring, but he'd never wanted so badly to kiss a woman. Here. In public.

But that would scandalize her and he'd lose all chances of...

Of what? He wasn't sure exactly what he wanted, but stealing another kiss certainly wouldn't attain it.

Her serious grey eyes returned to him. "Will you give me an honest answer if I ask you a direct question?"

"I'll tell you anything you want to know."

"Who were those men threatening you? And why?"

He stilled. Anything but that.

He'd distracted her the last two times she asked him that question, but he suspected she wouldn't be satisfied until she had a believable answer.

"Leandro and his right hand man, Santos, have been trying to kill me for years. Leandro blames me for the death of his half-brother, Macy. He also believes—erroneously—that I withheld some of the plunder our ship took during the war, and that I secretly hid it away instead of turning it over to the prize courts or dividing it up with the crew."

He glanced at her, but she only watched expectantly. "When you came upon us, he was trying to force me to give up the coordinates of the island where he thinks the cache was hidden."

"You mean like pirate's treasure?" She looked more intrigued than disapproving.

He smiled disarmingly. "I wasn't a pirate, I was a privateer. And there is no hidden treasure. I turned it all over to the government. The admiralty knows he's after me, but he's so slippery, they can't catch him."

"I'm sorry I didn't stop him when I had the opportunity." She looked troubled.

He grinned at the thought of her protecting him from Leandro. "No doubt you could have. Fear not. He's probably gone back to sea in search of easier prey."

"I'm glad to hear you weren't truly a pirate."

"Did you honestly believe me when I said that to Colin?"

"I hadn't quite decided."

He chuckled. "I do appreciate your honesty. Most women seem to think it unladylike to speak their mind."

"I've grown even more outspoken since Edward died."

"Oh? He didn't appreciate your forthrightness?"

"He had a calming influence upon me." Her brow creased.

"Calming or quelling?"

She shot him a look of annoyance. "His presence was a soothing reminder of how I ought to comport myself."

"That wasn't an answer."

"I wanted him to be happy, and I did what I could to be the kind of wife he deserved." Her voice grew testy.

"So for him you buried every desire of your heart?"

She stared as if he'd just suggested a scandalous liaison.

Druesdale maneuvered himself to her other side. He greeted Jared civilly and promptly turned his back on Jared to greet Mrs. Berkley. He turned on the charm so completely that Mrs. Berkley's attention remained focused on him to the exclusion of anyone else, affording Jared only the view of the back of her head, and on occasion, her profile.

With frustration chewing a hole through his insides, Jared silently cursed Druesdale.

Out of habit, Jared made a quick scan of

everyone's present location. As he eased Aries back, he tried to stop grinding his teeth. He cared nothing if the widow exchanged a few pleasantries with another man.

Surely the attention of the beautiful lady had nothing to do with his desire to run a blade through Druesdale.

The riding party stopped in a grove of trees. An army of servants hastened to lay out a meal on tables and chairs already set up. Druesdale placed himself next to Mrs. Berkley and shot Jared a challenging grin. Refusing to rise to the bait, Jared seated himself nearer the circle of men and covertly eavesdropped on their conversations. Meanwhile, he dug into a truly superb luncheon; another benefit of polite company.

"My shipping company lost another ship this week," a male voice grumbled.

Jared's ears perked. He gazed out over the horizon as if enjoying the view of the rolling hills and then glanced at the direction of the speaker. Mr. Bradford, the young widower who'd been eyeing Mrs. Berkley, wore a mournful expression.

"Perhaps shipping is no longer a lucrative investment," Lord Von Barondy suggested. "I've lost quite a few myself. Thinking of selling my shares."

Mr. Bradford raised his eyebrows. "Are you? Know anyone who might be interested in buying?"

"Could be. I've discussed it with an investor. Merely preliminary, but I can ask him, if you wish. I've dealt mostly with his solicitor, but I'm convinced they are both honest men."

Something about the overly smooth way Von Barondy made the suggestion set Jared's teeth on edge.

"I'd be happy to contact him, if you're serious," Von Barondy added.

Mr. Bradford thought for a moment. "If it's a fair

offer, I'd certainly consider it. I can't afford to lose much more. This is the third ship this year."

"Storms or pirates? Or both?" Von Barondy affected the expression of a concerned friend, but a greedy light briefly touched his eye.

The hackles on the back of Jared's neck rose.

"Pirates, surprisingly enough. Thought they'd been eliminated," said Bradford.

"I don't think that breed can be truly eradicated. They'll probably plague humanity for as long as there are riches to be had," Von Barondy said in an oily voice.

Jared avoided looking in Von Barondy's and Bradford's direction lest he give himself away. He scanned the crowd and found Greymore seated with his wife. Greymore looked up, met his eyes, and gave an almost imperceptible nod of understanding.

"Thank you, my lord," Bradford said to Von Barondy. "I would like to at least hear what he has to offer."

Jared located Von Barondy's wife, the viscountess, sitting in a circle of ladies showing off a new ring. The other ladies gushed about it, and she preened under their admiration.

Elise Berkley murmured something polite, but the glitter of envy remained noticeably absent in her eyes until she glanced at Mrs. Greymore just as she gave her husband a look of worship. Then Mrs. Berkley's face changed. A shadow of sadness and longing passed over her fair features as she watched husband and wife exchange smiles of affection. Mrs. Berkley looked away and visibly swallowed.

Had she loved her husband and missed him? Or did she wish such affection had existed between her and her late husband? Beauty such as hers should not be wasted on widowhood.

Too bad Jared was in no position to remedy that difficulty just yet.

Jared blinked. Where had that thought come from? He had no desire to marry anytime soon. He already faced the prospect of giving up his ship and therefore whatever sense of freedom he enjoyed. He'd seen how his married friends spent less time in their favorite pursuits, and more time in those of their wives' choosing. Moreover, shackling himself with a wife would not only give his enemies a weakness where they could strike him, but he'd lose whatever freedom he'd gained by ridding himself of his obligation to the Secret Service.

Once he finished working for the government, he would enjoy whatever liberties became available to him as a private citizen, not give them up for a woman.

After giving himself that reminder, he squared his shoulders and refocused upon Von Barondy and Bradford, but their conversation turned to other matters. Neither of them made further mention of shipping.

After luncheon, servants set up equipment for an archery tournament. Most of the gentlemen, and half of the ladies, clamored to take part.

Druesdale approached with a forced smile. "Amesbury? Care to join in as well?"

Jared smiled darkly and wished he could aim an arrow upon Druesdale. "You'd just love to see me humiliated, wouldn't you?"

Druesdale lifted his shoulder. "You humiliated me at fencing."

"That was years ago."

"I've a long memory. I'd love to see you lose at something."

Jared snorted. "If I were to lose at something, archery would be it. I haven't held a bow and arrow since I was a lad."

"Glad to hear it!"

"Your comradery is most heart-warming," Jared

said dryly as he got to his feet.

Mrs. Carson sidled up to him and actually fluttered her eyelashes. "I knew you'd be participating, Mr. Amesbury. One has only to look at you to know that you excel in any athletic pursuit."

He grinned wryly. "I believe you are about to be disabused of that opinion, Mrs. Carson, as archery has never been a strength of mine. And I am rather out of practice, as well."

"I'm certain your areas of expertise are vast. I have no doubt such a virile man is exceedingly skilled in all other manly pastimes," she cooed.

Amused, Jared raised a brow at her obvious innuendo. "Some more than others."

"Modest besides?"

"Not modest, merely honest." He almost added 'for a change.'

"You are a treasure."

Jared couldn't deny a certain pleasure in being openly pursued, but a woman such as she failed to capture his interest. Heaven only knew how many other beds she warmed. He wondered if Mrs. Carson's husband knew how thoroughly he'd been cuckolded.

"The others await me." He inclined his head in a slight bow and left the huntress.

Jared's aim lasted through the first three archery rounds, but failed on the fourth. He good-naturedly accepted the spectators' jeers, deftly extracted himself from Mrs. Hogan's praise, and dropped down next to Charlotte Greymore near the others who cheered or heckled the remaining contenders. Mr. Greymore remained among those in the tournament.

"You've attracted some attention, I see." Mrs. Greymore smiled at Jared and pointedly looked at Mrs. Carson who continued to send him come-hither looks.

Jared shrugged.

"Not even tempted?"

"She's comely. But no."

"Ah. You prefer more discreet women?"

"I prefer more principled women." He bit his lip before he said, 'like Elise Berkley.' "Moreover," he added. "I've no wish to give her husband reason to call me out."

Charlotte Greymore tilted her head and studied him. Jared returned her frank stare. Greymore had done well for himself. His wife had a sweet face and a disposition to match. Her china-blue eyes watched him unblinkingly.

"I believe I've misjudged you, Mr. Amesbury."

"Oh?"

"I'm sorry to say that I found you something of a rake when I first met you."

Jared felt his mouth curve. "I seem to give that impression."

"Unfounded?"

Jared paused. "I have not been a paragon of a gentleman, but I think 'rake' takes it too far."

"Yes," she said slowly. "I can see that. There is more to you than meets the eye, Mr. Amesbury. And my husband thinks very highly of you. Few men earn his good opinion."

"He's certainly one of the finest men I've ever known. His opinion matters much to me," Jared replied in all sincerity.

The fourth round ended, and Greymore returned amid the jests. He grinned at Jared and sat on his wife's other side.

"You made a respectable showing, Mr. Greymore," she said lovingly.

He kissed her hand. "Why, thank you, Mrs. Greymore. I live to impress you."

The final round had only two archers; Lord Druesdale and Mr. Bradford. Jared cast a surreptitious eye at Elise Berkley, but she did not appear to be raptly watching. She merely observed the proceedings with polite interest. Both contenders cast a glance her way and then glared at one another.

Ah. A pair of contenders competing for the favor of the lovely widow. Lord Druesdale, stocky, starting to grey at the temples, still presented a pleasing form. Moreover, he was wealthy and titled. Mr. Bradford, younger and fair of complexion, taller and leaner, also possessing of a respectable estate. All social circles welcomed the good-natured young widower. Either gentleman would be considered a smart match.

He glanced at Elise again, but she only watched the proceedings with calm reserve, her hands folded in her lap. He felt a certain satisfaction knowing she favored neither potential suitor.

Mr. Bradford nocked his arrow, took careful aim, and let it fly. It hit almost in the middle of the bull's-eye. He accepted congratulations with a modest smile and tilted his chin toward Lord Druesdale in challenge. Then he glanced at Elise for her approval. Her expression remained passive.

A feral glint touched Lord Druesdale's eyes as he glanced at his opponent. He, too, took careful aim. His arrow landed in a perfect bull's-eye, winning the tournament. Members of the riding party encircled Druesdale to offer congratulations.

Elise applauded politely, but appeared slightly removed from it all; not bored, just not entirely a part of the group. He wondered why. She'd been with these people all her life, and she should be perfectly comfortable with them.

To his surprise, she arose and strolled to the edge of the clearing. She climbed upon a cluster of boulders, and stood precariously on the highest one. With her face lifted toward the sun, and her arms straight at her side and slightly behind her, she looked poised for flight.

Charlotte Greymore stood, shaking him out of his musings, and went to offer her congratulations to the competitors. The moment she was out of earshot, Greymore glanced at Jared and raised his brows.

"Learn something?" he asked quietly.

"Von Barondy."

Greymore nodded. Jared knew he would contact the Central Office. Another operative in the organization would discreetly investigate the viscount and send Jared word. He'd know where to go from there. He redirected his attention to Elise Berkley on the rocks.

She turned with a sigh and leaped lightly down from the boulder. She joined Mrs. Greymore and was soon encircled by Mr. Bradford and Lord Druesdale, who alternately glared at one another and smiled at Elise. Druesdale said something to Elise, and her clear laugh rang out.

Jared stilled. When had he taken to calling her Elise? He almost groaned. Not a good sign. Smiling, she glanced his way, and the sight nearly undid him.

Definitely a very bad sign.

CHAPTER 7

Elise stood at the window and watched her son stroll to the lake next to Jared Amesbury; a small boy with gangly limbs and blond hair that never quite allowed a comb to tame it, and a tall, broad-shouldered man who walked with unusual athletic grace. They stopped, turned, and faced each other. Mr. Amesbury crouched down to Colin's eye level.

From this distance, she could not see their expressions, but Colin waved his hands about in his usual animated fashion. She could only speculate on their topic of discussion, or what the earl's son must be thinking about Colin's eager discourse. A moment later, Mr. Amesbury arose. As they walked, Colin slipped his hand into Mr. Amesbury's.

The gesture of affection made a lump rise in her throat. Turning away, she firmly shunned any thoughts that her son might need a father-figure. She liked her orderly life, liked overseeing her son's inheritance, managing the estate and the people upon it. She had no time for foolishness that included a man

Pirate indeed!

His changeable nature gave no credence to any theory. One moment, he appeared the perfect gentleman; restrained, polite. The next, a roguish grin lit his face, and his eyes shone wickedly. And whenever he addressed a child, gentleness softened his features. Yet through it all, wariness remained as if he lived continually poised to explode into action. Clearly, he was unpredictable and untrustworthy.

Elise met with the steward, forcing herself not to look at the clock, not to listen for signs that her son's fishing companion had left, not listen for his step.

Spending time with Mr. Amesbury would lead nowhere she wished to go.

She turned her attention to her correspondence. Had she ever found that task so tedious? After struggling through two letters, she laid down her pen and put on her bonnet. Going for a walk would do her good. And if she happened to walk by the lake...well...Colin might enjoy showing her the fruits of his labor. Certainly, she had no thought whatever of Mr. Amesbury.

When had she taken to lying?

Opening her parasol, she stepped outside and blinked in the bright sunlight. As she approached the lake, she paused, scanning the shoreline. Her heart thudded at the thought of being in his presence again. She spotted two figures sitting in the shade of a giant oak tree at the edge of the lake.

Leaning against the tree trunk, Mr. Amesbury sat with her son tucked up under his chin, carefully working out a knot in Colin's fishing line. His long legs were stretched out, one bent at the knee, his posture relaxed.

They looked up at her approach. She returned Colin's smile and glanced at Mr. Amesbury. A slow smile stole over his features. No wickedness danced in his eyes today. No aloof boredom. Only pure joy.

In that moment, she saw him not as a pirate, not as a proper gentleman; but as a man enjoying the simple pleasure of fishing with a boy.

Her lips curved as warmth and softness stole over her.

Colin said, "Mother, I caught two fish, but then I tangled my line."

Mr. Amesbury seemed to remember himself, and

the façade of the aloof gentleman reappeared, as did that edge of watchfulness. "Mrs. Berkley." He shifted and started to set Colin aside so he could rise.

She held out a hand. "Don't get up on my account. May I join you?"

"Please."

Within that cool reserve, a spark of genuine warmth lurked. Those aquamarine eyes followed her as she settled herself on the ground. His smile deepened before he returned his attention to the snarled fishing line.

Colin made no move to leave Mr. Amesbury's lap for hers. Elise could not decide if that bothered her. Her son relaxed with his new friend as if he'd spent the whole of his life there.

With his arms around her son, Mr. Amesbury's focus remained riveted on the tangled line in his hands. His lashes hid his eyes, and a tiny frown creased his brow as he concentrated on the fishing line. Those large hands deftly untangled a knot Elise would have thought impossible.

"You did it," Colin exclaimed.

"Amazing," she said. "I'd have just cut off the knot and moved the hook."

He grinned. "I enjoy a challenge."

Colin unflinchingly impaled a worm on his hook, stood, and cast. The line made a graceful arc and landed with a tiny plop in the water. Rings rippled back toward them. Colin resumed his seat on Mr. Amesbury's lap. Unperturbed, Mr. Amesbury merely resettled Colin and rested his chin on the top of the curly head. For a change, Colin didn't wriggle like a puppy, but remained content to sit quietly within the circle of Mr. Amesbury's arms, his eyes fixed upon the lake.

Afraid she'd break the magical spell by speaking, Elise observed them. If two people could appear more unlike, she couldn't recall. Mr.

Amesbury's skin was deeply tanned, his hair rich and dark, his features all square lines and hard angles, his body large and muscular. Colin, fair of skin and hair, with delicate features, and though of average size for a boy his age, he appeared decidedly fragile against the foil of Jared Amesbury.

No one would ever mistake them for father and son by their appearance, but at that moment, they appeared so much at ease together, one would wonder if they were some relation.

If only Edward could be here to see what a fine son he had. But then, Edward would never have spent the afternoon fishing with Colin. He would have considered the pastime unproductive. Pity. He would have missed some of the greatest joys of fatherhood.

She doubted Jared Amesbury would ever make that mistake with his own children. She could easily imagine him clamoring about with an adoring herd of dark-haired children.

Firmly stopping her thoughts from continuing down a road she did not wish them to venture, she pulled her eyes away from the magnetic gentleman, picked a sprig of jasmine and inhaled.

"What is that flower you are holding?" Mr. Amesbury asked.

"Jasmine."

"Jasmine," he repeated. "It smells good."

Birdsong accompanied the comfortable silence that fell, and the leaves murmured as a breeze blew.

"Do you have a son, Mr. Amesbury?" Colin asked presently.

"No."

"Why not?"

Amusement touched Jared's face. "I've not yet taken a wife."

"But some men have sons even when they don't have wives."

Jared's mouth twitched on one side. "Yes. Some do. But that comes with its own set of problems."

"Don't you want a son?"

Elise stifled a laugh.

"When the time is right." He glanced at Elise, his gaze guarded. "Contrary to my apparent reputation, I do not leave by-blows in my wake everywhere I go."

But Colin had gotten up to skip stones across the water and hadn't heard that last comment.

Elise smiled with exaggerated sweetness. "How refreshing. My late husband would never have done that, of course, but many gentlemen of the *beau monde* think nothing of such disreputable behavior."

His gaze caressed her. "I'm relieved you do not put me into the class of men who have disreputable behavior."

Though not close enough to Jared for any sort of impropriety, she felt his presence keenly, aware of his body's every movement, every pull of his mouth. That mouth that had touched hers and brought it back to life.

She swallowed. "I did not say that."

"What? That I'm a reprobate or that I'm not?"

"I have not yet decided what you are."

He chuckled softly.

Her heart made odd little skips, and her cheeks heated. She edged away. It didn't help. She looked out over the lake. That didn't help, either. What power did Jared hold over her?

She stilled. Jared? Mr. Amesbury, she meant, of course.

"What's disrepa'ble behavior?" Colin asked, wandering back.

Elise's face warmed as she wondered what else Colin had overheard. "Ungentlemanly conduct."

Puzzled, Colin stared back at her.

"I'll explain when you're older."

He sighed. "You always say that. You'll be explaining a lot of stuff when I'm older."

Jared laughed heartily.

As she suppressed a smile, her gaze slid to Mr. Amesbury again. She almost regretted her decision to join her son and his disturbing fishing companion. However, she could not place the blame at his feet. He'd done nothing, said nothing, which would be considered as inappropriate. At least, not lately.

Jared, indeed! When had she become so familiar with him in her thoughts?

Colin straightened. "I think I got one."

On their feet, Colin and Mr. Amesbury both worked the taut line until a wriggling fish appeared. The fish flapped about madly until Mr. Amesbury's large hands captured it.

He freed the hook from the fish's mouth and held it up for Colin's inspection. "Is this one big enough?"

"He's a beauty," Colin declared exuberantly. He turned to Elise. "Don't you think so, Mother?"

"I agree. Well done, my love."

The fish chose that moment to make a last desperate escape back into the lake. It shot out of Jared's hands and flopped about on the bank with both the man and the child frantically trying to recapture it. Elise laughed until her sides protested.

Finally, they subdued the errant fish, and Mr. Amesbury added the new arrival to a rope threaded through the gills of two other fish at the edge of the lake. "I believe this has been a successful day of fishing, young Master Berkley."

Elise realized then that only one fishing pole had been put to use. Jared's leaned untouched against the tree. He put away the hook, wound up the lines and retrieved the poles.

Like the triumphant victor, Colin carried the fish as they turned back toward the house.

Donna Hatch

The cooper's son ran up to him. "Colin! The cat in the dairy had kittens! We've only just found them. Come see?"

Colin turned to Elise with shining eyes. "May I go see the kittens with James, Mother?"

"Of course, love."

His grin nearly split his face. He handed the fish to Jared and then paused. "You'll remain for dinner, won't you, sir?"

"Colin, Mr. Amesbury might already have a previous engagement," Elise hastened to say.

Jared's gaze moved to meet hers, and for an instant, uncertainty flickered there. She realized she must have sounded as if she did not welcome him at their table.

Jared straightened. "I don't believe—"

"You are certainly welcome to join us for dinner, Mr. Amesbury," she broke in. "If your schedule allows."

Colin turned to him beseechingly. Only a heartless cad could refuse those big blue eyes.

Mr. Amesbury grinned. "I can think of nothing I'd rather do than remain in your charming company, young sir."

Colin flung his arms around Jared and hugged him before trotting off with the cooper's son.

Jared stared after him as if dazed. He spoke in a hushed voice. "You have a remarkable son."

"I must agree." She fingered the tassel at the handle of her parasol. "I hope our invitation does not inconvenience you."

He turned to her, his grin returning. How could such a masculine man be so beautiful? The sight of him smiling nearly sapped the strength right out of her knees.

"My alternative is to go home and have dinner at an empty table. I think I can bear to give that up for a bit of company."

104

"We are rather informal here. I know it simply isn't done, but unless I have guests, I usually eat dinner in the nursery with Colin." She smiled. "My alternative is to have dinner at an empty table."

He chuckled at her echo of his own words.

"I'm afraid he's expecting you to join us in our usual fashion," she added.

"Perfect."

She eyed him, judging his sincerity. "In truth?"

"Nothing would please me more than to have an informal dinner with my newest young friend and his beautiful and charming mother."

She looked away.

"Is it possible that you are unaccustomed to compliments, Mrs. Berkley?"

"They are empty and easily-given."

"You speak of flattery. I speak of heart-felt compliments."

She stopped and turned to him as an uncomfortable thought occurred to her. "You aren't using Colin to court me, are you?"

He blinked, clearly taken aback. "You find me insincere? Or do you fail to see your son's charm?"

She resumed walking, and he fell into step beside her. "Grown men don't normally choose to keep company with a seven-year-old."

He grinned. It came so easily to him. Edward had been a positive, optimistic person, but he hadn't smiled so often. "He invited me to fish. How could I refuse?"

"Be serious." Harshness crept into her voice.

He let out his breath. "I have been accused of many things, but using a child for my own agenda has never been one of them. I like Colin. I find him honest and uninhibited. He reminds me of my youngest brother, Christian, when he was a boy."

Elise waited, hoping for a glimpse inside the mysterious Jared Amesbury.

"We teased him mercilessly and often called him the 'perfectly perfect Christian.' But, actually, he is. I've never known a more pure soul."

"Were you close?"

"I regret that we were not. My fault, entirely. I was so jealous of his perfection, and how much my parents favored him, that I actually plotted to get rid of him; everything from having him press-ganged to feeding him to a tiger."

She chuckled softly. "How many children are in your family?"

"Six living. I have two older sisters, an older brother, and two younger brothers." His voice softened, and the light in his eyes dimmed. "A brother died as a child."

Elise made a sound of sympathy.

He visibly pulled himself back to the present. "Christian is all of us at our best. He's the only one of whom my father truly approves. And my mother positively adored him."

A gentle breeze stirred the air, and a songbird trilled. As she watched, a barrage of emotions traveled across his face so quickly she couldn't name them. Regret? Sorrow? Loss?

"What happened to Christian?" Elise asked softly.

A thoughtful frown touched his face. "He's changed. Perhaps he merely grew up, but he's lost that dreamy-eyed innocence. He's still perfect, but at times he's...guarded, as if protecting...something." He shook his head with a frown of puzzlement.

"A broken heart?"

"Who knows? He won't talk about it. But when we were children, I longed to be more like him. When I wasn't plotting to kill him, that is." A wry smile touched his expressive mouth. "Anyway, Colin reminds me of Christian as a child. Blond. Happy. Without guile. Sensitive. Totally loving."

"Colin is my world. I hardly take a breath without thinking of him. I'm afraid I'm terribly protective."

"I barely know Colin, and I already feel that way, too." Jared made a quick scan of the area that she would have missed had she been watching less closely. Again that watchfulness.

"You're an uncommonly attentive mother," he observed.

"I hope it's enough."

She led him to the kitchen door. Just as they reached the house, Jared shifted the fish and the poles to one hand and opened the door for her. Inside the house, two servants appeared. One relieved Jared of his poles and fish. The other bowed to him.

"This way, sir. I'll show you where you may wash."

"Thank you." Jared followed the servant out of the room.

Elise watched him cross the floor with predatory grace. At the door, he glanced back. She blushed that he'd caught her watching him. He grinned, winked playfully, and left the room.

She wondered how she would manage to eat with her stomach flipping about. No man had ever disturbed her so keenly. Or been such a study in contradictions. Or changed from rogue to gentleman to something in between.

It left her asking again: who, really, was Jared Amesbury?

She wondered if she'd ever solve that riddle.

CHAPTER 8

Jared leaned back in his chair and set down his napkin, amused by Colin's animated description of his last game of cricket.

Empty plates and serving dishes littered the small round table in Colin's nursery. The setting had been cozy, intimate even, without the stiff formality of a dining room and a dozen servants. A bowl of jasmine and roses adorned the table, the only centerpiece. A cheery fire crackled in the fireplace. The candles had burned low, and yet, he felt no desire to leave.

Jared glanced at Mrs. Berkley. An indulgent smile tugged at the corners of her lips as she watched Colin. Fascinated with those lips, Jared traced each curve with his gaze. The lower lip was slightly fuller than the upper lip, giving her a mouth a pouting illusion.

The desire to again taste those sweet lips crept over him. He controlled his impulse. She was a lady. He could not simply swoop down upon her like a hungry predator and devour her, despite his impulsive kiss at their first meeting.

His gaze moved from her lips, over the upturned nose, to her soft, gray eyes. Heavily lashed, and large enough to give her an innocent appearance, they shone as she focused on her son with obvious affection.

Jared couldn't remember when he'd felt so relaxed. This afternoon fishing with Colin, and tonight, having dinner with the mother and child, had been the most agreeable day he'd enjoyed in ages.

The kind of peace and contentment he felt at the moment had been missing from his life. He desired a home and, more importantly, a family. He'd never realized it until tonight. He looked back at Elise Berkley and then at Colin.

His heart whispered that he wanted it with them.

"Are you the eldest in your family, Mr. Amesbury?" Colin asked.

"No. I'm the fourth child."

"Oh. Then you're not the heir?" He sounded not only disappointed, but apologetic.

Elise gasped. "Colin!"

Jared grinned. "No. Not the heir. Just the spare. Good thing, too. The heir has much more responsibility and obligation. As the second son, I have freedom to do things such as piracy, you know."

Colin beamed while Elise frowned. Jared wondered if she frowned in disapproval for him continuing to feed her son's unhealthy hero worship of pirates, or because she thought he might truly be a pirate. He enjoyed keeping her uncertain and putting a wrinkle in the smooth fabric of her orderly life.

But that was stupid. He needed to play the perfect gentleman, at least until he completed this assignment, without anyone becoming suspicious of his true reason for living in this quiet part of the country.

He could figure out his identity later.

And the idea that she'd believe he fit into that category of unconscionable cutthroats disturbed him. Even if it were true.

He never, ever wanted her to look at him with revulsion and fear. He gave himself a good mental shake and vowed then to suppress his foolhardy impulsiveness.

"Colin, you know I'm merely playing when I say I used to be a pirate, don't you?"

Colin blinked. "You never were a pirate?"

Jared wanted to squirm under that focused stare. Only a monster could lie to this sweet, trusting child.

"During the war I served aboard a privateer, Colin. Everything I did at sea, I did for king and country."

He spoke honestly, for even his brief stint posing as a true pirate had been for king and country. Unfortunately, that role required him to behave as a reprobate, which made him unworthy of the company he kept tonight. A myriad of memories poured over him and he guarded his expression under their watchful eyes.

Colin digested Jared's declaration, and Elise's posture relaxed. She sent him a grateful smile.

"Were you the captain?" the boy pressed.

"I became the captain, in time. I went to sea at the age of thirteen, and I had much to learn before I could take command."

Colin turned to his mother. "You would never let me go to sea, would you?"

"You would break my heart if you did, my love."

Colin's face fell. Poor child. Tonight had brought the disillusionment of many of the boy's fantasies.

A plump, matronly woman appeared at the doorway of the nursery. Elise arose. Jared scrambled to his feet and Colin followed suit.

"It's time for bed, my love." Elise leaned over, gathered the child into her arms and kissed him soundly on the cheek.

Colin glanced at Jared, clearly embarrassed at the unmanly display of affection. Then, unable to resist his mother's affection, he snuggled into her.

Jared didn't blame him. He wouldn't be capable of resisting her, either.

110

Colin turned to Jared and threw his arms around him. Jared hugged him back and ruffled his hair.

"Say your prayers, Colin." Elise turned to Jared. "We have a fine Madeira in the study, if you are interested."

Jared quickly recovered from his surprise. He'd assumed Colin's bedtime would mark the end of the evening. "Thank you."

As she led him down the stairs, he kept pace with her, unable to keep his eyes off her. Her gown alternately clung to and flowed around her full, slender body. He admired the feminine lines of her neck and shoulders. His eyes moved downward to the womanly fullness of her breasts, the curve of her waist, the gently swaying hips.

He pulled at the suddenly strangling cravat and wondered when it had gotten so warm in the house.

Inside the study, she poured him a glass of Madeira. He accepted it without taking his eyes off her face. Heat flared as their fingers brushed.

A flush crept over her face. She sank into a large armchair. "How are you enjoying your stay in our quiet little corner of the country?"

He felt his mouth turn up on one side at her obvious attempt to break the tension. "Very much. More than I expected."

"I understand you've only let the house for the summer?"

"The terms of the lease are somewhat lax in this case. I've committed to the summer, with the option of keeping it longer if I so desire."

She nodded, her lashes hiding her eyes. "Do you plan to extend it, then?"

Jared took a sip of the Madeira. It was, indeed, noteworthy. "I have not yet decided."

Without looking up, she folded her hands in her lap. "Colin will be sad to see you go, I am sure."

"I can't believe how quickly I've fallen for his charms."

"You like children. There's no shame in that."

"I suppose I do."

"You have affection for the boy who was with you that day we, er, met."

Jared resisted the urge to groan. "I can't imagine a more awkward circumstance in which to make an acquaintance."

Her lips curved. "It's not the way I normally go about doing it."

Chuckling, he seated himself in a chair near hers by the fire. "I'm not quite sure how I would have extracted myself from that difficulty. I'm grateful you happened along. And had the courage to intervene."

"Who is the boy?"

"José. He's my tiger, of late. My cabin boy, formerly."

"He looks young for such roles."

"He's small for a ten-year-old, but very bright."

"How did he come to be in your care?"

"His father served as my quartermaster before his death. The mother died years ago. So I kept him on. He had no one else." Jared stared pensively into his drink. "He's seen far too much violence. I wish I could have spared him all that. A ship is no place for a child." Especially a pirate ship. "He likes the horses and the head groom treats him well. He'll be all right. Of course, with me as a master, the odds are stacked against him."

"Is it fashionable for gentlemen to speak unfavorably of themselves, or do you really have such a skewed opinion of yourself?"

The softness in her expression gave him pause. He wondered if he'd let down his guard too much and thought over his words.

He froze, the icy fingers of dread squeezing his

stomach. He'd let slip that he had a quartermaster. Would she know what the position entailed? He watched her carefully, but her expression only revealed mild curiosity.

Jared took a drink to allow himself time to form a reply. In her presence, he seemed to be revealing all sorts of things without thinking.

She smiled gently and spared him from having to answer. "What have you done since the war?"

"A great deal of no good, I'm afraid."

Elise nodded slowly. "Charlotte Greymore told me the man who is now her husband returned from the war a changed man. He spent the first year after his return trying to outrun the ghosts that seemed to haunt him. One of Edward's friends came home and literally drank himself to death."

"The atrocities one witnesses, and even commits, during a war are appalling; nothing any decent human would believe. We all must deal with the aftermath in our own way." He rubbed his hand down his face, hoping his own war would end soon.

"I'm sorry," she said softly.

He almost cursed in front of the lady before he caught himself. In all his years since he'd left home, he'd never spoken so openly with anyone. How had he managed to be an effective operative for twelve years without letting anything slip, yet in this lady's presence, start babbling like a half-wit?

Dismayed, he managed a wry smile, but the compassion in her expression made him want to weep. He finished the Madeira and pulled himself together.

"I do like it here. Greymore and I are old friends, and Lady Standwich has been dutiful in her attentions."

"She is a dear lady." She fixed a steady gaze upon him. "I'm sorry I questioned your motivations regarding Colin. It was foolish of me to think you'd go to so much trouble to court me."

He grinned. "I must admit though, your idea is rather ingenious. If ever a man wanted to court a reluctant widow, it would be through her son. I wonder if Druesdale or Bradford will think of that, since archery didn't seem to turn your head."

She shook her head. "Lady Standwich's machinations, no doubt. She seems to think now that she's about to remarry, I should, as well."

"She's a persistent lady. Almost as much as my Aunt Livy."

"She must have been lonelier as a widow than she admitted, for she seems unable to imagine anyone happy outside of wedded bliss," Elise said with a sigh.

He raised a brow. "You don't agree."

"I was happily married. But I am content not to wed again."

"Why? You are clearly lonely, too."

"Lonely!"

Jared stared at her sudden display of anger from such a gentle soul.

"How dare you tell me what I feel! I am quite happy caring for my son and I don't need a man to disrupt my life. I was happy with my husband. I'll never find another man like him."

His own ire rising, he struggled to control his voice. "I hope you don't find someone like him. You'd be smothered again like you were the first time."

"Smothered?"

"You like your freedom now that no one is here to censure you, but you crave being touched, you crave love. You have so much love to give, and no man to give it to."

"I don't want a man. I have my estate and my son and people who count on me. It's enough." But the conviction had fled her voice, and doubt shadowed her eyes.

Jared was tempted to point out all the times he'd witnessed her loneliness and how badly her son needed a man's guidance, but he resisted. It didn't matter. After he completed this final assignment, and not before, he would consider seeking a wife, all his earlier temptations notwithstanding. Forging any kind of attachments now would be dangerous. To all concerned.

Leandro or one of his cronies might be watching him even now. He would be foolish to gamble upon the chance Leandro had returned to the sea. Knowing that was an uncertainty, Jared shouldn't have come.

But he'd wanted to come. He wanted to be with them. With her.

He leaned forward. "Forgive me. I spoke out of turn."

Her anger softened, but her chest heaved. "I've grown weary of people advising me to remarry."

Jared kept his voice soft. "Perhaps they don't wish to see you alone for the rest of your life."

He reached out and took her hand. She stiffened but did not pull away. He caressed the back of her hand with his thumb. She looked torn between wanting to relax into his touch and fleeing his presence. He traced his fingers across the back of her smooth hand, over her knuckles, down her slender fingers. She went perfectly still.

Very softly he said, "You startle whenever anyone initiates contact, but you clearly enjoy being touched."

"It's not appropriate to be so familiar with others." Her voice sounded oddly hoarse. Her pulse throbbed in her neck and her breath came in tiny gasps.

Smug satisfaction crept over him. He put a teasing note into his voice. "You were quite familiar with me that day we met. I haven't been touched in

115

such a way in many, many years."

"I was trying to help you. And you returned the gesture with improper conduct."

Jared grinned at the blush that crept over her face. "That's another thing. You're very concerned with propriety, and yet you often break the manners and mores when it suits you. I believe there is a bit of a rebel deep down inside you, longing for freedom from the strictures of society."

"I admit I have a somewhat *laissez-faire* attitude about certain things, especially concerning my son, but I assure you, I have no intention of suddenly becoming a woman of scandal."

His grin widened, and he continued rubbing his thumb over the back of her hand. "I would never suggest such a thing. And widows, of course, are less closely censured than unwed young ladies. In a few years, you can call yourself an eccentric and be excused for almost any behavior."

She smiled faintly, her hand relaxing in his. Her focused gaze remained on his face and her expression softened further. "You seem to take delight in provoking me."

"I admit that I do. And I like soothing you afterward." He skimmed his fingers down her cheek.

She closed her eyes and tilted her head toward his hand. Yet some inner warning seemed to make her open her eyes and pull away.

He held up his hands in surrender. "Relax. As much as I'm tempted, I'm not trying to seduce you."

She blinked. "You admit you are tempted to seduce me, but you aren't going to make the attempt. I'm not sure if I'm relieved or terrified."

"The thought of seduction terrifies you?"

"I..." Twisting her hands, she arose and turned away, hiding her expression.

He stood behind her and put his hands on her shoulders. She flinched. He dropped his hands but leaned in, his body almost touching hers.

He whispered into her ear, "Do not fear me, Elise. I would never, ever hurt you."

She turned slowly to face him. Innocent desire, trepidation, and confusion all shone in her eyes.

"I should go." Before he ravished her right here. "Thank you for a most enjoyable evening. I truly can't remember a more wonderful dinner. Good night, Mrs. Berkley."

"Good night, Mr. Amesbury."

He kissed her chastely on the cheek. She caught her breath. He smiled, almost undone by the tenderness growing in his heart for this woman. Unable to resist, he leaned in slowly, allowing her the opportunity to pull away if she wanted. She didn't.

He touched her smooth cheek, leaned in, and kissed her lightly. Her unpracticed mouth remained tight at first, but it grew more pliant under his. Fighting all his inclinations to the contrary, he eased back. She looked dazed. And delightful.

If he ever decided to woo and win this lovely lady, he'd have to go very slowly. He wished he could tell the Secret Service to go to the devil so he could be free to pursue Elise Berkley.

He inclined his head in a brief bow and left while he possessed the strength.

CHAPTER 9

On a low hillside, Jared lay on his stomach, ignoring the insects crawling over him, and watched the Von Barondy house. A bramble scraped his back and a rock dug into his ribs, but he remained motionless. One by one, lights extinguished as servants went to bed, leaving the house in total darkness. Soon, he'd make his move.

After a lonely dinner spent wishing he could enjoy it with the charming Elise Berkley and her equally charming son, he'd gone to bed. Once the house was quiet, he'd risen, dressed all in black, and made his way to the Von Barondy residence. The viscount might be wily enough not to keep anything incriminating at his residence, but one never knew.

Jared studied the watchmen and dogs as they made their rounds until he could predict their pattern. After they passed by a third time, he arose. Using the night and his black clothing to conceal him, he crept soundlessly from his hiding place. He climbed over the stone fence, passed through the gardens, and approached the house.

Predictably, all the windows on the ground floor were locked. No matter. After picking the lock at the kitchen door and easing in, he waited, listening, but heard nothing more than the steady beating of his own heart.

He smiled wryly. Breaking into houses no longer even quickened his pulse.

He wondered if his lack of excitement had more to do with the fact that he'd frequently done far more dangerous acts, or if it stemmed from weariness of his career. This may be the last time he'd ever have to play burglar. Relief to be rid of the whole nasty business mingled with doubt as to whether he could actually give up the adventure.

When his eyes adjusted to the kitchen's inky blackness, Jared stole forward. At the door, he paused again to listen. All remained quiet.

He crept down the halls and opened several doors before he found a likely study with an imposing desk at the center of the room. Jared shook his head. Too obvious. But he'd check it anyway in case the man had no imagination.

After making sure the draperies were closed and would block out any light for the watchmen to see, Jared lit a candle and set it on the desk.

He found three hidden compartments in the desk, read a great deal of useless correspondence that he couldn't imagine why Von Barondy would hide, and gave up on the desk. He found a wall safe with legal documents and some jewels, but nothing incriminating. After a thorough sweep of the room, Jared blew out the candle. He waited until he could see well enough to navigate silently through obstacles in the dark room before he moved.

At the door, he paused, listening. Assured all remained quiet, Jared slipped into another room.

And realized his error.

A feminine gasp met his ears. The shadowy form of a woman stood silhouetted by the moonlight pouring through a window. She turned from an extinguished lamp, its wick still glowing. If he'd arrived a second sooner, she would have clearly seen him in the lamplight.

As the woman inhaled to scream, Jared leaped forward and placed a hand over her mouth.

She let out a frightened squeak.

Tightening his grip on her, he turned them both to put himself in the shadows. If they ever met in daylight, she would not recognize him. He hoped. Even with the moonlight on her face, he could barely make out her features, but her ragged breathing and heaving chest revealed her terror.

He felt like a beast frightening a woman.

He thought quickly. "Shhh, my dear," he crooned, his voice barely above a whisper. "Forgive me for startling you. I could not keep you out of my thoughts. I had to see you again."

She went utterly still.

Wondering how he was going to get out of this one, he stepped closer. As he leaned down to nuzzle her neck, he removed his hand from her mouth and caressed her cheek.

"Give me hope, dearest. One kiss is all I ask, and then I'll leave."

She caught her breath.

His pulse throbbed. If she screamed now, he'd have to leap out the window and try to outrun the dogs.

Her eyes fluttering closed, she leaned against him and lifted her mouth up toward his.

Jared could hardly believe his good fortune. Not that there'd been a terrible shortage of willing women, of course, but to have her capitulate so quickly seemed too good to be true. His charm must be even better than he'd imagined. Unless she truly thought he was someone else.

He kissed her softly. She sagged against him and placed a hand on his chest. This time she kissed him.

His conscience stabbed him that he'd kissed Elise Berkley only last night, and yet stood here kissing a stranger. There were no promises made or asked with Elise, but he felt as if he were being unfaithful. Not to mention using an obviously innocent girl.

He pressed his lips to the girl's cheek, then

backed away. "You give me hope, my dearest," he whispered. "Until next time."

Without a doubt, he had to be the most heartless cad in all of England.

He let himself out of the room and moved to the nearest alcove. As he flattened against a wall, he waited, hardly daring to breathe. He knew full well she may realize his deception and sound an alarm, yet he doubted he could bring himself to knock a woman unconscious even if she should prove to be a danger to him.

One of his former shipmates had taught him a Chinese method of rendering a victim unconscious with only a touch, but Jared had never tried it on anyone before. With pounding heart, he waited, sickened that he was even considering attacking a woman.

Of course he wouldn't. He'd simply run like the devil.

Several moments later, the girl came out. She let out a dreamy sigh. Then, pulling her dressing gown closer around her, she moved to the rear of the house. Her light footfalls on the servants' stairway faded. Once again, the house fell silent.

After letting his breath out in relief, Jared turned the opposite direction from where he'd encountered the girl. A library. Again, it might be too obvious, but he'd try. The first few compartments he discovered, one behind a picture and another in the mantle, revealed nothing interesting.

As Jared moved across the floor, he paused. Listening, he took one step back. The floor creaked oddly at that place. It sounded hollow. He knelt and traced the outline of two suspiciously symmetrical floorboards. Using a pocketknife, he pried up the two floorboards that revealed a compartment.

Inside sat a small, wooden locked box.

With quickening pulse, he reached in and lifted

the box. After picking the lock, he opened the lid. A stack of papers, all written in numbers and Greek symbols, met his eyes.

Anticipation raced through his veins and his heart pounded. This was it! This had to be what he sought; proof that Von Barondy was *O Ladrão*, the elusive fox he'd been hunting for over three years. He wanted to shout in triumph. All that work would soon pay off.

Then he would be free.

He lifted the papers from their hiding place, and traced the symbols with shaking fingers. Tingling with excitement, he rummaged through a small secretary desk until he found paper, pen and ink. He took a calming breath and set to work. After meticulously copying every character contained in the first two papers, he glanced at the mantle clock. Almost four in the morning. Servants would be rising soon.

Still reveling in the thrill of his victory, he sanded the ink and tucked the papers into his coat. Replacing everything with utmost care, Jared glanced about to ensure he hadn't disturbed anything. He blew out the candle and waited with his ear to the door before he slipped back down to the kitchen. From a window, he watched the bobbing lantern of the guard and dog pass by before he crept out of the house. He realized with alarm that the direction of the wind had changed. Aware of the dogs, he darted through the kitchen garden toward the back fence.

The dogs began barking with a ferocity that chilled his blood.

Jared tore across the yard. Shouting men and snarling, barking dogs pursued. He stumbled over an obstacle in his path but managed to keep on his feet. He steadied his balance and sprinted with renewed speed.

The baying dogs drew closer.

As Jared reached the high stone fence, he launched himself upward. His fingers gained purchase on the top just as the jaws of the nearest dog closed over his leg, but the teeth grasped a fold of his breeches just above his boots. With pounding heart, he kicked backward and the cloth tore.

A gunshot roared. Stone debris exploded in every direction.

He scrambled up the wall. He threw himself off the top and landed hard on the ground on the other side. Rolling to his feet, he kept running.

The dogs' barking fell further behind, but Jared ran without pause until he reached his horse tethered in the trees some distance from the house. As he vaulted up on the saddle, he looked back.

There was no sign or sound of pursuit. Still, he urged Aries to a full run.

With each mile he put between himself and the Von Barondy house, he relaxed. Then he grinned. Exhilarated, he threw back his head and laughed. Then he wished he could tell someone about it.

Elise would no doubt disapprove.

Or would she?

He galloped to Brenniswick, circling the tiny village several times, alert for signs of pursuit. His muscles relaxed and his heart slowed, leaving only fatigue in its place.

By the time he arrived home, concealed the coded papers in his room, and changed out of his black clothing that surely would have sent his valet into vapors, his fatigue drove him straight to bed. He'd attempt to decipher the code after getting adequate rest tomorrow. Er, later today.

Despite his weariness, rest came fitfully. Images of Elise Berkley hovered before his eyes, taunting him, tempting him, preventing restful sleep.

He dreamed of her. He dreamed of touching her

luscious body, losing himself in her sweetness. In the dream, she opened sleepy eyes. With a cry, she recoiled in horror from him as she saw him for the monster he truly was.

The dream changed, and Leandro held her captive. Leandro looked at Jared with malice and gleefully stabbed her just to spite him. She screamed.

Jared bolted up bathed in sweat.

****

"What makes you think I didn't sleep last night?" Jared snarled at Greymore. The man looked altogether far too smug.

Greymore chuckled. "As you are in a decidedly foul mood today, I'll assume it wasn't pleasant activities that kept you awake?"

Jared muttered something about Greymore's questionable parentage, but Greymore only laughed.

"Are you going to help me with this or not?" Jared shoved the paper into his hands.

Greymore took the paper and studied it, sobering. He glanced up at Jared. "Where did you get this?"

"From a box underneath a floorboard in Von Barondy's house."

Greymore whistled. "He wouldn't have a coded message if he weren't involved in some kind of criminal activity. Have you tried to break it?"

Jared shot him a glare that left Greymore holding up his hands in surrender. "All right, all right, I know; you wouldn't have come to me if you hadn't already tried." He clapped Jared on the back. "Take heart, if we can't crack it, we can always forward it to the main office in London."

Jared loosened his cravat and nodded. They worked on the code for the remainder of the day without success. Greymore's temper grew short, and Jared began to think they should concede the battle and send the code to London.

Mrs. Greymore entered with whisper of skirts. "Mr. Greymore, perhaps we should feed your guest."

Surprised, Greymore looked up at his wife. Immediately, his face softened and he beckoned to her. As if just now noticing the darkness outside the windows, he gave Jared a look of apology.

After settling herself upon Greymore's lap, Mrs. Greymore smiled at Jared. "Won't you please join us for a late dinner?"

"Thank you." He glanced at Greymore. "I apologize for keeping your husband so long."

"Secret business, no doubt." Her smile turned knowing.

Jared raised a brow.

Greymore grinned at his wife. "You know I'm retired from military service. We're just looking over a bit of a puzzle."

"Mmm." She clearly did not believe them, but chose not to dispute it.

They dined on a simple meal and Jared relaxed as he traded stories with Greymore and his delightful wife. The more time Jared spent here, the more he realized he missed the simple joys of home and family. That he might obtain them seemed a tantalizing dream.

When had he turned into such a sentimental fool?

CHAPTER 10

Elise trotted Prince out of the manicured gardens. Once out in the open, she let him have his head and they galloped across the fields. She relaxed into his smooth gait, letting her body melt into his. How easy to lose herself in the pure joy of motion, the thrill of speed, the allure of freedom.

When she spotted the main road bordering her land, Elise realized she'd ridden much further than she'd planned.

If she failed to return soon, Matthews would worry and no doubt lead a search party. She paused at the top of a rise and looked out over the land. The clear day allowed an unimpeded view.

A solitary rider cantered along the main road as it wound along the hills and vales, the figure little more than a speck in the distance. She let her eyes rove, taking in the green, rolling hills, the neatly furrowed fields, the faint shimmer of the ocean in the distance. She imagined herself a medieval queen surveying her kingdom, with brave knights vying for her favor.

Shaking her head at her fanciful thoughts, she turned Prince around and let him gallop toward home. A lurch in his gait gave the only warning before Prince stumbled and went down.

She sailed over Prince's head, flailing, and landed hard. Sharp pain shot up her foot and leg.

The terrible scream of a horse sent chills through her limbs as she lay stunned, desperate to draw a breath. Her chest seized convulsively. Dark panic overtook her.

Finally, with a gasp, air flooded her lungs. Grateful to breathe, she opened her eyes. That chilling scream continued. Prince lay with his back to her, writhing and shrieking.

"Oh, Prince."

She tried to rise, but pain shot through her foot and up her leg. She crawled to him, calling him and murmuring comforting words. When she reached him, she caught him by the reins.

"Easy boy, easy. I'm here."

She tore off her gloves and rubbed his quivering neck. Under her touch, his screams faded to cries of distress. She ran her hand down his neck and heaving side, her eyes following the lines of his legs. His left foreleg hung in a sickening angle, broken beyond repair. Her stomach lurched.

"No. Oh, no."

"Elise!" a distant voice called.

Only then did she hear hoof beats. Through her tears, she saw a blue roan gallop toward her. Jared Amesbury reined and leaped from his horse. He fell on his knees at her side. His anxious gaze swept over her.

"Are you hurt?"

"No. But Prince has broken a leg," she managed.

When he saw Prince, he let his breath out slowly and turned sorrowful eyes to her. "He'll have to be put down."

With tears distorting her vision, she rubbed her hand over Prince's quivering sides. The stallion whimpered.

"I'm sorry," Jared added.

Through her grief came the burning need to know why he'd fallen. She'd ridden over her land countless times without mishap. She looked back at the divots made by his hooves, but saw nothing that could have caused such a terrible fall.

Jared followed her gaze and went to investigate.

127

"A snake hole."

The utter senselessness of it left her alternating between rage and despair. She pressed a hand over her mouth.

He ran his hands along Prince's neck. "He's suffering. Do you want me to do it?"

She heaved a breath and nodded. "I couldn't."

The compassion in his expression almost undid her. Unable to speak, she rubbed Prince's face, whispering a goodbye.

Jared helped her to her feet. When she tried to take a step, she cried out as pain lanced her ankle. In her distress, she'd forgotten her injury.

Alarmed, he lowered her to the ground. "Where does it hurt?"

She held out her left foot.

He carefully removed her shoe and rubbed gentle hands over her ankle. It had already begun to purple and swell, but his touch did not aggravate the pain. It soothed.

"I don't think it's broken, only sprained." He scooped her up, and she shivered within the warmth and safety of his arms as he carried her to his horse. "Wait for me in that grove. I'll be with you shortly."

She settled herself sidesaddle as well as she could on a saddle not meant for a lady in a riding habit. Once she found a position she could maintain, she urged his horse forward. After a few steps, she looked over her shoulder.

Jared had retrieved a gun from his coat pocket. He looked back at her and waited.

She clicked to his horse and headed for the grove. Just as she reached the stand of trees, the gunshot cracked. She jumped. Jared's horse didn't flinch.

Tears fell openly then, and her shoulders shook. Prince had been a wedding gift from Edward. Losing him reopened stark pain as another part of Edward vanished. And Prince was one more friend to leave her. Their rides together would be no more. He'd never give her one of his affectionate hugs. He'd never nicker in greeting when she came to him. He'd never nose about her pockets looking for an apple or a carrot. She would never again feel his velvety coat, his sweet scent, his hairy nose tickling her neck as he nuzzled her. Her shoulders shook.

As Jared approached, she pulled herself together and wiped her tears, but fixed her gaze downward. Jared removed his gloves, took her hand in his and ran the pad of his thumb over the back of her bare hand. His rough hand was warm and soothing.

"Thank you," she whispered.

"Let's get you home so you can have that ankle tended."

Grimly, he swung up behind her and settled her in front of him. When they were comfortable, he urged the horse forward. At first, she sat stiffly, aware of the impropriety of their close contact. Yet the warmth of his body against her side and his arms encircling her was comforting. Her muscles unclenching, and the knots in her stomach easing, she relaxed against him. He tightened his arms. Well-being crept over her, calming her, easing her grief.

As they rode, her ankle throbbed in earnest. She hooked her right foot behind her injured ankle to keep it from being jarred unnecessarily. The roan danced against the reins, but Jared kept him at a walk. Elise wondered if he held her so close because he feared she'd fall riding across on a gentleman's saddle, or for another reason entirely. She rested her head against his chest.

His scent tantalized her, and she turned her face toward him, inhaling his smell. His muscles flexed as his arms tightened around her. Her heart thudded with more vigor.

After a moment, he loosened his grip on the reins and put his hands on her hips. She drew in her breath. He shifted her slightly and moved behind her. When he had her settled more comfortably in front of him, he removed his hands from her hips and simply put his arms around her, holding the reins in one hand, the other resting benignly on her arm.

She let out her breath, relieved and yet, unexplainably disappointed.

He leaned down and spoke into her ear, his breath tickling her neck. "You're trembling."

She tilted her head back to meet his blue-green gaze. His mouth hovered tantalizingly close, his lips slightly parted. The urge to trace the contours of his face almost raised her hand. She'd never wanted to be kissed so badly in all her life. She wanted that, and so much more.

And it terrified her.

His expression softened. "You have no need to fear me, Elise."

She didn't fear him as much as she feared herself.

A wicked, yet familiar glimmer entered his eyes. "I'm not going to ravish you right here and now."

"Are you planning on ravishing me elsewhere?" She snapped her mouth closed, horrified she'd just uttered such a scandalous statement.

His mouth slowly curved. "You wouldn't believe how badly I'm tempted to do just that. But I won't. Not unless you wish me to." His lips pulled into a sly smile. "Do you?"

Fearing her expression would give her away, she turned forward. "Certainly not."

His chin brushed against the top of her head. Her body tingled in awareness of his nearness, his virility.

He moved the reins into the other hand and smoothed her hair back. The contact felt achingly pleasant. Only then did she realize she must have lost her bonnet in the fall. She no doubt looked a sight with her hair sticking out in all directions. He gave no hint that he noticed. Instead, he pulled her in closer and pressed his lips to her temple.

The quiver in her stomach intensified. She felt both safe and threatened. Relaxed and alarmed. Aroused and frightened.

"You're still trembling." His chest rumbled against her.

She closed her eyes. "I'm not afraid of you."

"I can't tell you how relieved I am to hear that."

They rode without speaking with his arm wrapped around her. His heart beat against her shoulder. Strong. Steady. Safe.

Every nerve ending throbbed in awareness of him. She craved more of him, yet feared what more entailed. She'd never been so keenly aware of a man, or ached so badly. He was thrilling and forbidden.

And yet, underneath it all, a sense of belonging arose. She closed her eyes and burrowed against him.

As they crested the next hill, hoof beats pounded toward them. Elise opened her eyes. Matthews thundered to them, his expression murderous. He reined in, eyeing Elise in concern, and sent Jared an open glare. His eyes moved back to hers.

"Are you all right?" he demanded angrily.

"Prince fell, Matthews." Her voice shook as sharp sorrow returned.

The groom paled. "Are you hurt?"

"Just a sprained ankle. But Prince broke his leg. Mr. Amesbury came to assist." Elise swallowed and battled her tears. "Prince's leg was snapped," she managed through her tears.

Matthews's pallor became almost grey. "Where

is he?"

"At the eastern border near the road."

"I'll go take care of him." His voice sounded strangled.

"I've already seen to him," Jared said quietly.

Grim and tense, Matthews nodded. "I'll get someone to help me with the body." He paused, glancing alternately at her and Jared.

"I'll see her safely home," Jared assured him.

Matthews appeared to size up Jared. Whether he approved of something he saw in Jared, or whether Elise's expression convinced him, she did not know. He nodded again and spurred his horse back to the stables. By the time Elise and Jared had arrived in front of the house, Matthews and another stable lad were racing off together.

Jared dismounted, turned, and scooped her up. She put an arm around his neck, feeling safe and protected. How good it felt to depend on someone else instead of being always the one to whom everyone looked for decisions. Before Jared mounted the front steps, the doors opened and a small army of servants poured out.

The head housekeeper, Mrs. Chambers, led the group. "Matthews sent me word you'd been thrown. Are you all right?" Her eyes moved to Jared and narrowed in suspicion.

"Nothing worse than a sprained ankle. Mr. Amesbury kindly aided me."

Mrs. Chambers' eyes moved back to him. "Come inside. You can put her on the settee in the parlor."

Jared raised a brow at Elise. "Wouldn't you rather lie in your bed?"

"Oh, for heaven's sake, you can't go into her boudoir!" Mrs. Chambers cried.

Jared directed an amused smile toward Mrs. Chambers. "I'm not going to compromise her, just put her in her bed where she'll be more comfortable."

Blustering, Mrs. Chambers turned an interesting shade of red. Some of the servants looked horrified, others stifled laughter.

"Would you prefer to have one of the servants carry you up?" Jared asked Elise.

"No. You may take me. If you don't mind?"

"I don't mind at all." Jared showed no sign of expending effort. His breathing remained even and he spoke in a normal voice.

Mrs. Chambers sent for Elise's maid. Continually protesting the indecency of a gentleman in her lady's boudoir, she led the way up the stairs and opened the door. She stepped aside and glowered at Mr. Amesbury as he carried Elise inside.

"A moment." Mrs. Chambers pulled back the covers and stacked the pillows. Resigned but watchful, she gestured toward the bed and stepped back.

Under her glare, Jared carefully placed Elise upon the bed. He paused and looked deeply into her eyes. "Will you be all right?"

She finally gave into the impulse to touch him and laid a hand on his cheek. "Yes. Thank you. For everything."

"I'm glad I happened along when you needed me." Sympathy shone in his eyes, as if he somehow understood how much Prince meant to her.

She swallowed hard and looked away.

He straightened and stepped back. With a grin at Mrs. Chambers, he said, "I leave her in your most capable hands, madam." He bowed slightly, paused at the doorway and flashed a brilliant smile before he quit the room.

Mrs. Chambers humphed. "Scoundrel. To even suggest such a thing as to enter a lady's room."

She continued to expound on Mr. Amesbury's faults as she brought pillows to prop under Elise's foot. Her tirade lasted until Elise's maid entered the room.

Elise lay back, smiling, and closed her eyes.

Rescue by a handsome man wasn't such a bad thing. Then guilt dimmed her pleasure that she could be thinking that on the heels of Prince's death.

CHAPTER 11

Against his better judgment, Jared returned to Elise Berkley's house a few days after her fall. He should not be thinking about women; he needed to concentrate upon his mission.

But he and Greymore had given up on their attempts to decipher the code and had sent it to the home office in London. He had little to do at the moment but wait for word. In the meantime, courtesy required that he to call upon Mrs. Berkley to ensure she'd suffered no lasting injury after her fall.

Shaking his head at his feeble excuse, he marched up the stairs to the front door.

The stoic butler led him upstairs to the family quarters. Elise sat in a cheerful sitting room flooded with sunlight. Her feet rested upon a footstool, covered with a blanket.

"Mr. Amesbury. What a pleasant surprise."

She smiled and raised her hands to him. Her warm and genuine smile nearly undid him. She was beautiful. More than beautiful. Lovely in every way. Speechless at the sight, he swallowed against a dry mouth.

How she managed to reduce him to such a state without effort, he could not say. In his most secret dreams, he'd never imagined a lady of grace and courage and gentleness would look upon him with such a welcoming expression.

Hope that he might not be beyond salvation tapped him on the shoulder.

Jared called forth his mask of composure,

stripped off his gloves and took her hand in his. Her cool, soft hands conjured memories of the way they'd stroked his hair the first time they'd met. He probably held it longer than he should have, but he craved her touch. He raised her hand to his lips and kissed the back of it.

She blinked and looked away, but Jared caught the unmistakable light of pleasure showing in her face.

He released her hand and pulled a chair closer to her before he sat. "I wanted to discover for myself how you fared."

"My ankle is sore, which is why I have not yet ventured downstairs. Otherwise, I'm quite well."

"May I see?" He indicated the injured foot.

She hesitated, no doubt wrestling with the propriety of letting him see her ankles. With a weak smile, she inclined her head.

He pulled back the blanket. Resting upon a cushion, her swollen, black and purple ankle looked as bad a sprain as he'd ever seen. "Gads, are you sure it's only sprained?"

"The doctor assured me it was." At the pained expression he must have been wearing, she smiled. "It doesn't hurt much unless I try to walk on it."

Jared looked back at her foot. Grinning wickedly, he made a great showing of looking at her bared ankle. "Mrs. Berkley, how indecent of you to reveal your ankle! It's so desirable."

She let out a laugh, half embarrassed, half indignant. "You are indecent!"

"It's such a lovely shade of purple, and has swollen so beautifully. I'm not sure I can control my baser instincts now that I've seen such a tempting sight."

Her lips twitching in an effort to suppress a smile, she picked up a nearby chair pillow and threw it at him. Jared deflected it with one arm. Then he retrieved the pillow and brought it to her.

"Here is your ammunition for the next time you feel the need to do me bodily harm."

She laughed softly. "Most chivalrous of you, I must say."

As he replaced the blanket over her feet, his gaze fell upon her needlework in her lap. "May I see?"

She handed him the linen. The needle had been carefully threaded through the edge to mark her place and keep the needle secure. He doubted he'd be much of a judge, but the stitchery looked as fine as he'd ever seen.

"This is truly a work of art. My mother's work adorns tablecloths, bed linens, pillows. I believe if she were to see this, she'd be impressed." He handed the linen back to her.

She accepted it thoughtfully. "She's passed on, is she not?"

He sobered, nodded. "Nearly three years ago. Father never quite recovered from her loss."

Her voice hushed. "It's not easy to go on without the other half of your heart."

"Is that how it feels?" he asked gently, thinking not only of his father's grief, but of the husband she continued to mourn.

She put away her sewing. "It's fortunate I have my son to care for. In the beginning, he was the only reason I arose in the morning." A faraway look came into her eyes as she lost herself in memories for a moment. She offered an apologetic smile. "Forgive me."

He squelched a sudden flare of jealousy for her husband who still held her heart captive. Knowing how difficult Elise found it to reveal weakness or emotion, and not wishing her to linger on her perfect husband's memory, he searched for a way to change the subject, and he indicated a vase of flowers on a nearby table.

"Cheerful. From your garden?"

"Mr. Bradford's, actually. He heard of my fall and brought them to me. They do brighten the room."

Jared laughed when he wanted to gnash his teeth. "Oh, ho! I knew he had an interest in you. I'm surprised Lord Druesdale hasn't called as well."

"He has."

"The dog!"

She laughed.

"They both have excellent taste."

She shook her head once, her lips pressed together briefly.

"Why don't you believe me when I tell you that you're beautiful?"

She made a coughing sound which, coming from one less lady-like, might have been called a snort. "Because I own a looking glass."

"Clearly defective." He cocked his head to one side. "Perhaps you need the constant companionship of a man to convince you. Day and night."

"Rake!" But her smile betrayed her pleasure.

"Careful. I might have to prove you right."

She laughed softly. "You are the most changeable man I've ever met. One moment, you are the perfect gentleman. The next you act as a scoundrel. Then you're as playful as a child. Do you always act on whatever impulse seizes you?"

He grinned. "Not always. You'd be surprised how often I restrain my reckless nature."

"You are an adventurer."

"I am. But my wanderlust has been fed, and then some. I'm ready to settle down."

She eyed him. "I wonder if you'd find staying home too dull and stifling. Then you'd be off on some grand adventure again and leave your poor, unsuspecting wife and children alone."

"She'd have to understand me and not be caught unsuspecting. Or go with me. But I don't believe I would wish to go. I could be content in one place. I tire of not belonging."

The truth of his words rang through his soul. He did want to belong. And not just to a place, or a cause, but to a woman.

To this woman.

****

In the reflection of the darkened window pane, Jared saw a footman standing uncertainly in the doorway of his study. He dragged his thoughts away from Von Barondy and the intelligence he'd just received about the viscount's many recent purchases of shipping companies using false company names. No one had cracked the codes yet.

He turned. "Yes?"

The footman held a silver tray with an envelope on it. "A message just arrived for you, sir."

Jared waved toward the stack of correspondence on the edge of his desk. "Add it to the pile."

"Ah, sir, this one is trimmed in black."

Jared's heart jumped into his throat. With trembling fingers, he snatched the letter off the tray and tore it open without bothering with the letter opener. After scanning the words, he stumbled to the nearest chair and collapsed.

"Sir?" the footman took a few hesitant steps forward.

Jared waved him back. The door closed softly. He got up and poured himself a drink, but hardly felt the brandy's burn as it ran down his throat. He'd always thought there would be enough time to make things right with Father.

When he'd received word of Mama's death, he'd been half a world away, alone. Rebecca was gone and he'd had no one to turn to, no one to share his grief. Surrounded by strangers who called him by another name, who believed him to be whatever guise he happened to wear at that moment, he was alone. Always alone.

One day he'd be consumed by loneliness.

CHAPTER 12

Elise brushed a curl back from Colin's sleeping face. Awake, he attacked life with exuberance and mischief. In sleep, he glowed with angelic innocence. No wonder Jared Amesbury adored him. The man clearly had good sense.

Colin had spoken of little else but his afternoon fishing with Mr. Amesbury two weeks ago. He would be broken-hearted when his new friend left for the more exciting bachelor life in London with clubs and other manly entertainment.

She sighed. Perhaps she should limit Colin's contact with Jared Amesbury. The more affection he developed for the man, the harder his departure would be on her son. Not only her son.

As she left the nursery, limping on her tender ankle, Elise nodded to Nurse Robbins who looked up from her sewing and smiled in return. Though it was late, Elise went to the library to find something to read until she could sleep. After choosing a book, she curled up in an armchair by the fire.

Before she'd read more than a few chapters, a footman appeared in the doorway. "Forgive me, ma'am, but you have a caller."

Elise closed the volume on her lap. "At this time of night?"

"It's Mr. Amesbury. He seems rather distraught."

Filled with trepidation, Elise stood. Why would Jared come so late at night? Surely he wouldn't have an indecent proposition, would he? With Jared Amesbury, one never knew. She looked down at her dressing gown. Though not entirely appropriate to receiving guests, it would adequately preserve her modesty. She chewed her lip, wondering at the wisdom of receiving Jared.

"Elise."

She looked up. And blinked.

The sight nearly stopped her heart. Disheveled, rumpled, his cravat awry, Jared Amesbury leaned against the doorway as if he depended upon it to keep himself upright.

The footman appeared alarmed. "Sir. You cannot—"

"What has happened?" She crossed the room to Jared.

The footman discreetly left.

"I…" Anguish twisted his face. He dragged his fingers through his hair and let out a long, ragged breath. Then he seemed to gather himself. "I shouldn't have come. Forgive the interruption."

Closing his eyes, he took a breath. After appearing to find some hidden reservoir of strength, he squared his shoulders and turned away.

"Wait. Please come in."

He turned back. In his eyes, hope and desperation mingled with haunting grief.

Elise resisted the urge to put her arms around him and offer the comfort that he so clearly needed. Instead, she motioned to the settee.

"Please have a seat."

He collapsed upon it, leaned back and pressed the heels of his hands into his eyes.

She sank down next to him, frightened at his display of emotion. She touched his arm. "What is it?"

He lowered his hands. The bleakness in his expression brought a lump to her throat. "My father has died."

"Oh! I'm so sorry."

"He died thinking I was a disgrace to the family. I wanted to win his approval. I always hoped he'd...that we'd reconcile. That some day I'd become someone of whom he'd be proud." He leaned forward and hung his head, his forearms lying limp on his knees. "I'll never have that chance now."

Elise put a hand on his back. "I'm sorry."

He turned and pulled her into his arms, burrowing his face into her neck.

He needed her. At that moment, nothing else mattered.

Without hesitation, she gathered him close. The warmth of his body soaked through her. He smelled of masculine, earthy smells, all underscored by a touch of brandy.

"All my life, I lived in constant fear of failure, of never quite measuring up to my brothers. My father was a highly respected peer. He thought I'd never amount to anything, that my impulsive nature would be my downfall. For a while, I delighted in proving him right. I probably gave him all his gray hair. Then that day..."

He paused again, and the tension in his body seeped into Elise.

"A prank went terribly wrong. I hadn't meant to hurt anyone. It led to an ugly row with Father..." again he stopped. "I said terrible things. Then Cole and I both left and I swore I'd never return. I made good on my vow." His voice broke, and he stopped to steady it. "Mother's gone, and now Father. I'll never have a chance to say I'm sorry. To prove myself to him."

Weeping silently in sympathy for his suffering, Elise cradled his head against her shoulder and stroked his hair. She wondered why he'd come to her, an acquaintance of barely a few weeks, and bared his soul. Had he no one else?

"I shouldn't have come."

"Of course you should have," she soothed. "It's all right."

She continued holding him, stroking his hair. He needed her. She reveled in the sensation.

How long since someone other than Colin truly needed her?

He gradually relaxed against her, his head growing heavy on her shoulder, and his breathing deepened in sleep. She never would have thought a man of Jared's ilk would have let down his guard enough to sleep in the presence of a lady.

Surprised, but touched that he'd actually fallen asleep in her arms, she rested her cheek against his forehead and simply held on, overcome by the moment's intimacy.

Edward would never have unbent enough to bare his soul to her this way. Even when he'd received news that both of his parents had died suddenly, he'd nodded and immediately set about making the arrangements for their burial. He'd always remained in control.

Even in matters of love, he had kept a tight reign on his desires. He'd loved her as a man, but with restraint, almost apologetic about the act necessary to create a child. He seldom spoke of his desires, or his feelings.

She knew intuitively that Jared would not normally have opened up in this way, either. He kept everything close, guarded, as if he carried a hundred secrets that meant the difference between life and death. Either he was completely undone to open up now, or a man of great passion and expression searching for an outlet.

The idea of a man loving her passionately, without restraint, held tremendous appeal.

Elise absently stroked his hair. She watched the firelight shimmer in the dark waves, and played with the strands in her fingers.

Mrs. Chambers came in to check the windows, her nightly ritual before retiring, and stopped at the sight of Elise holding a man on her shoulder. Her eyes opened wide and the color drained from her face. Elise wondered if she would give notice at that very moment and go find employment with a lady who did not behave in such a scandalous manner.

Then, Mrs. Chambers' expression softened and she whispered, "He's very handsome, isn't he?"

Taken aback, Elise smiled.

"Men look deceptively innocent when they're sleeping. Like children," the housekeeper added wryly.

Elise looked down at Jared's slumbering face. Even in sleep, he failed to look innocent, but his features did soften.

"It's about time you came out of mourning. Do you need anything, before I retire, ma'am?"

Speechless at her normally prudish housekeeper's apparent approval, Elise shook her head.

Mrs. Chambers paused, pressed her lips together, and then clearly came to some sort of decision. She left, her skirts swishing.

Elise decided she would take whatever may come for the simple, sublime joy of holding Jared Amesbury during his moment of need.

Elise watched the fire die in the hearth and listened to the clock tick. Jared drew a shivering breath and shifted, nestling his face against her neck while his arms tightened around her. Emotion welled up and nearly overflowed. As she held this man, warmth and contentment settled over her.

She wanted to hold him all night. Every night. For a long, long time.

If Lily felt this way in Mr. Harrison's arms, no wonder she wanted to remarry. Elise smiled ruefully to herself. Not that she was ready to leap into marriage, but the thought was no longer as unappealing as it once was.

Mrs. Chambers returned carrying a tray with a cup. "In case he wakes," she whispered. She paused at the door. "Do you wish me to remain?"

"No, that's not necessary. Good night."

"Good night, ma'am."

Elise knew it was a bit late to be concerned with propriety now. Perhaps her status as a widow would shield her from whatever repercussions might arise out of her rather compromising position. At the moment, she hardly cared. Holding a hurting man in her arms seemed worth any embarrassment.

No, not a man. This man.

Somehow, he'd wormed his way through her defenses and into her heart. The softness that stole over her threatened to reduce her to tears again.

Whatever else he might be, he was a good man. She had no doubt. And he'd won Colin's affection. Seeing them together seemed right. Having him in her arms seemed right. Keeping him in her life seemed right.

She held him close, not knowing if she could bear it when he left. In a few months, the world traveler would tire of this quiet country life, and return to the more exciting London or other parts unknown. And her life of order would return.

The thought made her want to weep.

She wasn't certain she could tempt him to stay. Surely he had some feelings for her, or he would not have come to her at his hour of need. But she doubted they were enough to entice him to remain here with her.

Could she trust this impulsive, unpredictable man with her heart?

He raised his head. Then he closed his eyes and let out his breath.

"Forgive me."

"There is nothing to forgive."

With obvious reluctance, he removed his arms from around her and sat up. He pushed his hands through his hair and tugged at his already crumpled cravat.

"Did I really babble as badly as I fear I did?"

"You grieved for your father."

He took a steadying breath. "I don't normally reveal things of such a personal nature."

"It takes courage to speak of your feelings."

"I'm not sure why I did. I wasn't even drunk."

"Thank you for trusting me enough to come to me."

He watched her gravely.

To distract him, she offered him the cup Mrs. Chambers brought. "My housekeeper made one of her famous hot toddies for you in case you awoke." She offered it to him. "It's still warm."

A corner of his mouth lifted up in a strained attempt at humor. "Mrs. Chambers made it? Did she poison it to be rid of me?"

She shook her head. "Believe it or not, she accepted your presence here tonight with aplomb."

"I must be losing my touch."

She smiled, but felt his unease.

Without taking his eyes off her face, he accepted the drink. Vibrating with tension, he gulped it down and solemnly handed back the cup.

"Your confidences are safe with me, Jared."

He managed a brief, humorless smile. "If only I'd known all I had to do to hear you say my Christian name would be to bare my soul and weep like a child, I'd have done it sooner." He attempted a light-hearted tone, but it sounded forced.

She summoned a smile for his benefit. "I like children."

He studied her, not rakishly, not guardedly, he simply gazed at her. "I don't remember when I've ever felt this comfortable with a woman. With anyone."

"Why is that, do you think?"

"I'm not certain. Women usually find me dangerous."

"I don't doubt it."

"But you aren't afraid."

She took his hand between hers. "I think you are capable of many things. But hurting me is not one of them."

A smile stole slowly over his face and finally touched his eyes. "I've only known you a few weeks and already you know me better than..." he paused, "than most women care to."

With gentleness that matched the feeling in Elise's heart, Jared caressed her cheek and traced his thumb over her lips.

"So soft. So beautiful."

She shivered at the gentleness, at the hot, swirling ache that started in her stomach and spread outward.

"Elise." He cupped her face in his hands.

She breathed in his heady masculine scent, reveling in the feel of his rough hands on her face and his thumbs caressing her cheeks. Painfully slow, he leaned in. The unconcealed passion in his eyes should have frightened her. Instead, excitement coursed through her veins and her heart pounded in anticipation.

The instant his lips touched hers, she shivered at the desire flooding her. Ever so softly, he brushed his lips over hers before pressing more firmly. She yielded.

He deepened the kiss and Elise's heart soared. Edward had never kissed her in such a manner, had never stirred her to such heat. Jared captured her mouth, taking command, demanding more. His hands moved down her shoulder, along her side, and

148

encircled her waist. He pressed her against his hard, muscular body. Fissions of need rippled through her. His arm muscles flexed as he held her. The raw power of this man would have been daunting if she'd been any less hungry for him. She clung to him, no longer frightened by her own desire. He shivered and moved his mouth from her lips to her cheek, kissing his way to her temple.

He groaned softly. "I should leave. This is far too tempting."

"Don't go." Oh, gracious, what had she just said? "Ah, I mean, the guest room is at your disposal. You needn't go out this late."

He crushed her to him. "I can't stay without..." He pulled back and brushed her hair away from her eyes. "I shouldn't be here."

"I trust you." The words came out of her mouth before she realized it. But, oddly enough, she meant them.

He looked pained. "I'm a bad man. I've done things that would horrify you."

"Charlotte Greymore's husband came home from the war suffering for the acts of violence committed in battle. That faded in time."

Smiling faintly, yet with sadness still shading his eyes, he pushed himself away as though it took great effort. Elise had the feeling she'd just missed a crucial puzzle piece.

He rose and stood over her with a tender smile. Tender. Not rakish, not playful, not wicked. Tender. The softness in her heart crept outward.

"Thank you." He kissed her hand and pressed it against his cheek with his eyes closed. He quivered again, released her hand and strode quickly away.

She heard his rich voice as he conversed briefly with the footman by the door before he left. Without him, the house seemed dreadfully empty. Elise sat in stunned silence at the power that man held over her.

Exhilarating.

Heaven help her, the temptation to run after him and beg him to remain with her, loving her all night long in the way only he could, was nearly overwhelming. She clenched her fists while her heart thudded and a strange yearning coiled deep within. She struggled to banish all those warm, wicked, delicious thoughts. Then, she stopped struggling and let them envelope her in all their glory.

CHAPTER 13

Jared stood shoulder to shoulder between his brothers Cole and Christian, drawing strength from their presence. Emptiness seized Jared's chest each time he looked around his childhood home and failed to find either of his parents.

He'd been wrong to stay away.

Foolish and proud and wrong.

And now it was too late.

Jared knew he made a grim trio with Cole and Christian when the fourth guest who ventured an approach seemed to think better and turned away.

Sipping his drink, Jared glanced at Cole. His eldest brother, as usual, remained impassive but the lines around Cole's mouth had softened since his marriage. Impeccable as usual, Cole wore all black for the funeral, except for the white cravat and sapphire stick pin glittering from among the snowy folds. He stood with the air of authority only possessed by an heir bred for the role of earl.

"It was a nice service," Christian said, clearly feeling the need to break the silence.

Cole only grunted in reply.

Several irreverent quips popped into Jared's head, but he stifled the impulse to voice them. Instead, he merely said, "It was."

Standing to Jared's left, Christian ran his thumb along his lower lip. Jared wondered if Christian knew how much he looked like Father when he did that. Christian was a younger, almost pretty version of Cole; 'pretty' being the ultimate insult in the Amesbury brood and a taunt they'd hurled at each other all their lives. The only thing which saved Christian from the horror of being truly pretty was a small scar near one eye.

Every inch the height and breadth of Cole, Christian dressed as impeccably as the eldest, perfectly at ease with his black tailored clothing. And, unlike the child he'd been, Christian now stood with an air of quiet confidence. Perfect, as always. Everything about Christian was gold, from the color of his hair to the quality of his heart. Even the cravat looked good on Christian. The dog. Jared resisted tugging on his own neck ware.

"The solicitor wants to meet with us all tomorrow at eleven o'clock, if convenient," Christian said with a glance at Cole.

"Of course," Cole replied.

Relatives, many with names Jared could barely remember, mingled with the guests. The murmur of voices and soft laughter filtered through the sun-drenched air. If the guests hadn't been dressed somberly, this would appear a garden party instead of a funeral luncheon.

Jared finished his drink and set it on a passing tray. As he glanced at a nearby path, he wondered if it would be bad form to disappear into one of the many gardens that graced the Tarrington ancestral grounds.

Yet, he couldn't help but feel as if he were intruding. Everywhere he looked, he noticed things that had changed since he left. Everything was steeped in memory; some clear, others the dimmed memories of a child who'd taken home and family for granted. The few times Jared had returned to England over the years, he'd visited his mother and siblings when they were in London, but he'd kept the visits brief and carefully timed so as to ensure never coming face to face with Father.

How he longed to go back and reclaim the years

lost.

As if sensing Jared's regret, Christian gripped his shoulder briefly. "It's good to have you home."

Jared sent him a look of gratitude. Christian met his gaze and Jared noticed in him a new intensity.

Grant, Jared's junior by three years, sauntered to them. He normally scorned fashion and convention by wearing attire more appropriate for stalking hapless footpads in London's seediest alleys. Yet, for the occasion of attending the funeral of his own father, a prominent earl, Grant had dressed in a tailored black superfine. Jared imagined Cole had threatened to throw him in the stocks if he didn't appear in suitable clothing.

Secretly, Jared agreed with Grant's preferred attire, and had gleefully shunned gentleman's clothing while he'd played a pirate. Openly, Jared often taunted Grant's lack of decorum. Not that Grant ever seemed to care, curse him.

At the moment, Grant seemed almost amused. Well, amused for Grant. He lifted a brow as he looked at each of them in turn. "Funeral luncheons are supposed to be solemn, not drive guests to suicide."

Jared smirked. Cole turned a baleful glare on Grant. Christian ignored him.

Grant looked the least like the Amesbury brothers. Like them all, he shared Father's build, but his eyes were silvery-gray instead of blue, his features sharper, more angular, and his hair was almost black, a good reflection of his soul, Jared thought. A wide, ragged scar ran from his forehead to his jaw, narrowly missing his eye, making his appearance truly forbidding.

Grant's assessing gaze took on a calculating glint, and Jared waited for the cynical wisdom he would no doubt spew forth, making them look like illiterate babes.

"Wait. Here, you should stand thusly." Grant grasped Jared by the arm and tugged. Curious, Jared did not resist as Grant moved him to the other side of Cole. "There. Now you're in ascending order of pretty, beginning with Christian."

Jared laughed. Christian glanced heavenward, no doubt communing with angels mere mortals could not see, and calling down a holy amount of patience. Jared expected some kind of witty retort from Christian but he remained silently impervious to Grant's barbs.

Growing reflective, Jared pitied Christian for the torment he'd suffered at the hands of his brothers. From Jared, especially. They'd called him 'pretty boy,' the 'perfectly perfect Christian,' and 'Mama's favorite.' The last, of course, was spoken purely in jealousy, since Mama's attention was a coveted prize. Her soft hands and soothing voice were memories Jared had most treasured when he'd been far from home.

Grant turned to Cole. "And I suppose now that you're the impressive Sixth Earl of Tarrington, you expect us to call you 'My Lord?'"

Cole cuffed Grant on the back of the head. "Remember your manners, whelp. As head of the family, I can cut you off now, should I so choose. Unlike Jared and Christian, you've no investments of your own."

Grant yawned. "None that you know of. My Lord." His voice dripped with sarcasm. "Perhaps you're disappointed that Christian's still prettier than you?"

Christian turned to Cole. "I like your idea of cutting off his portion."

Jared couldn't have borne it had he been the target of Grant's merciless onslaught. Yet despite all Grant's attempts to ruffle him, Christian remained impassive, almost bored, like a tower standing against a storm.

As Jared took a good look at his youngest brother, he realized, except for his blond hair, Christian simply looked like a younger version of Father. His lips were slightly fuller, and his cheekbones more prominent, but there was truly nothing feminine about Christian, certainly nothing to warrant the insult 'pretty.' He'd certainly grown into a capable, dignified man.

"Any new directives you wish to make, O wise head of the household?" Grant taunted Cole.

"Leave him alone, Grant," Christian said wearily.

Grant folded his arms and fixed a blank stare at Christian. "But of course, anything you say, Pretty Boy."

Christian's calm exterior slipped as he faced him and his tone turned mocking. "Did we hurt your feelings when no one invited you to stand in the pretty line?"

Grant let out a snort but before he could say another word, Cole interjected with a decisive, "Enough."

Though Grant and Christian had never been close, this animosity between them was becoming increasingly heated. Had something happened between them?

The twins, Margaret and Rachel, approached. As if sensing the tension, Margaret lifted her head and looked at them with the condescending gaze one might expect from a queen. Marriage to a marquis had only encouraged her haughty demeanor. Or perhaps it was the decided lack of happiness she'd found in her wedded state.

Rachel shadowed her, her expression bland, but tragedy shimmered around the edges. Normally vibrant, she'd taken Father's death very hard, especially since it came so close on the heels of Mother's.

"I still can't believe he's gone," Rachel said. "I keep expecting him to walk around the corner."

Christian examined the ground, his golden head lowered. "I'd hoped he would rally at the seashore."

"I suppose a broken heart will do that to you," Rachel said with a faraway look.

Decidedly preoccupied, Christian wandered away, probably in search of something to eat. Though nearly four and twenty, he still ate like a colt.

"Few find a love like theirs, outside of fairy tales," Margaret said with a hard note to her voice.

Rachel turned to Cole. "You did, though, didn't you? Find a love like Mama and Father?"

Cole's expression softened so dramatically that Jared had to laugh. "You poor, besotted fool."

Cole grinned, looking decidedly smug. "Better than a lonely fool."

Jared scanned the crowed until he found Cole's wife, Alicia. Poised and gracious, she moved among the guests who'd attended the funeral. Though no one would ever consider her uncommonly beautiful, Alicia was uniquely lovely, and glowed with quiet joy. Even in her mourning attire, she looked radiant. She called everyone by name, and fixed her attention upon them as if they were the only one with whom she wanted to converse, whether a member of the nobility or the most humble field worker.

Jared had liked her immediately when they'd met a year ago and knew Cole had found a remarkable woman. He thought of Elise Berkley and decided she and Alicia would like each other. Both possessed courage, inner strength, and uncommon gentleness.

The thought of introducing Elise to his family filled him with warmth, and suddenly the estate felt like home.

Alicia moved to Christian who stood leaning against a tree, removed from the others, and staring off in the distance.

Jared frowned. It was unlike Christian to isolate himself unless immersed in the throes of painting. Was he so affected by Father's death? Or something else?

At Alicia's approach, he turned to her with a ready smile. Within moments, they were laughing together like old friends. As if unable to remain from her side for long, Cole went to his wife and took her hand. The smile she bestowed on him would have melted a marble statue. Lucky devil.

As Cole and Alicia left arm in arm, Christian turned away to stare thoughtfully out over the landscape.

Keenly missing the years lost between them, Jared sauntered to Christian and slung an arm around his youngest brother's neck. Jared mentally shook his head over how tall and broad-shouldered Christian had become. "You know, I've actually missed you."

Christian eyed him warily. "Indeed?"

"I met a little boy who reminded me of you as a child."

Christian lifted a brow in a perfect imitation of Cole. "You tried to feed him to a tiger?"

Jared laughed. "No. I took him fishing."

"So you tried to drown him?"

Chuckling, Jared tightened his arm around Christian. "I deserved that. Ah, Chris, you're too good for this ugly world. Think you'll ever find a woman worthy of you, or will you be transformed into a real angel first?"

Christian touched the scar by his eye in an unconscious gesture. "You don't know me at all, do you? I'm no saint."

A shadow passed over Christian that gave Jared pause, but he swiftly brought up a façade as practiced as any operative. Jared took his arm from around Christian's shoulders and led him apart from the others. They followed one of the garden paths away from the house.

Jared eyed him. "What's amiss between you and Grant?"

Christian shrugged but failed to appear as casual as he'd no doubt intended. " 'Tis nothing."

"Nothing? He's been taking shots at you all day."

"He usually does."

Jared eyed him. "Since when?"

"Years."

Jared waited, but Christian volunteered nothing further. Still missing the lost time between them, Jared finally said, "I'm sorry I wasn't there for you."

Christian made a slight choking sound. "So you could keep tormenting me?"

Jared winced. "I wasn't the best brother."

"I don't know what you mean." A playful glint surfaced in Christian's eye. "Surely not the time you dug a hole and planned to trap a tiger so you could feed me to it? Or when you locked me in the gardener's shed after telling me it was haunted and then banged on the walls and wailed? Or when—"

"I see your point."

Christian grinned wryly to show he bore no hard feelings.

"I was terrible." Jared blew out his breath and tugged at his cravat. If he'd had any decency, he never would have picked on a child six years younger than himself, especially one as tender-hearted as Christian had been.

"It was a long time ago," Christian said dismissively.

"You must have been glad to see me go."

"Would you believe I missed you when you and

Cole left?" His voice quieted. "Especially since it was so soon after Jason fell."

Instinctively, they both glanced toward the garden where their brother had lost his life as a child. Christian's jaw tightened and he looked away. Jared shied away from the helpless terror of watching Jason fall.

He cast about for anything to change the subject. "Have you decided to truly become a man of the cloth?"

Christian let out a slow breath, his forehead creasing. "I know everyone expects it. I'm just not sure I'm meant for the church."

"Cole won't force you do it if you don't want to."

"I know." Christian looked miserable. "But Father wished it for me. And Mama had her heart set on it."

Jared eyed him. "They are no longer here to disappoint. What do you want?"

Christian's pale blue eyes briefly met Jared's. "You'd laugh."

"All right. Make me laugh." Jared loosened his cravat and waited.

Christian took on that unfocused look he wore before he immersed himself in painting for hours on end, creating some pastoral scene existing at a level above mortal eyes. "What I really want is to go to the Royal Academy and study art under a true master."

Jared nodded pensively. Christian had talent. His paintings had graced the halls of some noted art collectors. To Jared's knowledge, Christian had given them as gifts, rather than being so gauche as to sell them, but their prominent displaying revealed their value. To study art at the Academy would be an unusual act for the son of an earl. However, their family seemed to delight in unconventional behavior.

Christian added, "Sometimes, though, I long for adventure. I wish I could go to sea with you."

Donna Hatch

Jared groaned. "Trust me, Chris, you don't."

Christian leveled a gaze at him that came as close to a glare as he'd ever seen from his youngest brother.

Jared held up his hands. "I'm not saying you couldn't do it. You're bigger than half the crew. And you probably shoot and swordfight better than most of them, too. But it's not the fun you think it is. I can't wait to leave it."

"You're not really a pirate, are you?" His tone landed somewhere between fascination and horror.

It suddenly mattered a great deal that Christian might think him a true pirate with all it entailed. They walked in silence, their feet crunching on the gravel. The scent of jasmine and honeysuckle filled the air, reminding Jared of Elise and the day he'd fished with Colin.

"I tell you this in utmost confidence." Jared waited until Christian met his eye to let him know he spoke in earnest.

Growing grave, Christian nodded.

Jared ordered his thoughts. "I'm a member of a secret government organization formed during the War. I played many roles as I spied for the crown. The one I've played since the war with Boney ended is that of pirate. So yes, I'm a pirate and have been for over three years. But it's under orders to expose a pirate ring. And I'm leaving the organization after this last assignment is completed."

Christian silently digested Jared's words. That he actually believed Jared came as a relief. "You've lived a life of adventure. A hero. I've lived mine as companion to Mama and Father."

"Father was proud of you and ashamed of me."

"He misplaced his pride. I didn't serve in the war. I've done nothing to uphold the family honor. And what's sad, is now that Father's gone, I feel liberated. Terrible, isn't it?"

"No," Jared said soberly. "It must have been awful watching him decline."

Christian made no reply, but his tension was tangible. Something dark and desperate entered his eyes.

Jared scowled at his feet. He'd missed so much at home; things that really mattered. Regret chewed a hole in his insides.

They walked in silence through the gardens designed to retell favorite Greek myths, each garden more magnificent that the rest. By the time they'd circled back to join the others, the shadows had grown long.

After bidding farewell to the guests and having dinner together, the family gathered in the drawing room. Jared, Cole and the girls conversed easily while playing a game of whist. Alicia worked at her needlepoint. Christian's eyes took on that unfocused look he always got when the Muse inspired him, and picked up a sketchpad and pencil. Grant sat apart from the others and silently drank.

As the evening waned, Cole caught Jared's eye and nodded toward the door. Jared stood.

Cole turned to Alicia. "If you'll excuse me, I wish to speak with Jared."

She nodded. "Of course."

Cole kissed his wife full on the mouth, his hand resting protectively over her abdomen where his child grew within her.

Margaret sniffed. "Don't be vulgar, Cole."

Cole merely smirked at Margaret as he led Jared out of the room to his private study. He poured drinks for them both and handed Jared a glass. "How long do you stay?"

Jared relaxed in an armchair. "I'll leave in the morning as soon as the estate matters are settled."

"So soon?"

"I have an assignment to complete."

"And a lady to woo?"

Jared raised a brow.

Cole grinned. "I caught you staring off into space, grinning like a half-wit. No one is supposed to look that happy at a funeral."

Still holding his drink, Jared went to the window and looked out at the sunset. "She's out of my reach."

"The only daughter of a duke? Or married?"

Jared set down his glass and tugged at his cravat. "She's a proper lady. She's also still in love with her deceased husband."

Cole said nothing.

"She's brave and beautiful and kind." Jared tore off the cursed cravat. "She's too good for me."

"Her opinion or yours?"

Jared uttered a sharp laugh devoid of amusement and collapsed into a chair. "She has no idea what I really am."

"The son of a respected earl?"

"A pirate!" he said tightly. "Deuce take it, Cole, I'm a thief and a liar. I've committed atrocities in the name of duty that give me nightmares. I've lied, deceived and betrayed my way through the years. I've killed more men than I can remember. Some even my own countrymen. And I did it to keep the image of a pirate for some greater good I don't even believe in anymore."

No sound beyond the ticking of the clock interrupted. Resting his forearms on his knees, Jared hunched over and absently wound the cravat around his hand.

Finally, he glanced at Cole, half fearful of the truth. "That makes me a monster, doesn't it?"

"No. It makes you a loyal Englishman." Cole sounded so convinced. If only Jared could be that sure.

Jared raked a hand through his hair. "My

superior officer has promised after I complete this last task, I'll be free. But I swear, there are days when I think I should have chosen the noose instead of this partial exile."

Cole said quietly, "No seventeen-year-old should have to make that choice."

Jared closed his eyes. At seventeen, facing hanging seemed more terrifying than war. Rebecca's offer to join the Secret Service in exchange for escaping the noose seemed easy at the time. He'd had no idea he'd be enslaved by them for the next twelve years of his life, engaging in acts of villainy no gentleman would ever dream of committing.

"What are you going to do about the lady?" Cole's voice brought him back to the present.

"Elise Berkley, a friend of Lady Standwich. I'll do nothing, I suppose. Complete my assignment and then try to figure out what civilian life is all about. She may never remarry. If she does, she'll probably wed a proper English gentleman who understands and appreciates her orderly life." He let out his breath. "She deserves a husband like Christian."

The thought left Jared with an intense desire to go plant his fist in Christian's perfect nose.

"She seems too tame for you." Cole got up and refilled his glass.

Jared felt his mouth curve. "I wouldn't call her tame. The first time I met her, she was threatening Leandro with a gun."

Cole coughed into his drink. "I think I want to hear this."

Jared recounted the events of their first meeting and each encounter since. Cole refilled their drinks and encouraged Jared to keep talking. Jared even related the night he'd gone to her after receiving word of Father's death.

"You know, it's odd, but I've played so many people, I'm not sure who I really am." He stood and went to the fireplace. Resting an arm on the mantle, he stared down at the floor, absently following the patterns on the carpet with his eyes. "But I like the man I become in her presence. She brings out a noble side of me I didn't know existed. I didn't even seduce her that night."

Cole chuckled. "That is noble of you."

"And when I'm with her and her son, I actually feel, well, relaxed. I can truly let down my guard and say whatever I think."

"Maybe who you are when you're with her, is who you really are," Cole suggested.

"It's all a pretense. If she knew…"

"I think she does—not what you do for the government—but she sees the man you are. I sailed on your ship for a year, remember? I know how you acted as a pirate. You had opportunities for ruthlessness that you didn't take. You never allowed torture. Or rapine. And when your prisoners cooperated, you set them free. Unharmed."

"Even I have scruples."

"Exactly. Despite the colorful rumors we spread about you, you were rather gentlemanly about piracy."

Jared snorted. "That has to be the worst contradiction in terms I've ever heard."

"You have much to offer a lady. She already knows your character. If she likes the man you are, she'll accept your sordid past, especially since you did it for king and country."

"But there were times when I enjoyed it," Jared confessed. "Having my own ship, men at my command, the freedom to go anywhere, do anything, not worry about the censure of society…"

"Of course you did. I enjoyed it. It was fun. How many men get to do anything they want?"

Jared grimaced.

"You told me once being an effective operative

means throwing yourself into the role. You excel at that. Being a good man doesn't mean you have to hate every second of a distasteful assignment. If you murdered just for fun, or abused your captives or women, then yes, I'd say you'd become the monster you fear. But you didn't. So stop torturing yourself."

Jared lifted his head and eyed Cole hopefully. He wanted to believe Cole. He wanted him to be right. He wanted to go back and tell Elise everything.

Yet a niggling fear whispered that the truth would drive Elise away.

That would be better for her anyway. She needed someone who deserved her. Not that he'd be introducing her to Christian.

Still, perhaps Cole was right. Perhaps he could be worthy of her. He'd served king and country diligently. He'd braved death and terror and laughed in its face.

Did he have the courage to place his heart in the hands of a woman?

Jared thought of Lord Druesdale; wealthy, titled, deeply entrenched in society, unsullied by war and death. He thought, too, of Mr. Bradford; young, sober, stable.

The idea of either of them winning her heart and hand made him want to go sharpen his sword.

He wanted her. He loved her.

Jared went utterly still. He loved Elise. Loved her! The truth did not leave him feeling trapped, but freed. Hope and optimism swelled in his heart.

Cole was right. Determination overcame him and Jared straightened. He refused to be the gentleman and step aside. He'd fight for her. Even though he didn't deserve her.

He'd confess his love and lay his heart at her feet.

And hope she didn't grind it beneath her heel.

CHAPTER 14

"You're in a fine mood, today, ma'am."

Elise looked up from her sewing at the maid who'd addressed and realized she'd been humming. "I am, Mary. It's a lovely day."

Elise smiled as she resumed her sewing. For the first time in years, she felt truly alive. Colors were more vivid, and she noticed details she had missed before; the lemon scent of the furniture oil, the maids' soft chatter in the room across the corridor, the shimmering dust particles in the slanted sunlight streaming in through the windows, the birds' sweet songs.

Her heart felt light. She'd been kissed—and awakened—by the most handsome and passionate man of her acquaintance. He'd needed her on many levels. He'd trusted her enough to reveal to her his heart. He'd touched her with unsurpassed gentleness and passion. He'd needed her comfort, needed her solace, needed a safe place where he could share his grief and unload his sorrow, his regret.

He'd needed her.

The hunger remained there, the lust, but more, he'd turned to her for comfort. That knowledge filled her with wonder. After he left that night, she had thrummed with such vibrancy that she'd doubted she would ever sleep again. Instead, she'd burrowed into her empty bed, smiling, and drifted off into a dream world where Jared held her close all night.

Could it be possible she was falling in love with this man?

"Mrs. Greymore to see you, madam," the butler intoned.

Elise clasped her friend's hand when she entered the room.

Charlotte smiled broadly. "Why, you look positively radiant. I'm glad to see you so well."

Elise smiled. "I am well. And you?" She peered at Charlotte's face.

"Very well, thank you."

"Charlotte," Elise said quietly.

Charlotte waved away her concerns. "I had a bad spell last week, but I am quite well now, not to worry. I simply had to get out of the house and I wanted to see you."

Elise felt a twinge of guilt. She'd neglected her friend and hadn't known she'd been ill. She made a mental commitment to visit her more often. They chatted over tea and cakes.

"I received an invitation from Mr. Bradford for a family picnic," Elise said.

Charlotte nodded. "We received one just this morning."

Elise let out her breath. "Oh, good. Then it's just a gathering of families in this area."

Charlotte looked at her curiously. "Were you concerned it would be a large affair? Or a small one?"

"Mr. Bradford paid me a visit yesterday afternoon and he's never done that before. Then he mentioned that he'd decided to remarry. I suspect he thinks I'd be a suitable wife."

"Would you?"

Elise laughed uneasily. "Charlotte, you know I will love Edward to the grave."

"I know, but you don't have to spend the rest of your life alone. If I died, I'd expect Charles to remarry. After a respectable period of mourning, of course." She smiled faintly.

"I couldn't do that."

"Even if the offer came from Jared Amesbury?"

Elise leveled a sober gaze. "I have no understanding with Mr. Amesbury. Besides, he's too much a man of mystery. I liked the predictability of my Edward. It made me feel safe."

"Don't you ever long for adventure?"

Elise swallowed the desire to reply with a resounding yes. "I have too many duties to indulge in adventure. Colin deserves a prosperous estate when he comes of age and inherits."

Charlotte's smile turned mysterious. "One can be both responsible and a bit unpredictable. Charles manages to do it."

"What do you mean?"

"He's always here for me when I need him, and he's as attentive as I'd hoped. Yet, there is still an aura of mystery about him, and he manages to surprise me on occasion." Charlotte leaned back against the settee, smiling.

Perhaps Jared had more in common with Charles Greymore than Elise had previously realized. Could it be possible Jared would be a steady and faithful companion the way Charles Greymore was to Charlotte?

Elise imagined herself married to Jared. The ways he'd make her laugh. The times he'd play with Colin, guiding him as he grew into adulthood. The unrestrained passion they'd share.

It was not an unwelcome thought.

****

Luncheon at the Bradford home had been set up at the edge of a lake which spanned the border between their lands.

After greeting the host and his sister, she accepted lemonade from a passing tray and scanned for Colin. She found him skipping rocks. Several servants hovered nearby, keeping a sharp eye out on the children near the water.

"Elise, I'm so glad to see you." Charlotte Greymore clasped her hand. Her china blue eyes shone.

Elise noted with relief that her friend's face had more color than the last time they'd visited. "How are you feeling?"

"Never better." She smiled and put a hand over her abdomen. Then, peering more closely at Elise, added, "Why, you look positively radiant." Before Elise had made a reply, Mr. Greymore came.

"Mrs. Berkley, how lovely you look. Is that a new gown?"

Elise looked down. "Yes." She'd had new gowns made now that she'd officially come out of mourning. She wondered if Jared had a favorite color.

Lord Druesdale greeted them all cordially. His eyes rested longer on Elise. "What a fetching bonnet, Mrs. Berkley. It's fitting for such a beautiful lady."

Elise couldn't remember when she'd had so many compliments all in the same day. Yet a compliment from Lord Druesdale sounded empty. She looked away and murmured an appropriate reply. They spoke of trivialities and exclaimed over the uncommonly fine weather.

Each time a new person arrived, Elise looked for Jared Amesbury. She chided herself. He'd made no effort to contact her in the week since he'd come to her grieving for his father. And kissed her in a way that brought heat to her face each time she recalled it.

'Twas possible Jared had merely needed the companionship of another person to comfort him that night. His kiss may have meant nothing more. And that hadn't been his only kiss, either. He'd kissed her the first moment they met, and again after dinner; therefore his kisses had no meaning. He probably kissed any female within reach. She'd been foolish to believe his heart had been engaged. A hollow ache sank deep inside, weighting her until she could hardly lift her head.

Jared arrived. He drew her gaze like a magnetic pull. Her breath stilled. Was it possible he'd actually grown more handsome since she'd seen him last?

Jared's gaze slid first to hers, then to Lord Druesdale standing next to her. Jared's eyes narrowed. Then he returned his focus to Mr. Bradford and whatever anger she thought she'd seen vanished. All that remained was calm aloofness. Disappointment flooded her.

Hers was a foolish, wayward heart!

"Good day, Mrs. Berkley." Lord Druesdale withdrew.

With embarrassment, she realized she'd been rudely neglecting Lord Druesdale. She made a vague reply and immediately, like the fool she was, sought Jared again. Wearing a black mourning armband, he spoke at length with Mr. Bradford. As Jared posed questions and listened to the replies, his intensity gave Elise the impression he remained completely focused on the speaker. Then, in fleeting instances, his gaze would flick about. Though his stance appeared casual, watchfulness remained just below the surface.

She drifted toward him, trying to appear merely strolling rather than being so unladylike as to approach a gentleman. When Jared glanced at her a second time, her heart fluttered in response.

He nodded to her once impassively, and returned his attention to Mr. Bradford.

Stung, she swallowed against the hurt swirling inside.

Mr. Bradford called to his guests. He welcomed them again and bid them be seated at the long tables set up near the terrace. Mr. Bradford invited Elise to sit at his right. Jared sat across the table from her and further down.

An ice carving of a swan graced the table in an impressive centerpiece. Crystal and silver sparkled in the sunlight.

Elise turned to Mr. Bradford. "This is beautiful."

He smiled. "I admit I imposed upon my sister a great deal to help me prepare."

To his other side, his sister beamed. "It was a pleasure."

He turned back to Elise and touched her hand. "I'm so glad you like it."

Startled at the familiarity, Elise looked up, but he only smiled benignly, no hint of the suggestiveness or rakishness Jared often displayed. Mr. Bradford was the picture of propriety. Comfortable. Familiar. Safe.

At the moment, the prospect of spending her life with a man such as he seemed empty instead of comforting.

She shook her head at her own loss of reason. When did she begin to like danger and the unexpected?

Since they came in the form of a grinning, impertinent man of passion. Her gaze moved down the table to Jared who conversed animatedly with his dinner companions, generously flashing that lethal smile.

As the first course arrived, Elise removed her gloves and draped them over her lap. The men discussed hawking and the races. Lord Von Barondy admitted to an enjoyment of cock fighting, which made Elise shiver. Mr. Bradford described a recent trip to Scotland where distant relatives introduced him to the game of golf. His dry humor, as he described his rather unimpressive game, kept Elise and the others laughing.

Time and time again, her eyes moved to Jared's. He often met her gaze briefly but his expression could not be deciphered.

She swallowed against the lump in her throat. He regretted his kiss. He regretted coming to her. He regretted the way he'd bared his emotions that night.

She looked farther down the table toward Lord Druesdale. He caught her gaze and lifted his glass to her with promise smoldering in his eyes, a promise which failed to incite a physical reaction.

She'd always prided herself on her ladylike reserve, her lack of immoral desires. Now she knew her restraint sprang from the lack of a man capable of inspiring passion, not from her self-control.

Stunned by that revelation, Elise stilled. Even her breath froze. Perhaps here lay the real reason she'd chosen not to remarry. Yet, she'd been happy with Edward. Hadn't she?

"Mrs. Berkley?"

Her eyes shot to Mr. Bradford who watched her in polite concern. She forced her lips into a semblance of a smile and drank deeply of her glass. Forcing air into her lungs, she glanced at Jared and found him watching her.

Perhaps there was still hope. Perhaps the kiss was not entirely meaningless. He broke eye contact and returned his attention to the lady at his side.

Perhaps she was a fool.

After a superb luncheon, Mr. Bradford stood and announced a game of bowls on the south lawn. Cricket for the children would be held on the east lawn.

Again Jared met her stare. Uncertainty glimmered around the edges of his façade.

She knew it! He regretted kissing her. Too bad she didn't share the sentiment. Once again, she'd proven herself an idiot. She bit the inside of her lip.

"Do you care to play, Mrs. Berkley?" Mr. Bradford bestowed a winsome smile upon her that did little to lift her spirits.

She tried to muster a modicum of enthusiasm. "I'd love to."

Gentlemen, and a few ladies, called wagers. Jared stood talking with Lord Von Barondy, his focus intense.

Elise glanced toward the east lawn where the children were choosing teams. Colin darted away from his friends to Jared and grabbed his hand. Jared looked down at him, grinned, and after another quick word with Lord Von Barondy, allowed Colin to lead him to the cricket field. The children danced around Jared who laughed and called out taunts to the other team.

Soon, other men joined the children at cricket, shedding their frockcoats to allow greater freedom of movement. Some of the older, more proper adults criticized this lack of decorum.

Elise managed to play a respectable game of bowls, despite dividing her attention between her own game and cricket played on the next lawn.

Several spectators wandered over to watch the animated cricket players. Mrs. Carson watched raptly and Elise realized it was Jared, not the game, which Mrs. Carson watched with such enthusiasm. Elise couldn't blame her. His athletic grace mocked all the other men present.

His smile flashed, brightening his stunning face, and his easy laugh rang out. He good-naturedly heckled the other players, and accepted their jeers in return with equanimity.

"Your son is a fine player," Mr. Bradford said, mistaking her.

Guiltily, Elise dragged her gaze off Jared and found Colin among the players. "He does love to play."

"He's a delightful child. My girls adore him."

The game ended amid cheers and groans. Mr.

Amesbury hefted Colin on one shoulder and another boy on the other. The rest clamored around him.

"The younger set appears to have fully accepted Mr. Amesbury."

Elise hoped her expression betrayed nothing. "Indeed."

"He seems a decent sort, despite his lack of restraint."

A brief flash of annoyance surged at the unintended word of censure toward Jared. Then she felt ashamed as she realized she'd recently echoed those same sentiments—especially his lack of restraint. But now she found those qualities endearing.

"Lady Standwich thinks highly of him," Elise replied calmly. "As do Mr. and Mrs. Greymore."

Lord Druesdale sauntered up. "A fine afternoon, Mr. Bradford. Even the weather cooperated."

"Nice of it to be so obliging." Mr. Bradford's voice remained cordial, but his stance stiffened.

With Colin perched on one shoulder, another boy on the other, and a third hanging down his back, Jared staggered to them, exaggerating every motion, drawing squeals from his passengers and the boys who danced around him. Jared swung the boys from his shoulders to the ground.

Colin's hair was mussed and his cheek smudged, but the happy glow in his face dissuaded any scolding. He threw his arms around Elise. "Mother, did you see my winning hit?"

"A fine showing, my love." Elise gave him a squeeze.

Jared shooed the boys off in search of drinks. They scattered, followed by a cluster of giggling little girls.

Mr. Bradford winced. "I must speak with my daughters about not chasing boys."

Elise laughed. "I don't think you need be

concerned yet."

Grinning, Jared pushed his hand through his tousled hair, but failed to arrange it into any sort of order. A light sheen of sweat shone on his forehead, dampening a few strands that clung together around his face. His cravat lay in sad creases. He looked wholly male and thoroughly pleased with himself. No man had ever looked so blatantly desirable.

He accepted his coat from a footman and donned it. The muscles in his chest and arms flexed as he pulled on his frockcoat over his shirt and waistcoat. He glanced at the men flanking her with one eyebrow raised slightly in amusement. Despite his lazy grin, a brief flash of annoyance appeared in his eyes as he looked at the others. Tension crackled in the air as the three men mentally squared off.

Charlotte Greymore and her husband arrived. "What a lovely party, Mr. Bradford," Charlotte said. "How kind of you to invite us."

Mr. Bradford replied appropriately and the Greymores made their excuses and made ready to depart. With one hand tucked in the crook of her husband's arm, Charlotte smiled at Elise in farewell.

Elise called to Colin, who came reluctantly. They both bid their host a good day.

Mr. Bradford held Elise's hand a moment longer than necessary. "I'm so glad you came."

"I had a lovely time. Thank you for the invitation." Elise gently extracted her hand and glanced at the other men nearby. "Lord Druesdale. Mr. Amesbury."

They answered with perfect civility and shot deadly glares at one another.

Mr. Greymore extended his free arm. "Shall we escort you to your carriage, Mrs. Berkley?" Elise nodded and linked her arm through his. Holding Colin's hand on the other side, she walked with them toward the carriages lined up along the drive.

"I thought they were going to come to blows," Charlotte said with a smile. She glanced back. "They still might."

"Quite a competition is lining up for you, Mrs. Berkley," Mr. Greymore said.

Elise focused on the ground, secretly glad that Jared had shown animosity toward the other men. Surely that meant interest in her at some level.

"It was rather awkward, I'm afraid."

Charlotte's smile broadened. "I know you're unaccustomed to such attention, but you cannot be entirely surprised by it. They are all attractive men. Are you going to choose one?"

"I'm not sure what it is they want."

Greymore chuckled softly. "I believe they all want your favor, Mrs. Berkley. The question is, to what degree? That may vary from man to man."

Elise had no answer. Lord Druesdale's interest no doubt involved nothing more than an empty affair. She wondered if Jared and Mr. Bradford wanted her for a wife, or a lover, or merely a friend.

No. She was certain none merely wanted her friendship, more's the pity. Friendship would be so much more convenient.

Colin sighed dramatically. "I wish Mr. Amesbury could play with me every day. He makes me feel like I do everything good!"

"As though you do everything well," Elise corrected.

"That, too."

Elise moved toward her carriage further down the line. A hand appeared under her elbow and a familiar presence awakened her senses. She turned to face Jared.

He offered a brief smile, but his eyes slid over her almost as a caress. "I went home."

She blinked. "Oh."

"For the funeral. I should have sent you word. I

176

meant to."

She looked down. "You owe me no explanation."

"I felt that I did after—" he glanced at Colin, "—after your aid the last time I called upon you. I didn't want you to think it meant nothing to me."

The warmth from his gloved hand seeped through her afternoon gown into her arm. It continued to spread until his touch bathed her in warmth. She met his gaze and fell into his aquamarine eyes.

"It meant more to me than you can know. You saved me." His voice, hardly more than a whisper, brushed against her very soul.

She wanted to ask which part of the night meant so much to him. The things he confided to her? The way they held each other? The kiss? All of it? It suddenly mattered a great deal.

And worse, she wanted nothing more than to be back in his arms, feeling both needed and desirable as no man before him had made her feel. Unable to drag her eyes away, she remained captured by his gaze and tried to look deeply enough into his eyes to see all the way to his heart, not even caring if he saw hers. Not caring if he saw that she did, indeed, love him.

She stilled. She loved him. Her heart turned into something warm and liquid.

His lashes hid his eyes as he ruffled Colin's already disheveled hair. "Well done today, Young Master Colin."

Colin threw his arms around one of Jared's thighs and hugged him. "Thank you for playing with us. You made it so fun."

Jared patted Colin's back. "Glad to be of service."

She loved him. She swallowed hard.

He helped them into the carriage. For another lingering moment, his gaze held hers. In that instant, his shields lowered and she saw uncertainty, desire, and determination all warring inside. She wondered what he wished he could tell her, what he feared to reveal.

"Good day, Mrs. Berkley. Master Colin." He shut the door and stepped back.

Elise leaned back against the seat. She bit her lip and wondered if she had the courage to piece together the puzzle of Jared Amesbury.

She had no doubt the finished picture would be worth the trouble, the picture of the man she loved.

CHAPTER 15

Jared bid a good evening to the Greymore's after enjoying a delightful dinner with them, and climbed into the curricle. They'd managed to bring up the subject of Elise Berkley during every course. He'd feigned disinterest at first, but finally gave in and listened to anything they would tell him. Secretly, he was flattered that the elegant Charlotte Greymore thought him worthy of her friend. Still grinning, he glanced behind him where José perched behind the seat in his role as tiger.

Jared waved him over. "Come sit up here on the seat with me."

The lad clamored over and settled in next to him. Jared snapped the reins and guided the curricle down the moonlight-bathed road. José remained silent for so long that Jared glanced at him to see if he'd fallen asleep.

"Captain?" José asked in Portuguese, his young face solemn.

"What is it, lad?" Jared replied in the same tongue.

"Are we going back to the ship soon?"

Jared looked down at him. "Do you miss the sea?"

"A little, I suppose. But I like it here. I feel safe."

"Safe? After that incident with Leandro?"

He nodded. "Even so. I don't fear any of the servants. The stable lads treat me well and I like the horses. I muck out the stalls a lot, which I don't like, but the head groom is also teaching me how to care for the horses. He thinks I could be a groom someday. I'd like that."

"You didn't feel safe at sea?" he asked gently.

"The boatswain terrified me. And some of the others, too. Sometimes I wondered if the storms would finish us. And every time we went into battle, I always wondered..." he trailed off, tears welling up in his eyes.

"What? You wouldn't have been hurt; I never let you fight."

"If you'd be killed." He sniffled. "Like Father."

Jared wrapped an arm around José and pulled him against his side. He held the boy as well as he could and still maintain control over the reins.

Circling overhead, a night bird called and glided away. Moonlight flitted through the trees. The steady clop-clopping of the horses' hooves broke the stillness.

Jared's heart felt leaden. On board the ship, he'd tried to care for the boy, to shield him from the ugliness of their life, and indeed José seldom voiced any complaint. But Jared had failed. No child his age should be subjected to that kind of life. He'd seen deceit, thievery, violence, death.

Jared drew a steadying breath. "I have no plans to return to the sea. In fact, I plan to give up piracy forever."

José looked up at him, hope glimmering in his dark eyes. "Could you?"

"I'm making every effort to do just that."

José wiped his nose on his sleeve. "You were a fierce pirate. But you're different from the others. More honor."

Jared snorted. "Honor?"

"You never hurt your enemies who didn't fight back. You were never cruel to your crew like Captain Macy was."

In pure astonishment, Jared looked down. He gave José a little squeeze. "You honor me." His father had been a good friend, a good man, and Jared had mourned his death. He'd be proud of his son. "If I'm forced to go back to sea, I'll see to it that you remain here with someone who will care for you until I can return. This I vow."

José rested his head against Jared's shoulder and snuggled in close. Jared tightened his arm around the lad. He knew it was unseemly to be so familiar with one's servants, but at the moment, he cared little. Within minutes, José fell asleep.

Guided by moonlight, Jared drove silently and worried over the boy's fate. He could take him with him when he left Brenniswick, of course, but he hated to drag the lad all over until he found a place to settle down. The boy needed stability. Jared only had the estate for the summer and it was entailed, so he couldn't purchase it. He didn't know if he could arrange for José to continue to work in the stables for the owners. He'd have to check into that. If not, perhaps Elise's overprotective groom would be willing to take him as a stable lad.

He grinned at the mischief José and Colin would no doubt combine. Imagine, if José ever confessed he'd lived all his life aboard a pirate ship! Colin might die of rapture. Either that or his fascination with pirates would be cured once he heard the truth from José's mouth.

A lone rider galloped down the middle of the road toward him. Jared eased his gun out and cocked it. Then, recognizing the rider, he slowed the team.

José stirred and lifted his head.

"It's all right, lad. Dubois is here."

José rubbed his eyes. When Jared's first mate pulled abreast, he gave a nod. "*Bon soir, Monsieur*," José said.

If any good had come from his life at sea, the boy had picked up a goodly amount of foreign tongues besides his native Portuguese.

"*Bon soir*, to you, you little imp." Dubois gave a toothy grin. He sobered as he turned to Jared.

"Leandro's still looking for you. Two of his men tried to sneak on board the *Mistress* and cause trouble. Apparently, he wanted to hold the ship and crew on board hostage until you arrived."

Jared cursed. "Do you know where he is?"

"No. He and Santos have been seen in Port Johns, at the Wild Boar, but he's not staying there. We didn't find where his ship put down anchor. She may have gone further out to sea and will rendezvous with him later."

Jared loosened his cravat. "At least that means he doesn't yet know where I am. Is it possible he found me by chance that last time?"

Dubois shrugged. "*C'est possible.*"

"Find him. Then send me word. I need to finish this."

Dubois nodded and spurred his horse to a gallop. Jared snapped the reins.

He felt José's penetrating gaze. "You're going to kill Leandro, aren't you?" His sober tone made Jared's heart heavy.

"I showed him mercy last time, and he's tried to kill me twice since then," Jared replied quietly. "And you. Neither of us will be safe until he's dead."

CHAPTER 16

Elise strolled through the gardens, admiring the rain-swept view and the water droplets shimmering on the plants as if a tiny rainbow rested inside each one. Briefly, she glanced at the stables as she passed by, but continued on foot, unable to bear the thought of riding without Prince.

Turning her attention to the cloud-dappled sky, she drew a deep breath. The rain always revived the colors, and reawakened the scents of roses, jasmine, honeysuckle, and violets. As she passed beyond the gardens and out into the wide open fields, she watched the long grass bend in the wind. Sunlight glinted off select blades making them dazzle. Upon climbing a low rise toward a grove of trees, she stopped short.

Jared Amesbury leaned lazily against the trunk of an oak, his arms folded. Dressed in buckskin breeches and a sea green waistcoat, with the wind ruffling his dark hair, he looked unbearably handsome.

She quickened her steps toward him.

"I'd hoped to find you here," he said by way of greeting. He took her hand in his and raised it to his lips. Then he unbuttoned her glove. Surprise arrested all movement, and she simply stood motionless and allowed his actions. He lightly kissed the inside of her bare wrist.

She shivered and her knees wobbled. "I...don't think you should do that."

"Does it displease you?" His languid voice rippled over her.

"On the contrary. That's why I think you shouldn't do it."

A mischievous grin tugged on the corner of his expressive mouth while unconcealed desire glinted in his eye. "In that case..." He stepped in closer.

A quiver vibrated in her stomach. He ran one finger along her cheek down to her chin. Eddies of warmth undulated through every nerve. He tilted up her chin and leaned in.

The thudding of her heart could probably be heard for miles around. Her breath came in gasps. He gently kissed her once, his lips soft and warm. Shamelessly, she leaned into him. He kissed her again and this time he lingered, teasing, coaxing. He rested his other hand on her waist. His lips continued tugging gently, but each kiss grew in intensity, in hunger. His hand moved to the small of her back and pulled her in closer. He slid his hand from her face to the back of her head, holding it firm.

She pressed herself against him, letting him take command of her mouth. He deepened the kiss. Her desire circumvented any shock at their behavior.

They kissed in a world of their own making. Elise had never felt more vital in her life. Every nerve tingled, every sense reeled. He tasted of lemon and honey tea. His clean masculine scent mingled with fragrance of the heather in an earthy blend. His heart beat quick and hard against her in a cadence that matched her own. She felt the cool breeze, the warmth of his hands, the heat of his body against hers.

His demanding lips brought her to a height of pleasure totally unknown, and yet familiar, as if she'd longed for it all her life and only now discovered what had been missing.

His breathing turned ragged and he uttered a groan. He pulled her to him desperately. The intensity of his passion left her breathless and aching. She lost contact with reason. All that remained was the fierce pull of his mouth. Urgently, he deepened the kiss. Then she began to make demands of her own, her kisses bold and hungry. With a groan, he shivered. His lips moved across her cheek, down her throat. His fingers traced her sensitive skin, skimming over her neck and shoulders. His lips followed. Her knees weakened, but his arms held her secure. Kissing a path down lower across her flesh, he slipped the sleeve of her gown off one shoulder.

Elise's morality nudged her and she shifted into clear thought.

She did not want an empty affair.

Her breathing hard and uneven, she caught his wandering hand with hers and pulled her mouth away from his.

He blinked as if dazed. With his eyes half-opened and his moist lips parted, he looked thoroughly desirable. And hungry.

"Jared," she managed.

The heavily-lidded expression faded and he visibly snapped into reason. "Forgive me. I shouldn't have taken such liberties."

"What exactly are your intentions toward me?"

He drew a breath. "I'm not in a position to make you a formal offer just yet. Despite my better sense warning me away, I cannot seem to keep my thoughts from you. And my feet seem inclined to agree with my thoughts."

"I see." Stung by his non-committal answer, she shrugged out of his grasp.

His hands tightened on her upper arms, preventing her from leaving. "You don't understand. My life is rather complicated right now. I have problems that I need to resolve. It requires my full attention. I shouldn't have let myself be distracted.

Yet, you've distracted me most thoroughly. You're too good for me, but I want you anyway."

She was only a distraction to him? Angry, hurt, she looked away.

"Elise. No, that's not what I mean. Look, I didn't intend to tell you like this. I..." he blew out his breath and muttered something in a tongue she did not understand. "I'm doing this all wrong." His gaze moved away as he gathered his thoughts. An instant later, his aquamarine gaze held her fast. "I love you."

She stilled.

"I love you with all of my heart."

Dumbstruck, she could only stare.

"I don't deserve you, but I vow if you'll have me, I will spend my every moment trying to make you happy. But I need to clear up some issues. Will you wait for me? Will you give me the time I need before I can make you a formal offer of marriage?"

The loneliness she'd suffered all these years faded and a tremendous sense of belonging overcame her. She'd never wanted anything as badly as spending her life with Jared.

Joy and hope bubbled out of her. She laughed and threw her arms around his neck. "Yes. Yes, of course I will."

He joined in her laughter and squeezed her so hard that she squeaked. Then he pulled back and smoothed the hair away from her face. "You'll really have me? With all my flaws and my tainted past?"

"Oh, Jared. I love you. All of you."

His face transformed into such happiness that he looked like a man who'd just been offered the world. "You've made me so happy. I never dared believe I'd ever be this happy."

She laughed again just out of sheer bliss.

"For now, we'll make it a secret betrothal. But I promise you, very soon I'll make it formal. And public."

"I'll wait for you. Take all the time you need. It's taken me this long to find you, I can certainly wait a little longer."

And she realized she'd wait an eternity for this man who completed her. He pulled her into his arms again and kissed her so thoroughly she wondered if she'd actually left the mortal bounds of earth.

When he pulled away, he grinned. Mischievously, he cocked his head to one side. "How is it that you were married for five years and don't know how to kiss?"

Taken aback, she blinked. "Edward thought it vulgar to kiss on the mouth."

"Nothing about you is vulgar. How could he think that? What kind of man did you marry?"

She said defensively, "He was tender. He often kissed my hand and my cheek; he just didn't like to kiss on the mouth. But I assure you he was very loving."

Jared grinned. "He'd be an idiot if he weren't loving toward you. I, however, harbor no such opinions. Here let me show you." He drew her close and kissed her until she thought she'd soar.

And she'd never been happier.

****

As Elise strolled along the streets of Port Johns, gulls spiraled overhead, and a light mist hung on the air. The clean, refreshing smell of the sea blew in on the breezes. Fortunately, the odors of the wharf remained below and did not carry to the hill where the shopping district lay.

Elise left the pearl Jared gave her with a jeweler who would make it into a brooch. She realized she was smiling incessantly, but she'd never been so filled with contentment. More than contentment. Pure exhilaration.

When her purchases piled up, her two footmen

following behind had to begin making return trips to the carriage to put the packages away.

Elise browsed inside a milliner, but none of the bonnets caught her eye. As she emerged from the milliner's, she caught sight of Jared Amesbury's unmistakable tall, muscular form as he stood speaking to someone across the street. Her heart rose up and shouted with joy. She hurried across the street toward him.

He wore his usual tasteful attire, although the cravat looked a bit battered. Keeping to the shadows, he spoke intently to a shadowed figure for a moment and then put his hand on the other man's shoulder, spun him around, and ushered him toward a narrow alley between buildings. Something about the furtive nature of their behavior awakened Elise's imagination.

She hesitated, but curiosity ruled and she followed them. Two male voices guided her toward the end of the alley, so near that they sounded as though they were just around the corner.

Intuition warned her to be discreet. Holding her breath, Elise flattened herself against the wall, crept to the edge and listened.

In annoyance, she realized one of the footmen had followed her. He opened his mouth to protest, but she laid a finger over her lips to silence him and waved him away. He moved back, but kept her in sight.

"Then why are you here?" a male voice demanded in a lilting accent Elise could not place.

"I told you, I'm here on a lead. I've had to assume this identity so I could follow it," replied Jared.

"So you aren't really the son of an earl."

Jared laughed, sounding disgusted. "No, Anakoni, I'm merely posing as one."

Anakoni paused. "You've just made up this

name Amesbury? Don't these noble blokes all know each other?"

"Oh, there really is a Jared Amesbury. Or was. His family thinks he's still abroad. But he's dead."

Elise caught her breath as her heart skittered to a halt. If he weren't Jared Amesbury, who was he?

"How do you know?"

"Because I killed him."

Jared's voice took on a chilling tone that Elise never would have recognized. Disbelief and a vague fear crept over her. She clenched her hands together and held them against her fluttering stomach.

"Of course," Jared added, "I waited until after he handed over all his money to ransom his own life. Spineless coward. He deserved to die. You should have heard him pleading for mercy. He'd have sold his own sister to save his miserable skin."

With her back pressed against a wall, she slid to the ground.

No. No this couldn't be. This was the gentle and exuberant man to whom she'd pledged her heart. Not an imposter. Not a killer. This couldn't be happening.

Breathless, and suddenly terrified they would discover her, she sat motionless.

Anakoni's musical accent drew her back. "And no one else knows he's dead?"

"No, and as long as I avoid anyone who might have known him, my alias will remain intact."

A long pause followed and Elise's heart thudded so loudly she feared they would hear.

"Why didn't you just tell me? I know you keep things to yourself, but this..."

"You know me. I never trust anyone. Nothing personal."

"Aye." Anakoni sounded resigned.

"I just need another week or two and then we'll all be richer than Midas."

"Midas?"

"You know, the man whose finger turned everything to gold?" Jared made a huffing sound. "Never mind. Suffice it to say, we'll be so rich, we could live like kings the rest of our lives and never have to step foot on a ship again."

"Won't you miss the adventure?"

"Aye. Some. But I'm tired of always looking over my shoulder, watching out for the Royal Navy or some pirate hunter. I'd like to live long enough to enjoy my wealth."

"I'm surprised you'd be willing to give up the freedom."

"I'd be trading freedoms. Money can buy a new life. And if I get an urge for adventure, I could always hire a crew and take the ship out for a little fun. But not because I need the money."

Anakoni snorted. "You don't need the money now."

"This is big, Anakoni. Trust me. It will be worth it. Just keep Leandro off my back long enough to make this deal. You'll thank me later."

"Very well, Cap'n, but we're running out of blunt. We'll need to put to sea soon."

"Give me another week," the man she'd known as Jared said. They moved off in another direction and parted company.

Elise sat stunned and shaken.

He'd grown tired of avoiding pirate hunters.

Because he was a pirate.

Her head spun as memories swirled. Jared, dressed like a pirate, being hanged by two men also dressed as pirates. The duality she frequently sensed in him. The predatory way he moved. Colin's intuitive statement that he thought Jared a pirate.

Jared was a pirate.

A killer.

She had to do something. He might hurt her

friends. But what could she do? He was a murderer, capable of anything. Such a man would kill her without hesitation if he suspected she knew his ruse.

But the thought of Jared harming her seemed so contradictory to the gentle man she knew. She touched her lips with her fingers and relived his passionate kisses, the way he held her, needed her, the sheer joy and completion she'd felt in his arms.

If she hadn't heard him utter those words, she never would have believed it. But the more she thought of it, the more pieces fell into place; his constant state of wariness, the way he always remained guarded, listening, watching.

With the skill of an actor exceeding anyone on the stage, he'd donned a new name, a new identity, and duped them all. He had to be a natural mimic to have fooled them so perfectly. Somewhere in the back of her mind, she dully wondered his true name.

She pressed her hands over her eyes, her thoughts churning. She would have to contact the authorities. What to do? To whom should she go? The constable? The magistrate?

But could she really? She quailed at the thought of seeing him hang, this man who'd touched her so gently. Kissed her so passionately. Fished with Colin and treated him with such affection and respect. Rescued her when her horse had fallen.

His face haunted her, its chiseled, masculine beauty, eyes as deep as the sea, infectious laugh, gentle hands, soft yet hungry lips.

As much as she wanted to believe otherwise, she'd heard Jared say in his own voice he had killed the real Jared Amesbury in cold blood and stolen his name to work further evil.

Tears squeezed out of her eyes and ran down her cheeks.

He'd murdered. He'd deceived them all. He no doubt planned to carry off a scheme far more nefarious than any of them suspected. A man such as that deserved to be punished.

How could she have been so easily taken in? What an utterly gullible simpleton she'd been to fall prey to a handsome face and a glib tongue. He'd lied to her. He'd deceived her. He'd used her! Anger boiled through her and she leaped to her feet.

A sound to her right turned her head. Rough hands grabbed her and clamped a strange-smelling cloth over her mouth. She bucked and kicked, but her limbs quickly lost their strength. A dark face under a wide-brimmed hat leered. All faded to black.

CHAPTER 17

Jared lounged in an armchair in Greymore's study. "The codes returned by special messenger last night."

Greymore raised his brows in anticipation. "Don't keep me in suspense, man, out with it."

Jared retrieved a packet of papers from an inner pocket of his waistcoat. "This lists three ships scheduled to leave within the week, the names of their captains, cargo, and destination. All are from different shipping companies."

Greymore whistled softly. "What are our orders?"

"Confront Von Barondy and persuade him to reveal his informants. Then turn him over to the authorities. I suppose we could offer to allow him to be a gentleman and shoot himself. We could arrange for it to appear an accident so his property isn't seized and his wife is spared both poverty and the scandal of having a traitor for a husband."

Greymore looked revolted at the thought of condoning the heinous crime of self-murder. He rubbed his temples. "And the ships?"

"In addition to their cargo, they'll be filled with navy sailors spoiling for a fight. Other naval ships will wait nearby. It will be spectacular. The pirates won't have a chance."

Greymore eyed him. "Wish you could be there?"

Jared sighed and stopped his hand just as it touched his cravat. "No, not really. I'm through. I've seen enough bloodshed to last several lifetimes. But it would be satisfying to see the pirates meet their end."

"I sense a personal interest in this." Greymore leaned back in his chair and steepled his fingers.

Jared felt a twinge of remorse that he kept so much from his closest friend. "I'll tell you about it some day."

Greymore nodded. "When do you wish to approach Von Barondy?"

"Now?"

Greymore stood. "Very well. Now."

He kissed his wife goodbye and told her he and Jared were calling upon Lord Von Barondy. She nodded gravely, clearly sensing the tension. They rode on horseback side by side to the Von Barondy house. Jared quivered with anticipation.

Von Barondy kept them waiting half an hour.

"He's reminding us he's a peer and we're beneath him," Greymore muttered as they waited in the front parlor.

A pretty parlor maid slipped in to straighten and dust the room. When she saw them, she straightened. "Begging your pardon," she said bobbing a curtsey.

Jared narrowed his eyes. She seemed familiar.

She glanced his way and did a double take, a puzzled frown touching her brow. She passed a searching gaze over him.

Jared realized with a jolt she was the girl he'd startled the night he'd found the evidence against Von Barondy. Affecting a cool demeanor absolutely devoid of any recognition, he raised a brow as if to chastise her for her bold perusal.

Blushing, she stammered an apology and fled.

Jared took a silent breath of relief that she hadn't recognized him.

Greymore glanced at him inquiringly.

Smugly, Jared shrugged. "It happens all the time. Women just can't keep their eyes off me."

Greymore let out a snort. "Blind, all of them."

Lady Von Barondy fluttered in, greeted them with a flash of jewels, and fluttered out. At last, the butler invited them into Von Barondy's private study.

The red and gold brocade upholstery and wallpaper looked overwhelming rather than elegant. A portrait of a younger Von Barondy, painted in a manner to make his likeness more noble and handsome than accurate, hung over the mantle, next to one of his wife, similarly inaccurate.

Von Barondy greeted them with condescension. "May I offer you a brandy?"

They both demurred. Greymore glanced at Jared. Normally Greymore would take the lead, but this had been Jared's assignment for far longer, and he was considered the senior operative in this case.

Jared cleared his throat. "My lord. You've recently purchased a large number of shipping companies. You own an alarming percentage of all the privately owned ships in England."

"You are mistaken. I only own a few."

"Many of them are under false business names. With patience, they were all eventually traced to you."

Von Barondy stilled. "There's no law against owning ships."

Jared withdrew a paper from his waistcoat pocket. "I have here a copy of a code that I retrieved from your floor safe."

Von Barondy's eye twitched.

"And here is a copy of the code after the experts at Headquarters broke it. As you can see, you are clearly named as the leader of the pirate ring who has been receiving information about cargo, embark dates, and destinations of several merchant ships." Jared pinned him with a stare. "*O Ladrão*, is it? You realize, of course, consorting with pirates makes you a pirate. But since you are a peer, the charges become more serious. It makes you a traitor."

Von Barondy turned pasty, and turned an imploring look upon Greymore. "We've been neighbors since our youth. How can you believe this of me?"

"The evidence is irrefutable," Greymore replied evenly.

As a calculating light entered Von Barondy's eyes, Jared calmly folded the papers and put them back inside his pocket. "Yes, our superiors know of this. Their experts broke the code. We're here under orders to speak with you. Sorry, old boy, killing us would not help you. It will only further affirm your guilt. Not that proof is lacking."

Von Barondy's shoulders slumped and he passed a hand over his eyes. He turned to stare out the window.

Jared pressed on. "The pirate ships who received this information will meet with the navy. Those not killed in battle face the hangman's noose."

"I suppose there's nothing left for me to say," Von Barondy said dully.

"Do you wish to bear the consequences alone, or will you tell us who your accomplices are inside the shipping companies?" Greymore interjected.

Von Barondy's breathing became irregular. He reached into a drawer. In a flash, Jared and Greymore both had their guns out and pointed at the viscount.

Von Barondy froze. "I merely reach for paper." With shaking hands, he retrieved parchment and a pen. He wrote four names neatly on the paper, carefully sanded it and poured off the sand. His eyes, when he lifted them, looked tortured. "My wife..."

Surprised that a man of such a criminal nature would think of his wife at a time like this, Jared faltered. Then he poured scorn into his voice. "Will suffer social ruin and poverty, as all your property and possessions are seized."

Jared picked up the list, read over it, and tucked it away. He waited to let Von Barondy suffer. Because of this man's greed, Jared had endured three years as a pirate. Seeing it all come to an end seemed dream-like.

Jared sent a meaningful look at Von Barondy. "You could choose to die as a gentleman."

The viscount nodded as if he'd already considered that alternative. He moistened his lips. "Allow me a pistol with a single shot. I'll make it appear as an accident. Please. I beg you. Spare my wife the shame. She is innocent."

Suddenly drained and unexpectedly moved by the man's apparent concern for his wife whom he obviously loved, Jared glanced at Greymore who looked utterly defeated. "Very well. If you wish to add suicide to your many crimes, we will not prevent you." He leveled his gun at the viscount to ensure no trickery.

Gray and shaken, Von Barondy went to a cabinet where he retrieved a gun and all his cleaning supplies which he laid out in a meticulous row. He stopped and looked hard at Greymore first, and then at Jared, before carefully loading it.

If the coroner suspected suicide, Von Barondy would be a murderer in the eyes of the crown. The consequences to his wife would be as bad as if he were executed for treason. To avoid that, they'd have to make sure his death really did appear accidental.

"Tell my wife, my final words were of affection for her."

Greymore nodded.

Jared stood, hoping he appeared unmoved by the sorrow in Von Barondy's voice, while his conscience stabbed him for the savage delight he took in seeing this traitor meet his end. But the viscount did not deserve pity; he was only sorry to have been caught. He felt no remorse for his crimes. That Jared actually felt sympathy for the blighter came as a surprise.

Perhaps his love for Elise and the hope she offered him had softened his heart.

"I'll wait until you've left the house to avoid any suspicion." Von Barondy heaved a deep breath and began cleaning his gun.

They nodded and left him alone, bidding good day to the servants as they took their leave. Riding beside Jared, Greymore turned to him. "You enjoyed that," he accused grimly.

"I'm sorry if he was a friend."

"That's not what I mean."

Jared kept his focus straight ahead. "I've been on this assignment for three years, impersonating a pirate to find the leader; by far, my most distasteful task. I'm glad to see it end. And yes, I am glad to see the man behind it meet his own defeat."

Greymore remained silent.

Jared added, "If it makes you feel any better, I did actually pity him at the end."

A moment later, the sound of a gunshot roared.

"But I'm free now." Jared wondered why the sound failed to satisfy his sense of vengeance.

****

A few hours later, Jared and Greymore rode side by side after the ugly business of setting the record straight with the authorities had been completed. Their superiors had come from London and they'd managed to keep the distasteful incident surprisingly quiet. The coroner declared the shooting a tragic accident; unfortunate, but unsuspicious. It never failed to astonish Jared what the Service could accomplish.

"What will you do now?" Greymore asked.

"Resign." He hesitated, haunted by doubts.

"Court Mrs. Berkley. Hope she can overlook my evil past."

Greymore raised a brow, satisfaction edging past his grimness. "Ah."

Jared grimaced, waiting for Greymore to begin gloating.

"She's a fine woman. Think you could really give up all the adventure for someone so entrenched in the quiet life?"

"Without a doubt."

A gunshot crackled, echoing in the hills. Greymore grunted and slumped over in his saddle. A bolt of terror shot through Jared.

Not Greymore!

Still alert for further danger, Jared put a hand on Greymore's back to keep him from falling off. He grabbed his pistol and did a quick scan of the terrain. Greymore's labored breathing quelled Jared's blinding fear that his friend had been killed.

Moaning, Greymore straightened. "I can ride."

"Head for cover."

Greymore's face paled but he remained in the saddle as they galloped to the nearest copse of trees. Inside the cool, protective shade, they waited for further sign of danger. Greymore collapsed onto his horse's neck.

Jared felt for Greymore's pulse. It was there, erratic but strong.

"I'm still with you," Greymore managed.

A lone rider galloped away, long black braids flapping behind.

Jared cursed. "Santos."

He must have shot Greymore accidentally. No doubt Jared had been his target. Fortunately, he lacked Leandro's determination to kill the right person or he would have remained behind and finished the task.

Greymore opened his eyes. "A friend of yours?"

Jared pursed his lips together. "Can you make it home?"

Greymore nodded. Sweat beaded on his upper lip. They rode as fast as Greymore could tolerate, but by the time they'd reached his home, he barely clung to consciousness. Jared yelled for help and practically carried his friend into the house.

The butler ushered them into the nearest room and Jared lowered Greymore on a settee. Charlotte Greymore hurried in and came to an abrupt halt.

Jared forced himself to look her in the face. "He's been shot." He nearly choked as the full realization hit him. He drew a steadying breath. Now was not the time to fall apart.

She gaped in disbelief, but quickly collected herself and sprang into action with all the calm efficiency of a trained operative. "Mawbry, send for the doctor and have Standage come help me. Bring clean cloths and water."

She continued with her instructions while the servants scrambled to obey without question. She peeled back layers of Greymore's blood-soaked clothing while the color continued to drain out of the man's face. Blood bubbled from a wound in Greymore's side below his ribs.

Jared ripped off his cravat and used it to help stem the flow while Mrs. Greymore continued calling instructions. Clenching his teeth, Jared pressed the cloth over the wound.

It should have been him. He had no doubt Santos meant to kill him. And now, Greymore could die. His lungs seized at the thought.

Greymore caught his wrist with surprising strength. "Stop it."

Keeping steady pressure on the wound, Jared met his gaze.

"Stop blaming yourself. It's not your fault," Greymore said.

"He was after me."

"I'm glad to have ruined his plans."

The doctor arrived shortly and Jared was ushered out. Unwilling to leave until he'd heard the doctor's prognosis, Jared paced, alternately cursing Leandro, and his own lack of vigilance.

Would there be no end to the lives at risk for his sake?

Black anger boiled inside him. He'd been foolish to believe that exposing Von Barondy and his informants would buy his freedom. He still had to deal with Leandro, which meant he'd be returning to the sea. If Greymore died, Jared would live up to his reputation as Black Jack when he sought vengeance on Leandro.

Elise would be horrified if she had any idea how truly bloodthirsty he felt at the moment.

Mrs. Greymore emerged. She and the doctor spoke in hushed tones, and then the doctor left.

She turned to Jared. Blood soaked the front of her gown, and a streak smudged her cheek. But her posture was dignified and her expression resolute. "I need to speak with you in private."

Heart-sick, he followed her down the corridor. Inside the study, he slumped into a chair.

She poured Jared a drink and handed it to him. "You look as though you need this."

Jared gulped it down and eyed her miserably. "How is he?"

"Sleeping. He's lost much blood, but the ball passed right through. The doctor has high hopes for his complete recovery." She sat with her hands folded in her lap and watched him with an assessing stare. "Don't blame yourself. He does not wish it."

"I was the intended target."

She smiled gently. "He would have thrown himself in front of you if he'd known. It makes no difference that he protected you inadvertently."

201

Jared loosened his cravat. "It makes a difference to me. And to you. I'm not married. That makes me expendable."

"I'm sure your family would disagree. And Elise." She bowed her head a moment. "Charles has told me very little about his service to the crown. I know he served as a spy during the war and that he helps the government at times on a limited basis. But when his superiors informed him you were involved in a difficult assignment, and might need him, he changed to active status to assist you."

Jared leaned forward, resting his forearms on his thighs, and hung his head. "He shouldn't have."

"You needed him. That's all that mattered. He knows the risks. I shall be sure to use all my feminine wiles to discourage him from any further involvement." A faint smile flitted over her mouth. "I assume your task is not completed? Or is this shooting an unrelated incident?"

"They are related indirectly. The actual case has been solved, but I've made some enemies along the way." He stood. "Take care of him. I need to see to this last detail."

She fixed upon him a stare that left him with the urge to squirm. "Be careful."

He forced his mouth into a semblance of a grin. "I won't let his sacrifice be for nothing. It would insult his honor if he took a bullet meant for me, and then I did an ungracious thing like get myself killed."

"See that you remember that." She saw him out. At the door, she touched his arm. "And Elise?"

"I have to finish this first."

"Have a care with her heart."

"I have no intention of hurting her."

Keeping a sharp eye out for hidden gunmen, Jared rode home. When he arrived, he called out commands to the servants. "Saddle a fresh horse. I'll be leaving within minutes."

He took the stairs two at a time. Hunting a pirate dressed as a gentleman would not serve, so he changed into his pirate's garb.

His valet, Gibbs, came in with raised brow and said dryly, "Interesting attire. Are you trying to ruin my reputation and destroy any hope that I'll obtain employment with another gentleman?"

Normally Jared appreciated humor in all its forms, but he could not bring himself to smile. "I'm going to be absent for an indeterminate period of time." He pulled on his scarred and creased boot and wriggled his foot back and forth until the boot slid on.

"You might want to see this, sir. It just arrived. The messenger said it was urgent." Gibbs held out a note. Jared pulled on his second boot and took the note.

Meet me at the Fox & Hound. Do not delay.
Dubois

Jared swore. That could not be good. Leandro was probably causing havoc again. Jared tucked every gun and knife he owned about his person, ignoring Gibbs's look of trepidation.

"Should I not return by the time the lease is up, inform my brother, Cole Amesbury, the Sixth Earl of Tarrington."

Gibbs started. "Are you in trouble, sir?"

"I often am." He grabbed a cloak and strode out.

José led a fresh mount to Jared just outside the stables. "What's wrong, sir?"

Jared squatted down to the boy's eye level. "If I don't return before my lease expires, ask to remain here as an employee of the owner."

With tears shimmering in his eyes, the boy nodded.

"When I return, I'll look for you here. I'd make the arrangements myself, but I have to go after

Leandro before the trail grows cold."

José threw his arms around Jared. "You will come back?"

"I have many reasons to do so."

Jared pulled José close, kissed the top of his dark head, and thrust him back. He mounted and spurred his horse.

Acutely alert, he wound his way through the streets to the Fox & Hound. As he entered, he pulled his hat low over his face and took a chair where he could keep the door in sight.

The smell of bread and ale greeted him. The inn had two windows in front and one on the side. All were large enough to climb through if necessary. Tallow candles guttered on the tables. A door to the back led to the kitchens. No doubt, a back door could be found there.

A girl far too young for her role brought him a drink without making eye contact and scurried away.

Dubois came in looking grim. He strode to Jared immediately and took a seat.

Speaking quietly, he came right to the point, "Leandro has your lady."

Jared rocked back. Black rage nearly strangled him. He curled his hands into fists and struggled against the bile rising in this throat.

"His demands are simple. 'Come get her, if you dare.' His ship left two hours ago, reportedly for Isla de Tiburon."

"Of course."

No doubt Leandro thought it some kind of poetic justice to take Elise to the same place Jared had killed Macy.

Jared pressed shaking hands over his eyes. First Greymore and now Elise. Leandro, the blackguard, must have been tailing him for days to know where to strike.

Dubois broke into his thoughts. "All hands are readying the ship and preparing to disembark. If we hurry, we may catch him before he reaches the island. At least we know a heading. I've told the crew nothing about your lady. They only know we hunt Leandro. They're spoiling for a fight."

"Supplies?"

"Stores are full. We've been prepared for days to leave. By your command."

Jared called for pen and paper and wrote a note to Cole, warning him that Leandro might have discovered his true name and may seek retaliation by threatening his family, and to take precautions. Cole, no stranger to peril of that kind, would know what to do.

After extracting a promise from the innkeeper to have the letter posted, and handing him a goodly amount of coin to see to the task, Jared nodded to Dubois. "Let's go get him."

Under cover of darkness, they rode by the main highway toward Port Johns. Fear coiled in the pit of Jared's stomach as he considered Elise at the mercy of Leandro and his men. Leandro was ruthless and unpredictable; he might do anything to her.

Sickened at the thought, he pushed his horse to a reckless speed. Dubois remained at his side.

An eternity later, they clattered into the silent town. For a port and former smuggler's cove, the cobblestone streets were surprisingly clean. Shopkeepers had already closed up and retreated to the second level where they lived with their families. The salty, fishy smells of the ocean mingled with cheap perfume worn by passing members of the *demi-monde* who awarded him seductive smiles and swaying hips. Fog rolled in, softening all the sounds. From somewhere up ahead, a bell clanged.

They made their way to the pier. Shadows flitted along buildings as thieves lurked, awaiting easier targets than two armed men. Fog swirled around ships that creaked and moaned like restless ghosts.

Holding a lantern, Anakoni met them at the dock with a longboat. His teeth flashed in the darkness. "Captain. Glad to be making way at last. My purse is empty."

"How far out is the ship?"

"She's anchored just beyond the rocky island at the mouth of the cove."

Grimly, Jared said, "We're going after Leandro."

CHAPTER 18

Elise swam through gray haze. Her stomach lurched at the smell of unclean linen and the lingering scent of unwashed bodies. Her bed felt strangely hard. She battled to open her eyes, but could only force them into slits. Struggling to sit, she pressed her hand to her throbbing head. After a moment, the room stopped spinning, but continued to rock. She squinted against bright sunlight streaming in through tiny, round windows.

Where was she?

She remembered a vague struggle, but nothing else. She had no idea how she now found herself in this strange room.

Her tongue stuck to the root of her mouth. Using the bedpost to steady herself, she swung her feet off the side of the mattress and pushed to a stand. Though tempted to sink back down, her throat aching with thirst drove her onward. Praying the pitcher upon the trunk contained water, she lurched her way across the rocking floor to the pitcher and peered in. Water.

Though the cup next to the pitcher was smeared with grime, she filled it and gulped greedily. Fresh, cold water ran over her parched tongue and spilled down the side of her mouth.

After drinking, she washed her face and hands. The water refreshed her but failed to steady her legs. She leaned on the trunk until she stopped shaking. The floor continued to rock.

Rising up on tip toe, she peered through the windows cut out of rough, wooden walls, and saw only sea and sky. The horizon moved up and down. She blinked.

She was on board a ship. She'd never stepped foot on a ship before in her life. She still had no idea how she came to be here. At least a ship explained the rocking floor. She didn't know if she'd been unconscious for hours, or days. Judging from her state of weakness, she guessed days.

The conversation she'd overheard between Jared and the man called Anakoni returned to her mind.

She wondered if Jared had discovered her and taken her aboard his pirate ship. Would she ever see Colin again?

Male voices shouted from outside her room while heavy footsteps thundered past the door. More curious than frightened, Elise opened the door and peered through the gloom. She followed a narrow passageway, illuminated only by an opening at the top of a steep stairway. Legs and feet disappeared up the steps and pounded on wooden planks over her head. She hesitated.

Fear of the unknown grappled with fear of remaining in ignorance. Determined to find answers, she lifted her skirts and climbed the narrow stairs, holding tightly to a rope on one side. Blinking in the harsh sunlight, she stepped onto the deck of a boat with two masts.

"My glass!" someone shouted.

Elise shielded her eyes with her hand. Men in canvas pants made adjustments to the sails. A boy scampered to a raised deck and handed something to a man whose plumed hat shadowed his face.

The boy darted away as the man put a spyglass to his eye. That man looked familiar somehow.

She saw no sign of Jared.

"It's the *Sea Mistress*," the man in the hat said. "Weak fool, I knew he'd come." A faint Spanish accent laced his voice. In another time and place, she would have found the accent charming. He laughed darkly and chills ran down Elise's spine. Then he raised his voice and called, "Come about and set a course to intercept."

A man with long braids at his side repeated the orders, and then shouted in a language she did not understand.

The man calling the commands turned to Elise. With a mocking smile, he swept off his hat and made a grand bow. "How convenient that you are awake. Welcome aboard the *Venture*. Do join me here on the quarterdeck."

Elise's knees nearly crumpled as she recognized the Spaniard as one of the men who'd been slowly hanging Jared and threatening the boy. She had no reason to believe he'd show her mercy.

He gestured impatiently. "Come, come."

Elise's nearly paralyzing fear left her sick and light-headed. Yet to remain where she stood seemed pointless. A sailor laughed, low and guttural. Mangy ruffians grinned dangerously. Some eyed her as if she were a juicy steak. Others looked at her with open hostility and fingered their weapons.

She fought the urge to give into her rising fear and simply run back down the stairway. Such an action would be futile. After all, aboard a ship, she had nowhere to hide. Though her heart pounded, she raised her chin and squared her shoulders in false courage. She strode with dignity through the gauntlet of villains to the raised deck, mounted the steep stairs, and approached the man who'd spoken.

He watched her with glittering eyes and a chilling smile.

Battling the bile rising in her mouth, she looked him full in the eye and hoped her voice sounded confident. "Might I assume you are the captain of this vessel?"

"You do indeed, *Señora*. Captain Diego de

Leandro, at your service." His tone mocked her.

"Then please be good enough to explain how I've come to be here." She concealed her trepidation behind an imperious façade.

His grin left her with the desire to wash. "You are here as bait to draw out my enemy."

"Your enemy?"

"Black Jack, Captain of the *Sea Mistress*."

Black Jack. She'd heard stories of this merciless pirate. Articles detailing his cruelty frequented the newspapers. Puzzled, she shook her head. "What makes you think he would come for me?"

"You are his lover. I've seen him with you. Going to and from your house at all hours of the night." Leandro's grin revealed yellowed and broken teeth, and Elise had to resist taking a step backward.

"She's adjusted her heading, Cap'n," called a man perched up high.

Captain Leandro took another look through his spyglass.

Elise went to the railing, shaded her eyes with her hand, and peered out over the water. A white, shapeless speck bobbed just on the horizon.

Leandro collapsed his spyglass with a snap. "Spread the sand! My steel will taste his blood today."

Another sailor shouted orders in more than one language. Men wet down the deck and poured sand, amid much ribald talk and laughter.

Elise turned to Captain Leandro and drew herself up further. "You must have mistaken me for another. I only know Black Jack by reputation. And as I never consort with pirates, I could not have met this—" she allowed her voice to revealed her disgust, "—Black Jack."

"Hasn't told you, eh, *Señora*? He used the name of a...how do you say...a blueblood. Amesbury, I think, no?"

Elise felt the blood drain from her face.

"Ah, I see you know that name, *Señora*."

Weakly, she said, "Jared Amesbury is Black Jack?"

"Aye." He watched her with impassive curiosity.

Aghast, she stared. "You're lying."

Shrugging, he leaned against the railing. "You see for yourself soon."

What possible motive Leandro would have for telling her such a thing, she couldn't imagine. He seemed to have no reason to lie.

And yet his words were too horrible to believe.

As she grappled with the awful reality, horror sapped the strength in her knees. She gripped the railing to remain upright and pressed a shaking hand over her mouth. She knew all too well of Black Jack, of his acts of brutality to those who defied him.

According to the papers, when a merchant had refused to obey Black Jack's demands, he had plundered the cargo, disemboweled the captain, and then set fire to the ship with the crew tied up on board, leaving them to burn alive. Other stories of equally monstrous acts jostled against her memory until her stomach squeezed. That her Jared could be capable of inhuman cruelty to that magnitude seemed incomprehensible.

Sick with dismay, she stumbled backwards and fell against a barrel. Jared was the pirate Black Jack, the most ruthless renegade to plague the seas since the war.

"It's a bit...eh, how do you say...ironic, that you would save him once, only to lure him to his death later, *Señora*, no? Perhaps now you be happy to watch him die. He used you. He lied to you, eh, *Señora*?" He made a tsking sound. "No way to treat a lady. Still, for you he comes." He jabbed a thumb toward the direction of the approaching ship.

Numbly, Elise wondered why Jared would come

for her. It couldn't be possible that he had any true feelings for her. It must all be part of some grand plan she had yet to understand. She might be perfectly irrelevant to his purpose. Apparently, both pirate captains had some score to settle and would soon attempt to destroy one another.

Some tiny part of her quailed at the thought that Jared might be killed. Despite the pain of betrayal that left her shaking, she couldn't abide watching him die.

She shouldn't care. Pathetic fool, she did care. Even now. He had shown her that she'd been living in a state of numbness since Edward's death. He'd made her feel alive again. And oh, how badly being alive hurt now.

Jared was a pirate. Not just any pirate. Black Jack.

Waves of dizziness washed over her. She gripped the top of the barrel to keep from falling off while despair and revulsion burned a dark hole through her soul.

She'd kissed him. She'd fallen in love with him. She'd agreed to marry him.

Battling tears, Elise turned away to hide her anguish and focused on forcing air into her constricted lungs.

A nearby seaman with long, black braids shouted commands. The memory of that same seaman holding a knife to the throat of the boy José leaped into her mind. She recoiled.

All around her, sailors strapped on an assortment of guns, knives, and swords, and hurried to carry out orders. Instead of grimly preparing for battle, they gleefully made ready the *Venture* and themselves to engage in an act of war. Leandro turned his attention to his ship and crew, leaving Elise to despair.

Had Jared's touch been genuine, or all part of

the ruse? Not that it mattered. He was a pretender. A murderer. The thought that Jared could be of the same ilk as Leandro and his filthy, crude men made her skin crawl.

The other ship steadily neared. Sitting on the barrel, she tried to school her expression into a proper English lady's passiveness, knowing she must be failing miserably.

"Cast loose the guns!" the first mate called. "Take out your tampions and run out your guns." He repeated orders in a foreign tongue.

The pirates readied the cannons lining the deck of the ship.

Leandro returned to her and made a slow perusal of her body. "You will provide welcome entertainment when I celebrate the death of my enemy."

Despite the disgust at the thought of that beast touching her, she pressed her lips together and lifted her chin. Some inner reserve gave her courage. Despair gave way to righteous anger. "I will do no such thing."

"What makes you think you have a choice?"

He turned to his nearest men. "We can't let Black Jack think we treat his woman courteously. Tie her to the foremast."

Two pairs of hands seized her roughly. Her first thought was to fight, but their hatred-filled eyes promised abuse if she resisted. And really, even should she break free, where would she go? Trapped here on the ship, she had nowhere to go but overboard. Nothing would drive her to the unpardonable sin of taking her own life.

And somehow, she must live to return to Colin.

Despite her lack of resistance, the pirates dragged her with unnecessary force to the nearest mast and tied her. As the ropes cut into her skin, she bit her lip to keep from crying out. She refused to

213

give them the satisfaction of knowing they hurt her. One of her captors appeared younger than the others, barely out of boyhood, but just as hardened.

When he spoke to the others, Elise stared. "You're an Englishman."

The young pirate's lip curled. "England never did nothin' fer me 'cept treat me like a slave. 'igh society ladies like ye never cared fer the likes o' me or mine."

He gave the ropes a vicious jerk. Violence, not lust, radiated from him. She shrank from his hatred. To her relief, the men turned away and ignored her as they saw to their tasks.

The sun beat down upon her while the chill wind whipped her hair. Constricted by the ropes, her limbs throbbed and then numbed. Slowly, the other vessel neared.

Captain Leandro called, "Now, Santos!"

"Prime your guns," the man with the braids shouted. "Fire!"

An unwarranted surge of concern flittered over Elise's heart at the thought that Jared might suffer injury. She stamped it down. He did not deserve her concern.

He was a liar. A pirate. A murderer.

A deafening roar erupted from the nearest cannon. The concussion pressed Elise against the mast. Her ears rang. The *Venture* rocked slightly while a puff of smoke rose up from the muzzle and the smell of gunpowder stung her eyes and nose. Her heart beat an unsteady staccato.

With a brief flash of orange, a gun on the *Sea Mistress* replied and a cannon ball sailed toward them. Her mouth dried. If Jared's ship were firing at them with her on board, he must not be overly concerned with her safety. His motive must truly be revenge, not rescue. The realization saddened her more than she cared to admit.

The cannon ball blasted through the side of Leandro's ship near the rear. Splinters erupted. The *Venture* trembled below Elise's feet, throwing men to the deck. Terror choked her. She could die in this battle, a mere pawn in some deadly game these pirates played. What would happen to Colin if she died?

Swiftly, the pirates sponged out their cannons, rammed in cartridge and balls, and sparked the powder before sending out another volley. Most of the balls failed to hit their intended target. The *Sea Mistress* sent another salvo hurtling toward them. The right side of the *Venture* near the back of the ship exploded, showering wreckage in all directions, and ripping into an unlucky few men. Despite their abhorred profession, the men's screams wrenched Elise's heart.

Leandro's crew retaliated, but not before another round of deadly missiles battered the ship. The *Venture* shuddered, and the nearest gun was blown into the center of the deck under a shower of fragments, killing or wounding those who manned it.

Choking smoke swirled above the deck, reducing visibility. The screams of dying men and the horrible crash of balls tearing into the ship dulled Elise's senses.

As they drew closer, the vessels no longer fired cannon balls. Instead, the *Sea Mistress* launched metal shards and nails. The shards rent the sails into tatters, and tore with equal deadliness into men in their path.

Appalled at the destruction, Elise stared in mute horror. Her heart hammered in her deafened ears and her gown dampened with perspiration. Vaguely, she noticed that all the fire coming from the *Sea Mistress* focused on the rearward part of the ship, even though the *Venture* had turned and exposed its broadside to the enemies to give all its big guns the ability to fire.

The cannons fell silent as the *Sea Mistress* sailed ever nearer, and pirates shot one another with personal firearms. Men crumpled, and others took their places. How they could see their targets clearly enough to hit anything through the drifting smoke, she couldn't imagine. The *Sea Mistress* drew alongside.

Grappling hooks clawed onto the railing as sailors pulled their ships together, while others swung onto *Venture*'s deck on long ropes. Combatants threw down their spent guns and hacked at each other with swords, knives or clubs.

Sickened at the carnage, but unable to look away, Elise watched as murderers and scoundrels clashed with a fervor that exceeded her imagination. As bodies piled up and blood flowed freely, Elise saw the grim wisdom of using sand on the deck.

A dark form landed lightly in the middle of the deck and cut a swath of death around him. Many of Leandro's men fell back rather than face the terrible blade and its ruthless wielder.

"Leandro! Come and fight me man to man, you cowardly dog!"

The smoke cleared. Jared stood with his feet wide apart and brandishing a bloodied sword. Wind ruffled his dark hair and whipped his shirt about his muscular form.

He'd survived the battle. An appalling and unwarranted relief poured into her.

Jared's mouth twisted into a cold sneer. No, not Jared—a pirate who used that name. But even now, she could not think of him by any other name.

Captain Leandro chortled. He dispatched his opponent and turned to Jared.

Sailors drew back as the opposing captains faced each other.

Leandro hurled insults at Jared, some in

English, many in Spanish. They circled. Jared feinted. They came together with a clash. The clang of their swords cut through the noises of battle around them. No mere fencing match, these were two mortal enemies clearly bent on killing one other.

The Spaniard taunted and made a great deal of noise with flamboyant moves, but Jared remained silent, focused and lethal. He moved with deadly grace, warily watching, keeping his defense tight, striking out with accuracy.

Leandro howled in pain as Jared's blade cut his shoulder, and he shifted his sword to his other hand, adjusting his stance. Jared came at him again. Leandro fell back. Their swords flashed in the sunlight as they struck with bone-jarring force. They leaped back and circled. Leandro lunged, aiming for the heart.

Elise let out a gasp of alarm.

Jared parried and drove him back. Leandro fought with increasing desperation. Jared fought with more savagery.

Leandro's shoulder bled freely and he showed signs of tiring. He no longer lunged, but merely kept Jared's sword from driving home. His breathing grew ragged, his eyes desperate and wild. "Dog! You die today!"

"One of us will surely die. It will not be me." Jared's calm voice carried over the *mêlée*.

"Before your body has cooled, I will ravish your woman," Leandro taunted. He leaped forward driving in his sword.

Jared's blade deflected Leandro's. They remained locked together while their swords slid down with a hiss. They disengaged and sprang back. His sword arm bleeding from a fresh wound, Leandro hurled another series of insults at Jared as they thrust and parried, but again, Jared remained silent. As the battle raged, the Spaniard breathed

217

with more effort. Snarling and dancing, Leandro wormed through Jared's defenses and nicked him on the chin.

Elise caught her breath.

Jared gave no reaction. Unheeded blood dripped off his chin and onto his shirt. Leandro let out a cry of victory. They came together. Jared plunged his sword through Leandro's heart.

Leandro dropped his weapon. It clattered on the deck. Jared wrenched his sword out of his foe's chest and watched impassively as Leandro fell forward and landed on his face.

With a battle call, Santos flew at Jared.

Jared dispatched him with less effort. He calmly surveyed the battle around him while his opponent fell at his feet.

"That's for Greymore," he said to the body so quietly that she barely caught the words.

All sinewy grace and raw strength, Jared climbed to the quarterdeck. Blood dripped from his sword onto the deck. He stood fierce and deadly and handsome.

Even though she'd witnessed how coolly he delivered death, her heart skipped at the sight of him.

She must be losing her mind.

Looking over the men, he raised his voice and spoke in Spanish, and then in another language Elise did not recognize. Portuguese, perhaps? Then he shouted in English. The wind made it difficult to hear, but she caught the words of invitation to join him and share in his plunder.

Sailors who'd been trying to kill each other moments ago now brought out bottles and passed them around, sharing drinks like old friends.

Jared swaggered purposefully toward her and stopped to slowly look her over.

She stared back in uncertainty. If she had not

known his face and form so well, she would never have recognized this dangerous, battle-hardened man. Sweat ran off the ends of his disheveled hair. A few days' stubble shadowed his face. His open shirt, dirty and spattered with blood still dropping from his chin, clung to his muscular chest. He smelled of gunpowder, blood and death. But at the moment, he seemed a welcome relief from the terrifying Captain Leandro.

Jared picked up a loose piece of a sail and carefully wiped his sword before he thrust it into the scabbard at his hip next to a long knife and a pair of pistols. He eyed her as if she were a horse, and without even a glimmer of recognition.

From over his shoulder, she saw pirates behind him, watching. Men of all nationalities, they looked equally vile. Some handed their bottles to others and advanced upon her hungrily.

"A fair prize for a fair day's work," Jared drawled as he looked at her. He turned back to the pirates and unsheathed his sword in a flourish. With his sword raised, he shouted, "I claim the woman."

More than a few of the men looked disappointed as others translated.

"What about equal share?" someone muttered.

"That don't apply to women, half-wit. It's in the articles," came a low reply from another.

Jared's back stiffened. Whatever expression he wore silenced the pirates. No one else spoke against him.

"Dubois, make sure the new recruits understand the articles of agreement. Anakoni, see that whatever plunder we take from the *Venture* is divided. I'll count the woman as my two shares."

With a turn, he advanced upon Elise. She searched for any sign of the Jared Amesbury she thought she knew, but he remained as impersonal as if they'd never met.

He pulled out a knife. Her heart leaped into her throat. He wouldn't actually harm her, would he? The knife came closer, aiming for her chest. She shrank back, her breath coming in ragged gasps.

He used the knife to saw on the ropes binding her. Her relief lived only until he paused and leaned in with an ugly grin almost identical to Leandro's. All hope of rescue from this hardened, ruthless man fled.

Perspiration ran down between her shoulder blades. How could she have ever cared for this vile man? Anger surged, and she glared in defiance rather than fear.

The last rope snapped in half under his blade. Moving too swiftly for her to react, he threw her over his shoulder. She thrashed against him, but his shoulder pressing into her stomach drained her strength. He strode between the pirates who parted for him, climbed onto the railing, waited for the next wave to crest, and leaped to his ship. He carried her across the deck and through a door. Only after he shut and bolted the door did he set her down.

As his eyes locked with hers, his face transformed from the ruthless pirate Black Jack to Jared the gentleman, looking as desperate as the night he'd come to her with news of his father's death.

"Are you hurt?"

She blinked at his sudden metamorphosis.

"Elise?" He touched her shoulder.

Too shocked to respond, she simply stared.

"Did they harm you?"

Numbly, she shook her head.

"Did they touch you?"

She understood what he meant and shook her head again.

"Elise." He uttered her name almost as a prayer of thanksgiving. He closed his eyes briefly. "I'm sorry you got dragged into this." With his eyes upon her, he raised his hand to her face.

Repulsed, she stepped back.

His aquamarine eyes searched hers. "I have much to explain, but I can't right now."

"I already know." Her voice sounded tight and hard even to her own ears. "You are the pirate Black Jack."

He glanced toward the door. "There's more."

She held up a hand. "I don't want to hear it. All along, I sensed that you played some kind of role. Now I know. How clever you must think you are to have fooled us all." Tears filled her eyes. She tried to curb them, but they streamed down her cheeks.

"I never lied to you."

"Everything was a lie." A sob ripped through her.

Voices outside the door drew his attention. He looked back. "I know this looks bad, but it's not what it seems."

She turned away and put her hands over her face. The real Jared Amesbury was dead. She'd never known him. A heartless pretender stood in his place. Any feelings she might have developed for the man she knew as Jared were for a man who did not exist. She might as well love a fictional character in a story.

Worse, he was one of those reprehensible monsters about whom she'd been warning Colin. And not just any pirate, the most violent of them all.

"Elise, please believe me."

She whirled on him. "You're a liar. A thief. A murderer."

Someone pounded upon the door. "Captain, come quick."

Jared remained still, but his image faded into swirls of light and color through her tears. She turned away. Without a word, he strode to the door, wrenched it open and slammed it shut.

Elise sank down to the floor, and wrapped her arms around her knees. What would he do to her? Would she ever see Colin again?

Defeated, betrayed, utterly lost, she sobbed like a child.

When her tears ran dry, and her shudders quieted, she lay motionless on the floor, completely spent. The room grew dark and her limbs stiffened.

She gripped the edge of a heavy mahogany desk and used it to pull herself to her feet. Dully, she looked over her surroundings. Brass lanterns hung from the ceiling, swinging with the motion of the ship. Shelves lined one side of the room filled with books and curious artifacts from the Orient, Egypt, and exotic cultures she could not identify. A table and several chairs hugged the corner behind the desk. The room had a professional feel much like that of a well-traveled attorney. How ironic.

A smaller door to the side opened onto a small bedchamber. Elise looked in the doorway without entering. A thick rug with an oriental design lay upon the floor. Outside a leaded glass window shimmered a glorious sunset.

Someone entered the main cabin. Elise whirled around. Two sailors nodded to her deferentially and set about pushing the desk against the wall and moving the table into the middle of the room. A third approached Elise. His tasteful clothing had a decidedly French flavor. He had a neatly trimmed beard and mustache, and bright, alert eyes. Extended exposure to the elements left his face weathered and craggy.

He removed his hat. "*Madame*, permit me to introduce myself. I am Jean-Claude Dubois, first mate." He spoke in the faint accent of a Frenchman who'd spoken English for many years. "The captain sends his respects and invites you to join him for dinner."

With vague surprise, she realized she did not feel threatened by the Frenchman. He eyed her with curiosity, but without the open leer she'd seen on the other pirates. Another, younger sailor entered carrying a bucket. Though too young to grow facial hair, he towered over her, and his bare arms bulged with muscle.

"With your permission, ma'am?" He thrust his chin toward the bedroom.

Elise stepped out of the doorway, and the youth carried the bucket into the room. The sound of water being poured reached her ears.

The large boy padded out carrying an empty bucket. She realized they all walked on bare feet and wondered if that were a common practice aboard ships.

"You may wish to wash first. Dinner will be served momentarily," Mr. Dubois said. He paused. "*Madame*, do let me know should there be anything we can do to make you comfortable."

Numbly, Elise nodded.

He affected a brief bow and stepped back. She went into the bedchamber and closed the door. Leaning against the door, she listened to the sounds of footsteps outside the room, but no one came near. For good measure, she bolted the lock. It would not stop a truly determined man, but the act made her feel better.

On the chest, she found a small wash basin and a clean, dry cloth. Next to the cloth lay a silver brush, comb and a hand mirror in a matched set. Perhaps he kept such things for all the other women he carried off from ships he plundered.

Villain.

A large bed occupied one corner of the room. Rich fabrics, blankets and pillows bespoke a preference for comfort and opulence. Odd, but that seemed to contradict the man she thought she knew. He'd always seemed to show a penchant for simpler things. That must have been part of the role he played. A ruse to break through the barriers around her heart.

The bed loomed large. She wondered how many women had occupied that bed with him. Grinding her teeth, she turned away. Another thought halted her.

He might expect her to share it with him.

Could he be the kind of man to take by force what he did not receive by seduction? The gentleman she knew as Jared Amesbury certainly would not. He'd had opportunities to do just that and had not taken them.

But a pirate remained an unpredictable mystery.

In an act of practicality, she washed her face and hands. After removing the few remaining hair pins, she brushed her hair, slowly working out the tangles. She braided it and wound it into a coil at the back of her head. She had so few hairpins remaining that she could not fasten it securely, but at least she felt neater, as if she had some measure of control. Control. Almost laughable, that.

A scratch at the door and a hesitant, "Milady?" called her to dinner.

She opened the door to the fresh-faced lad who'd brought in the water. "I'm not a titled lady. Mrs. Berkley will do."

Blushing, he ducked his head, murmured something, and stepped back to allow her to pass. The captain's cabin had transformed into an elegant dining room. Candles flickered, silver shimmered, crystal and china graced the table. Platters of fragrant food waited, tempting her stomach.

Elise sensed Jared enter the room. Her heart pounded, whether from dismay or anticipation, she did not dare examine too closely. No sound came from behind her. She steeled herself and turned to see him leaning against the doorframe, his arms folded over his chest, a hint of a smile hovering on his mouth.

The hardened conqueror on deck had vanished. He'd bathed and changed into clean clothes resembling those he'd worn the day she first met him; a white linen shirt and leather breeches. The cut on his chin had been sewn with black thread, but was enough below his jaw line that it barely showed. The first signs of a beard shadowed his jaw. Tonight he walked barefoot. And yet, he looked so much like the Jared Amesbury she knew that she wanted to weep again. It was like seeing the ghost of a loved one.

She pressed her hand to her stomach and commanded herself not to fall apart. With lowered eyes, the youth pulled out a chair for her and waited. Too hungry to refuse, she accepted the offered chair. When she had comfortably settled, the boy poured the wine.

"Thank you, O'Brian, that will be all," rumbled Jared from the doorway.

He pushed off from the wall and closed the door behind O'Brian. He approached like a great cat stalking its prey. She felt his gaze but refused to meet it.

His chair scraped as he sat. "I think you'll find the food more suitable than usual. I insisted the ship's cook work in a reputable tavern while we were on land in the hopes that he could produce something edible. His apprenticeship appears to have improved his skills."

She heard the amusement in his voice, but refused to look at him.

"If you'd been on board the *Sea Mistress* before, you would appreciate the improvement," he added.

Donna Hatch

She twisted the napkin in her lap.

"Perhaps it is the company that chases away your appetite." The softness of his voice drew her gaze. A teasing smile played around his mouth. He looked so like his former self that a lump formed in her throat and she had to fight back her tears.

The tightness in her stomach made the thought of eating unappealing, despite her earlier hunger.

"I'm hungry. I cannot force you to eat, but I'm not willing to starve." He dug into his meal.

She had no idea how long she'd been in a drug-induced sleep, but she was beginning to feel weak from lack of food. As she smelled the tempting aromas, her stomach reawakened feeling painfully empty. Despite her wishes to appear mutinous, she tasted the first dish. Not up to her chef's standards, but certainly quite good.

She pointedly kept her eyes off him and they ate the first course in silence. After the second arrived, Elise could no longer stand the silence.

"Would you be so kind as to reveal to me your intentions?" Her tone came out more plaintive than she'd hoped.

He lowered his fork. "My intentions?"

"Toward me."

He sipped his wine and leaned back in his chair. Holding the glass, he regarded her a moment before he spoke. "I intend to show you every courtesy and make your voyage aboard my ship as pleasant and comfortable as possible."

"And how long do you plan to hold me on board?"

"My dear Mrs. Berkley, I am not holding you. You are a guest, not a prisoner." The outer corners of his eyes crinkled.

"I am here against my will."

His lips twitched. "You'd rather I left you aboard Leandro's ship?"

Her shoulders slumped. "No."

"I thought not."

"Then, if I'm not a prisoner, you'll take me home?"

"All in good time."

Desperation edged through. "I need to get home to Colin."

He paused. "I'm confident he's receiving the best possible care from your ever faithful servants. You will be returned to him soon, not to worry."

She swallowed. "Unharmed?"

The humor left his face. "Do you believe I'd turn my men loose on you?"

She cringed. She had feared he'd keep her for his own pleasure, but the thought of those savage-looking men overpowering her left her sick. "Would you really do that?"

He frowned. "Of course not."

"Then what do you mean to do with me?"

He pressed his lips together briefly. "Allow you full use of my ship. These quarters are for your comfort while you remain on board."

"Alone?"

"Well, you are using my cabin," he drawled, looking her over with a wicked grin. "Where do you expect me to sleep?"

She leaped to her feet. "If you think I'll share your bed with you, you'd better come in wearing armor or you'll find a knife in your ribs!" She picked up her butter knife and brandished it at him.

He laughed. "Good girl. Nice to see your spirits returning. That passive, timid creature a moment ago barely resembled the Elise Berkley I know."

She blinked, her indignation fading. Then she realized what he'd done and she grew angry all over again. "You! You deliberately provoked me."

"Of course. I had to shock you out of your shell somehow." He grinned. Then his face softened. "Fear not. Once I've escorted the *Venture* to a safe place where she can undergo repairs, I'll take you home. That is, if you still wish to go there after seeing the liberty afforded by the open seas."

She sank back into her chair. "Take me home, I beg you. Colin will be terrified when I've turned up missing."

He let his breath out slowly. "I'm sorry. I truly am. I wish I could take you home immediately, but I'm commandeering the *Venture* and she needs repairs. We damaged her in battle and she looks as though she hasn't been in dry dock in a decade. I can't send them off in her alone and unprotected. There are so many unsavory characters who might take advantage of a crippled ship, you know." He grinned at his own joke.

She was not amused. "Are there any worse than Black Jack?"

His tone light, he said, "Worse? I suppose that depends on your point of view. Leandro was worse. Our former captain was worse. I killed both, so I've done the world a favor by ridding it of them."

She shuddered at how casually he spoke of taking another man's life. Although, she could not mourn Captain Leandro's passing. "Is that what you plan to tell the real Jared Amesbury's family?"

He stilled. "The real Jared Amesbury's family?"

"I overheard you in town talking to one of your men. You admitted that you'd killed the real Jared Amesbury and have been using his name when it suits you."

He appeared to carefully choose his words. After a furtive glance toward the door, he replied, "There are times when having an alias becomes necessary."

"Is murder necessary?"

He met her gaze evenly. "I have killed more men than I can remember. Many in the war. Others since then. Some today. It happens in battle."

"Then you do not deny that you are indeed the

pirate Black Jack."

"I do not deny it. I've been a pirate for the past three years." Gravely, he drank the rest of his wine.

"Another alias?"

"Does it matter?" All trace of humor vanished from his face. Even his eyes lost their sparkle.

"So you've stolen and lied and killed. All for a bit of treasure."

"We are all pawns in some greater game." He stared off at some unrevealed memory. "If it means anything to you, I'm retiring now that I've completed this last task."

"And how many died from 'this last task?'"

"A great number, no doubt."

Her mouth fell open. "How can you be so complacent about human life?"

"Some things cannot be changed," he replied grimly. "A price must be paid for everything."

The next course arrived. After the servant—or perhaps sailor would be more appropriate—had left, she picked at the food.

"Elise." He waited until she looked up. "You have seen me at my worst and at my best. You've even seen me grieving. Whatever man you glimpsed in those moments is still here," he tapped his chest with his fingertips. "I believe you found him not objectionable then."

"That was before I knew all this." She made a sweeping motion that took in the ship. The truth seemed almost too horrible to admit. Tears filled her eyes.

He reached over and lifted her chin. She glared at him. Her tears overflowed and ran down her cheeks.

"I never thought I'd see the immovable Elise Berkley reduced to tears," he whispered.

"I trusted you. But everything about you is a lie." She sat with tears streaming down her face, absolutely lost. She hated her weakness, her helplessness, her inability to control her emotions. The man she loved never existed. He'd been an illusion. A fraud. A lie. The loss cut more deeply than if he had died. "You killed a man in cold blood and stole his name."

"I've never killed in cold blood. Lives have been lost, but only in the heat of battle."

She let out a huff but it came out more like a sob.

His voice gentled. "I will return you home. Unmolested. No one you love, or even know, will be hurt."

A true sob broke through. She turned away and put a hand over her face.

"Elise..."

"Please. No more." She stumbled into the sleeping chamber, shut the door and leaned against it. She heard the outer door open and then close.

Desolation crept in.

Despite his familiar face, he remained a stranger. A pirate. One who made a profession of stealing and killing.

CHAPTER 19

Jared slung his coat over his shoulder. Leaning against the mainmast of the *Sea Mistress*, he stared up at the vast array of brilliant stars. The pilot skillfully guided the ship through calm waters. A white and silver moon held court with the stars. Two points off the port quarter sailed the *Venture*, silhouetted by the starlight.

He looked back up at the glittering lights, mentally naming the constellations. His brother Cole had been mad for astronomy and knew each mythological story to accompany the constellations. He always seemed to find life's lessons paralleled in mythology. Jared wondered what advice Cole would offer in his current predicament.

A light breeze ruffled his hair. He filled his lungs with the smells of the ocean. No mist marred the beauty of the sea this night. Not long ago, he'd believed nothing could be more perfect than such a night. Now he would gladly give it up for the love of one woman. A woman who wept in his cabin.

Seeing her reduced to tears tore out his heart. He hadn't believed he would ever see such a sight. And he'd caused it. Twice.

He could go in and simply tell her the truth, but he doubted she would believe him. She would no doubt think he'd simply made up an elaborate lie as part of some evil scheme.

More importantly, the bulkheads were decidedly thin and he couldn't risk someone on board the ship overhearing. He'd be immediately killed.

And Elise would be left to the tender mercies of

231

his men. He'd weeded out the worst of the villains from among his own crew over time, but Leandro's former crew, some of whom were now aboard, were the worst of the lot.

A small part of him wondered if she could still love him now that she knew of his role as a pirate. For all intents and purposes, he truly was a pirate. That he committed all those acts under orders made little difference. He could never bring back all the lives he'd taken. His chest tightened.

He should just take Elise home. The government would never approve of him helping pirates and would order him to return immediately. Once he saw to Von Barondy, he should have gone to London, received his decommission and kept both feet firmly on land. Leaving in his ship, leading a band of villains to rescue Elise, and turning over a ship to them would surely be seen as a rogue act. It would be in his best interest to get back to England quickly.

Elise needed to return to her son. His ship was certainly no place for a lady.

But he wanted to leave the ships to Dubois and Anakoni, who had been faithful friends, despite their station. If he could convince them to give up piracy and accept the pardons he'd been promised for them, they could sell their ships and make a tidy profit; enough, he hoped, to start an honest life.

Perhaps truth would change Elise's mind about him. Whether or not he deserved her affections was an entirely different matter. He was just selfish enough not to care.

Below deck, a cacophony of laughter rang out as the crew continued to celebrate their victory and toast their new alliance. Rum flowed freely, the best pirate's reward.

Jared doubted any of his men would be so bold as to break into his cabin to get to Elise. They'd all signed the articles protecting women, and Jared fiercely enforced penalties for breaking said articles. Besides, he'd proven himself as a good leader, making most of them ridiculously wealthy. Or they would be, if they could refrain from frittering it all away on drink and women the instant they set foot on land.

Yet leaving a beautiful woman alone invited trouble; drunken sailors were capable of almost anything. She'd hate him if he entered the cabin, but that couldn't be helped. He'd risk her wrath to protect her.

Jared spoke briefly with the pilot before returning to the main cabin. Inside, he paused. O'Brian had cleared away dinner and set the cabin to rights. He heard nothing from behind the shut portal to his sleeping cabin.

At least she wasn't throwing things. Or audibly crying. That had to be a good sign. Right?

He snuffed out the candles and opened the portal. Inside, all was still. Only moonlight from the porthole illuminated the interior. A vague lump in his bunk indicated Elise's sleeping form.

He moved forward until the back of his neck prickled. He spun around just in time to catch an object hurtling toward his head. He seized the object with one hand, stopping its forward motion, and seized the arm that wielded it with the other. That fragile hand could only belong to one person on board. He wrested what felt like a candlestick from her and discarded it. It made a dull clank as it bumped against a bulkhead and landed on the deck.

"Trying to kill me, or merely render me senseless?" he drawled as he jerked her hard against him.

Her breath came in gasps. "I knew you were coming."

"Of course. This is my cabin. I sleep here."

"If you were a gentleman, you'd sleep in someone else's cabin."

"And inconvenience them? How thoughtless."

"Let go of me." Her voice rose in pitch.

He tightened his grip and pulled her lush body against his, awakening his ardor. "I rather like you where you are."

Her breasts heaved as she breathed in harsh gasps. Her body trembled. Oh, anything but that! He pulled her in closer and rubbed her back.

"Shhh. It's all right."

Instead of relaxing against him, she tensed further. Her icy hands pushed at him, but he had her effectively pinned. The softness of her body tempted his resolve. He battled it. She was angry and frightened; hardly ideal emotions for seduction. Hoping to soothe her, he wrapped his other arm around her and laid his cheek on top of her head, breathing in the sweet fragrance of her hair. She remained rigid, her hands curled into fists trapped between them.

"I won't hurt you," he whispered. "Regardless of the name I use, I'm not such a different man as that."

"I don't know you at all." He heard the tears in her voice. "I don't know what you're capable of doing. Or what you want."

He smoothed her hair. "I just want to hold you."

"Please don't ask this of me."

"I won't do anything you don't want me to do."

"Then I beg you to release me."

He let his breath out in frustration. How could he argue with a plea like that? He loosened his grip a little. In the semi-darkness, her wide, frightened eyes stared unblinkingly up at him. He opened his arms and let her back away. She flattened herself against the bulkhead. All the warmth left with her.

"We both need rest. And you're cold. Come." He

took her hand and pulled her toward the bunk.

She dug in her heels. "No."

"Just sleep." He pulled the top blanket off the bunk and wrapped it around her. "Your teeth are chattering." He repositioned the pillows. "Nice deception. I thought you were actually sleeping in my bunk."

She stood hugging the blanket, poised to flee.

He tugged on the blanket she clutched and drew her to the bunk. "Rest. It will comfortably sleep two."

"How many times has it done that?" She sounded more like the Elise he knew. It gave him heart.

He grinned. "Jealous?"

She made a scoffing noise. "I'd have to care to be jealous."

"You wound me." It was only a partial jest.

"You're a liar."

"You've no idea. Get in bed, woman."

"I will not salute you and obey your every order. Captain." The mockery in her voice made him grin again.

"This is a pirate ship. No one salutes." He scooped her up in his arms and dumped her unceremoniously on the bunk.

"Blackguard," she snarled.

"Guilty."

She struggled inside her blanket cocoon to get into a comfortable position. If he were a true gentleman, he'd sleep on the floor. But at the moment, he took perverse enjoyment in discarding the guise of a gentleman. He pulled off his shirt and climbed in next to her wearing only his breeches. She stared in fear rather than fascination. His pride took a blow.

He rolled her over to her side facing away from him, and wrapping his arms around her, snuggled against her spoon position.

She lay rigidly. "You have a lot of nerve."

"See? You do know me."

She remained quiet for so long he thought a miracle had happened and she'd accepted his presence. "Please."

The angry, courageous woman had been replaced by the frightened lady again. He liked the angry one better.

He sighed. "It's cold in here. I'm only trying to warm you. Go to sleep, Elise. I will not attempt to seduce you."

Her voice shook. "Seduction is not what I most fear."

He raised up on his elbow and rolled her over on her back. She stiffened further. He peered into her face and lifted her chin, waiting until she made eye contact. Even in the semidarkness, he saw fear shadowing her eyes.

Solemnly he said, "I will not lay a hand on you. I swear it. Not in lust. Not in violence."

Her brow furrowed, her eyes searching his. He battled the increasing need to love her as a man. He settled for a chaste kiss. She remained stiff. He teased her lips with his, keeping them soft, light. She softened for only a moment and then stiffened again. Heaving an enormous mental sigh, he ended the kiss and traced his finger down her cheek, battling with the man he wanted to be for her, and the man he wanted to be for himself.

Her wide eyes stared back at him as if she expected him to sprout horns. "You said you wouldn't lay a hand on me."

"I said nothing about not laying my lips on yours.

"Untrustworthy." She sounded exasperated instead of frightened. That was good. Progress.

"Pirate."

"Don't remind me," she huffed.

"Are you in danger of forgetting?"

"Not even if you hit me over the head with a candlestick."

He laughed softly. Against his better judgment, he kissed her again. Despite her fear, her lips remained surprisingly pliant. She was becoming very skilled at kissing. He kissed her until he thought he'd incinerate.

A very primal, possessive part of him enjoyed the idea that she'd never been kissed the way he kissed her. Or pleasured the way he planned to pleasure her. Just as soon as he got her to stop hating him.

Wishing he had a handy bucket of cold water to dump over his head, he groaned. She went rigid and stared at him with large eyes.

He rolled her over and pulled her against his chest. "You're safe with me, Elise," he whispered against her ear, making a silent vow to be a man of his word.

"You'll have to prove that to me." She said nothing more, but her body finally relaxed against him.

He stroked her hair, marveling at its silken texture, and raised a fistful to his lips. Inhaling its lavender scent, he kissed it, kissed her temple, and then simply held her.

As he cradled her blanket-wrapped body, the fire cooled. In its stead, peace and well-being stole over him. He vowed to protect her at all costs, even with his very life, if necessary. It would be no great sacrifice; she was so much more worthy of living than he.

He agonized over his need to assure Elise, and his need to protect himself from discovery. He couldn't stand the thought that she believed him capable of cold-blooded murder. She no doubt envisioned him tying up a nobleman, extracting all his wealth, and murdering the man as he lay bound and helpless. He'd never done anything so ruthless and he wanted her to know it.

He put his lips next to her ear and whispered, "Elise."

Though she made no reply, he knew by her breathing that she was awake.

He continued in a whisper, "I didn't murder Jared Amesbury. I am Jared Amesbury."

Her breath stilled.

Praying that the walls didn't have ears, he whispered, "I swear I'll tell you everything as soon as it's safe, but for now, please believe me, I've never murdered an unarmed man. I am Jared Amesbury. I use the name John Black, or Black Jack, to protect my family. I can't tell you more."

She made no reply for a very long time. Up on deck, the watch bell clanged.

Finally, she drew in a breath and whispered. "How do I know that's not just another lie?"

"You'll have to trust me."

She made a huff of annoyance. Defeated, but glad to have at least tried, he lay perfectly still. And wished he could take them both far away.

****

On the quarterdeck of the *Mistress*, Jared squinted up at the sun, idly watched a gull soar overhead before turning his attention back to Dubois.

"The repairs on the *Mistress* have been completed." Dubois glanced toward the ship sailing just off their port bow. "But the *Venture* takes on water as quickly as they pump it out. She needs repairs we cannot complete at sea."

Jared nodded soberly. "Providing the wind and the weather hold, we'll be in port in two days. We'll careen the *Venture* and leave her for repairs while we go back aboard the *Mistress*. I intend to return

Mrs. Berkley home as soon as possible."

Dubois stroked his beard. "The men spent all their booty in Port Johns before we came after Leandro. Should we land now, we'll have hungry, thirsty men with no means to buy food or entertainment. The *Venture* had plenty of stores, but little cargo that we could sell. If I thought the *Venture* could last that long, I'd advise taking another merchant ship."

Jared frowned. Now that his assignment had officially ended, he had no intention of engaging in piracy for real. Even to prevent a mutiny.

Surely no one would be stupid enough to take a crippled ship into battle. Some of the crew had houses and families on the island, and would simply go home. Others lived at tavern in between voyages and had only their share of the plunder to support their needs. Leandro's men would only see it as another port call and fall into their customary disorderliness of wenching and drinking. But if they landed without any coin, Leandro's men might ransack the smuggler's port on the island his crew used as their haven.

He couldn't wait to rid himself of the whole business.

"The men may insist upon it," Dubois added.

"We can't go after a ship with the *Venture* so badly damaged, and I don't want to leave her behind unprotected while we go without her."

"If it comes to a vote, they'll be in favor of it. Empty purses make reckless men."

"We don't dare risk it and they know it," Jared snapped. But Dubois had a point. At times, the democratic way pirate ships operated was a confounded nuisance. He sighed and ran his fingers through his hair. "Empty the safe in the main cabin and have the quartermaster divide it among the men before we land."

"You're giving up your share?"

"Only what I have on board."

Dubois shrugged. "We'll bring it to a vote, but I think they'll agree."

Jared paused as Dubois indicated with his chin at something over his shoulder. Jared turned to see Elise coming tentatively from his cabin.

Blinking in the sunlight, she rested her hand on the bulkhead to steady herself against the motion of the ship. The wind stirred her dress, making it cling to the contours of her delicious body. Her rumpled clothes and unbound hair flowing around her shoulders invited images of her arising from her lover's bed.

Who would have thought an angel would be such a temptation?

Jared rubbed a hand over his stubbled face. Such thoughts would only challenge his resolve. Keeping his baser desires at bay last night had been one of the more difficult things he'd ever done, but holding her all night had been a dream.

"It is good we have just come from port or the men would be sniffing around her like a pack of hungry wolves." Dubois watched her. "She's a fine-looking woman, *non?*"

Jared glowered. "She's my woman, and I'll skewer anyone who challenges that."

Grinning, Dubois held out his hand in surrender. "But of course, *mon capitaine.*"

Wearing his best smile, Jared went to Elise. "Good morning. Did you sleep well?"

She eyed him with trepidation. "Very well."

"Were you warm enough?" He grinned roguishly, taking delight in reminding her she'd slept in his arms.

A faint pink tinged her cheeks. "Quite warm."

Jared smiled broadly. "I can't remember when I've slept so comfortably."

Her color deepened and she looked away.

Jared took her hand. "You're cold. O'Brian!"

"Sir?"

"Fetch my coat."

The boy trotted to Jared's cabin and returned carrying a dark brown wool coat. The youth looked carefully at Elise. As he turned away, he frowned. Jared wondered if O'Brian harbored the superstitions of many sailors.

As O'Brian returned to his duties, Jared laid the coat across her shoulders. She clutched it together and offered a hesitant, grateful smile.

"The wind is almost constant. We hope. Otherwise we sit dead in the water. But it can take some getting used to." He led her to Dubois who watched her with appreciation, a crooked smile on his weathered face. "Mrs. Berkley, I believe you've met my first mate, Jean-Claude Dubois."

"We meet again. *Enchanté, madame.*" Dubois raised her hand to his lips.

Her smile appeared more relaxed. "What is a civilized Frenchman doing on a pirate ship?"

Dubois laughed. "I'm afraid I'm a pirate, as well, *ma cherie.*"

"Oh, too bad. I'd hoped to hear you were a 'guest' here as well," she replied ruefully.

"*Mais oui,* we are all guests here, *madame.* Some of us have stayed longer than others, *non?*"

"Captain. A word?" One of the crewmen called.

Jared sent a meaningful look at Dubois. His first mate gave a brief incline of the head in reply and tucked Elise's hand in the crook of his arm.

Confident Dubois would watch over her, Jared stepped aside and listened to the crewman with one ear and Dubois with the other. Jared frowned as Dubois poured his French charm upon Elise.

"*Madame,* despite sailor's superstitions, I must say, I'm delighted to have you aboard. You much improve the scenery."

Silently cursing Dubois, Jared shot his first mate a warning look. Dubois grinned in reply and returned his gaze to Elise.

"You flatter me, sir," came Elise's voice.

"Oh, no. I'd love to prove my sincerity, but the captain has a powerful temper, and he can best me in swords. Half the men follow him because they believe he's the best man to do it. The other half fear him too much to vote him out."

Jared ground his teeth. Perfect. All he needed was for Elise to have continuous reminders of what he was. Or had been. And presently still was. Even if it weren't precisely true.

What a twisted mess.

The crewman who'd called him away paused. "Captain? Did you hear me?"

Jared snatched his attention away from Elise and Dubois. "Yes. We'll leave the *Venture* careened on the island. Anyone who wishes to remain on shore may do so. The rest will accompany me back to England."

"The missus will be glad of that."

Jared sent him an understanding grin and the crewman returned to his duties. Jared noticed young O'Brian hanging around, alternately watching Elise and Jared with furtive glances. Jared had never seen O'Brian so edgy.

Catching O'Brian's attention, Jared motioned him over. He slung his arm around the boy's shoulders. "What's the problem, lad?"

O'Brian hesitated. "Nothin'," he replied glumly.

"Speak up, lad. I won't eat you for dinner."

Miserably, he looked back at Elise speaking with Dubois. "The lady, sir. You've never taken a lady prisoner before. You uh...you don't normally treat the fair sex in such a manner. Least, not since I've been aboard."

"You're right. The ship's articles are very specific about the treatment of women. And we never take prisoners. But she was Leandro's prisoner. What would you have me do? Leave her on the *Venture*?"

He ducked his head. "She..." he swallowed. "She's your prisoner now, sir."

Jared nodded, understanding the problem. Who would have thought the boy who chortled at the thought of battle and plunder would be so tender-hearted toward women? Jared folded his arms and fixed him with a stern scowl. "Does she look to you like a woman who'd been brutalized?"

O'Brian paused, and then took a longer look at Elise. Jared did, too. Her skin glowed in healthy radiance and she stood in a relaxed and open stance as she smiled up at Dubois. Her hair shimmered golden, honey-brown in the sunlight and blowing in soft waves in the wind. Her laugh rang out.

O'Brian gave a brief shake of his head. "No, sir."

Jared nodded. "A woman will give you the greatest pleasure when you've pleased her. Seduction is satisfying. Rape is not. And if she isn't ready to be seduced, you must give her time to accept you. It will always be worth it. If not, let her go untouched. There will always be another willing woman."

O'Brian nodded, looking enormously relieved. Jared wondered how long it would be before the entire crew learned their captain's softness toward women. However, Jared had always been adamant that his crew leave the women untouched, hence the articles which addressed that. It should come as no surprise.

Jared went back to Elise and Dubois. With a dark look at his first mate, Jared took Elise's hand from Dubois's arm and placed it upon his own.

"Dismissed, Dubois," he said crisply.

Dubois's eyes crinkled in silent laughter. He made mock salute and left them alone.

Elise made no move to pull away, but she seemed to withdraw in every other way.

"Did you breakfast yet?" Jared asked.

She nodded, her eyes moving to the horizon.

"Any seasickness?"

"No."

"You are fortunate. Most are sick for days or weeks when they first go to sea."

She nodded, her eyes taking on a far away look. "I suppose there is a silver lining to every cloud."

He gentled his voice. "What troubles you?"

She made a sound that might have been a sharp, mirthless laugh. Or a sound of despair. He could not decide which.

"Your men think I'm your prisoner. And therefore, your...ah...mistress."

"Who cares what a bunch of scallywags think?"

"You've compromised my honor. And now they might expect me to...to entertain them."

"Not unless they want to fight me. And I doubt any of them are that stupid."

He took her to the bow of the ship where their voices would carry downwind out to sea. Still, he lowered his voice.

"Dubois thinks we were already lovers even before you came on board. The rest of the crew sees you as a prize I won fairly. If I hadn't laid claim on you, the men would have considered you fair game. Now that I have, they won't dare touch you, unless we give them reason to believe I'm through with you."

She looked up at him, half hopeful, half doubtful. "Then you didn't publically claim me because you expected me to—?"

"No." He glanced about, but all the men appeared busily attending to their labors. "I know

I've turned your world upside down, but I'm not as different as you suppose. I didn't attack you on land. I won't do it on the ship."

"I have no reason to believe you."

Her words stung. "Last night offered no proof? At first, O'Brian assumed I raped you. Now he merely believes I seduced you."

"That's exactly my point."

"Would you feel better if I had?"

"No!" She looked utterly horrified.

That stung, too, as if the thought of being intimate with him seemed repulsive. Hurt gave way to anger. "You know me better than anyone on board. But if you want me to behave the barbarian, believe me, I can."

He grabbed her roughly by the shoulders and hauled her against him. She let out a cry before he brought his mouth down hard upon hers. She struggled against him, but he held her fast. A sound of distress escaped her.

His anger faded. He couldn't be rough. He couldn't hurt her.

He wanted to protect her, hold her, love her.

As he gentled, she stopped fighting him. He slid his arms around her, drawing her in closer and poured out every tender thing he could not tell her, showed her without words that he loved her as the man who'd asked her to wait for him. Her sweet mouth became pliant under his. With his hand behind her head, he changed the angle of their mouths and deepened the kiss.

She responded, tentatively at first, but with growing hunger. She wrapped her arms around him, her voluptuous body pressing against him. Her heart hammered against his chest, matching the rhythm of his own. He wanted nothing at that moment but to scoop her into his arms, carry her to his cabin and love her deeply, passionately.

245

When he thought he might explode, he ended the kiss. He cupped her cheek, caressing her soft skin with the pad of his thumb. With his eyes closed, he rested his forehead upon hers. Breathing raggedly, shaking with unfulfilled desire, he held her.

"I could never harm you, Elise," he whispered. "If my entire crew pointed guns at me and threatened to kill me unless I hurt you, I'd die gladly. My only fear would be leaving you unprotected."

She drew in a shuddering breath.

Jared opened his eyes. Hers were closed, her lashes laying against her cheeks. Her lips were moist, pink and swollen from his kiss. Her flushed face and disheveled hair gave the appearance that she'd been thoroughly ravished. How badly he wanted to complete the picture!

Becoming aware of his crew, he lifted his head and glowered at the raised eyebrows, knowing grins, and sly chuckles.

"As you were!" he barked.

They snapped into action, but they continued to toss his way knowing winks and smirks. Ignoring them, he released Elise slowly.

Half-dazed, she blinked up at him. A moment later, the softness vanished, and she stared at him in horror, backing away. Her eyes shimmered and tears spilled down her cheeks.

His gut clenched.

Wrapping her arms around herself, she turned away.

Jared steadied his breathing. She believed him a pirate. She wouldn't easily warm to him. If ever.

He took her hand and led her to an area shaded by the mainsail where he made her a seat with a coil of rope and a folded piece of canvas.

She sat stiffly without meeting his eyes.

"My cabin is at your disposal, of course. Or, if you prefer, you may stay on deck. The crew knows to leave you be." He caught O'Brian's attention and motioned him over. "Your task is to see to Mrs. Berkley's every need."

"Aye, sir." The youth plopped down at Elise's feet and looked up at her worshipfully.

Jared went to consult with the pilot and made a slight course correction. Then he climbed aloft to help adjust a sail. He normally let the smaller, nimbler members of his crew climb the rigging, but he needed something with which to occupy his mind other than Elise.

She sat with all the dignity and grace of a lady in a drawing room, despite her lose hair blowing in the wind. He dragged his attention back to his task.

Aloft, while tying a knot, he felt a change in the air. From his perch high in the rigging, he peered into the horizon.

As he opened his mouth to sound the alarm, the lookout called, "Storm abrewing!"

All hands sprang into motion. Though a disreputable lot, they were undoubtedly proficient sailors. Jared clambered down and called for his glass. After he reassured himself that the *Venture* had seen the storm and had begun preparations, he turned back to lend aid. Amidst the activity, he found Elise deep in an earnest discussion with O'Brian who motioned below deck, no doubt pleading with her to go below.

She met Jared's gaze with wide, frightened eyes.

He strode to her. "Go to my cabin. It will be all right. We'll weather the storm, and with any luck be in port much sooner. Go on."

"Then, you don't think it's a bad one?"

"Fear not; I'll get us safely through it. I've faced plenty of storms." He flashed a grin. "You don't think the notorious Black Jack could be bested by a bit of wind, do you?"

She frowned, but appeared reassured.

Black clouds boiled, darkening the heavens, dimming the sunlight. Within moments, the wind whipped up. Jared looked back toward Elise. O'Brian towered over her, his hand under her elbow to steady her as she tottered on the pitching deck toward his cabin.

Praying he'd get Elise and his crew safely through, Jared turned back to face the storm.

CHAPTER 20

Elise awoke to the sound of a door opening. Pale, early morning sunlight filtered through the windows, illuminating Jared's haggard face. They'd battled the storm half the day and all night, and his exhaustion showed. He offered a tired smile as he closed the door to the cabin and began peeling off his dripping clothes. Each layer he removed showed more of his perfectly sculpted body. His clothing landed with a wet plop on the floor.

Elise's face burned and she turned her head, wishing she could turn off her imagination as he continued undressing.

"The storm is over, I see," she said, stating the obvious.

"We're through." Weariness dulled his voice.

Hinges to his sea chest creaked and then she heard the rustle of cloth. Moments later, he padded quietly to the bed. Elise glanced back, almost afraid at what she'd see. His half-open eyes and drawn face revealed his fatigue. Wearing only breeches, he staggered forward and fell face-first onto the bed beside her. At least he hadn't come to bed naked as she'd feared. Or had that been her hope?

The mattress sank under the weight of his body and Elise stiffened to keep herself from rolling into him. His eyes closed before his head found the pillow. Seconds later, his deep breathing filled the cabin.

Elise turned on her side and studied him. His tousled wet hair clung in dark waves to his face and neck. Seawater droplets seeped out of the ends of his hair and ran down his sculpted back, so hard and muscular even at rest. The raw masculinity of this man touched her on an elemental level.

He looked much as he had the day she'd first seen him. Only today, a new beard shadowed his face, making him look raw, savage, and so very male. She wanted to reach out and touch him, soothe him as she had when she'd freed him from the noose. But at the moment, he only needed rest, not whatever comfort she might provide. She touched his hand. It was cold.

Moving slowly, quietly so as not to disturb him, she pulled a blanket over him and lay close enough to warm him with her body heat. A small place deep inside questioned why she bothered.

His breathing never broke rhythm. Her own trepidations quieted and she slept.

Elise woke to sunlight streaming in the windows. She lay curled up against Jared. Jared. It could be his real name, as he'd said. Or another in a very long list of lies he'd told. Even so, she had no idea how else to think of him. Black Jack, an admitted alias, probably had little to do with his real name. 'Captain' seemed too impersonal after all they'd been through together. He would always be Jared to her.

She admired his face, the curve of his brow, the feathered lashes, the shape of his mouth, the patrician features. How easily she'd believed him to be nobility. Perhaps he had some noble blood in his veins. Not that it mattered. His large, calloused hands, so strong, so gentle, lay limp and open. Her eyes followed his neck down to the ruthlessly honed muscles of his shoulders, back and arms.

She wondered if the real Jared Amesbury had been so handsome. Or if the real Jared Amesbury lay next to her. He'd seemed earnest when he'd told her he truly was Jared sailing under an alias.

Perhaps it was true.

She stilled, her mind working carefully. He had come to her grieving for his father. Two days later, she'd read in the paper that the Fifth Earl of Tarrington had died in his seaside home. Then Jared had disappeared for over a week, the same time the funeral took place. All part of the act? Or the truth?

She let out her breath in a huff. Whether or not his name was Jared Amesbury, born the son of an earl, mattered not. He was a pirate. The facts were indisputable. And he'd admitted it.

Elise climbed to her feet. His trunk lay open, its lid resting against the wall. Inside, she found a clean shirt and donned it over her own very rumpled gown. It hung down to her knees and she had to roll up the sleeves several times to uncover her hands. His wool coat lay on the floor in a wet heap, tangled with the shirt and breeches he'd worn fighting the storm. She scooped them up and went out. The deck was deserted. No one even stood at the helm.

She draped his wet clothes over a barrel in the sun and went into the galley to find something to eat. Tiptoeing, so as not to disturb the cook who slumbered in his hammock, she raided a half-empty barrel of apples in one corner, and broke off a hunk of bread. After making herself comfortable at the prow of the ship, she ate in the sunlight with the breeze in her face.

In the distance, the waterspout of a whale blew white foam into the air. The sheer stillness whispered peace into her heart. She saw the allure and the splendor of the sea, both its danger and beauty. Here she was truly free from the stifling strictures of society. This must be why Jared loved the sea.

How she wished she could share this with Colin, minus Leandro and battles and danger, of course. With such a fascination with pirates and everything about sailing, Colin's eyes would shine in wonder. She pictured him scampering about the deck and asking questions of everyone.

Perhaps when she arrived home, they could take a ship to Ireland or France, and give him something to feed his adventurous soul. After all, she'd dreamed of travel as a child, something she and her father had planned to do when the war ended. Colin harbored the same dreams. Soon, she would indulge them. Perhaps Jared would accompany them. She sighed at the wistful hope.

Then she wondered how Colin fared and if he were well.

Of course he was well. His nurse loved him like her own son. In fact, he had the fierce protectiveness and devotion of the entire household. They would care for him until her return.

"Mrs. Berkley."

She smiled up at the first mate. "I was beginning to think you'd all jumped ship, Monsieur Dubois."

The Frenchman grinned. "We sleep late after fighting the storm so long. And we got separated from the *Venture,* so we put down anchor to wait for her to find us. If not, we'll turn back for her and send up signals."

She raised her brow. "Loyalty among pirates? I assumed it was every man for himself."

Dubois squinted up at the sunlight, his weathered face puckering. "The captain has his own set of ethics. We are a sort of brotherhood. We never leave ours behind." He gazed out over the horizon. "In Havana, Anakoni and I were captured and stood trial. Long story. But the captain led a raid to free us before we were hanged."

Elise could easily imagine Jared brandishing his sword and rushing recklessly into a fight. "I see. So murder and plunder are acceptable, but abandoning shipmates is not?"

"You don't know our good captain well, do you?"

Bleakly, she shook her head. "I don't know him at all. He's not the man I thought."

He watched her. "You think because he's a pirate, he has no heart. No conscience. You're wrong. He has no thirst for blood. He's determined, smart, resourceful. He always gets what he seeks, and he gets it in the most efficient possible way."

"Regardless of whom he hurts."

Dubois studied her for so long that she grew uncomfortable. "Do you know anyone who never hurts someone? Rich landowners living in wealth to rival your king while his tenants live in poverty? Factory owners who care nothing for the women and children who work long hours and die caught in their machines? Is what we do even as bad?" His faintly French accent lilted his words.

"But you kill," she protested.

"*Oui*, sometimes, but most surrender without a fight the moment they see our captain's flag. When they heave to and let us board, we only take cargo and supplies, not hurt the crew."

"And if they resist?"

"We cripple the ship, make much smoke, board during the confusion. Once we are aboard, their captain usually surrenders."

"But all those stories about Black Jack torturing those who resist him..."

Dubois chuckled. "Aye, good stories, *non*? They aid in the deception. Captains surrender without a fight if they think resistance is both useless and will guarantee a painful death. No fighting means no one gets hurt on either ship."

She blinked. "Then they aren't true?"

He sobered as he realized she was in earnest. "I've known Jack since before he took command of the *Mistress*. Been at his side at every battle. Never

253

saw him torture anyone. We spread those stories ourselves when in port." He grinned. "His brother told the best stories."

She digested his words. All those tales were fictional. Mere stories so lives would be spared. She looked out over the water. Jared hadn't tortured anyone. He hadn't killed them slowly and painfully to make an example of them. He'd only created those tales to prevent bloodshed.

She should have known.

"But you steal. It's wrong." When he appeared unmoved, she tried a different argument. "Don't you worry that you'll hang?"

"Death is inevitable. For a sailor, it comes quickly. We face storms, uncharted shoals, and sandbars, and disease such as scurvy, dysentery, and smallpox." He shrugged. "Hanging is a small threat."

"If life as a sailor is so bad, then why do you do it?"

"It's all we know. Some of us are craftsmen; carpenters and such, but most served in the navy or on a privateer during the war. Wages were low, the officers had absolute rule and many were cruel. Living conditions were very bad. Sometimes we went months before we found fresh water. Often food ran out or spoiled. We were kept prisoner on board while at port. But never for the officers, oh, no, they never suffered."

He toyed with the hem of his coat. "But on a pirate ship, we are all equal. We sign articles of agreement which promise equal share of the plunder. Now we never go hungry or lack for water because we take provisions from ships we board, or we head for land. The captain is no better than anyone else aboard. We have wealth. There is no cruel punishment on the whim of an officer. The only time we obey the captain without question is during battle. Otherwise, we all decide what we do."

"I had no idea."

"Our captain's one of the few men aboard who can navigate, work a quadrant, and read charts. He can steer a steady course. He knows where the best shipping routes are, understands trade winds and currents. He's aggressive, but not reckless. Never risks men unnecessarily. We follow him because we choose to. It's why we elected him captain."

Elise blinked. "You elected him captain?"

"*Oui.* It is a democratic system."

Perhaps she'd had too much sun, but she actually understood his reasoning. She knew the war had left many military and navy men unemployed. If the picture Dubois painted of life aboard a civilized ship had really been so bad, she understood the lure of a ship offering equal say and equal division.

Elise idly watched sailors who appeared and saw to their duties.

Dubois gestured to a young, fit man wearing a knotted scarf around his head to protect it from the sun. He stood several inches shorter than the others but had a broader chest and shoulders. "Dawson, there, was an indentured servant before he joined us. This is freedom for him. We rescued him from a ship we plundered." Dubois gestured to another. "Now Anakoni, he is quartermaster. He divides up plunder. He keeps everyone honest. He can read and do figuring faster than anyone I ever saw."

Anakoni had rich brown skin and untamed black hair. Elise recognized his name from the conversation she'd overheard in Port Johns. The quartermaster looked like a boy not even old enough to shave, perhaps the same age as O'Brian. Dubois indicated an enormous man with shining, black skin. "The gunner makes sure we have all the weapons we need and that they stay in working condition. He ensures there's enough gunpowder and cannon balls.

He also commands the gun crews during battle."

"Everyone looks so young."

"Aye. Most are in their teens or twenties. A sailor's life is too grueling for many. I'm the oldest aboard."

"You don't look much over thirty."

"Only just." Something caught his eye, and he inclined his head in a brief bow. "Excuse me, *madame*, but I have duties as well." He joined the surprisingly orderly ship's operations.

She tried to stay out of everyone's way, amazed they were so industrious. She'd imagined pirates an indolent lot. According to the stories, many pirates had been captured or killed because they'd been too drunk to fight. Whenever she pictured pirate ships, she'd envisioned floating dens of sin and debauchery. But no other women were on board. She saw no signs of gambling or riotous living. These men were hard-working sailors first and thieves second.

At noon, she ate a cold luncheon in the galley, chatting with the cook who'd lost both an eye and a leg. Disease had pocked and scarred his face, but he spoke to her with courtesy she did not expect to find from such a frightening-looking man. After she finished, she went back up on deck.

O'Brian made a seat for her near the prow of the ship and brought her a coat. "It's a fine wind. Don't be chilled."

She smiled up at him. "You're very kind."

Blushing, he stammered, "A pleasure, ma'am."

"How old are you?"

"I'm about seventeen, ma'am."

"Don't you know?"

He looked away. "I come from murky origins."

"No matter. You are a fine young man and I'm grateful to you. I see why the captain thinks highly of you."

He blinked and a slow look of joy overcame his

features. He squared his shoulders and actually puffed out his chest.

"I'm glad you're seeing to her comforts, O'Brian. I knew I could depend upon you."

Elise inwardly groaned at the way her heart fluttered at the sound of Jared's voice. Wearing his smug, lazy smile, he lounged with his arms folded, one shoulder resting against the nearest mast. His shirt whipped around him in the wind and his skin-tight breeches hugged his long, muscular legs.

O'Brian murmured something about seeing to his duties and beat a hasty retreat.

Jared prowled closer, looking very predatory. How could a barefoot man appear so dangerous?

He stopped an arm's length away and smiled down at her as if she were the most beautiful woman alive. She couldn't help but return the smile.

"You were gone when I awoke. I missed you." He reached out and tucked a strand of hair behind her ear. His thumb traced a line down her cheek; tender, intimate, possessive, invoking eddies of pleasure.

As she looked up at him looming over her, feeling safe rather than threatened, she realized she still loved this man. Desperately, completely. He made her feel cherished. Protected. Desirable. Loved.

She loved him.

She loved him despite the shadows of his profession. He would stand between her and all danger. She would do the same for him. Loving him did not catch her in a trap. It freed her.

She looked away lest he see the tears in her eyes. Other women prided themselves on crying at will to appear poetic, or romantic, or to coerce others into bending to their whim. Elise prided herself on her decorum yet Jared turned her into a weeping ninny.

Absently watching a crewman mop the planks of

the deck, she said, "You certainly keep your ship clean, Captain."

He grinned. "You expected a slovenly bunch, no doubt. To be honest, we don't swab the deck to keep it clean; we do it to keep it wet."

"Why?"

"Dry wood shrinks. Shrunken wood makes big cracks. I swim well, but not enough to get me all the way to land. Do you?"

"I don't swim at all."

"You don't know what you're missing. I spent a great deal of my youth in the lake." He held out a hand. "I need to go to my cabin for a moment. Would you care to get out of the sun?"

She took his hand. "I would."

Inside the captain's quarters, Jared spread out a map and weighted the edges while he studied it. Elise perused his library.

She took up a book and settled down to read, but found it more interesting to watch Jared. The men came freely in and out as if they had as much a right to the cabin as he. They spoke with him regarding the ship, asking his opinion, informing him of matters. They never asked his permission, but sought his approval, nonetheless. The crew might see themselves as equals on the ship, but they deferred to his judgment.

She followed him back up to the quarterdeck. He raised an astrolabe to the horizon and sighted along it. After checking the reading and then both a timepiece and compass, he looked over the Nautical Almanac and carefully recorded his readings in a log.

"Is something wrong?" Elise ventured.

"Finding our bearings after a storm can be tricky. It's difficult to determine how far off course we've been blown."

At high noon, Jared checked the sextant, a

timepiece, and compass again, and made a chalk mark on a chart.

He looked up at Dubois with a wry smile. "Just my best guess, but I think I know where we are. I used dead reckoning too, and both came in pretty close."

Dubois shrugged. "I'd trust your best guess."

"My brother does this better," Jared admitted.

"The *Venture*!" called a lookout.

Jared let out his breath in relief. "She weathered the storm."

Elise smiled in bemusement. Yesterday, they'd been trying to kill one another. She'd never understand men.

The *Venture* drew alongside and Jared leaped gracefully over to the other ship where the other crew crowded around him. "Are all hands accounted for?"

As they spoke animatedly, Elise shook her head, part puzzled, part amused. They were ill-kempt and rough-looking, but failed to fit the image she'd conjured of pirates. None looked particularly evil or bloodthirsty. They didn't appear to be contemplating murdering Jared. They looked happy to see him. Although, most of Leandro's crew had probably died in the bloodbath as the two pirate captains and crews battled. From what she'd heard, Leandro's crew had suffered heavier casualties than Jared's.

Jared laughed and talked with them, perfectly relaxed. He exuded confidence, authority, and an air of dignity the others lacked. Otherwise, except for his handsome face, he seemed little different than the others. He fit in with them as easily as he fit in with the landed gentry.

Did he play a role when he played the gentleman?

Or when he played the pirate?

How could one ever know? The man was a

human chameleon.

Jared leaped back to the *Mistress* with the power and grace of a great cat, landing lightly on deck. Some of the men traded places on the ships as they discussed damage the storm caused. Jared gave the heading to the man holding the wheel and Dubois relayed the course to the other ship. Jared winked at her and returned to his work.

He was always moving, always active, working right along side his crew, as hard at work as they. She saw him amid the men hoisting a sail, or moving ropes she'd been informed were called 'lines.' He climbed the rigging at dizzying heights.

Jared's eyes sought her often, his face always softening, and sometimes when he passed by her, he touched her surreptitiously. Other times, he stopped to speak with her. Either Dubois or O'Brian checked on her frequently to inquire as to her needs.

Late that afternoon, the lookout called from above, "Land ho!"

Amid a flurry of activity spurred by the announcement, Elise shaded her eyes and looked out over the prow.

Jared shimmied down a rope and dropped lightly on deck, calling out orders to the helmsmen.

Elise watched the land draw steadily closer, thinking she'd never seen such an inhospitable-looking place.

Jared appeared next to her. "Our safe harbor."

"This is where you go when you aren't plundering?" Then she winced. She hadn't meant it to sound so harsh or judgmental.

He did not appear disturbed by her choice of words. "Our haven. Not exactly paradise, but it serves our needs."

"Don't you worry the navy will find you here?"

"We're several leagues off a main shipping route. The lee side of the island, what we see now, looks totally uninhabitable, so even if someone were to get off course, they'd never look twice at this place. The cove and the habitable part lay on the other side. The cove is deep enough for the *Sea Mistress* and sloops like the *Venture*, but not deep enough for a navy frigate. There are also several off-shore shoals which can be tricky to navigate if you aren't familiar with them."

By the time they'd rounded the island, darkness had fallen. Lights dotted the darkened land. As they put down anchor in the harbor and made ready to disembark, the men gathered up personal effects and pulled on coats and boots while others lowered longboats.

Jared steadied her as she stepped into the longboat. She sat between Jared and young O'Brian, with Dubois at the prow. Moonlight rippled on the water and the oars made a soft sloshing sound as they rowed toward shore. The winking lights grew progressively larger and brighter. As they reached the island, several men jumped out and pulled the longboats up onto the beach. The sand made a scraping sound on the bottom of the boat.

Jared's hand steadied her as she stepped out. "This way." He put a hand under her elbow and guided her, holding up a lantern.

He led her through the darkness with the men tramping behind, following a path through overgrown vegetation. Jared, O'Brian and Dubois parted branches and held them aside for her to pass through so nothing touched her. After climbing a steady rise, they broke through the brush to a clearing. Lights and music greeted them. Small buildings crouched drunkenly along the road, light spilling out of their shuttered windows to illuminate patches of the bare ground.

All the men broke off into different directions, calling out farewells, or predictions of the greeting they anticipated receiving. A group of the men headed for the open doors of a large, noisy tavern with tawdry women lounging about in various inviting poses that made Elise's cheeks burn.

She and Jared were alone by the time they arrived in front of a two-story building at the end of the road.

Jared opened the door. "Home. Sometimes."

"You live here?"

"I only come to the island for repairs and to sell my plunder. I sleep at the tavern while I'm here. There are several rooms on the second floor."

Alarm arose and she took an involuntary step back. "You don't sleep in a brothel, do you?"

Amusement danced in his face. "You'd be surprised where I've slept. But seriously, I would never bring you to a brothel. It's a perfectly respectable tavern with soft beds and decent food. The locals come for the exceptional ale."

Despite the tavern's poor illumination, she could see several tables filling the room. Smoke hung in the air, mingled with the pungent odor of bodies, tar and cheap wine. Underneath the unpleasant odors, she caught the smell of onions, beef and a faint hint of basil.

"Jack! Yer 'ome!" A portly woman with a broad, toothless grin lumbered to Jared and clapped his arm.

"How's business, Nan?" Jared asked in a hearty voice.

"Can't complain. 'Ungry?"

"Aye. Bring us a bowl of whatever you've got that smells so good."

She chuckled. "Don't never get 'customed to yer fancy talk, Jack. Ye almost sound like a confounded gentleman." Her gaze slid to Elise.

"Mrs. Berkley, meet Nan," Jared said by way of introduction.

Elise nodded.

Nan eyed her slowly with a look of speculation. "Welcome, Mrs. Berkley." After sending Jared a sly smile, she trundled off into another room.

Jared exchanged greetings with two men drinking. At another table, three men played cards. Jared guided Elise to a vacant table as Nan returned balancing two bowls of stew and a board of bread. Elise tasted the stew and looked up at Nan who hovered expectantly.

"It's very good, thank you," Elise said.

Nan's toothless grin appeared again. "Glad ta 'ear it." She turned to Jared. "Lor, Jack, she talks jus' like ye. Ye gonna give up a-piratin' and settle down wiff 'er?"

Jared grinned and glanced at Elise before returning his gaze to Nan. "What makes you think she'll have the likes of me?"

Nan snorted. "Shor, Jack, she ain't blind. I'd take ye and I'm old 'nuff to be yer dam."

Elise choked on her bread. Nan waddled off to bring more drinks to the other patrons.

After they finished their dinner, Jared took a lamp and led her upstairs under Nan's knowing grin. Elise's cheeks heated in embarrassment, knowing Nan assumed they were lovers.

Elise found the idea not objectionable.

She stole a glance at Jared as he unlocked a door at the end of the passageway.

He stepped back and waited for her to precede him. "This is my room."

"You have your own room? You must be a generous customer."

"I own the place. Nan just runs it for me. The agreement was a fifty-fifty split, but she hasn't paid me my honest portion in years. Still, I always have a room and a meal when I come, and I can trust her. Except with my money." He set the lantern on a small table.

Elise found the room clean and aired, with a large, comfortable bed. The linens appeared freshly laundered and crisp.

Jared opened the window and leaned out for a long time, silhouetted by the pale moon. He turned back and looked at her thoughtfully, leaning against the windowsill. The sound of the waves crashing on the beach reached her ears, and a gentle, balmy breeze flitted in, stirring the curtains.

"I don't dare sleep in the room next door. We're on the second floor so the casual passerby wouldn't think of entering. Still, a ladder would make for an easy climb. And this is the first night on land, so there's likely to be a lot of revelry. There might be trouble."

The wolfish, plotting pirate with seduction on his mind was nowhere to be found. In his place stood a gentleman who hesitated, torn between wishing to honor her sensibilities and what he thought he had to do to protect her from others.

She should assure him she would be well here in her own room and remind him she could always call out for help if she needed aid. Yet she wanted him near. She'd grown accustomed to having him next to her, curling up against him, listening to the sound of his breathing. She trusted him. He hadn't ravished her before. He wouldn't do it now.

But if he tried seduction, would she have the fortitude to resist? Did she care?

She moistened her lips. "Perhaps you should stay here."

He gazed steadily at her. "I shouldn't be here. You shouldn't trust me."

She held back a smile. "No, indeed. You are indisputably a rogue and a pirate."

"I'll sleep on the floor." With disappointment in his eyes, he pushed off from the window and pulled a blanket off the bed.

She put a hand on his arm, halting him. "If you give me your word you'll continue to behave as a gentleman, you may sleep on the bed."

He eyed her, part hopeful, part disbelieving. "I won't lay a hand on you."

"Perhaps I am a bit touched in the head, but I do trust you," she whispered.

Gratitude and relief leaped into his eyes. He skimmed one finger down the side of her face. Then one corner of his mouth lifted in a wry smile. "Your trust doesn't say much for my virility."

"I doubt there's any question of that."

"Men don't normally like to be told by a beautiful woman that she trusts him not to seduce her while they're sleeping in the same bed."

She couldn't help but smile. "Yes, I know. You want to be seen as a dangerous rake. But even though I believed that of you at first, I think that was just another act."

"Another act?"

"You seem to play many roles. You seldom let down your guard and show your true self."

Jared digested her words silently. "You're surprisingly astute." He stood lost in thought, and she wished she understood this man she loved. He slipped into his irrepressible pirate persona and grinned wickedly. "But remember that there's a limit to my ability to withstand temptation."

She nodded, only barely repressing a smile.

Jared sat on the bed and pulled off his boots. "You needn't fear for your reputation. No one here has ever mingled with the *beau monde*. Word of your circumstances here will never reach the ears of polite company."

"I daresay, my reputation is already tarnished. Once it's discovered I've been captured by pirates, people will assume I'm a fallen woman."

He looked sharply at her. "Will they make trouble for you?"

"I'm a widow. The scandal won't be as damaging as if I were an unmarried miss."

He leaned over and rested his arms on his thighs. "I'm sorry you got dragged into this. Because of me, Leandro took you from your home and your son. He frightened you. Ruined you socially."

"My true friends will stand by me. Lady Standwich will probably view it all as a great adventure. And she's influential enough that if she remains my ally, the others will eventually come around. And Charlotte Greymore will be at my side. My questionable adventure will be forgotten by the time Colin is old enough to be affected by it."

She tried to keep her tone light, but she knew she would be given the cut direct by many. The reputation of a fallen woman and the inevitable rejection would not only hurt her, but may affect Colin's future. Probably more than she could predict.

Jared sat with his head in his hands. "It's my fault. I knew Leandro was after me. That you'd be in danger if he found me again. I should have stayed away. Kept you safe. He could have killed you. Or let his men have you. They could have hurt your son." The last word was spoken with dismay.

She sat next to him on the bed and rubbed circles on his back. His muscles tensed under her hand.

"I hold you blameless."

He looked away. After a moment, he stood and pulled his shirt over his head. "Don't hog the covers again." His gruff tone failed to fool her.

"Perhaps you'd stay warmer if you wore more to bed."

The irrepressible rake reappeared. "I can think of more interesting ways to stay warm."

"I'll just bet you can, you cad. Where's my

candlestick?"

He chuckled, his tension dissolving.

They lay on opposite sides of the bed, wrapped in separate blankets, but by morning, Elise found herself cradled within his arms. She opened her eyes to see him watching her.

Something akin to pain crossed his features. He rolled away and got up. "I need a bucket of cold water."

Elise arose and watched out the window as Jared stalked away amid the townspeople who carried out their tasks like in any other town. People of every color and manner of dress strolled about and she caught snatches of conversation in a dozen different languages. The buildings were all newer, and more sloppily built than Port Johns, but everything else seemed the same. She saw a fishmonger, a baker, a tanner, heard the clanging noises of a smith, everything one would normally find in a town like Brenniswick. Oddly, she felt at home in this simple, quiet place which harbored pirates.

Briefly, she wondered if she could live here. If Jared asked her to stay here with him, would she be able to give up her life as the widow of a gentleman, and live as the wife of a pirate? For Colin's sake, she couldn't. He deserved an education and a future.

But if she were alone, without the responsibility of a child?

The answer would be a resounding yes. She'd stay with Jared. Whether here on the island, or on board his ship, it mattered little. She wanted to be with him. She would gladly give up her safe, stifling world for him.

She turned from the window. It didn't matter. Since they'd left England, Jared had not professed love, nor had he asked her to stay with him. He desired her. Perhaps even cared for her. But nothing suggested he meant to settle down. On his ship, he was totally free, unbound the by the strictures of polite society, and he was respected by his men. She doubted very much he'd give it up for her. Or anyone, for that matter.

Elise saw to her morning washing, dressing and grooming to the best of her ability, a fruitless effort considering she hadn't changed her gown in a week and had no toiletries of any kind. After seeing to her personal needs, she went downstairs to find a nearly deserted room.

Flecks of dust swam in the sunlight streaming through the open door and windows. From outside came the stamp and cries of animals, voices of shopkeepers and customers, the occasional rattle of a wagon or cart, the shouts and laughter of children.

Nan lumbered about trimming the lamps and wiping off tables. She greeted Elise with a grin, the effort distorting her wrinkled face. "Morning, yer ladyship. Don't have nothin' fancy, but there's fruit and bread, if yer 'ungry." She motioned to a table in the far corner near a window.

"Thank you, Nan. I am hungry." Elise sat. Since no silverware graced the table, she ate with her fingers, feeling oddly barbaric.

"I 'spect yer be wantin' a bath, too?"

"That would be lovely. I don't suppose it would be possible to also find a change of clothes?"

She heard a footstep at the door a moment before Jared's voice rang out. "It's possible." He tossed a bundle of clothing to her lap. "Not what you're accustomed to, I'm sure, but it's clean. Nan here would be happy to wash your things."

Elise's eyes flew to him. The man was simply stunning. Her heart beat a quick staccato. Then he grinned and her heart nearly leaped from her breast.

She wondered again if he'd been truthful about truly being Jared Amesbury. In a moment of clarity, she realized it didn't matter. She didn't care if his father was a duke or a cobbler or a highwayman. She wanted to know about his family, where he'd grown up, what had driven him to this risky, illegal way of life. She wished to understand him, to know him, to see him when he did not play a charade. But whether his blood flowed from common or royal origins, it mattered not. She loved him as he was.

Nan stood. "I'll just go get some water aheatin' for yer bath, and wash yer things while ye git clean."

Jared pulled a chair out, flipped it around backwards and straddled it. His hair had gone wild, and a week's worth of beard darkened his face. He wore an open shirt and breeches, with a sword on one side and a gun on the other. She wondered how many of their friends would even recognize the man they knew as Jared Amesbury. He tore off a hunk of bread with his fingers and stuffed it into his mouth. He seemed to be deliberately immersing himself into the uncivilized pirate guise.

Elise set down her cup and leaned back in her chair. "Who are you when you aren't playing a role?"

He froze, his eyes locked with hers while suspicion and wariness leaped into the depths of his aquamarine gaze. Remembering himself, he finished chewing.

When he made no reply, she added, "When you played the earl's son, you seemed quite convincing, but there were moments when I could tell it did not come quite as naturally as you attempted to portray. And now, again, you seem to be trying too hard to project an image that isn't quite who you are. So, who are you really?"

He glanced in the direction Nan had gone and replied in a hushed voice. "I have no idea. I haven't seen the real me in years." He leaped to his feet. "I need to see to the ship." At the door he paused, "For your own safety, stay near the tavern. There are

Donna Hatch

worse reprobates than I who live here. Nan will get you anything you want. I'll return for you when I can."

Jared strode out the door in graceful, silent strides, but Elise couldn't shake the impression that he'd fled scared.

Nan re-entered the room, humming off-key. "Never thought I'd see our good cap'n fall for the charms of a lady." She snickered. " 'E's fallen hard, 'e 'as."

"I doubt very much he's fallen for me, Nan."

" 'E's never brought 'nother lady 'ome, I kin tell ye that."

"The circumstances of my presence here are somewhat unique."

"Not just that, yer ladyship. It's the way 'e looks at ye. Oh, 'e don't want to, but 'e is."

"He is...?"

"In love wit' ye."

Elise looked away.

"And yer in love wit' 'im just as much, but yer scart. 'E's not the man ye thought ye wanted. Least, not on the outside. But in 'ere," she tapped her chest in the proximity of her heart. "In 'ere, 'e's a right good man. Better 'n most." She hummed off key as she trimmed the lamps and swept the floor.

After eating her fill, Elise arose. "Thank you for breakfast."

Nan paused with the broom in her hand. "Yer bath water's warm. Ye kin bathe in the kitchen, I'll stand watch out 'ere. Leave yer things to be washed and I'll see to 'em."

"You're very kind."

Nan shrugged and made a pshaw sound. "Jack gave me the place and don't never ask for 'is share back. Just wants food and a place to sleep, when 'e come, is all. Least I kin do is take care of 'is lady."

Elise murmured something appropriate, she

270

hoped, and went into the kitchen. She sank in the warm tub, thinking she'd never felt so heavenly in her life. The soap was rough and unscented, and the tub too small to truly immerse herself, but having clean skin eclipsed any disappointment that may have arisen from the unsophisticated surroundings.

Nan came in humming, scooped up Elise's discarded clothing, and went outside.

After scrubbing her skin and hair, Elise dried and dressed. Jared had been most thorough. In the bundle he'd brought her, she found all the appropriate undergarments and a gown which fit reasonably well. Simple and unadorned, but clean.

She wondered if Jared had enlisted help, or if he truly knew this much about a woman's unmentionables. Whatever else he was, the man she knew as Jared certainly had moments of thoughtfulness. A great number of them, truth be told.

If only she could sail away with him forever and be totally free.

CHAPTER 21

Jared glanced down at Elise. She leaned on the bulwark into the wind, smiling slightly as the salt sprayed her face. Several strands of hair had escaped the braid hanging down her back and blew about her riotously. He liked the less-than-immaculately coiffed Elise standing next to him even better than the perfect lady in England.

"Colin would love this," she mused.

"I'll have you home within the week," Jared assured her.

She looked up at him searchingly. "I have to admit, I am beginning to understand why you love the sea. Minus the danger of storms and reefs, of course."

"Of course." His smile warmed her.

They'd restocked the ship on the island, made arrangements for Leandro's former ship to be refitted, and departed for England.

He ached to tell her the truth about himself; that he served his country as a spy for the crown. That he wasn't really a pirate. But if the crew learned his plan to turn the ship over to the authorities and that he'd negotiated for the end to their way of life, they'd shoot him immediately. Or worse. Sailors had any number of horrible and painful ways to administer death. He knew they would not hesitate to use one of those methods upon him.

Except possibly Dubois. The man had been a good friend from the beginning, but Jared could not predict with any confidence what Dubois would do when faced with the truth about his captain. Would he cheerfully agree to the terms of the pardon, thanking his fortune that he was being spared the noose? Or would he give Jared a cold stare and condemn him as a traitor to their brotherhood?

Either way, his friendship with the Frenchman would soon come to an end. The knowledge filled him with a hollow pain.

And Elise, how would she react when he told her? Women were unpredictable. Would she be angry he'd kept such a big secret from her? She appeared to have affection for him, even though she believed him to be a pirate. If that were true, her love would be boundless.

Soon, they'd be in England and he'd tell her everything. Once she knew the truth, his heart would be completely at her mercy. He would be asking her to marry his very flawed self, which might be difficult for her to accept in a husband.

"You're looking very serious, Captain." Elise's soft voice washed over him.

"Sail ho!" the lookout called.

"Where away?" Jared shouted up.

"Fine on the larboard bow."

Jared grabbed his spyglass. He focused the glass on the sails and waited for them to come near enough to reveal their ship's identity. If she were a merchant ship, his crew would demand they take her. Jared could not condone the act. Not now.

The other ship approached. It wasn't a merchant ship, but something far worse. His stomach gave a lurch.

Dubois appeared at his side. "Is that what I think it is?"

Jared swore under his breath. "British Navy."

"All hands on deck!" Dubois ordered.

With pounding heart, Jared thrust the glass back and ran to the captain's quarters, swearing all the way.

The arrival of the navy could not have come at a worse time. In a few days, this ship would be sold, refitted, and employed in honest work, and he would return to being Jared Amesbury the gentleman. His crew would be pardoned and given enough money to find legitimate employment.

The Secret Service had made no promises for intervention if he were apprehended and tried for piracy. He fit into the category of a non-uniformed spy, which meant no aid would come if he were in danger. Moreover, his mission technically ended the moment he and Greymore exposed Von Barondy as O Ladrão. Everything he'd done since then had been without orders from the Secret Service. They'd view him as a renegade. A pirate.

If he couldn't outrun the frigate, he'd be forced to stand and fight his own countrymen. Otherwise, they would be captured and executed. He would die with his crew.

He unlocked his trunk and fished through the different flags he stowed there. He chose a Portuguese flag. To his knowledge, the British Navy had no particular quarrel with Portugal, nor would there be much chance anyone on board the naval ship could speak the language. He ran back up and handed it off, shouting for it to be hoisted immediately.

"Gutierrez, make yourself visible. You, too, Anakoni!" Anakoni's Hawaiian features would help him pass for a Portuguese man. Jared hoped. "Pray they see our Portuguese flag and nothing else," he added to no one in particular.

"Why?" Elise asked.

"Because we don't look like a merchant ship."

"What do we look like?"

"A ship built for speed and modified to carry more guns. A pirate ship. We're a lot bigger than the normal pirate sloop, but if they take a good look, they'll figure it out."

"Why not just raise a British flag?"

"Because they might come over to socialize. Or exchange mail. And we do not want to get friendly with them."

He'd rather draw a knife across his own wrist than fight the British Navy. He couldn't bear the thought of firing upon his own countrymen, nor did he wish to risk injury and death to his crew.

And Elise. Between shot, flying debris, gunfire, and the risk of fire or sinking, she could be harmed. The thought left him cold and shaking.

He'd been forced to fire on the *Venture* while Leandro held Elise prisoner, and had ordered the gunners keep their fire away from the proximity of the foremast where she'd been tied.

The navy had no reason to have a care with their aim.

He whirled to face Elise, noting she wore the clothing he'd gotten for her on the island. "Go change into your gown. You need to be dressed as a lady. O'Brian!"

"Sir?"

"If they come after us, we'll try to outrun them. If they engage us in battle, take Mrs. Berkley on the longboat and head away from us. When it's over, come back. If we lose, flag down the frigate and get her on board. Tell them you helped her escape during the battle."

"You're asking me to desert you?" O'Brian said, aghast.

"I'm asking you to protect the lady."

"I am not abandoning you," Elise said with a determined glare.

Both men ignored her.

"I could take her to the island we passed an hour ago." O'Brian gestured over his shoulder.

Jared shook his head. "It's uninhabited and it may be weeks or months before a ship passes by and can pick her up."

Elise folded her arms. "I am not jumping ship."

Jared looked steadily at her. "Tell the navy captain you were my prisoner and O'Brian helped you." To O'Brian, he said, "If you're charged with piracy, you can become the king's witness and testify against us."

O'Brian paled. "You want me to betray my own shipmates?"

Elise grabbed Jared's arm, her eyes narrowed in indignation. "I am not—"

"Elise!" Tension made him speak more harshly than he'd intended. He took her hand and softened his voice. "We may not have to resort to that. I'm just trying to think of the worst possible situation. If we have to fight, you cannot stand with us."

"I can help. I can shoot a gun, you know I can."

"And fire upon your own countrymen? Your friends' brothers? Their husbands? Their sons?"

She froze. The determined glint in her eye faded. "I...I don't want to leave you."

"Are you willing to die here with us? Or later at the gibbet?"

She paled.

"Think of Colin. You must get home. He needs his mother."

Her features crumpled in agony.

"She's changed her heading, sir," reported the lookout. "Intercept course."

Dubois, who'd been silent throughout the exchange, glanced at Jared. "Retreat?"

"Run!"

The Frenchman shouted orders. A cacophony of voices and running feet erupted as they adjusted the lines, changing the sails until the ship heeled. Jared called out the coordinates and they laid in a course for the island they'd just passed. He hoped to hide there among the many inlets and outlets, if they could get there in time.

With all sails unfurled, and her superior sleek design built to outrun an enemy, the *Sea Mistress* pulled ahead.

The navy frigate gave chase, but fell behind. The tightness in Jared's chest did not ease.

Dubois watched him narrowly. "It appears we've lost them."

"It does appear so."

"But?"

Jared shook his head, uneasiness tying in knots in his gut. Grimly, Dubois drummed his fingers on the bulwark.

Less than an hour later, the island they'd passed that morning came into view. Careful of the shallows and an offshore reef, they headed around the end of the island toward one of the many inlets; a perfect hiding place they'd often used in the past. They rounded the tip of the island.

And sailed right into the waiting guns of another navy frigate.

Jared's heart dropped. This would not end well.

In minutes, the first frigate would catch up to them, and they'd be hopelessly outgunned with nowhere to run.

He glanced back at Elise. Wearing her afternoon gown and slippers, Elise sat under a sail rigged as shade on the quarterdeck. She pulled her eyes from the frigate and met Jared's gaze, her face ashen.

"O'Brian! Now!" Jared shouted.

"Aye, sir." The boy moved toward Elise.

The frigate guns fired, and a spread of shot landed a few feet from the bowsprit, sending a spray of water upward like a geyser.

Jared shouted orders he'd hoped, only hours ago, he would never again have to say. "Clear the deck and spread the sand. Douse the galley—" He stopped mid-sentence.

All hands froze. Every head turned to him, waiting.

He drew a breath and looked each one of them in the eye while a second volley from the frigate fell into the ocean.

"Gentlemen. We face two British Naval frigates. We are outnumbered and outgunned. We could surrender and throw ourselves upon the mercy of the law."

A few nervous chuckles came in reply.

"We can fight, most certainly to the death. Or you can take the longboats and jump ship. You might make it to the island."

Another volley hurled toward them. One landed at the bow, tearing into the bulwark of the forecastle. The *Mistress* pitched slightly. No one moved. The faces of the men revealed their indecision and fear.

Jared swallowed against a dry throat. "Know this. No matter what you each decide, it's been a pleasure to know you." He turned. "Raise our true colors!"

Someone hoisted Black Jack's colors, a blood-red dagger on a black field. An unreasonable surge of pride swelled at the sight of his ensign waving defiantly in the wind.

Three hands jumped ship and rowed toward the island. The rest prepared for battle. For death. They understood no quarter would be given.

Jared seized Elise and crushed her to him, molding her body to his and plundering her mouth in a fierce, possessive kiss. When he released her, she stood stunned and shaken. Tears filled her eyes.

He cupped her face. "Tell Greymore what's happened. He'll notify my family."

She nodded while tears streamed down her

cheeks.

"Go home to your son, Mrs. Berkley." He thrust her into O'Brian's arms. "I'm counting on you, lad."

"I won't fail you, sir."

"Do not, under any circumstances, board any ship during the battle."

Gravely, O'Brian shook his head.

A longboat cast in the water near a naval battle would be a perilous place, but on board any ship while being fired upon by another, would be worse. Jared turned away and gave the order to prepare the guns.

The master gunner called, "Cut loose the guns and remove the tampions!" After the gun crews ran to remove the plugs protecting the muzzles, the gunner ordered, "Run out your guns!"

Jared glanced over his shoulder to see O'Brian guiding Elise to a longboat. "Fire at will," he ordered.

"Fire as your guns bear!" shouted the gunner.

Jared braced himself for the concussion as the gun crews on the port side of the *Sea Mistress* lit the fuses and sent their projectiles toward the frigate. Before the shot reached their target, tongues of flame flashed from the guns of the frigate and a volley sailed toward them.

The sound of the guns firing reached his ears a moment later. He held onto the bulwark, anticipating the impact. It blasted with teeth-jarring force, tearing into the hull, overturning two guns, killing and maiming their crews. Screams of the wounded and dying filled the air. Gunpowder and smoke burned eyes and nostrils.

"Right the guns and reload!" Jared ordered.

The gunner shouted at the port gun crews to reload and fire again. Several hands ran to right the upset guns while others either pulled bodies toward the center of the ship, out of the way or threw them overboard. The guns sent out another round. Their shots hit the target, but the frigate answered with its own. Wood splintered and rained down upon them. The *Sea Mistress* shivered under the onslaught. Sailors fell wounded and bleeding. Some stared sightless into the blue sky. A boy lay in pieces at his feet.

Jared refused to number the dead, or even name them. He could grieve later, should he live that long.

The *Sea Mistress* continued to fire, inflicting her own devastation on the naval ship, but the damage paled in comparison to that exacted by His Majesty's finest. Another round blasted his ship, killing the lucky ones, maiming the unlucky. The dead and wounded outnumbered the living. Throughout it all, he shouted orders and encouragement to his men. The crew struggled admirably to obey. Dubois rushed in to assist manning a gun.

When the master gunner fell during the next round, Jared leaped to take his place and kept all hands moving in a smooth rhythm of cooling, loading, and firing the guns. The *Mistress* sent out a volley that ripped a gaping hole in the broadside of the frigate and blew apart the main topmast.

The first frigate they'd been outrunning caught up to them and fired her forward guns.

Pinned between the two vessels, the *Mistress* shivered under the dual onslaught. Her mizzenmast exploded, raining wood, rigging, blocking, and torn sails upon the deck.

Then the first frigate circled, heeled sharply, and presented her broadside to the *Sea Mistress's* bow.

His heart sank. "No. Please no," Jared whispered.

She open-fired with all her starboard guns. A volley sizzled through the air and raked the *Mistress* from stem to stern.

Jared slammed into the deck. Another round from the other frigate blasted into their port broadside, destroying guns and crews. One ripped through the mainmast, sending a shower of splintering wood.

The mast twisted, hovered, and fell like a great tree. It smashed what little remained of the starboard bulwark and slid slowly across the deck, making the whole ship list dangerously.

"Cut loose the mast! Move the guns to port and tie them as a counter-weight!" Jared leaped in to work alongside his decimated crew.

Despite their efforts, the *Sea Mistress* continued to list almost horizontal. Barrels, buckets, and anything loose bumped across the deck and over the edge into the churning sea. The dead and dying slid down and disappeared beneath the waves.

Jared made a controlled slide to the mast, inched out to the rigging, and began sawing through the lines. Nimble hands rushed to assist. Freed ropes whipped through the air with whistling sounds, some floating downward to the water.

Abandoning the guns, the crew pushed at the fallen mast in an attempt to shove it overboard. Agonizingly slow, the mast slid into the water with a horrible groan. The *Mistress* hung on its side for a few heart-pounding seconds before she righted herself.

"Man the guns!" Jared shouted.

Despite their hopeless odds, his men fought with a savage ferocity he'd never seen. Dubois and Anakoni manned the guns along with three tattered remnants of gun crews. Only five of the fourteen starboard guns were operable. Jared considered moving the guns to the other side, but he lacked the manpower to operate them even if they could spare the time to move them.

Another round from the navy, and the *Mistress's*

hold filled with water, making her list drunkenly.

The smoke cleared long enough to reveal the second frigate pulling up alongside. British sailors threw grappling hooks and pulled the ships together.

Jared made a quick head count. Seventeen of his men remained standing. Seventeen out of a crew of one hundred and twenty.

The navy boarded the *Mistress* amid smoke and chaos.

Dubois rushed to Jared's side, and they stood back to back as the British swarmed on board.

Jared fired both guns and then pushed impatiently at the liquid running into his eyes. Wiping it with the back of his hand, he realized it was blood from a head wound he didn't remember receiving.

Dubois went down with a gunshot wound to the leg.

A grim-faced lieutenant engaged Jared sword-to-sword.

Jared fended him off half-heartedly. He had no quarrel with this navy officer. And what would it matter? He was defeated. How many other officers would he kill before they finally overpowered him?

The pirate inside him snarled he'd take with him as many as possible before they killed him.

The loyal Englishman within reminded him they fought on the same side, even though the navy didn't know it.

"Lieutenant, I have no desire to kill you."

The officer blinked, but never missed a beat in his swordplay. "I have no such compulsions about you, pirate scum."

Jared stepped back and dropped his sword.

The lieutenant's eyes widened.

"I am yours. You may kill me, or take me back to London and have the pleasure of seeing me hang. Your choice."

Confusion crossed the officer's face, and he lowered his weapon. "I do not kill unarmed men."

"Ah. A man of honor, just as I had hoped."

Loathing returned to his expression. "Do you surrender, pirate?"

"I do. You have the unprecedented honor of effecting Black Jack's capture."

CHAPTER 22

Half-blinded by smoke, stinging gunpowder, and her own tears, Elise struggled to climb the ladder. Her skirts kept getting in the way and her hands trembled so badly she had little success.

O'Brian climbed behind her, keeping her steady, murmuring encouragement.

Coughing and sobbing, she missed her footing, but O'Brian caught her before she fell.

Hands reached and drew her upward. Uniformed British officers helped her onto the deck of the naval ship and then roughly seized O'Brian as he climbed aboard.

"Please!" she cried. "He helped me escape. He was forced onto the ship against his will, as was I. He's innocent."

A gray-haired captain wearing gold epaulets pushed through the crowd. His shrewd gaze took in her torn gown, noting the cut and fabric. Earlier, O'Brian had suggested she tear her afternoon gown at the sleeve to further verify her story. She knew dirt and tears streaked her face, and that her hair hung unbound in riotous disarray. She could probably pass as either an uncivilized heathen or a victimized lady. At the moment, she almost didn't care which they believed. Or what they did with her. Her terror for Jared overshadowed everything else.

Then a single light of reason pierced the haze; she must get home to Colin.

He eyed her warily. "I am Captain John Randolf of His Majesty's Navy." He spoke in the clipped accent of the British gentry.

"Captain," she gasped. She took herself in hand and tried to calm herself. "I'm Elise Berkley."

Her hands shook and her voice quivered. Though her fears lay with Jared, she hoped the navy captain would attribute her distress to her harrowing experience as a prisoner of pirates.

She glanced back at the *Mistress*. Smoke hung in great clouds over a battered hull barely resembling a ship. Not a single mast remained standing. Sending another prayer heavenward for Jared's safety, she returned her attention to the captain.

"I escaped the pirate ship during the battle, with this young man's help." She indicated O'Brian. "He was pressed into service. He is innocent."

"Are you now?" the navy captain swung on O'Brian. "And what skills do you possess that would be so desirable to a pirate ship?"

"I'm a carpenter, sir. And they were in need of repairs at the time."

"So they pointed a gun at your head and told you either die or join them?"

O'Brian's ears reddened. "Something like that."

Elise's heart sank. He wasn't doing a convincing job of lying. "He feels terrible that he didn't choose an honorable death, but consider what you might have done at his age, Captain. Please, he aided me and protected me from the others. Can you not show him clemency?"

"That's for the Admiralty to decide, Ma'am."

She turned to O'Brian apologetically, but he only shrugged. Another round of coughing seized her. A gust of wind blew her skirts and hair, cleansing the smoky air with sweet, salty ocean smells.

The captain eyed her with an assessing stare. "Are you in need of a doctor, Miss Berkley?"

"No, Captain. And it's Missus. I am widowed."

She turned anxious eyes toward the *Mistress* again.

The wind blew away the smoke, but she could not spot Jared. The sight of so many bodies made her ill. She knew most of them. Unlike Leandro's sailors, Jared's had been decent men, despite their chosen profession.

Misunderstanding her fearful glances, the captain said in a gentler tone, "You are safe here under my protection, ma'am."

She heaved a shuddering breath, trying to convince herself Jared lived. "Thank you, Captain."

The captain assigned her quarters, no doubt moving some of his men around to accommodate her. She lost sight of O'Brian.

She followed a young officer below deck. Alone in a cabin barely large enough to turn around, Elise collapsed upon the bunk and wept. A wish that Jared had abandoned his honor and run away with her warred with her admiration that he'd remained behind and taken a last stand with his men.

If he lived, she'd do anything to free him, to protect him from the law, but suspected her chances of negotiating a pardon were woefully small. She wondered if Greymore could help. Or would he be horrified to learn his friend was a pirate? Not many friendships could transcend such a dangerous secret.

She pounded the bed with a fist. Why didn't she tell Jared she loved him? She might never have the chance now. She'd wasted her time with him. She would have done things differently if she'd known their days together were so limited.

She froze. His fate was her fault.

If he hadn't rescued her from Leandro, Jared would not have been at sea that day. The navy would not have captured him. The thought left her cold, and she sobbed anew.

What would she tell Colin had befallen his friend?

The portal showed a sinking sun when a knock shook the door. She opened it to find a sailor holding out a white shirt to her.

He kept his eyes averted. "The first mate thought you'd want this, Ma'am. It belongs to one of the junior officers; he's the smallest man aboard. It's a man's shirt, but it's clean and will offer you...ah... covering. And I've got fresh water for you to wash." He indicated a bucket sitting on the deck next to his feet. "The captain invited you to be his guest at dinner tonight. If your...ah...in a frame of mind to..." He trailed off, not meeting her eyes.

"May I come up for a bit of fresh air?"

"Not yet. Flogging's a messy business. No place for a lady."

Elise shivered. She certainly had no desire to witness a flogging. Thanks to Dubois, she knew discipline on a naval ship was cruel and absolute. She hoped to avoid such an example.

"What's your name, young man?"

He glanced up at her quickly and then looked away. "Murphy, ma'am."

"Thank you, Mr. Murphy. Tell me, do you know how many pirates were captured?"

He paused, "Only about a dozen, Ma'am. The rest fell in battle."

Elise's heart seized. "And...the captain...did he perish? Or is he a prisoner?"

"I'm not certain, ma'am. What shall I tell the captain?"

She fought her first inclination to refuse the dinner invitation. She did not wish to spend time in the company of the man responsible for Jared's imprisonment or—she choked—death, but this might be the best opportunity to learn of Jared's fate.

Besides, the navy captain was only doing his duty; a duty, under normal circumstances, she'd applaud.

She let out her breath in a small, mirthless laugh at her absurd heart. She resented a naval officer for serving his country. She loved a pirate. When did the world turn on end?

The sailor looked at her as if he thought her mad.

She swallowed. "Thank you, Mr. Murphy. Tell the captain I accept his generous offer."

Elise washed, combed her hair and donned the clean shirt over her torn and soiled gown. An hour later, young Mr. Murphy knocked again and led her to dinner. When she entered the officer's dining room, all the men arose, wearing crisp uniforms.

She blinked at the sumptuous surroundings. The walls were painted blue, with bright white trim. A gleaming mahogany table with silver, china and crystal filled the table in perfect order.

They treated her with cautious respect, but clearly felt awkward by her presence. They asked her polite questions, but spoke quietly to one another more than to her, an arrangement which suited Elise. She found it difficult to converse with Jared's enemies.

Once dinner had ended, the officers excused themselves and Elise found herself alone with the captain and his first officer.

"Mrs. Berkley, I know you have suffered a terrible ordeal, but it is my duty to ask you a few questions."

"Of course."

He sipped his wine. "You seem much calmer now."

"I apologize for my state of agitation when I came on board. I was overset by my experience at the hands of the pirates."

"I can imagine."

"You and your men have made me feel very safe

here. Thank you for your hospitality."

"How did you come to be in the company of pirates? Were you a passenger on board a ship?"

"Actually, no, it is a rather long story."

He exchanged glances with his first officer. "I have only time on my hands."

Elise nodded and set down her glass. "I live in Brenniswick, about a two hour carriage ride from a small town called Port Johns."

"I am acquainted with Port Johns," he said dismissively.

"The last thing I remember, I was shopping in town. Someone grabbed me from behind. Then I woke up on a ship called the *Venture* with Captain Leandro in command."

"Leandro!"

She blinked. "You know him?"

"I know of him. He's the one of the cruelest, most bloodthirsty pirates ever to curse the seas. He takes great delight in mistreating the crew of ships he plunders. Tales of his exploits are as widespread as those of Black Jack."

"I believe it." She shivered. "They were vile!"

The captain looked very grave. "If you were his prisoner..."

"They did not harm me, Captain, though I'm not certain of their reasons. Perhaps they planned to hold me for ransom. And only minutes after I awoke, they engaged in battle with the *Sea Mistress*."

"From the frying pan into the fire."

Elise's first instinct was to rise to Jared's defense and declare that he and his men never touched her. But she feared the captain would suspect she'd been in league with the pirates. They might hold her for an inquiry, or a trial. She could not allow them to detain her, thus separating her from Colin.

"I am most fortunate you happened along,

Captain. They hadn't harmed me, yet, but I was terrified. I have a seven-year-old son, and I feared I might not ever return to him."

The captain leaned back in his chair thoughtfully. "I have heard rumors that Black Jack never hurt innocents, or those who cooperate when he boards their ship. I also know that he shows no mercy to those who resist him." His expression turned thunderous.

"I believe both are true."

He appraised her searchingly. "Then you are unmolested?"

"Yes. Apparently, there is something in the articles on the *Sea Mistress* about not harming women. Although, I must confess, I could not be confident they would honor their own rules. I don't entirely trust the word of a pirate." She added the last bit in hopes that the captain would be convinced of her innocence.

"The pirates strictly enforce their articles. Offenders are punished ruthlessly. They have their own version of honor, I suppose."

"Captain, I am most anxious to return home to my son. Will I be detained in London to testify against the pirates? I understand you have some captive."

"We have eleven in the brig. Most died in battle rather than surrender and face the hangman. The Admiralty will determine whether your testimony will be needed."

Elise knew asking might sound suspicious, but she had to know if Jared lived. "Is the captain in your possession, or was he among those who perished?"

"He's in the brig. Wounded, but he'll live long enough to face trial. And hang."

Elise's heart flittered between concern that Jared was hurt, and relief that he lived.

"The blackguard. That's one hanging I'll not miss." The captain's eyes glittered.

Elise blinked, surprised at the sudden outburst. "I confess, I know little of him. Is he so notorious, then, or is this personal?"

"Both. He's cut a swath through the Caribbean and all around Africa. He boarded a ship captained by my best friend, who'd also married my sister. He wouldn't yield to the pirates, so Black Jack and his crew killed him. Left my sister widowed with two children."

She gasped. "Oh! How terrible!"

She did not doubt he spoke the truth. Jared had admitted he'd killed any who refused to cooperate. Yet meeting a victim of his actions made his actions more immediate, more horrifying. She put a hand to her head. How could she love a man who'd killed so many?

Yet, those truths contradicted the man who shielded her from danger and held her so tenderly in the night.

"Don't worry; we gave him a proper welcome when he came aboard."

His venomous expression chilled her. What had they done to Jared? "A proper welcome?" she repeated.

He smiled grimly. "Nothing I should discuss with a lady. I wouldn't want to offend your delicate nature."

Her heart dropped to her feet. Was Jared the one they'd flogged?

She shouldn't care. He was a pirate. The very thing she'd warned Colin against. Yet, she would do all she could to negotiate a pardon for him.

Then she'd return home to Colin in her safe little corner of the world and try to forget Jared.

She knew she'd fail miserably.

And love him all of her life.

CHAPTER 23

"Visitor to see you, pirate scum. Get up!"

The voice of the guard jarred Jared out of his nightmare, and brought him right back into another. Only this nightmare continued.

He lifted his head. The swelling had gone down enough for him to be able to see out of one eye. He ached all over and his tongue stuck to the roof of his mouth. He struggled to rise, but movement sent agony knifing through him.

"Careful, ma'am," came the voice of the guard. "He's dangerous."

"He never harmed me while I was his prisoner. I doubt he'll offer much of a threat now that he's injured."

Jared closed his eyes as Elise's soothing voice washed over him. Just having her near eased his pain. He heard a tiny gasp and the rustle of her clothing as she bent over him. She raised her voice and said angrily, "Don't you give prisoners water?"

"Ah..." came the voice of the guard.

"Bring some at once!"

"And leave you here alone with them?" He sounded horrified.

"They're chained and injured; hardly a threat. Water. Now."

"Yes, ma'am." Heavy footsteps moved away.

Her scent filled his nostrils as her silken hair brushed against his cheek. "Jared," she whispered.

He opened his eyes. She leaned over him. Tears trickled down her cheeks. She did not seem repulsed by the filth in this hole called a brig, only concerned for him.

She guided his head to her lap, despite the dirt and blood crusting his face and body. "It was you they flogged."

He heard the tears in her voice. A cool hand pressed against his brow and another lay against his cheek.

"Nothing the legendary Black Jack doesn't deserve," he croaked. "You shouldn't be here. They'll believe you have sympathies for pirates."

"Let me worry about that."

He tried to swallow, but his dry throat prevented it. "Are you all right?" he rasped.

"The captain believes I was an innocent prisoner."

"And so you were." Even though the view had grown so appealing, the effort of keeping his eyes open proved too difficult.

"He's given me quarters and extended every courtesy." At approaching footsteps, she said, "Thank you."

She pressed a cup against his lips and water dripped into his mouth. He lapped it greedily, never more grateful in all his miserable life for the blessed gift of water, stale as it was. He coughed when he swallowed too much, the cough sending a fresh wave of pain through his battered body.

"We'll be in London tomorrow. What can I do for you?"

"Send word to Greymore. Then go home and wash your hands of this. And us."

The guard cleared his throat. "Ma'am. Please. I cannot give you any more time. If the captain found out I'd let you in here..."

"I understand. Thank you for indulging me. And for mercy's sake, give these men food and water. You'd treat animals better."

"They're worse than animals. They're pirates,"

the guard snarled.

"Be that as it may, they saved me from the horrifying Captain Leandro and his men, who were true savages. They treated me with courtesy and respect while I was aboard their ship. I'd be grateful if you'd do the same for them. They will face justice soon. That should be good enough for you."

She rested a soothing hand on Jared's cheek for a moment, and he wished he could immerse himself in her softness. "I'll do everything I can for you," she whispered. She lifted his head from her lap and set it back down on the deck. With a rustling of her skirts, she arose and left.

Her scent lingered and sustained him. He faded in and out of sleep, vaguely aware of pain and thirst and cold, yet steeped in the memory of an angel with soft hands.

Someone shook him and held a cup to his lips. He gulped and opened his eyes.

Dubois met his gaze. "Her charms worked. They brought us food and ale."

Jared tried to push himself to a seated position, but failed before he made it to his elbows.

Dubois grimaced as he straightened his wounded leg. "You are a lucky man."

"Because we've been captured when, for a change, we were not engaging in acts of piracy?" Jared returned dryly. "Or because the captain thought it good sport to beat and then flog me after I'd surrendered?"

"Because a lovely and gentle lady loves you."

Jared snorted, sending a new bolt of pain shooting through him. He had to wait a moment before he replied, "She knows better than to love a wretch like me."

"She loves you," Dubois said with conviction. "I see the way she looks at you. And she wouldn't risk coming down here to see you if she didn't."

Anakoni scoffed. "Lot a good it'll do you, Jack. You'll dance the hempen jig, soon enough."

"I will. But you won't," Jared said with conviction. "I'll bargain for your lives."

Young O'Brian lifted his head with hope and disbelief in his eyes.

"There's nothing you can do for us," Anakoni grumbled.

Jared glanced at the other pirates languishing about in various parts of the cell and lowered his voice. "I'll give them the coordinates for Isla del Tiburon in exchange for pardons for all of you."

"You wouldn't," Dubois said, aghast. "Half our stored booty is there."

"Won't do you any good if you hang, will it?" Jared retorted.

Dubois closed his mouth with a snap.

Jared tried to rise, and failed. He rested his head on his arm and breathed through the pain. "The rest of the crew is dead. You'll be able to access the hoard on Marquette Island. If you split it evenly, you'll live like kings. The authorities will agree to pardon you in exchange for my information, provided you swear to forsake piracy."

"You are not sacrificing yourself for us," Dubois growled.

"I'm a dead man no matter what. Nothing I could offer them would be worth trading the glory of executing Black Jack. At least this way, I can bargain for your lives. Go retrieve the plunder on Marquette Island and sell the *Venture*. Change your names. Settle down with a lusty woman and grow old."

Dubois slammed his fist into the wall and swore as only an old sea dog could. In a rare moment of exposed emotion, Anakoni squeezed his eyes closed and rested his head against the bulkhead. Young O'Brian looked as though he were about to burst into tears.

Chained in the brig and awaiting almost certain death, Jared realized he'd never known truer friends.

For the first time in years, he prayed. Truly prayed. He prayed he could ransom his friends. He prayed that Elise would be well. And he prayed that Greymore and the British Secret Service would break their vow and free him.

Yet he suspected his prayers would only be heard by the devil.

CHAPTER 24

The Admiralty sent for Elise the moment she arrived in London. Uniformed sailors escorted her from the ship directly to the building housing the Admiralty.

Three men awaited her inside a plush office. One of the men was decorated as an admiral. A second, a captain. The third appeared to be a clerk. They greeted her coolly and made the introductions. Then the inquiry began.

"State your name for the record, ma'am."

"Mrs. Edward Berkley."

"Your place of residence."

"Berkley Manor, outside of Brenniswick, which lies southwest of Port Johns."

The admiral eyed Elise with detachment. She kept her gaze fixed unswervingly upon him, knowing he would decide her fate. And probably Jared's.

"And how did you come to be in the company of pirates?"

Elise repeated the same story she'd told to the navy captain, emphasizing how the pirates had left her unharmed. "The captain, Black Jack, assured me their articles protected women from assault. I believe it was his intention to return me to England uninjured."

"Is it possible he planned to ransom you, Mrs. Berkley?" asked the captain.

"If that were his intent, he never revealed it to me."

"Did these men who held you captive ever engage in any acts of piracy while you were aboard?"

"No, sir. They attacked the pirates who captured me, and took me on board, but it may have been an act of pirate hunting, for all I know. We sailed to an island to obtain provisions, and had just left the island when the naval ships intercepted and engaged them."

They looked disappointed. "Then you cannot truly testify they were actually pirates."

"No, Admiral."

"Very well. You may go, Mrs. Berkley. We have no reason to suspect you were willfully involved with them. And as you cannot be used as a witness against them, your presence is not required at the trial."

"Thank you, Admiral. May I inquire as to when the trial will take place?"

"We'll need time to gather the evidence and the witnesses. Probably a few weeks."

Elise nodded, hoping she had enough time to bargain for Jared's life. She secured a room in a hotel, bathed, ate, and hired a post chaise to take her home the following morning. She'd been captured without any money, but the hotel manager arranged a line of credit for everything she needed once she gave him the name of her man of business.

After a fitful night haunted by visions of Jared being flogged, beaten and hanged, Elise took a chaise home. They stopped only to change horses and drivers at posting inns along the way. Elise ate with little appetite as she waited for her transportation to be arranged and then resumed her exhausting journey over bumpy, rutted roads. Elise paid a fortune to travel day and night without stopping longer than necessary to change horses and drivers.

Just after dawn, Elise arrived at the Greymore estate. Exhausted, cold and hungry, she stepped from the carriage and stumbled up the stairs to the manor door. A weary footman admitted her, took one look at her disreputable appearance, and hurried away. Only a moment later, he returned and showed her upstairs.

Charlotte and Charles Greymore had donned dressing robes, looking sleepy and alarmed.

"Elise! Good heavens! Where have you been? Are you all right?" Charlotte put an arm around her and drew her further in the sitting room just off their bedroom.

A maid hurriedly built up the fire while another brought in a tea service.

Elise let Charlotte seat her at a small settee near the fireplace and leaned against her, grateful for her friendship. Elise laced her fingers in an attempt to appear calm. "Jared is in trouble."

Fear for him, combined with her state of fatigue, finally defeated her. She broke down crying and could not speak further.

Charlotte held her while shoulder-shaking sobs battered Elise until she finally controlled her tears.

Greymore handed her a handkerchief. "Tell us."

Charlotte thrust a teacup in her hand. Elise gulped down the hot tea. It burned her mouth, but she hardly felt it.

Elise began with, "Mr. Greymore, how long have you known Jared?"

"Since the Peninsular War."

She paused. "So long ago? Did you know he's the pirate Black Jack?"

Greymore's eyes narrowed. "I suspected it. He always did everything grandly."

"He's in Newgate Prison."

Greymore pressed his mouth together. Only then did Elise notice he seemed to favor his arm. "Tell me everything."

She did, and got as far as telling him that they'd flogged Jared after they captured him. Tears made speaking impossible again.

Mr. Greymore took her hand. "Mrs. Berkley. Elise." He waited until she calmed enough to understand him and look him in the eye. "Whatever else he may be, know this; he is a loyal Englishman, instrumental in Bonaparte's defeat."

Elise blinked. "Loyal Englishman? He's a pirate."

"He's no pirate. He works for the British government. I was working with him on the assignment."

Everything came too fast. Jared was not a pirate? Or rather, he was, but his actions were sanctioned by the government? She put a hand to her head. "But I heard him telling a member of his crew he'd killed the real Jared Amesbury and was using his identity, and that he was here to do something that would make them all rich men."

A ghost of a smile flitted over his mouth. "You don't think he'd reveal his real name to a pirate, do you? He used an alias to infiltrate the pirates. They'd have killed him if they knew he wasn't truly one of them."

She stared stupidly at him. Deep in her heart, she'd believed Jared when he'd professed his identity. Yet she'd feared it was a lie. "He's not a real pirate," she said numbly.

"No. He was tracking down the head informant selling information to a pirate ring. Believe me, he's no pirate. No amount of evidence against him would ever convince me otherwise."

Elise pressed her hand to her forehead. Jared was not a pirate. Relief warred with shame. "I should have known better. I can't believe I truly thought it of him." She paused, frowning. "He should have told me."

"Someone might have overheard him. He couldn't risk the mission. Lives were at stake."

Daring to hope, Elise said, "Then he won't be executed. The government will clear his name and free him."

"It's not so simple. Covert operatives are not uniformed officers. And a field agent who's captured is on his own."

"But that's terrible! If he's done all this for king and country, why won't they save him?"

"It was the understanding from the beginning."

"Why would he agree to that?"

"He had no choice. It gets worse. His assignment was officially over before he boarded his ship and came after you. What he did is viewed as a renegade act."

Elise closed her eyes. He'd risked more for her than she ever would have imagined. Gathering herself, she fixed her gaze upon him. "What do we do?"

Charles rubbed his temples, looking weary. "This was to be his last assignment." He drew a breath. "I'll leave for London but I'm not sure what kind of influence I'll have. They're quite firm about doing nothing to reveal their presence."

"I'm coming with you," Charlotte said.

"And I," said Elise.

"Elise. Go home to your son. He's worried about you."

"I will, and then I'm coming with you to London. I cannot remain here and leave Jared to his fate. There must be something we can do."

Greymore arose and began pacing. "I'll notify his family. His brother Cole, as the new Earl of Tarrington, may have some influence. Their father was widely respected. His brother Grant is closely involved with the Bow Street Runners. He may be a better source of aid. In fact, he may already know Jared is imprisoned."

"I can be ready to leave in a matter of hours,"

Elise said.

"We'll leave in two days."

"Two days! No, we must leave at once."

Greymore put a calming hand on her arm. "There will be an inquiry and then a formal trial. We have a few weeks."

"But we can't just leave him locked up in that terrible place. I've heard such dreadful things about Newgate."

"If Grant's aware of Jared's imprisonment, he'll see to it that his accommodations are improved. I'll send messengers immediately and arrange for appointments with those who may be sympathetic for our cause. Two days here or in London will make no difference with those in authority to help him. We can't exactly stage a prison-break."

"I'd be willing to do it."

Greymore smiled. "Of that, I have no doubt."

In the end, she conceded the battle and went home. After a tearful reunion with Colin, she let Morrison put her to bed. Despite her exhaustion, sleep was long in coming.

If they didn't act quickly, Jared would die.

CHAPTER 25

Jared knew someone had paid a garnish and easement of irons for him when the turnkey removed Jared's heavy shackles and moved him into a private cell. The honorable navy officers had confiscated all his money when they captured him, so he'd had no hope of buying better conditions when he arrived at Newgate. His crew had likewise been relieved of their purses.

He wondered about his benefactor. Greymore wouldn't have come this soon. Elise probably hadn't even arrived home yet to tell him.

His new cell was clean in comparison to the hole he'd shared with thirty other ragged and hungry men. The garnish provided soap, a sponge, two basins of water, a clean towel, and candles. Clean clothes even awaited him on a cot that appeared free of fleas. Only one rat ran across the floor. Luxury. Better than some inns where he'd spent the night.

Jared drank fresh water from one of the basins. Then, despite the cold room, he stripped off what remained of his clothes and bathed, scrubbing until his skin felt raw. Everything on his body hurt. Each time he moved, pain shot outward. The freezing water made his teeth chatter, but the desire to be clean outweighed the discomfort. He carefully poured soapy water over his head and leaned over to let it run down his back where the naval boatswain's cat o'nine tails had bitten into his flesh. Standing on the cold stone floor in the puddle of water he'd created, he bathed again, using the second basin of fresh water.

The turnkey had offered to send someone in to shave him, but he'd refused. His hair and beard had grown long and scruffy, just as he wanted. It all combined for a good image of a pirate.

Moreover, he and Cole looked enough alike to be twins; he didn't dare taint the family name should someone chance to note the resemblance between a pirate and the new Earl of Tarrington. The law and the papers must never know his true name.

Behind him, the lock turned with a clank.

Falling into a defensive crouch, Jared faced the door, wishing he had a weapon. The door swung open on reluctant hinges to reveal a dark, ominous form in the doorway.

Jared's heart hammered in his throat. The figure approached. Jared tensed further, prepared to kill or die.

There was a pause. Then, "Well, there you are in all your glory," drawled a familiar voice. The figure stepped into the light cast by the lone candle.

Jared let his breath out, almost dizzy with relief. "Grant. I've never been so happy to see you." He dried quickly and pulled on clean breeches, gritting his teeth against pain.

"You've never been happy to see me." His brother folded his arms and leaned against the wall. "I see you managed to offend someone. What a surprise." No pity. No anger. Just sarcasm. That was Grant.

"You paid for the luxurious accommodations?" Jared made a sweeping gesture around the cell.

"Don't think I did it out of the goodness of my heart," Grant said. "I just didn't want to have to breathe your stench."

"Can't blame you. After two weeks in the brig on the ship and, er, I'm not sure how many more here, the smell was enough to make the fleas sick."

"A chat with the Royal Navy, I hear?"

Jared didn't bother to keep the disgust out of his voice. "They waited until after I'd surrendered to beat and flog me. They were real honorable and fearsome officers. The navy's finest."

At least they seemed to have treated Elise well. O'Brian and Dubois had assured him she'd appeared unharmed and in good health when she visited him in the brig, and she'd apparently had her freedom on board the ship.

Jared struggled to get his shirt on without opening the wounds on his back, or aggravating his broken ribs, but as pain flared, he sucked in his breath sharply.

"Baby," Grant accused scornfully. "Here."

In a rare sign of compassion, Grant was at his side, lifting the shirt up and over Jared's head and lowering it over his back, Grant's hands careful despite his gruff voice.

Grant looked Jared over, as if noting every mark on him. In a quiet voice, he asked, "You all right?"

Speechless at the unlikely display of concern, Jared nodded. Grant locked the compassion behind his customary sardonic exterior. Jared fastened the three buttons on the front of his clean shirt and tucked it into his breeches.

Grant removed his coat and threw it at him. "It's freezing in here. Wouldn't want you to sneeze on the Admiralty during your inquiry."

"How soon will that take place?"

"In an hour."

"Ah. Bath was well-timed." Jared put on the wool coat, trying not to wince as he moved his arms, and again, Grant helped him.

"I would have paid for your garnishment and easement sooner if I'd known you were here," Grant grumbled. "I came as soon as I heard."

Jared sobered, startled by Grant's confession. "I know."

It surprised him to realize that he truly did know. Despite Grant's gruffness, he was a brother who cared for his family. He just hid it beneath an impossibly hardened exterior. Grant had always been a cynic who preferred his own company to that of others, and he'd returned from the war positively hard-hearted. But not a complete cad, apparently. Who would have thought such a cold exterior would actually protect a beating heart?

Jared sat on the cot and pulled on the woolen socks. Grant helped him with his boots.

"Do you know the members of the Admiralty who will try me?"

Grant nodded. "Admiral Ruggle. Hard but fair."

"Will he be willing to negotiate?"

Grant uttered a sharp laugh. "With a known pirate? Hardly."

Jared sat hunched over, trying to plan a strategy.

"I can arrange for some female companionship for you later, if you like," Grant said.

Jared raised his brows.

Something akin to a dry smile touched Grant's mouth. "Or I could bring you some really bad and overpriced gin made from Newgate's own private still. Anything can be had for the right price here."

"Anything?"

"Except your freedom, of course."

"Are you sure that can't be bought?"

"For the legendary pirate Black Jack? Difficult. If you were unknown, I could bribe the right person and slip you out. They could say gaol fever claimed yet another victim. Typhus kills more prisoners than the executioner."

Jared nodded. "That's how I got out the first time."

He had the supreme satisfaction of actually surprising Grant. Probably an unprecedented event.

"The first time?"

Jared heaved a sigh. "Can you help me?"

Grant sat beside him. "Tell me the whole sordid tale."

Jared took a moment to order his thoughts. "As you know, when Cole left for the navy, I signed up with a privateer."

Grant nodded and waved him on.

"At first I loved it. I worked up to first officer quickly, something I wouldn't have been able to do in the navy. During one of our calls at port to re-supply, I stumbled upon a beautiful woman in peril. Her name was Rebecca. My aid turned into an adventure but I got her to safety. Then I returned to the sea and assumed I'd never see her again."

"How did you end up in gaol the first time?"

"My captain lost patience with the government. They were slow giving us our fair share of the booty we took. For some, we never received compensation."

"And?"

Jared paused as shame washed over him. "We decided to augment our pay. Sometimes we failed to report our takings and sold them directly to smugglers instead. Occasionally, we only reported a portion of the spoils and kept the rest."

Grant watched him impassively, without any judgment or condemnation. Nor understanding. Who knew what Grant ever thought?

"We began straying further and further from our approved area. Then we started attacking ships from other countries, not just the French as we were sanctioned to do. Once, against my better judgment, we preyed on a British merchant ship. We were caught."

Grant's eyes narrowed, but said nothing.

"We were arrested for piracy. Rebecca came with an offer. She was a covert operative for the British Secret Service and told me she could arrange to have my death falsified, provided I pledge myself to the Service."

He blew out his breath slowly and glanced at Grant, wondering if he'd made the right choice. "I can't tell you how many times I wished I'd just let them hang me. But I was seventeen and didn't know there were things worse than death."

Grant nodded, looking haunted. "There are."

Jared waited, but Grant did not elaborate.

"Go on," Grant said.

"I agreed to their terms. Basically, they owned me. They sent me on all the most dangerous missions, but I always returned." He stood and moved to the window as memory reopened old wounds. "Bonaparte discovered Rebecca was a spy and executed her."

He stared out the window, afraid if he turned around, Grant would see telltale signs of emotion. He watched the London fog swirl slowly across the bars like a live creature. He drew a steadying breath.

"After Boney was defeated, I remained in France to help with the mop-up effort, thinking my time with the Service would soon end. Then I received new orders." He swallowed. "They wanted to utilize my experience on the sea. So I hung around seedy taverns and grumbled about the lack of work for a former privateer until I met up with some pirates. They signed me up."

Jared glanced at his brother, but Grant never shifted, never made a sound. There was nothing but impassivity in his expression.

"The captain was a snake," Jared continued. "More interested in blood and terror than in plunder. He loved to torture his victims. I convinced the crew I'd make a better captain and we voted him out. It's all very democratic, you know. The captain didn't take kindly to losing his position and I had to kill him. I left his first mate, and incidentally half-brother, Leandro, in Havana."

Grant raised his brows. "You didn't kill him, too? How compassionate of you."

"I should have fed him to the sharks. He plagued me for years. My assignment was to expose a pirate ring and find the one feeding them information. I traced it to a nobleman outside of Port Johns. There I met a lady named Elise Berkley."

He heard the softening of his own voice. It seemed an unavoidable reaction whenever he thought of the angel who came to him with soothing hands.

Grant's face twisted in true disgust. "First Cole and now you. What a pathetic pair of lovesick fools you are. I thought you looked rather moony when you were home for Father's funeral."

Jared found it interesting Grant could listen to tales of betrayal, espionage, and piracy without comment and with no emotion other than mild sarcasm. Yet the mention of a lady brought a stronger reaction.

He moistened his lips. "Leandro found me, and learned about Elise. He nabbed her and used her as bait to draw me out."

Grant barked a sharp laugh, his eyes dark with anger. "Of course. And you, being the gallant hero you are, waltzed right into his trap."

"Of course I did. Haven't you heard of Captain Leandro? He made Blackbeard look like a kitten. He actually committed many of the tales I'm credited for doing. Yes, I went after him."

Jared relived his stark desperation when he learned Leandro had taken Elise. He took a moment to steady his breathing. "I killed him and took his ship. We were on our way back to England to take Elise home. This was my last assignment. If all went according to plan, I would receive my decommission and a full pardon for any of my crew I deemed fit to save."

"But the navy found you first."

"And the Secret Service made it clear all along they'd never help me if I got myself captured by either side."

Grant rubbed his temples.

"It gets worse. My assignment was technically over once I exposed the leader of the ring. Leaving England on the ship and using my pirate guise to rescue Elise was an unauthorized act."

Grant stood and went to the window next to Jared. For a long time, he stood looking out. Finally, he spoke. "If you have no documentation, and no proof, this is merely your story. It isn't much to go on."

"I know. The Service is very careful to never leave any papers that can be traced to them. Get word to Charles Greymore in Brenniswick. I asked Elise to contact him, but I have no idea if she's being held for questioning or if she's free. Greymore may be able to do something. I doubt it, though."

"I'll find out about your woman."

"Lady, Grant. She's a lady."

Grant blew out his breath in disgust.

Jared didn't remember Grant always having such a dark opinion of women. Something must have happened. Jared had been home so little in the last fifteen years that he hardly knew anyone in his family. He'd missed much.

"You could try telling Admiral Ruggle the truth, but he probably won't believe you," Grant said.

"Except for my name, and then I'll die publicly as Jared Amesbury. The entire family will be dishonored." He shook his head. "I must continue being Black Jack."

Grant snorted. "That's a stupid name."

Jared's mouth curved upward, but winced as the

motion pulled at his cut lip. "Cole agrees. It was all I could think of on the moment."

"Can this operative, Greymore, come through for you like the first time?"

"I'm not sure how far his connections reach. Besides, I was in a smaller gaol the first time, not Newgate, and I was unknown then. As you said, my notoriety complicates things."

Grant paused, his voice quieting. "You didn't really do everything they credit to Black Jack? Leandro did them?"

"He did some of them, but all the really good stories are rumors my men and I started so the ships we boarded would give up without a fight. Fewer people die that way. On both sides." He waited a beat. "Grant."

His brother looked him in the eye.

"I've committed acts which will haunt me all my life. But I did it all in the name of duty."

Grant watched him in that piercing, assessing way he had and slowly nodded. "I don't know what I can do for you. I have an idea, but it will probably fail. Even if it succeeds, there's considerable risk." He paused, deep in thought.

Jared leaned against the cold stone wall, grateful for Grant's coat.

Grant drew in a breath. "I agree you shouldn't give the Admiralty your name. Cole and Christian and the girls shouldn't bear the stain."

Jared's throat tightened as he thought of his brothers and sisters. They were all good people with untarnished names. "Will you tell them the truth about me?"

Grant frowned. "Don't you want me to?"

Jared considered carefully. His first instinct was to ask Grant to keep his secrets. Then he decided against it. "Yes. Do tell them. Cole already knows. So does Christian. I've told the girls nothing other than that I was a privateer during the war. If Father had known the truth, he might have approved. I hope."

"He approved more than you know."

Jared shrugged, but hoped Grant was right. "I don't want the rest of the family to think I was a disgrace." He drew a breath and forced himself to say the next words. "But if all efforts fail and I do hang—"

"Stop." Desperation touched Grant's voice.

Startled by Grant's show of emotion, Jared paused, but these were matters that had to be discussed. He pressed on. "As far as public knowledge..."

Grant drew in a breath, nodded, and gave a pained smile. "As far as public knowledge, I'll make up something about you dying at sea. Want me to say you were protecting a lady when you single-handedly fought off twenty pirates before they overpowered and killed you?"

"That would be spectacular." Jared thought it over, warming to the idea. "Actually, yes. That's exactly what I want you to say. But leave Elise Berkley's name out of it."

Grant looked away and nodded. His voice husky, he said, "If I fail you, I just want you to know..." he cleared his throat.

The tightness in Jared's chest grew more pronounced. "Don't get sentimental on me, little brother. Just get me out of here."

"Right. I'll hire a small army and we'll storm the prison."

"Sounds like fun."

Grant tapped on the door and waited for the turnkey.

"Grant, before you go, I need you to pay easement and garnishment for my crew. There are ten of them. Talk to Charles Grady at the bank."

"I'm not taking your money, you fool. Yes, I'll see to your men." As the door opened, Grant turned back and gave Jared a long look.

Jared swallowed against a lump. "My thanks, Grant."

Tight-lipped, Grant gripped Jared's shoulder in one of the few places where he didn't hurt, and left with the silence of a shadow.

Moments later, Jared was brought before the Admiralty Court. He was surprised they decided to try him so soon. Often, pirates remained in prison awaiting their trials for months on end. Many died from gaol fever before their case ever came before the Admiralty.

The captain involved in his capture and who'd ordered his flogging was present, along with his first and second lieutenants. They looked smug. Also in attendance were Admiral Ruggle, the governor, two merchant captains, and a clerk.

Jared vaguely remembered a few of the others who lined the walls, looking alternately angry and frightened; no doubt former victims called here as witnesses. Windows behind the admiral revealed grey, stormy skies. Though chained, temptation pulled at him to jump through a window and run, regardless of his abysmal chances at escaping alive.

Instead, Jared stood ramrod straight and looked Admiral Ruggle directly in the eye.

"Your name, sir?"

"My full name is John Black."

The admiral blinked as if surprised by his answer, or perhaps by his accent. "Are you also called Black Jack?"

"Yes, my lord."

The charges against him were read, beginning with 'not having God before his eyes, but being moved and seduced by the instigation of the devil,' and continued in great detail too long and numerous to follow, but included theft, piracy, and murder. Many of the charges were false, but any one of the true ones would be enough to sentence him to death.

When the clerk ended with, "Feloniously, and et cetera, did kill and murder, against the peace of our sovereign Lord the King, his Crown and Dignity. How do you plead?"

Jared took a breath. "I plead guilty."

Astonishment shone on all the faces present. A murmur rippled through the room.

The admiral leaned forward. "Then you admit to piracy?"

"Yes, Admiral. I have engaged in acts of piracy for the past three years."

The admiral sat back and looked him over. "You are well-spoken for a pirate. Who were your parents?"

"I am the illegitimate son of a member of the gentry, whose name I do not wish to tarnish. My mother was his mistress. My father paid for me to attend school."

"I see."

Disgust was written on the faces of the other navy officers. The merchant captains did not meet his gaze.

The admiral asked, "Do you have any final words in your defense before we pronounce the verdict and punishment?"

"Yes, my lord. I wish to bargain for the lives of my crew. Ten survived the navy's attack. In exchange for their freedom, I will provide you the coordinates of Isla del Tuburon, where we store much of our plunder until buyers can be found. Our own personal hoard is there as well; the accumulation of over two hundred men."

"Your freedom is not worth a bit of treasure," snapped the navy captain who'd captured Jared.

Jared met his gaze calmly. "I understand,

Captain. But surely the lives of my men are."

The captain's face darkened in anger. "You are not worthy of any mercy. Not you, nor your men."

"That will do, Captain." Admiral Ruggle glanced at the others.

Jared wondered if he were silencing them, or receiving their agreement.

The admiral steepled his fingers and stared unfocused at the wall behind Jared. "Very well, Mr. Black. In exchange for your information, we will pardon two of your men."

"All ten," Jared demanded.

A faint lifting of his brow was the only change in the admiral's expression, no doubt in reaction to Jared's cheekiness. "Three."

"Eight."

The Admiral's eyes narrowed. "Three. And that's my final offer. But they must swear to forsake piracy. They'll receive full pardons, but if they're caught again, there will be no leniency. And I want your full written and signed confession."

"Agreed."

"Their names?"

"Jean-Claude Dubois. Kaleo Anakoni. Timothy O'Brian."

The clerk recorded their names carefully.

"I'll have their pardons drawn up," Lord Ruggle said. "When our ship returns from the island with news of success, your men will be released."

"You won't be disappointed, sir." Knowing his audacity was probably already causing a stir, Jared pushed on, voicing his fears. "My Lord?" He hesitated and Lord Ruggle waited. "I do have your word? I'll be dead by the time a ship can get to and from Isla del Tuburon with news."

The Admiral drew himself up. "You have my word these men you named will be pardoned and freed. It is duly recorded and witnessed by this jury."

Jared nodded. "I have heard you are a fair and honorable man, my lord. I will trust you to save these men who will most certainly be glad to become law abiding citizens if given the opportunity." Squelching the feeling he was somehow betraying his crew, he drew a breath and gave the coordinates to the island, warned about the offshore reef on the lee side, and described exactly how to find the cave where they'd hidden their hoard.

The clerk carefully wrote it all down and then handed the paper to Jared to approve. Jared read it over, made one correction, and a final addition. He handed it back to the clerk and looked at each man in attendance one at a time.

The navy captain appeared poised to spring at his throat. The members of the jury returned his gaze, some in newfound respect, others with blatant distaste.

After a word with the Admiralty court, the clerk stood and declared; "Your punishment to be hanged by the neck until dead, dead, dead."

CHAPTER 26

Inside the drawing room of the Greymore's London house, Elise dropped the newspaper and looked at Charlotte in dismay. "They've sentenced him and his crew to hang on Monday."

Charles nodded grimly. "Officially, he's an embarrassment. His brothers are working night and day to find some way to save him, but there's no help from any quarter. We've even tried bribery. All has failed." His voice was tight and angry. "All we've managed to do is ensure his family will gain immediate possession of his body instead of letting the ghouls who engage in dissection have it first."

Elise put a hand over her mouth. A cold chill passed over her.

Greymore cursed and came to her. "Forgive me. I shouldn't have said that."

A footman came to the door. "The Earl and Countess Tarrington and company."

"Show them in." Greymore turned to Elise. "His family is here."

Elise found herself nearly overwhelmed by the Amesburys. A handsome gentleman who could pass for Jared's twin crossed the threshold. He bore a regal, commanding air and his eyes were as blue as sapphires. He lacked the hardness she'd first noticed in Jared, but Elise attributed that to the tall lady on his arm whose sweet face glowed with gentleness.

"Lord and Lady Tarrington." Greymore bowed.

"Mr. Greymore, thank you for receiving us." The earl's rich bass could almost be mistaken for Jared's.

Behind the earl and his countess came a

younger gentleman. Elise gaped.

He was stunning. A younger, almost ethereal version of the earl and Jared, he stood every inch the height and breadth of his brothers. His eyes were a clear blue, so pale they almost seemed to glow, and his eyelashes were enviable. Unlike the other members of his family, his hair was golden. The only mar to his perfection was a white scar at his temple near one eye which somehow only made him more intriguing.

The ladies on his arms both had the same rich, dark hair as Jared and the earl. They were undoubtedly sisters. The ladies had similar enough facial features to place them as relatives, but did not look enough like one another for Elise to have guessed they were twins. One lady appeared older, haughtier, with sharper features and a thinner face.

Greymore introduced Charlotte and Elise to Lord Tarrington.

The earl gestured to his wife, his face softening. "My wife, Alicia, Lady Tarrington."

The lady put a hand over her slightly swollen abdomen in an unconscious gesture ladies who are increasing often do and held out the other hand to Elise. "I'm very happy to meet the lady who finally tamed Jared's wild heart."

The earl continued, "My sisters, Margaret, Lady Hennessey."

The haughty lady fixed an assessing stare upon Elise.

"And Miss Rachel Amesbury."

The other twin smiled warmly.

"And the youngest of our misbegotten bunch, Christian."

As Elise turned to the blond gentleman, he smiled, warming her like a ray of sunshine spearing a storm cloud. Endowed with the same athletic grace as his brothers, he bowed over her hand. When he straightened, his blue gaze swept over her in a surprisingly assessing stare.

Elise had the urge to straighten and wondered if she looked as tattered as she felt.

Christian said, "I knew you'd be a remarkable lady to have won my brother's heart. I see I was right."

He had an intensity about him that caught Elise by surprise. She didn't know why, but such high praise from this total stranger suddenly meant a great deal. Perhaps it was due to the affection Jared obviously felt for him. Or perhaps it was his air of quiet dignity normally only found in a peer.

Elise managed to reply, "He spoke of you often and with deep affection, Mr. Amesbury."

He smiled again and Elise marveled how one family could have produced such magnificent men. "If I have my wish, I'll be your brother-in-law soon. No need to stand on formality."

The thought of marrying Jared suddenly became an impossible dream; there seemed little hope he could ever be freed. Tears swam in her eyes and she could not speak.

Christian gently enfolded both her hands in his. They were as large and strong as Jared's but not nearly as calloused. "Courage," he said softly. "We will not allow them to execute our brother."

"Of course we won't," said the young Earl of Tarrington.

Christian released her hand as Tarrington approached Elise. He smiled down at her with a brotherly warmth that seemed at odds with his lordly presence. "I've been looking forward to meeting you. I wish the occasion of our meeting were more pleasant." He looked so much like a safe and happy Jared that Elise's eyes overflowed. His voice softened. "We'll see this through, I vow it."

Christian pressed a handkerchief into her hand.

Elise wiped her tears, ashamed at her lack of decorum. A pair of slender arms went around her shoulders. Through her blurred vision, she saw Lady Tarrington next to her. Lady Tarrington's eyes shimmered as she embraced Elise.

"What a load of ninnies you are! What's to be done?" demanded Lady Hennessey.

Tarrington's mouth twitched. "Quite right, Margaret. All right, Greymore, your friends got my brother into this fine mess. What are you going to do to get him out of it?"

Greymore looked pained.

The earl softened. "Sorry, old man, just a jest. I know he'd have hung years ago if it weren't for their intervention."

Charlotte rang for tea and they all sat.

No one suggested the ladies leave while the men discussed the ugly predicament at hand.

"I've gone all the way to the top," Mr. Greymore said. "I've been denied all aid. He was a rogue when he was apprehended and they refuse to sanction the actions he took after his assignment was completed."

No one sent a look of censure Elise's way, though she deserved it since he took those actions for her sake.

"We could force their hand by going to the press," Christian suggested. "Play up the angle of an honorable gentleman who served his country with loyalty is about to die."

Greymore shook his head. "I've been assured if any word of this leaks, Jared will be dead within minutes."

Elise drew in her breath sharply. "They'd do that?"

Greymore rubbed his eyes. "Of that I have no doubt."

A pall fell over the group. "Grant may have had success through his own channels," Lord Tarrington said. "He'll be here shortly."

Christian grumbled, "Must we endure his presence?"

Tarrington grinned. "He may be the very devil, but he's useful, on occasion." He turned to Greymore. "Why don't you fill us in on what you know while we wait?"

While Greymore parted with the somber news regarding his attempts at the Secret Service Headquarters, tea and a platter of sandwiches and cakes arrived. Despite the grave matters that brought them together, the family tucked into their meal. Eventually, they fell into jesting, taunting, and laughing, perfectly at ease. Their affection and camaraderie were infectious, in spite of the cracks they took at one another.

Christian had a quick wit that drew reluctant smiles out of Elise and pushed back the darkness that had fallen over her since Jared's imprisonment. Rachel frequently exchanged glances with Christian as if they shared private jokes.

Margaret presided over them all like a queen, and a single look from her might have reduced lesser men to ash, but Tarrington matched her, even setting her back a time or two. And when she sent those looks Christian's way, he only threw back his own playful shots, making the imperious Margaret smile in spite of herself.

Next to Elise, Lady Tarrington occasionally touched Elise. At first, the contact surprised Elise, but Lady Tarrington's touches were so full of support and understanding that Elise quickly warmed to her. Feeling as if she'd known this gentle lady all her life, Elise clung to her.

"Mr. Grant Amesbury," the butler intoned.

Grant Amesbury entered silently. Unlike his siblings, and in contradiction to his station, he wore the coarse clothes of a laborer and was dressed head to toe in black.

He bore only a vague resemblance to the Amesbury brothers. His hair was darker, almost black. Gray eyes held an aloof hardness and the lines of his visage were stern. A long, ragged scar ran down the side of his face. He would have made an even more convincing pirate than Jared.

As Lord Tarrington introduced them, his gaze passed over her, his expression chilling. Clearly, he blamed her for his brother's fate. Because of her, Jared was locked in Newgate awaiting his execution.

Grant glanced back to the others who waited expectantly. He shook his head once.

Elise's heart hammered in her chest as cold despair crept over her. "No," she whispered.

Lady Tarrington put a hand over her mouth. Tarrington put his arm around her, his own face pale and drawn.

Christian jumped to his feet. "You're going to let them execute him?"

"Calm yourself," Grant replied in a rough voice. "I know what's at stake."

Christian moved to stand only inches from Grant. "You can't simply give up."

"I've done everything I can."

Christian squared his shoulders, raising his head in determination. "Then it's up to me."

Grant let out a snort and said sarcastically, "Oh, of course, Chris, you have so much influence in my circles."

"I have influence in circles closed to you."

"Being the darling of society gives you influence to Almack's and other frivolous enterprises of uselessness."

"You don't have enough imagination to guess where I have influence."

Grant and Christian glared at one another with such ferocity that Elise feared they would come to blows. Seeing the gentle Christian so angry gave her pause. She wondered if they were lashing out at each other out of fear over the fate of their brother, or another matter entirely.

Suddenly, it became terrifyingly possible, despite his family and connections, Jared might truly die.

Her heart stopped at the thought. Elise leaped to her feet. "I need to see him."

"Newgate is no place for a lady," Mr. Greymore said firmly.

"I must see him. I must tell him..." She choked. "Please. If you won't help me, I'll go alone."

Wearily, Tarrington glanced at Grant and Christian who stood nose to nose as if locked in a silent battle of will.

"Hail a hackney," Elise ordered a footman when no one moved. She went for her pelisse.

Christian broke eye contact with Grant. "Don't go alone."

As he took a breath to say more, Tarrington interjected. "No, indeed. I shall accompany you."

Grant said, "I'll take her. I've been in and out enough that I can do it quickly and easily. Wouldn't want to sully your good name by having the new Earl of Tarrington visiting an inmate of Newgate." He spoke as if he meant it as an insult.

Tarrington nodded once. "Go."

Christian turned away, but not before she saw the frustration in his eyes. She wondered if his brothers were always treating him like the baby, instead of the man he'd become.

"We'll go after dark," Grant said, his chill gaze passing over Elise.

Elise glanced at Grant narrowly, knowing she should trust him, but almost afraid to be alone with this intimidating stranger.

"I'll see you safely in and out," Grant snapped as

if her mistrust besmirched his honor.

Lady Tarrington patted her arm and nodded. She smiled at Grant, something mysterious in her eyes, as if she knew a secret about him.

Grant glared at her in return.

Not the least intimidated, Lady Tarrington positively beamed. She leaned in to Elise. "Don't let Grant bully you. He likes to play the unfeeling cad, but he'll protect you with all the gallantry of a knight."

Grant folded his arms. "Your wife is delusional, Cole."

The earl grinned. "You just keep believing it, little brother."

Grant made a sound of disgust. "Women. Always making something out of nothing."

"I can't wait to see the day when you fall in love, Grant," Lady Tarrington said with an impish glint in her eye.

Christian choked. "Grant in love?"

"Over my dead body," Grant snarled.

"No respectable lady would have him," Christian said.

Tarrington grinned. "Perhaps he'll fall for a footpad, or a murderess. Someone disreputable."

All the Amesbury siblings snickered. Grant folded his arms and glowered until they turned the discussion to other matters.

Outside, darkness fell, and Grant finally gave Elise a brief nod. A hackney was hailed and they departed. An unusually thick fog, even for London, enshrouded the streets and swirled eerily around the hackney winding along the dark streets of London.

Elise watched Grant's shadowed face and repressed the urge to rub her hands over her arms.

"I understand you also served in the war," Elise ventured.

Grant nodded, sitting utterly still and staring

out the window.

Elise frowned. She'd always heard women speak wistfully of the strong, silent type, but after having met one, Elise decided she liked the playful, roguish type. Like Jared.

Jared.

Disbelief and hopelessness fell over her again.

Glumly, she eyed Grant. "You blame me for your brother's predicament, don't you?"

"He vows you were a victim, but no woman is ever innocent."

He shot such a freezing stare upon her that she held her tongue for the remainder of their journey. And rubbed her hands over her arms.

The hackney stopped in front of an innocuous brick building. Grant surprised her by handing her out. As she stared, he raised a brow, almost looking amused. Almost.

They were admitted into the office, a small room with two windows overlooking the Old Bailey. It seemed ordinary, like a professional office; neat, clean, with crisp wainscoting.

A respectable-looking man with graying hair greeted Grant with familiarity. "Weapons, Mr. Amesbury?"

Grant opened his coat and retrieved a frightening number of guns, knives and daggers, all of which he laid on the desk.

The man lifted a brow and attempted humor. "Traveling lighter than usual, eh?"

Grant fixed him with a cold stare.

The man cleared his throat. "Right. And my lady." He turned to Elise. "I'm sure you don't carry weapons."

Elise opened her reticule and retrieved a tiny pistol. She set it carefully on the table next to Grant's armory. "Just this one, sir."

Grant lifted a brow. "You can shoot a gun." His

voice reflected his disbelief.

"Ask Jared how we met, sometime," she said smugly.

The officer turned to a junior clerk. "Bring the turnkey, please. Who are you here to see tonight, Mr. Amesbury?"

"John Black."

The officer lifted his eyebrows. "The pirate Black Jack? A friend of yours?"

Without blinking, Grant replied evenly, "I have unusual friends."

The officer's laugh sounded more like a cough. "You're questioning him for a case, right?" Grant waited, giving nothing away and the officer uncomfortably cleared his voice. "Please sign your names here, sir." He indicated a large book.

After they signed and the officer had also affixed his signature, he put away their weapons. Moments later, a hunched man entered wearing a respectable suit and carrying a heavy ring of keys.

"Show these people to John Black's cell, if you please."

The turnkey nodded. "Thi' way, guv'nuh."

He led them to a heavy oak gate, bound with iron, and studded with nails. Another turnkey stood guard. They nodded to each other and the second guard opened the gate to a dismal passageway made of stone, which ran parallel to the Old Bailey.

The turnkey led them confidently along a maze of passages, turning at some junctions, passing straight on through others until Elise completely lost her bearings. If she'd been alone, she would have been terrified. She was actually grateful for the intimidating man at her side. Heavy doors and guards barred each new corridor. No prisoner could ever dream of escaping.

They followed the turnkey in and out of the shadows along a passageway. Her feet slipped with every step on the damp and slimy stone floor and she had to step carefully. Gloom battled with guttering, smoking candles set too far apart to give any real light. The stench of human waste and sickness nauseated her. Rats scurried at the sound of their footsteps and Elise clamped her mouth closed lest she cry out in alarm.

Beside her, Grant moved like a phantom, his grim presence as unnerving as the prison itself. The smells worsened. She'd never dreamed such filth existed. She nearly gagged, but left her perfumed handkerchief in her reticule, unwilling to show a sign of weakness in Grant's company. He would no doubt only sneer at her for coming.

Occasionally, a moan seeped from the other side of a doorway, reminding her some wretched soul lived in misery within these walls.

She glanced at Grant. Though his brother had been forced to live here for nearly two weeks, he maintained an expressionless façade. He either had no feelings on the matter or was masterful at hiding them.

The turnkey stopped at a door and fitted a key into the lock. The door opened with a squeal, revealing a tiny room lit by a single candle sitting on the floor. A form crouched by a low, narrow cot.

"Grant." Jared's voice met them as the shadowy form straightened and stepped forward. "Elise. What are you doing here? Grant! You shouldn't have brought her."

Grant held up his hands in surrender. "How well do you know this woman?"

Jared's teeth flashed in the dim light. "What'd she do, point a gun at you?" He turned to her. "Oh, Elise. You're a vision." With one stride, he came to her and enfolded her into his arms. He crushed her against him and turned his head into her neck, breathing deeply. "You smell good."

With her arms wrapped around him, she let him hold her as long as he wished, reveling in the completeness that overcame her each time he took her into his arms. When at last he pulled back, he brushed a hand across the side of her face and smoothed back her hair.

She laid a hand on his bearded cheek. He was thinner, but his eyes were clear and untroubled by fever, and his bruises had faded to a pale yellow. She'd worried he'd been ill and suffering from his injuries with no one to tend him. Seeing him well and whole left her weak with relief.

"Are you all right?" he asked.

She laughed weakly. "I'm not the one who's been beaten, flogged, and locked in the most inhumane prison in all of England."

Unsmiling, he put a hand on each side of her face and looked at her searchingly. "Did the navy captain mistreat you?"

"No. He was a gentleman. He brought me untouched to London, and arranged lodging for me until I could return home. I'm staying with Charles and Charlotte Greymore here in town."

"I'm glad they're helping you. How's Colin?"

"He's well. I brought him with me. I couldn't bear to be separated from him again. And we're visiting the museums and the zoo. He sees it all as a great adventure. We even took a hot air balloon ride at Hyde Park."

"I bet he loved it."

"He did. I felt terribly guilty engaging in such diverting activities with you in here, but I was trying not to let Colin know anything was amiss." She drew a breath. "He misses you. He asks about you often. I don't know what to tell him." She glanced back at Grant who stood stiffly, arms folded, scowling out of the narrow, barred window.

Jared pulled her in close again. He kissed her in

long, lingering kisses that left her breathless. His fingers traced her face, his lips following behind. Then he just held her.

Elise would have given anything to remain in his arms forever.

"A few more lessons, and you'll be a skilled kisser, Mrs. Berkley." His attempt to lighten the somber mood made her determined to play along.

She smiled, probably too brightly. "I look forward to more kissing lessons from you, Mr. Amesbury."

He grinned. "So happy to oblige."

He drew her in for a kiss again, playful at first, but becoming more desperate. His imminent death loomed over them and their passion grew, fueled by desperation and fear. A tremor ran through his body. He broke the kiss and crushed her against him.

"I love you," she whispered raggedly.

He let his breath out and shivered. "I thought I'd die before I heard you say that."

"I loved you aboard the ship. I loved you before then. I think I've loved you since that first scandalous kiss."

He gathered her in closer and rested the side of his face on top of her head. "Oh, Elise, I never thought I'd love anyone so deeply. If I manage to get free of this place, I'm going to throw you over my shoulder and carry you off to the nearest parson."

"Is that a marriage proposal, Mr. Amesbury?"

"No. Not giving you a choice."

She laughed softly even through her threatening tears. "Fortunate for you I want to marry you or I might give you a spot of trouble. I'm a pretty good shot, you know. Deadly with candlesticks, as well."

He chuckled but sobered quickly and pulled back enough to search her eyes. "Will you have me?"

"Yes. Come out of this alive and I will gladly be your wife."

"Are you just saying that because you know I'm condemned?"

"No, indeed. If you'd asked me on your ship, my answer would have been the same."

He raised his brows in surprise. "In truth? Even when you thought I was a pirate?"

"Even then. I knew you were a good man caught in bad circumstances. Each time you ceased playing a role and showed me the man you are underneath, I couldn't help but love that man even more."

He paused. "The man underneath?"

"A man of honor and decency and gentleness and strength. A man I love."

Jared closed his eyes. "As an operative, I donned so many disguises, played so many roles..." he stared at a fixed point behind her, seeing another life. "I feared once I dropped all guises, there'd be no one left."

She tightened her arms around him. "There is someone left. And he's the one I love."

"I killed a lot of men, Elise. I terrorized many others."

"You had no choice. It was a war, first against the French, then against the pirates, and you fought it for your country. Sometimes it's easier to forgive others than to forgive yourself. Let it go. I already have. And I loved the irrepressible pirate, as well."

"You bring out the best in me. I want to be a better man when I'm with you. You make me want to live by a higher code of honor." He drew a breath, his heartbeat steady against her. His voice hushed. "And I can be completely relaxed with you. It's like coming home. You've helped me find myself. You saved me, my angel."

She slipped her fingers into his hair and pulled his mouth down on hers, trying to prove to him with her kiss all the tenderness and passion in her heart.

He returned her kisses with a fierceness that

might have frightened her a few weeks ago. Now it only made her want him more. How desperately she wanted to free him and make a place for him in her life. She rested her cheek against his chest, wishing for his freedom, wishing for a future with him.

"Are you two finished?" came Grant's snide tone.

Elise blushed. She'd actually forgotten Grant was still in the room. She was more surprised he'd remained silent for so long. He seemed the type to interject derogatory comments during such a tender encounter.

"If you ever fall in love, I'm going to give you such grief," Jared threatened.

Grant made a sound somewhere between a cough and a choke. "I'll shoot my own foot before I'll ever fall in love."

The brothers exchanged a long look, Grant's expression transforming from sarcasm to distress. Jared's hands tightened on Elise's shoulders as his gaze locked with his brother.

Elise could almost hear them thinking Jared might not live long enough to ever tease his brother again. She swallowed a lump.

Grant hardened again and turned his back the same time Jared looked away. Jared kissed her again with a note of finality.

"Take Colin and go home. Stay away from the square Monday."

Elise nodded, biting her lip to hold back the tears. She couldn't bear the thought of not being there for his last moment, yet couldn't imagine being at the site of his death. "I love you."

Grant led her away. He held her arm as they followed the turnkey down the intricately twisted corridors which seemed more oppressive, the guarded gates more ominous, the moans of the prisoners more heart-wrenching.

She maintained control until after they'd

retrieved their weapons, signed out, and left the outer door. Then, as they waited in the suffocating fog for a hackney, Elise doubled over and lost the contents of her dinner.

Grant kept a steadying arm around her through her dry heaves and even during the racking sobs that followed. Without censure, he guided her to the coach and saw her back to the Greymore's home.

There she awaited Jared's death.

CHAPTER 27

The afternoon before the scheduled hangings, Jared's siblings paid him a visit.

Appalled, Jared could barely choke out a greeting. "What are you thinking? You can't come visit a pirate in gaol. It will be all over the papers tomorrow."

Ever cocky, Cole quirked an eyebrow. "You underestimate my influence, little brother."

Jared glanced meaningfully at the twins.

Cole only shook his head. "You really don't think we'd fail to come see you, do you." It wasn't a question.

Though still concerned about the scandal touching the family he'd worked so hard to protect, Jared had to admit their visit meant a great deal. The conversation lagged, stilted and uncomfortable, despite his family's attempts to tease him as they always had, and his own poor retorts.

Oddly enough, the girls managed to be more themselves than his brothers. Margaret, completely unruffled, looked him over in her usual imperious way. "Save a place for my husband in hell."

He offered a wry grin. "Are you sending him there, soon?"

"One can only hope."

Rachel described a cottage she'd found near the Scottish border where she planned to finish writing her book on herbology.

Christian was grim and tight-lipped. "Father would be proud of you," he said quietly. "He'd consider this a hero's death."

Jared looked away, unwilling to show how much Christian's words meant to him. "Yes, well, I'd rather live if given a choice. But at least they no longer chain pirates to the river and let three tides wash over their bodies. That'd be chilly."

Christian closed his eyes, his jaw hard.

At the sickened looks on his siblings' faces, Jared said, "Sorry. I keep making tasteless jokes."

Cole tried too hard to act as if nothing unusual were happening and traded jests with his brothers with zeal. When they were about to depart, Cole turned back. "I'll be there tomorrow for you."

Jared stared at him, astounded. "You can't be serious. No, Cole, don't."

"I will not leave you to face this alone. I was on your ship with you for a year. I wasn't even there under orders. I should be hanging right beside you."

"You came on board because I needed you."

Stricken, Cole dragged his hand through his hair.

"Cole." He waited until his brother looked him in the eye. "Go home and take care of Alicia. And your child. Don't speak another word of it."

Cole nodded miserably, his eyes suspiciously bright.

"Greymore may yet come through for me," Jared added.

Cole swallowed hard. "We've both already gone all the way to the top. They've washed their hands of you."

"Just as they promised."

Cole embraced him fiercely, then Margaret and Rachel followed suit. Grant offered a brief hug accompanied with a hearty back slap.

Lastly, Christian, looking utterly desolate, threw his arms around him. "Father was wrong about you. I'm sorry he never saw you the way I always have."

Jared couldn't speak. Christian pulled away without meeting his eyes. And then they were gone. Jared sank down on his cot.

Would he have done anything differently if he'd known this was how it would end?

He relived the events of his life. In a moment of humbling clarity, he realized even though he'd often cursed the Secret Service, he'd thrived on the danger. He loved immersing himself in the different roles he'd played. Even some aspects of piracy had been...well...fun. At least he'd rid the world of Macy, the cruel and ferocious pirate captain whose ship he later commanded, as well as Leandro and Santos, who were equally bloodthirsty, plus a number of other reprobates the world would never mourn.

If he could have gone back and relived his life, all the major paths he trod would have been the same. Except for killing Leandro sooner, he would have done little differently.

Even his time aboard the ship with Elise was precious. And now, with astonishing clarity, he knew who he was.

Underneath all the lies and espionage, he truly was the man he became in Elise's presence. She brought out that man from the deep place Jared had imprisoned him.

He stood and went to the window. Perhaps that wasn't entirely true. Perhaps his real self had more power than he'd suspected. Perhaps his real self influenced everything he did. The realization brought a peace he hadn't expected.

He hadn't vanished after years of portraying others; he had remained, guiding his choices all along.

Jared smiled. He would not have changed a thing. Except make amends with Father and visit his family more frequently.

And take a different route home to avoid the

navy.

Tomorrow he would die as a pirate, and there wasn't a thing he could do about it.

He straightened.

He'd hold his head up and go with the dignity of an honorable gentleman. A gentleman Elise would be proud to love.

CHAPTER 28

After a sleepless and tear-filled night, Elise broke her promise.

When Jared had pled with her not to go to his hanging, she'd had every intention of honoring his request. Furthermore, she had no taste for the macabre, and never read the newspaper accounts which relayed every morbid detail of executions. She'd always been disgusted at her countrymen's delight in the gruesome stories filling the papers and independent flyers.

Nevertheless, as she packed to return home, she suddenly had to be there for Jared. She couldn't bear the thought of him dying surrounded only by strangers who believed him a pirate.

She glanced at the clock. There was still time.

While a footman hailed a hackney, she donned her pelisse and bonnet.

"Mother, where are you going?" Colin asked soberly.

"I have an errand. I'll return shortly."

Colin went to her with solemn eyes. He'd seen through her forced cheer as she'd taken him to the various sites of the city.

She gathered him close. "You're a good boy, Colin. I'm blessed to have you."

He wrapped his arms around her neck and let her hold him, for once not wriggling away. "They're hanging a group of pirates today, Mother."

"I know, my love." Her voice quivered.

"Pirates are bad people and they do bad things. But I feel sad when I hear someone is going to die."

337

Elise shuddered. "I do, too."

"Do you think their families cry when they die?"

"Yes." She choked. "I'm sure they do. Those who have families." She wiped an errant tear, released him, and stood. "I'll return shortly and then we'll go home."

Colin nodded. "I don't like London so well."

"It's not always so dreary."

The hackney arrived and the footman handed her in. She sat rigidly with clenched fists as the coach wound slowly through the crowded streets.

The square was packed. Much of England viewed a hanging as a sort of holiday. Spectators came from far and wide, and bought food and drink and whatever else the street vendors sold. Merchants sold their wares in some of their most profitable days all year.

Elise ground her teeth, never more ashamed to be English than she was at that moment.

"This is as close as I kin git ye, m'lady," the jarvey said as he pulled the hackney to a stop.

"This will do, thank you." Elise paid him and began walking.

She hated every one of the revelers who'd come to watch the death of the man she loved. Her stomach clenched each time someone laughed. She glared at those who'd brought children. Rudely, she pushed her way through the throng to the square.

A group hanging was already in progress. The condemned stood on the gallows platform, each taking a moment to say his final words. With her heart hammering, she searched their faces. Jared wasn't among them.

She pushed closer, ignoring the others around her. There was a sickening drop and the crowd collectively gasped. Elise refused to look at the gallows until after they'd removed the bodies. When she drew close enough to be satisfied Jared could see her if he looked to her for strength, she stopped and waited.

Jared walked out in the next group. He strode with head high, his shoulders straight, moving with his usual athletic grace.

Her heart dropped. Until now, she'd held on to an insane wish he'd somehow be spared and had almost dared hope he would not be here.

"Elise. What are you doing here?" Christian threaded through the crowd to her.

She spread her hands in a helpless gesture. "I had to be here. For him."

Christian nodded, his expression filled with compassion and haunting misery. Dark shadows lay under his eyes. "I know. You couldn't *not* be here." He put a protective arm around her to keep back the jostling crowd.

There was a hush as the crowd pressed forward to hear the final words of the notorious pirate Black Jack.

Jared looked over the mob, his aquamarine eyes lifted to the horizon. "I lived my life, not as a spectator, but as an active participant. I have no regrets."

They waited. But he said nothing more. At that moment, he looked nobler than any king.

The executioner approached.

Elise's blood chilled.

The scene took on a surreal cast; sound fading, color dimming, joy evaporating into a faint memory.

Jared looked down and met Elise's eyes. His eyes widened, first in despair and then in gratitude. His gaze moved to Christian, and something akin to relief overcame his features.

Brothers exchanged a meaningful glance. Jared's eyes flicked to Elise. Christian's mouth tightened and he nodded once. Elise knew without words, Jared had just asked Christian to watch over her.

How like Jared to worry over her when his own life was in imminent peril.

A sob wrenched its way out of her.

Some of the other condemned men gave farewell speeches, some remained silent. They wore expressions ranging from fear to insolence. Only Jared stood in quiet dignity.

The executioner lowered the hood over Jared's face and placed the noose around his neck. Slow horror crept over Elise, leaving her profoundly cold. She leaned heavily against Christian who tightened his arm around her.

Jared stood tall and straight while the hangman moved to the other condemned.

"Oh, God, please save him," Christian moaned.

The fervency of his prayer was so strong Elise half expected to see a legion of angels descending from heaven to free his brother.

Despite the chill air, sweat trickled down the side of Christian's suddenly pale face. Elise put an arm around his waist in an attempt to be comforting, though her own heart crumbled. Christian looked down at her with desperately anguished eyes.

The executioner came back down the line and made a final adjustment to the nooses. Then he pulled the lever.

Elise's knees crumpled.

CHAPTER 29

Christian caught her to prevent her from falling. She turned and buried her face in his coat. Disbelief and despair plunged her into absolute darkness. He held her in a brotherly embrace while she sobbed.

A moment later, he leaned down and said into her ear, "It's over. Let's go."

Light-headed and shivering, Elise glanced up as the executioner cut Jared down. Another man helped dump the lifeless form onto a waiting wagon. Jared's body landed on the wagon with a thud.

Her stomach hit the ground and she let out a low moan.

The second man snapped the reins and drove through a cleared path. The hangman returned to the others, cutting them down and dumping them in wagons.

Elise pressed her hand over her mouth, cold clear down to her soul.

Christian half-carried her through the crowd and hailed a hackney. Elise remembered nothing of the ride home, only Christian close by, grim and stunned.

Jared.

She relived their first encounter, his playful grin, his sensual kiss. She remembered his thoughtful gesture when he'd given her a pearl of sentimental value. She recalled that moment of vulnerability in Lily's garden revealing a deeper man underneath. Memories flowed over her; his playfulness with Colin, his tenderness, his passion, the times he'd truly needed her.

341

How would she ever find joy without him in her life?

How would she ever *feel* again?

Christian saw her safely to the Greymore's house. At the stairs leading to the front door, her knees gave way and she crumpled. Christian silently swung her into his arms and carried her inside.

Emptiness engulfed her. Through a haze, she heard voices; Christian's and Charlotte's, among others. Christian carried her to her room and laid her on the bed. Without resistance, Elise drank the laudanum-laced brandy Charlotte gave her. She floated in a world of half reality, sometimes dreaming sweet visions, sometimes recoiling from horrifying nightmares.

The nightmares were real.

Jared was dead.

She'd never again see his beautiful aquamarine eyes gleaming with roguish charm or his unabashed grin. She'd never feel his arms around her, never enjoy his sultry, passionate kisses. She'd never feel that sense of home and belonging as she watched him play with Colin.

She'd never love again.

Somewhere through the fog of grief and pain, she felt Colin climb into bed with her. She pulled his small body in close and finally drifted to unfeeling darkness.

"Elise."

She tried to climb into consciousness, but failed.

"Elise. Christian Amesbury is here to see you."

Fearful of her waking reality, Elise turned from the light and sank back into the shadows.

A cool hand rested on her brow. "Elise." Charlotte's voice cut through the mist.

Elise opened hot, gritty eyes. Sunlight streamed through the gap in the draperies over the window. Colin had gone leaving her bed cold and empty.

The memory of Jared standing on the scaffold drew a groan from the depths of her soul.

"Elise. The Amesburys have sent for you. You need to get up."

Elise pressed a hand over her eyes as tears squeezed through her lashes. "No. No."

"Wake up, sister-in-law-to-be, there's someone demanding to see you," called an urgent, yet strangely cheerful voice.

"Mr. Amesbury! You shouldn't be in her room," scolded Charlotte.

Christian leaned over her. "Come. Don't keep Jared waiting."

Keep Jared waiting?

"I'm dreaming," Elise moaned.

Gently, Christian took her hand. "He's alive."

Elise blinked. "You're mad. I watched them hang him."

"Yes. Then they revived him." Christian's eyes were earnest, ringed by the shadows of a sleepless, tortured night. The horror of seeing his brother hang still clung to him, giving him a haunted look. Yet he smiled, and his eyes were alight.

Elise pushed herself up, looking to Charlotte as confusion and faint hope mingled in her heart.

Charlotte offered a teary smile and nodded. "It's true."

Looking haggard, Charles Greymore hovered in the doorway. When Elise met his gaze, he said, "He's had a tough go of it, but he regained consciousness a few minutes ago."

They left her in the care of her maid, Morrison. Numb with disbelief, Elise struggled to wash and dress. Fortunately, Morrison's hands were steadier than hers or she never would have managed.

As she tied her bonnet under her chin, Elise asked, "Where's Colin?"

"Two of the Greymore's maids and a footman

took him to the park," Morrison assured her.

Moments later, they climbed into the coach. She glanced from Christian to Greymore and back again, searching for an explanation. Greymore appeared bone-deep weary. Christian looked as though he'd barely survived a war and come home wounded.

"Tell me," she insisted.

Mr. Greymore rubbed his eyes. The poor man probably would go home and sleep for a week when this was all over. "The Secret Service came through for us. Unofficially, of course."

Elise stared, hardly daring to believe.

Mr. Greymore shot Christian a wry, albeit tired smile. "The youngest Mr. Amesbury has friends in high places, apparently."

Christian took a shuddering breath. "I thought I'd failed. They gave me no hope when I appealed to them."

"Apparently whomever Christian spoke with bullied the Secret Service. They arranged to have the hangman switched at the last minute with one with whom Grant is acquainted. This executioner knows how to tie knots a certain way to prevent the victim from dying immediately. The victims strangulate more slowly, and it's painful, but the this allows them to suffocate slowly enough to lose consciousness rather than die immediately."

Elise shivered at the thought of Jared suffering, but did not interrupt.

"When Jared appeared dead, the executioner cut him down. They took him to a tavern around the corner which was empty and ready. The Service had a man inside who is expert at reviving the nearly-dead."

"It sounds terribly risky," Elise said.

"It is. Many die anyway. Sometimes their windpipe is crushed. Sometimes they go without air too long. Sometimes their hearts stop and cannot be restarted."

Horrified, Elise shook her head slowly. "And they were willing to take the risk he would die?"

"Actually, I'm surprised they helped as much as they did." Mr. Greymore glanced at Christian in admiration.

"Is that why you didn't tell me? In case you couldn't revive him?" she asked.

"There wasn't time. The final arrangements were made less than an hour before the hangings were to take place. But, yes, even if I'd known, I wouldn't have told you. It would have been cruel to raise your hopes. If something had gone wrong..." He rubbed his hands over his face. His unshaven whiskers made a scraping noise against his hands.

She leaned back, absorbing all she'd been told. She tried to decide how she felt. Shocked. Numb.

It still seemed unreal that she'd seen Jared die. It seemed even less real that he now lived. Tentative hope mingled with a fear that this was all an elaborate hoax, but for what purpose, she could not guess.

Christian squeezed her hand briefly, his eyes intense. "I know this is difficult to believe, but all is well. Truly. Jared asked for you the moment he awoke."

The carriage stopped near a park in front of a stately townhouse with a tastefully elegant façade. With Grecian flavor, the entry boasted sweeping staircases and marble floors. It managed to be lavish without appearing ostentatious. Elise barely saw it all as Christian led them immediately upstairs.

Her pulse quickened, not in excitement, but in fear. Fear this would prove to be a cruel joke. Fear she would only be led to Jared's lifeless body. Fear she'd never feel anything but this utter desolation.

Steeling herself, she followed Christian slowly. At the doorway, she hung back, terrified at what she'd find inside.

Christian reappeared, his face revealing first puzzlement, then compassion. He took her hand gently, looking into her eyes with a sincerity she could not refuse. "I could hardly believe, it either. But he's alive and well. Come."

Elise let him pull her inside.

The room had a masculine feel, with rich, dark fabrics. The draperies had been thrown back from the windows, letting in London's intermittent light. The bed on the far end loomed, but Elise could not bring herself to look at it.

Lady Tarrington arose from a chair next to the bed and took Elise's hands, drawing her near. "Jared. She's here."

Trembling, Elise swallowed and finally made herself look inside the canopied bed. In the bed, half-inclined on pillows, lay Jared.

His face was pale, and horrible open wounds, surrounded by purple bruises, ringed his neck. He turned his head and the brilliance of his blue-green eyes flared. One corner of his mouth lifted as he held a hand out to her.

With a cry, Elise ran the last few steps and threw herself against him.

She inhaled his scent. Under her cheek, his heart beat in his solid, warm chest, assuring her he indeed lived. He wrapped his arms around her.

He was alive.

Great, shoulder-shaking sobs seized her. He pulled her in tighter until she lay next to the full length of him. Enfolded in his arms, she released all her grief, her terror, her despair.

Without speaking, he rubbed circles on her back and stroked her hair, occasionally kissing her brow.

Her sobs died down until she rested quietly against him. He was real. Solid. Whole. Alive.

And she would live again.

Only then did she realize the others had left and closed the door. Their lack of concern over propriety surprised her. They probably assumed after being kidnapped by pirates, her sullied reputation would suffer no worse by leaving her alone with Jared.

Grateful for the privacy so she could, without embarrassment, improperly enjoy her reunion with him, she kicked off her slippers and draped a knee over his leg.

She burrowed her face into his shoulder. "I hope you still mean to marry me, Jared Amesbury. After what you just put me through, you'll need a lifetime to make it up to me."

He let out his breath in a weak laugh. "Yes, ma'am," he whispered roughly.

She heaved a shuddering breath.

"Is it really over? Will anyone else wish you dead? Because I truly couldn't bear seeing you in a noose a third time."

In a hoarse voice he said, "The pirate Black Jack is legally and officially dead. The only one who might wish Jared Amesbury dead would be one of your jilted suitors."

Elise smiled in spite of herself. "I doubt either of them feel strongly enough about me to wish to challenge you."

She heard him exhale in a smile. Tears of gratitude and relief coursed silently down her cheeks. She'd never laughed or cried so much until she met this man. How numb and unemotional she'd been before him!

His breathing deepened, grew more regular. She held him as he slept. Elise anticipated Colin's reaction when he learned the man he'd grown to admire so quickly would be his new father. She wondered how much they'd tell him when he was old enough to understand.

She'd leave it to Jared. It was his story to tell.

But she'd demand a full explanation herself.

She wanted no more secrets between them.

As she snuggled against him, she suspected Jared had also tired of secrets.

CHAPTER 30

Jared bolted up with a hand at his throat. Seized by wild terror, he gulped air in ragged gasps, vaguely surprised he could do it.

"Jared. It's all right."

A soothing voice pushed gently through the horror that left him shaking and cold. Soft hands touched him. Perspiration ran down his face and back. For the moment, all he could manage was to breathe.

Slender arms went around him. "You're safe."

Pushing back the darkness, he focused on Elise's angelic face. Fear and despair receded. The ropes were gone; his neck was free, his arms unbound.

He touched his throat, fingering the welts and the open, raw skin and he flinched against the soreness. Swallowing brought a new wave of pain, but assured him he truly lived.

Elise's fingers combed through his hair and caressed his face. He let her pull him into her arms and guide his head to her shoulder. Finding solace, he leaned against her. Comfort and peace drove away the terrifying memories.

"Oh, Jared," Elise whispered. "What you must have endured." Her arms tightened around him and she wept softly.

Jared closed his eyes, moved beyond words that someone would weep over him, and thanked God for the gift of this angel whom he clearly did not deserve.

He'd never in his life felt so safe.

After a moment, she loosened her hold on him

and pressed a cup to his lips. When he'd drunk a few painful swallows, she arranged the pillows before she let him lay back.

Jared could not take his eyes off her. She sat next to him on his bed, wearing a rumpled gown, her hair slipping out of its hairpins. Her leg rested against his and her eyes were soft with affection. She was the most beautiful sight he'd ever seen.

Tenderly, she touched his face. "Rest."

"Stay with me?" he whispered.

She curled up next to him. "Always," she promised.

He drifted to a place of peace for a time. He thought he must be dreaming when he awoke with Elise in his arms. For a moment, he wondered if they were still aboard his ship, and if the capture by the navy, his flogging, imprisonment, and hanging, were lingering visions of a terrible nightmare.

But no, those were real memories.

He lay in his old room in the family London home in Pall Mall. At least he did, indeed, hold Elise in his arms. She lay unmoving, with one arm resting on his chest, and one leg over his thigh. Her body felt perfectly relaxed, but by the rhythm of her breathing, he knew she lay awake.

She raised up on an elbow and looked down at him. The love in her expression nearly made him break down and cry. She touched his face, her fingertips light and soft, and kissed him.

"Are you thirsty?" she asked.

At his nod, she reached to the nightstand and retrieved a glass of water. Frustrated that she saw him in such a weakened state, and fighting his natural instinct to be self-sufficient, he had no choice but to let her hold his head while he drank. A part of him he'd repressed for years enjoyed her attention. Her gentle hands soothed him.

She lay back down next to him, warm and

comforting.

He nuzzled against her and whispered, "Do you wish to run off to Gretna Green, or shall I obtain a special license?"

She raised her head to look at him, a gleam in her eye. "Any special reason why we're in a hurry to marry?"

"I don't want to give you opportunity to change your mind. Once the adventure of these last few weeks wears off, you might decide you don't want to marry me after all."

"There's no danger of that. But are you sure you can bear my quiet life?"

"My angel, as long as you and Colin are there, it will be heavenly." He looked at her soberly. "Will you marry me?"

"Oh, Jared, of course I will. You've asked me three times, now. My answer will not change." Her eyes danced mischievously. "And I promise to leave both my gun and my candlestick outside the bedroom."

CHAPTER 31

In the gardens behind Elise's manor house, serenaded by the heavenly strains of a harp, Elise smiled in awe. She'd just married the irrepressible Jared Amesbury. She counted herself blessed.

Still amazed at how close she had come to losing him, she looked up at her husband of only a few hours and tightened her grip on his hand.

He glanced at her with a smile and squeezed back.

Resplendent in his wedding superfine, with nary a mark from his brush with death, he laughed with his brothers Cole and Christian. The three brothers standing together made an impressive picture of masculine beauty, yet Jared stood out as if a light shone upon him. If she'd thought him handsome before, he was positively stunning now. She admired the shine of his dark hair, the breadth of his shoulders, the brilliance of his smile. Once again every inch the gentleman firmly entrenched in the world of aristocracy, he stood with the assurance of a nobleman. His usual undercurrents of watchfulness had faded.

More at ease than she'd ever seen him, he tousled Christian's golden hair and laughed at the objection his youngest brother raised.

The wedding breakfast had been consumed yet the guests lingered, enjoying the fine company and the fine weather.

She met Jared's gaze and he awarded her with a roguish grin. Tenderly, she smiled, hoping he saw the promise in her eyes.

Charlotte Greymore and Lily Standwich—now Mrs. Harrison—embraced her and wished her well. "I'm so happy for you, dear one," Charlotte said.

Elise smiled. "Thank you. I never imagined I'd be so happy."

Lily, with her arm through her husband's, said, "Now, isn't this better than widowhood?" Her eyes twinkled.

Elise laughed softly and somewhat sheepishly, remembering her reaction when Lily first told of her decision to remarry. "I should never have disagreed with you, Lily." She exchanged a loving glance with Jared, nearly melting at the tenderness in his expression.

Greymore called him from her side, and Cole and Christian also moved away to allow her to converse with her friends. As she stood talking, she cast longing looks at Jared standing in a circle of relatives and neighbors. He looked away from Mr. Greymore, who smiled knowingly, to meet her gaze. He sent her a look so smoldering that she felt breathless.

Grant stood apart from the others, darker and more contemplative than normal. In his immaculate superfine, no doubt thanks to Cole's intervention, he looked respectable and more like his brothers, except for the thunderous expression he wore.

After excusing herself, she went to Grant. On the way, she snatched a glass of champagne from a tray and handed it to him. "Weddings are supposed to be happy occasions."

He glanced at her coldly, his steely eyes making a sweep of her wedding gown as he fingered the glass she handed him. "Nice dress."

Elise smiled. High praise from Grant.

He sipped his drink and glanced at Jared. "Seems happy enough, for the moment. See that you don't change his mind."

"Oh, yes, sir." Her smile broadened.

His dark brows drew together and he tossed back the rest of his drink. With a low voice, he said, "Let me know if he mistreats you."

"Don't worry. I'll keep him in line. I'm a very good shot, you know."

Something which might have passed as a smile touched his lips. He bowed slightly and strode away.

A footman approached, holding a letter. "Forgive me, madam, but this just arrived for the Honorable Christian Amesbury. The messenger said it was urgent."

Elise glanced about until she found Christian, surrounded by a group of young ladies. "I'll take it to him."

As she approached Christian, she noticed that while his ready smile flashed frequently, it never seemed to quite touch his eyes. He often looked down as if shy around women. And yet, there was something more...something guarded that reminded her of herself when she'd been protecting her heart.

She shook off her musings and offered him an easy smile. "May I have a moment of your time, brother-in-law?"

"Certainly." Christian bowed to the ladies, who made sounds of disappointment, and offered her his arm.

As Elise fell into step with him, she held out the letter. "This just arrived for you." She stepped back to allow him the privacy to read.

He broke the seal, and after a brief perusal, looked up. "Where's Jared?"

Dread clutched at Elise's stomach as she searched for Jared's beloved face. "With Cole," she managed.

"Come. This involves you, as well."

Elise hurried to keep up with Christian's long strides, her heart thudding.

Please no. Please let his past stay buried.

When Christian reached Jared, he glanced about and lowered his voice. "I just got word. I made some inquiries as to the fate of your shipmates."

Jared blinked. "You did?"

Christian shrugged. "You were worried about them."

"I was. I...thank you." Wonder and gratitude reflected in Jared's eyes. "And?"

"Dubois, Anakoni and O'Brian were set free the day after your...er..." Christian winced, "hanging."

"The day after?" Jared went still. "Then, the Admiralty didn't wait to verify whether or not I'd been truthful about the cache on the island."

"Apparently not," Christian said.

Elise took Jared's hand. She wanted to weep each time she thought of him standing with his men against impossible odds, and later, bargaining his life for theirs. "They must have perceived you are a man of honor."

Jared took on a far-away look as if replaying his trial. "Perhaps."

"Then they are free." Elise, too, had worried over the fate of the pirates who'd been so kind to her.

Christian's eyes crinkled at the corners. "They're free. They boarded a passenger ship and left England a few days after their release."

Cole playfully punched Christian's shoulder. "Well done."

Jared smirked. "Good thing there were two islands and two caches; one for the navy and one for my men." Then he turned wistful. "I wish I could tell them I'm still...but no, Black Jack must remain dead to all who knew him."

"All but me," she murmured as she snuggled against his side.

Jared put his arm around her and squeezed.

Christian's eyes twinkled. "Apparently one of

your mates found you out. Dubois gave this to the man I hired to make inquiries." He held out a second note wrapped inside the first, addressed to 'The Honorable Jared Amesbury.'

Jared broke the seal and opened it, holding it so Elise could read.

Thank you, mon ami, for your sacrifice on our behalf. I'm happy to know you managed to cheat death yet again.

We recovered the cache, and refitted and sold the Venture. *Thanks to you, we will live like kings.*

Dubois

P.S. Please wish Miss Elise the best of luck. She's going to need it married to you.

Jared laughed with abandon until some of the guests turned to look. He put his arm around Elise and kissed her brow. "Indeed you will."

Elise rested her head on his shoulder, warmth and contentment swelling her heart.

Jared drew Elise away from his brothers and wrapped both arms around her, smiling down at her with undisguised love. "You're looking very happy, Mrs. Amesbury."

"You are as well, Mr. Amesbury."

"I'd be happier if we could shoo everyone away and be alone. Better yet, I'd like to take you on a long trip and keep you all to myself. For a year or two. "

"What about Colin?"

At that moment, a laughing Colin darted through the guests, chasing one of the children.

Jared grinned. "The younglings will keep him occupied. We can send for him in a week or so." He pulled her in and kissed her. "Mmmm. You don't need any more kissing lessons. You've grown skilled quickly."

"Surely I need many, many more lessons."

"No more lessons. No more practice. From now

on, it's the real thing."

She laughed and kissed him again.

Colin scampered in and threw his arms around them both. "This is even better than my birthday!" he declared rapturously.

Elise clucked over his mussed clothes and hair, and he ran off again, chasing a cousin by marriage.

Jared enfolded her in his arms and she melted against him. "I don't deserve you, but I'll do everything I can to help you overlook that painful truth."

She smiled. "Hurry. I'll only give you sixty or seventy years to do so."

"That might not be long enough."

Hardly able to contain her happiness, she nestled against him.

He kissed the top of her head, raised her chin and kissed her long and tenderly. As he held her close, he murmured, "I love you, Elise. I promise to love you forever."

She had no doubt he'd keep his promises. All of them.

A word about the author...

Donna has had a passion for writing since the age of 8 when she wrote her first short story. When in 10th grade, she wrote her first full-length novel, a science fiction romance. She wrote her second novel, a fantasy romance, during her junior year of high school. Needless to say, English and Creative Writing were always her favorite subjects. She fell in love with historical novels as a teenager and has loved them ever since.

In between caring for six children, (seven counting her husband!) she manages to carve out time to indulge in her writing obsession, with varying degrees of success, although she writes most often late at night instead of sleeping. A native of Arizona, she writes Regency Romance and Fantasy.

All of her heroes are patterned after her husband of over 21 years, who continues to prove that there really is a happily ever after.

Visit Donna at www.donnahatch.net

Thank you for purchasing
this Wild Rose Press publication.
For other wonderful stories of romance,
please visit our on-line bookstore at
www.thewildrosepress.com

For questions or more information
contact us at info@thewildrosepress.com

The Wild Rose Press
www.TheWildRosePress.com